Wicked Witches

Wicked Witches

An Anthology of the
New England Horror Writers

Edited by

Scott T. Goudsward
David Price
Daniel G. Keohane

Introduction by
Penny Dreadful

Maine - New Hampshire - Vermont - Massachusetts - Rhode Island - Connecticut
www.newenglandhorror.org

Introduction © 2016 by Penny Dreadful
"That Witch We Dread" © 2016 by Suzanne Reynolds-Alpert
"In Agatha Craggins' Defense" © 2016 by John McIlveen
"Welcome to the D.I.V." © 2016 by Errick A. Nunnally
"The Witch's Apprentice" © 2016 by Morven Westfield
"Going Home" © 2016 by James A. Moore
"White Witch" © 2016 by Catherine Grant
"Baskets" © 2016 by Paul McMahon
"The Saint of Regret" © 2016 by Nick Manzolillo
"Witch" © 2016 by Trisha J. Wooldridge
"Run in the Widow's Hell" © 2016 by K.H. Vaughan
"Portrait of an Old Woman With Crows" © 2016 by Peter N. Dudar
"Tilberian Holiday" © 2016 by Izzy Lee
"To Dance the Witches Circle Again" © 2016 by Morgan Sylvia
"Another Plane" © 2016 by Patrick Lacey
"Access Violation" © 2016 by Jeremy Flagg
"T.S. Eliot Burns in Hell" © 2016 by GD Dearborn
"Black Forest, Black Heart" © 2016 by Joshua Goudreau
"The Jatinga Effect" © 2016 by Doug Rinaldi
"The Place of Bones" © 2016 by Barry Lee Dejasu
"Creaking Through Salem" © 2016 by Ogmios
"Blessed Be and Kick Ass" © 2016 by Jan Kozlowski
"Moving House" © 2016 by Rob Smales

Cover Art and Interior Illustrations by Mikio Murakami
Published in October 2016 by NEHW Press
ISBN 10: 0-9981854-0-X
ISBN 13: 978-0-9981854-0-8
www.newenglandhorror.org
Printed in the United States of America

Other Anthologies of the
New England Horror Writers

Epitaphs
Edited by Tracy L. Carbone

Wicked Seasons
Edited by Stacey Longo

Wicked Tales
Edited by Scott T. Goudsward,
Daniel G. Keohane and David Price

*For Tom, Terry, Tanith, Melanie and Harper.
May your stories always live on....*

～ Table of Contents ～

Introduction
Penny Dreadful

I've been a witch for about 700 years, give or take. It's been fun, but I miss the old days when we'd make a cow's milk go sour or cause Goody Wilkins to break out in pustules. Those were good times! Now you have all these positive-type "witches" doing all this really "nice" stuff and it's like, "What?! This is what the scene has become??!" I mean, it used to be pretty cool back in the day, but now everybody knows about it. Where are the poppets and needles? Where are the flying ointments made from the fat of unbaptized babies?!!... Uh… Not that I ever made any of that myself, of course. I'm just saying.

What is it about stories of witches and warlocks that continue to fascinate? From age-old beliefs and stories, to Medea in Greek mythology, to fairy tales, to the witches in *Macbeth*, to Gothic tales like The *Witch of Ravensworth*, *Dreams in the Witch House*, and *The Necromancer*, to films like *The Wizard of Oz*, *Black Sunday*, *Suspiria*, *Snow White and the Seven Dwarves*, *The Blair Witch Project*, *Warlock*, and *The Witch*, to TV witches like Angelique in *Dark Shadows* or Willow in *Buffy the Vampire Slayer*, all the way to the present day with the unhallowed tome you hold in your hands, witches return again and again to entrance audiences with their spells.

There's something captivating about the magic witches wield, and that's part of their appeal. Witches can bend others to their will. They can know the unknowable. They can subvert the laws of nature itself. They are formidable, and sometimes frightening.

Witches of horror literature and films are typically presented as normal humans who either obtain supernatural powers via a pact with dark forces, or they are born with innate magical abilities. If we're talking about horror genre witches, it's often the former. When presented in this way, the witch is something terrifyingly "other" – a denizen of darkness who warps all that which is natural. Truly, witches such as Helena Markos in *Suspiria* or Princess Asa Vajda in *Black Sunday*, for example, are cut from the same ebon cloth as vampires, werewolves, zombies, and other gothic horrors.

But there are many different types of witches. Not all witches are creatures of dark sorcery and ill-intent. For example, there are witches like the wise and good Professor McGonagall in the *Harry Potter* books, or the absent-minded but kindly Madame Razz in the *She-Ra* cartoons. And, of course, who can forget Samantha, Endora, and the rest of the family in *Bewitched?* As we learned in the *Wizard of Oz*, some witches are very good and some are very, *very* bad. Either way, witches and warlocks can do things regular folks can't, and that's part of their draw.

And so, before you read this tenebrous tome or terror, I must warn you - have your torch at the ready (We hate fire!), take hold of your protective amulet (We love curses!), and remember to avoid that house made of candy and sweets (We love to eat kids!...um.. Well, not me, but some people I know). Prepare to be entranced and electrified by stories crafted by the many talented authors who contributed to this forbidden volume. Indeed, I have it on good authority that even Black Phillip fears the contents of this book, though I think he may have eaten my copy. Damned goat (literally).

Hexoxo,
Penny Dreadful
Television Horror Movie Hostess
Penny Dreadful's Shilling Shockers

That Witch We Dread
Suzanne Reynolds-Alpert

A witch, sometimes,
should be dark. Should wear
a crooked nose,
a frock black like ink;
murky and stale
as the corner of a root cellar floor.

Some witches exist,
to haunt your thoughts. Dive
gleefully into your mind,
unseat logic;
pulling up shadows
that were well-hidden, placed with reason.

This witch is not
Wiccan, not Goddess.

She is horrible.
The pit in your belly,
the earth falling away,
the dread that lives tightly coiled,
dormant; awaiting its moment with
grotesque implausibility.

For Caitlin –
Good Witch or Bad?

In Agatha Craggins' Defense

John McIlveen

[signature: John McIlveen]

Gloucester Massachusetts
June 1693

Agatha Craggins was a witch – or so many townsfolk thought – but I wasn't convinced.

It wasn't that she didn't look the part…she did, with her coarse, straggly hair as grey as bog mists, and her nose, long and crooked and arrow sharp with one perfectly grotesque wart just to the right of its tip. From it sprouted five crooked, black hairs, much resembling a spider, be it absent a leg.

Short and stout of body, she displayed anonymity of gender beneath her correspondingly formless wraps, which fell to her feet like ethereal drapes. To say Agatha Craggins was unattractive was a gross understatement.

She lived in a cabin along a swamp-lined path bordering one of the inland ponds, deep in the woods on the western part of town. Stagnant, insect-ridden, and festering with lichen, none traveled there without reason, and when reason existed, most formed even stronger reasons to avoid it.

Rather a recluse, Agatha stayed mostly to herself, but on Tuesdays, would waddle two miles into town to buy provisions, and then waddle the two miles back, for she had neither horse nor mule. Each time she would lug a wicker basket for her goods, with her shoulders draped in a heavy shawl and a dark kerchief on her head, regardless the weather. As she shuffled, she would mumble, murmur, ramble, and curse; but always under her breath and to herself, paying no heed to the stares, jeers, and jitters of the townsfolk, who would point and laugh. They would gossip and whisper silently—yet conspicuously—of the "withered old shrew" or the "wizened hag," who – unbeknownst to all – was only four years into her sixth decade.

From the markets, she would purchase roots, herbs, spices, and tonics, most by special order. With exotic names like elder, cassia, mandrake root, and linden leaf – not your average soup fixings, perhaps – her selections branded her, for *these*, the people embraced as evidence.

"Nightshade!" they'd accuse, knowing little of which they spoke.

Although no one could prove any misconduct on Agatha's part, they remained smugly righteous in their allegations and self-important in their religiosity. *For these are troubled times,* they professed, *when demons walked the day lit streets in the guise of common womenfolk, seducing and deceiving with the spells they cast.*

Agatha was the bane of the faint-hearted, the source of all illnesses, the root of misfortune, and a justification for iniquities. For her unattractiveness, she carried the blame for those enchantresses who were far more guilty than she, yet exonerated by the imbursement of beauty.

Parents would keep their children in check, threatening them and promising them the sufferings of Agatha's spells. Children would chase each other, brandishing crooked branches like wands, cackling and shrieking of the same woes.

And although many mocked her and participated in her denouncement, they let her be for fear of befalling the unseen terrors of which she mumbled...or of which they imagined she mumbled. Therefore, Agatha lived in peace...until the Tuesday that little Thomas Dobbins went missing.

At sixteen years, I was older than Thomas by a decade, but I would often see him playing near his home. Fair of hair and skin and handsome to the point of beautiful, he was a loveable and spirited child, pleasant and easily engaged. His mother said he was a reservoir of endearment and adventure, his father affectionately quipped that he was full of the devil. It struck me how wide-ranging that allegation was, for he said the same of Agatha.

Thomas went missing in full daylight, two houses away from his home, and a mere four blocks from the center of town. On that evening, a crowd had gathered on the waterfront of Fort Point to voice their outrage and conspire to destroy what they feared - which was usually anything they didn't understand. Our home faced the cold waters of the Atlantic Ocean and was the focus of those who gathered. The town folk raised their fists in protest and brandished their words like weapons. In their eyes burned the fires of sadness, fear, and excitement; in their hearts, the resolve to find reason or restitution. Some just hungered for the thrill of the hunt.

Randolph Fenton let the curtain fall back into place and shook his head. He was Gloucester's Marshal Deputy by title, and the simple fact that no other desired the post. He was also my father.

"What are they doing?" I asked.

"They want answers. They gather like gulls to form strength in numbers," he said. "Unfortunately, ignorance and rage in numbers often begets a lynch mob."

We pulled on our coats and I followed him outside to face the writhing throng of perhaps fifty strong, among which were Minister Burles, Judge Bernard Stern, and the child's parents, Henry and Abigail Dobbins.

"It was the Craggins hag!" charged the persnickety matron Fields. "I saw her near the harbor with my own eyes, not a block from the Dobbins' home." The very eyes of which she had spoken roiled with outrage from her equine spinster's face, gaunt and etched deep by her own acidity.

"And how might she have abducted him? In her little wicker basket?" father asked her.

"If she hacked him to bits, then yes," sniffed the unpleasant old busybody, casting the child's mother into racking sobs.

"Would have made a bit of a mess, I'd fathom, the likes of which I have not seen in my investigations," father said.

"Search the old crone's house! Surely she carried him off there!" demanded another voice in the mass.

"We have no grounds. Besides, the old sort can hardly carry

herself, never mind a healthy child," said father.

"Be aware, Randolph, you underestimate the power of the Devil and his acolytes," said Judge Stern, whose granite hard voice and surly countenance aptly depicted his name. "It is this brand of negligence that will be your folly."

"And it is this form of assumption that persecutes the innocent," my father responded, his indifference to Judge Stern's station bringing forth gasps from many of those present.

"What proof have you of her innocence?" challenged the judge.

"And what proof have you of her guilt?" replied my father.

"Be that as it may, it is your exact calling that requires you to differentiate the two," Judge Stern haughtily said.

"And I shall, lest we become the theater of blood the good city of Salem has."

*   *   *

Of Agatha Craggins' innocence, I had no doubt, for I had known her for nearly a year. On a late spring eve of our previous year, 1692, I had followed the biddy home, impelled by curiosity of this peculiar old bag, for I heard the stories and presumptions. I tracked her progress, taking precautions to remain from her sight, and I was certain I had until she paused on the narrow path to her house.

"Why do you stalk me, child?" she calmly inquired, not turning to confront me.

The power of her voice and her thick Gaelic brogue were disconcerting whereas I had only heard murmuring and mumblings prior. I was befuddled not so much by her acknowledgment of me following her, since she may have heard my movements, but by her regarding me as a child. Not once during her travels had she turned or even looked in my direction. I remained silent and still, veiled by the girth of a large oak and some low-lying brush.

"Come now, lass, what is your purpose?" she persisted.

Again, I said nothing.

"Very well," she said with a shrug and then turned in my direction.

Through the obstructed view of the brush, I saw her raise a hand towards where I hid and conduct the smallest of gestures with her index finger. A queer sensation, cool, but not unpleasant, traced up my spine and down into my legs, which then - of their own accord - carried me onto the path before her. A fear as I had never experienced before gripped me. My entire being longed to flee in terror, yet I could not move; I was bound as surely as if I were wrapped in burial sheets. She lowered her hand and a weight I had not been aware of fell from me, freeing my arms.

"My, what a lovely sight you are. What is your name, hen?"

Still in shock, I could not form words. The ancient ogress impatiently grimaced, rolled her eyes, and quickly flicked a finger my way. My name spilled from my open mouth like water.

"Evangeline Fenton," I said, despite my knowing that to give a witch your name gave her power over you.

"Aye, daughter to Deputy Marshal Fenton," she said. It was not a question.

"Witch," I managed. The single word sounded more an allegation than the precursor to the endless string of questions I ached to ask her.

"Some do accuse me of being such, ignorant clodpates they are, but I prefer *sorceress*," she said. Her eyes gleamed, looking youthful and wise within the confines of her otherwise repulsive face. "How old are you, kitten?"

"Fifteen," I said, accepting the futility of resistance.

She studied me for a moment and I felt uncomfortable under her scrutiny. Her suspicion seemed to ease, but not expire.

"You surpass your years. You have the face of a woman, the body of a siren, and the eyes of a temptress. Men will be wise to take heed…you have your own sorcery."

How can she distinguish my body under the many layers of loose fitting clothing? Can she see through to my naked form beneath? I wondered, not at all entertained by such thoughts.

"You have not answered me," she said.

"I do not recall a question."

"Why do you stalk me?"

Again, I paused under the truth of my answer, and then spoke before she could pin yet another hex on me and loosen my tongue.

"To see if it was true," I said. "What they say about you…that you are a witch."

"And now you know. I'm sure *they* will, too, once you report back," she said.

There was disdain and tired acceptance in her voice that told of a history of similar troubles, but her suggestion that I would "report back" opened a narrow window of hope. She stared at me expectantly and I kept an eye on her hand, waiting for the finger-flick that would permanently still my tongue or seal my lips. Maybe she was toying with me, like a cat torments a mouse. She would use that binding hex again and drag me into the depths of the pond, leaving me to be feasted upon by whatever resided in its dank waters.

"Are you going to kill me?" I asked, thinking that was the only way she could guarantee my silence.

Her eyes met mine, and when she saw my question was serious, she shook her head and released a loud cackle, a grating shriek like a rusted wheel hub.

"Your mind festers with the same absurdity as the rest of your people," she said. It was mockery, yet it contained profound sadness. "Because you are beautiful, you are not vilified; you are seen in a positive light. But since I am disagreeable to the eye, I am considered guilty of hideousness. Because I live a different style of life and reside in solitude, I am regarded with suspicion and am even assumed evil. Do you think I prefer loneliness? Do you think I enjoy such an existence?"

I had no answers for her. She lifted her basket and turned from me dismissively. She's leaving, I realized. She had no interest in me. I took a reflexive step towards her and was surprised the binds no longer held me. *How long had I been free?* I wondered. *Why hadn't I felt their release?*

"Wait!" I said. Agatha paused but didn't turn back. "Can you teach me...the things you do?" I asked.

The question startled me more than it did the old woman, but I remembered the feeling of immobility and the uncontrolled spill of words from my lips and I couldn't deny the lure of having that kind of ability. *What other things could she teach me?* Agatha turned to me.

"Now, why would I do that?" she asked. "I have lived in Gloucester for all of my fifty-three years, and have never been accepted as a daughter of this town. I ask nothing of anybody except to trade with the markets. I have been mocked, scorned, and at best, shunned by those who live here, yet you, the daughter of the Deputy Marshal, expect such a gift from me?"

I was speechless for a while, astonished by her confession of her age. I had assumed her in her eighties and had even entertained twice that, with her being branded as a witch. I knew I would have to appeal to her, or at least paint myself as worthy of her "gift."

"I have never done you harm," I said.

"You have never done me charity."

This was a truth I could not deny, but since she hadn't turned away or terminated our conversation, I took it as a victory.

"Maybe we can make a trade, my companionship for your knowledge."

"You consider that a fair exchange?"

"You confessed just a moment ago that you do not prefer loneliness, and I sense in you that you would enjoy the company or you would have already dismissed me."

A wistful look crossed her face. "I've been alone since my mother died twenty years yore. She was the last person to show me love, empathy, or humor."

"And your father?"

"Never knew the sod," she scoffed. "Nothing but a wayward roustabout, thick with the clap. He took advantage of my mum, who was excessively compassionate and desperately naive. He promised her the world and left her with an ugly disease, and an even uglier child in the womb. She could have hated me, but she showed me only love...and a knack for hexes and spells." She considered me for a moment. "You're a fascinating lass. Come back in two days, after your studies. Bring me something convincing. An object that confirms that you perceive me as others do not."

I searched for hours, clueless as to what I was looking for until I considered I was looking from the wrong perspective. If I were to appeal to Agatha's sense of self, I should be assessing with her eyes. Two days later, I returned to Agatha's cabin with a carving by one of the artisans on the wharf. Created from a whale's tooth, it depicted a heart engraved within a larger carved heart, and due to a flaw in the ivory, a ragged hole had collapsed within the inner heart. Because of this unsightly blemish, the artist gave it to me in trade for nothing more than my prettiest smile. I felt it was right, as did Agatha Craggins, who studied the perfectly imperfect gift with inquisitive eyes, and then wept.

From that day, Agatha painstakingly shared with me the gifts her mother gave her, all the while conversing with me and asking me questions I answered conscientiously. She taught me that there was not a black magic and white magic, as many believed, but only one neutral magic; the darkness or light within magic came from the intentions of those who implemented it.

"We must never undermine the free will of another soul," she stressed. "There within lies the darkness."

She tutored me in incantations, prayers, meditation, and the use of incense smoke, oils, charms, amulets, and talismans. I was a quick study, attentive, and sympathetic.

Of course, at Agatha's insistence, we kept our gatherings secret. "No sense both of us burning at the stake," she would joke, though her message severe and resolute. "Those not enchanted see all magic as evil. Fear and ignorance makes people crazy and makes them act rashly," she explained, which is the primary reason she avoided the people of Gloucester instead of trying to meld with them.

I saw the magical arts as freedom and as a confirmation of my being. I adopted them, lived them, breathed them, perfected them, and made them my own.

Agatha's teachings went fine for nearly a year, until little Thomas Dobbins went missing.

On *that* night, when Judge Stern and my father stood face to face and challenged each other as to proof of her innocence or guilt, I knew it was my time to speak up about Agatha Craggins. As I had mentioned, of Agatha's innocence I had no doubt, for she had never harmed a soul; her nature made it impossible.

"Instead of debating as to whether she is guilty or innocent, why not visit her home and ask for a look around?" I suggested to the quarreling men. "Why, if I were suspected of such a heinous act, but was innocent, I would surely give you a grand tour from the top of my loft to my *root cellar floor*."

I took special attention to emphasize *root cellar floor*, because that was precisely where Little Thomas Dobbins' body lay. It was quite easy, really. A little spell of attraction and little Thomas Dobbins would have followed me to the ends of our Earth, and follow me is exactly what he did on that Tuesday afternoon as an oblivious Agatha Craggins walked to the market.

"Why, that's a splendid idea," said Judge Stern.

"Indeed," said father. "I cannot see why she would deny us such, if she is truly blameless."

I reached into my dress pocket and felt the contents, which sifted like pearls between my fingers. I shivered with pleasure at the potential there, for what was better than a child's tooth for a witches cause but twenty teeth?

Agatha might have said there is no white magic or dark magic, only intent, but all will learn there is no intent darker than mine.

WELCOME TO THE D.I.V.

Errick A. Nunnally

I'm going to tell you a story. Are you listening? This isn't a fairy tale, not some anecdote or metaphor—it's the real deal. I don't care what your track record is, how many trades you're moving on the floor, whatever positions you've miraculously turned into millions of dollars. That's what got you here, it's *why you were chosen* for the next level of investment management at Löckumm & Fixe.

You've all heard of the D.I.V. department, I already know. Just like I already know that some of you have made inquiries—subtle or otherwise—to find out what the department's all about. And I already know the answers you found: *nothing*. Zero, zilch, nada— you found out dick squat! If you managed to get someone to give you a direct answer, I know what they told you: "I can't tell you anything about that." Do you know why they said that? Because it's all they can say about it. Literally.

You! Yes, you. I'm pointing because it's hard to tell one of you blue-shirted wonder boy pinheads from the other. Oh, are you proud of your work? From this point on, you've done nothing of note. The fact that you've managed to keep your mouth shut while I'm talking at least tells me you might have a chance at becoming filthy rich with the company.

Look out on the floor. See all those no-name lunkheads out there? That used to be the six of you. Play your cards right today and it'll never be you again. Ever. Your first real success after you were hired was signing up for this program.

You know why this conference room has a bank of glass looking over the trading floor? So that they can see us drop the shades, like so, and get started treating you real special. Like they want to be, like you wanted to be, once upon a time.

Now all of you quit squirming and keep your eyes up here. Lights! The slide I'm showing you now is the before and after P and L, before L&F developed the D.I.V. to when it was implemented. Settle down, settle down, you all sound like yaks in heat, trying to contain all that desire. I know it's a lot of money. That's the point, it's why you're here today.

Now, you should already know that Löckumme & Fixe has been in operation since before the crash of 1920. And since then, this company has turned a profit every year since. Oooooh, there's some shit you didn't know. That's how smart you're not. No one knows. Not the FCC, not the White House, not Congress, not even our clients. *No one can know this.* Cool story, bro. Right? You're fuckin' A right it is. The best story. That doesn't mean there haven't been ups and downs or that we haven't suffered some collateral damage.

Which brings us to Todd Markham. Maybe some of you met him when you started? Bright young fellow, wore blue shirts and dark suits just like the rest of you brilliantly ignorant twatwaffles. See the haircut? Fits right in, don't he? Fits right into the meat grinder too, from that perfectly coiffed cut down to the wingtips. It's no different for any one of you, it is a one-size-fits-all machine and your candy asses are prime cut.

Mr. Markham here joined the firm in—ah, it doesn't matter, you can reverse engineer that by his numbers. He did well enough and did it long enough to find himself sitting in this room, in one of those chairs. Mr. Markham, shortly after observing this very presentation, took full advantage of the D.I.V. department. It is a tool—you have to be ready for that, you need to be serious about this. D.I.V. will give you unprecedented access to market information that *no one else* has seen or will see. Ooh, you're really perking up now, eh? This has never been repeated in the market and we've taken steps to ensure that it never is repeated at another company. And it's not even illegal! Wonderful stuff, just wonderful.

You engage this department here and here alone, one-on-one. There is no porting this experience elsewhere, no duplicating the methods—you're in or you're out.

Now back to Mr. Markham.

This is a visualization of his returns after one year with the D.I.V.

Two years.

Three.

Four. I can hear you salivating from here. Good, good. That drive is what it takes. But here's the thing: Mr. Markham thought he had it, the drive. He didn't. He was just greedy. Greed without discipline is reckless, it's suicide. *And we don't care*. The company makes money off of your efforts, it will continue to make money when you're gone.

Here's Markham at year five. Look at his eyes, the color of his skin.

Year six. Look at his neckline, see that creeping rot? Look at the split in his lip, the sore just below his earlobe. Look at it! This is what greed without discipline gets you. Markham couldn't earn enough to pay himself back; he took the risks, reaped the rewards, and never recouped the costs, he overreached. It takes balance, boys, a delicate balance.

Here, I'll flip back; look again. Notice his weight?

185 pounds.

178.

170.

And, finally, 152.

Leasing your soul for profit is serious business, I'm warning you now, the repo is a bitch.

Oh, that gets smiles, hm? It's funny. Right? Who's got a soul in this business? Am I right? You'll find out. Markham did. Where's he at now, which firm? Hm? No answers? Good. Still keeping your mouths shut. It's that kind of self-discipline that keeps the D.I.V. humming. Take out those fancy phones of yours and look up 'Todd Markham.' Use all the extra keywords you want, put all that millennial Google-fu to work. Go ahead, I'll wait. It'll give me a moment to enjoy the warm glow of your phone screens on your melting faces as you smarten up.

Okay, I can see that you found him. Keep looking. Uh-huh.

Aaaaah, there it is. Where is he now? Nowhere. Gone. One moment he's there, the next: nothing. His story ends.

The D.I.V. puts it all on the line, boys. This is the career you make or *you* break. Get it? Probably not. That's fine, everyone figures it out in the end. You may be wondering where young Markham has gone. I'll tell you the truth, I have no idea and give not two shits. I know where he's not. He's not here, he's not redefining 'best' and screw the rest.

Here, look at this slide. The average broker earns this amount after three years in this business. Tidy, right? Five years, looking good. Then six, seven and statistical plateau. Unless you manage to dig a whale out of the one percenters, there's nothing left to squeeze out of the damned market. This is a side-effect of our industry, boys, a concentration of wealth means fewer big clients. With the D.I.V., you can find *all* the advantages, take advantage of all the angles. All. Of. Them. Hell, with the right planning, you can *make* advantages.

Our penultimate plan is to consolidate every last one of these billionaires. Even the most liberal among them is greedy enough to bite, just to create more wealth. Greed is your tool, it's a weapon, harness it, leverage it. All you have to do is show them the numbers, do your jobs and sell them. Just like I'm doing for you today.

Okay, next slide.

Can you see it? You might think it's blank right now, but look hard. See it? That's opportunity, boys, this is the part *you* write—the future. Of wealth. *Real* money. You know what you don't see in this department? Derivatives or any of that other made-up junk. You know why? Cash, boys, the cold hard truth.

Now, let me make something perfectly clear. The fact that you're in this room means you made a decision to commit to this company. Now's your last chance to back out. Everything I've shown you up to this moment doesn't mean you can't walk away. Right now. If you're not ready to bring in more profits than any company has ever seen before, get your ass up and get out now. And keep walking.

You can try to join the saps out there on other trading floors, and plateau in a couple of years. You might think having L&F on your resume would make other firms sit up and notice. They do. Sure. And they won't touch your radioactive ass. You get this far at *this* company and wash out? You're done.

Go do taxes for some poor slob, volunteer at a soup kitchen, spend more time at church. *We don't care.* Money's money, you've served your purpose. But not the highest one. Anyone ready to leave? How about you, pinhead? Or you? No takers? Good, I like that.

Here. The contracts I just placed at the center of the table have never changed, not once since the development of the D.I.V. There is no bullshit, nothing is unclear, it is just one sheet. Take one and read it. I'll wait.

By the skeptical looks on your faces, you now know the acronym stands for Divination Investment Viability and you also know what access to such will cost. Some of you may consider the cost to be nothing at all and others may consider it too high a price. All of you are correct. Access to this department starts here. Literally here. The private elevator behind me goes up to the top floor where the department is headquartered. What? You thought we kept it in the basement?

Excuse me, I shouldn't laugh like that, but it always amuses me. Everyone thinks it's in the basement after reading the contract. They're elemental, these folks, they like to see the sky, a little sunlight. They can see the world from up there. What they do is just for us, for the glory of L&F. And The Chairman. Time check!

Okay, in thirty seconds, I'll introduce our Director of Personnel for the D.I.V. She's been with us since 'go' and continues to maintain critical staff like nothing you've ever seen. The Chairman is a fan and you'll learn to be too, if you want to survive this business. Same rules apply, keep your mouths shut. I'll just add that her appearance is non-standard, so keep your expressions in check. If she decides to cut one of you from the program early, that's her business, entirely up to her. Stoicism, boys, learn it.

There's the ding, right on time, and here she is. Gentleman, meet Mrs. Kyteler. Give her your full, undivided attention; I leave you to her.

* * *

Kyteler swept into the room like a rolling cloud of kept promises. No hesitation, no consideration, one moment she was on the elevator, the next swallowing one-hundred square feet with her presence. She fixed them in place, captivated with her yellowed eyes, observed the chosen recruits. Waited. There was some shifting, a few self-conscious twitches: touching an ear, scratching a neck, folding and unfolding of hands. But none of them cracked, they ignored the way her long red hair moved of its own volition in the dead air, the uncanny luminescence of her milky white skin. She appeared almost translucent, ephemeral in her peasant beauty. All of this wrapped in a black skirt suit and white blouse, her only adornment was a black cameo choker, its stone seeming to absorb light rather than reflect it.

She took a deep breath, taking in their scents, their fear. When she spoke, it was a delicate breeze from a cave too deep to fathom, a promise of escape where there was none. She had a light Irish brogue, just enough of a hint to remind anyone listening of her true origins.

"There is no jest here. No play." Kyteler paused, no apparent urgency in her person.

The pause that followed was beyond pregnant. It swelled to odious proportions, gravid beyond belief and was interrupted only when Kyteler began pacing a slow circle around the room. She dipped one long-fingered hand into her coat pocket and began drizzling a trail of a granular white substance behind her.

"We have a bargain here, trusts within unbreakable trusts. Your soul is leased to us, to The Chairman, for the duration of your service or the end of your life, whichever comes first."

The barest hint of a hissing sound as she continued to pace and drizzle until the table and its occupants were encircled. She stopped, inside the circle, and brushed her hands slowly. The sound of dry skin against skin was loud in the room.

"Who among you doubts, which of you does not believe in the soul? You may nod or raise your hand."

No answer.

"Come, come, gentleman; there is always one. *Always.*"

A tentative hand went up. They were difficult to tell apart, she noted, they all wore the same style of hair, similar shading, clean-shaven, blue shirts and white collars. At her age, all of them started to look the same, regardless, but she would come to know this one until the end of his story was written. She would take a peek at his most valued possession.

Kyteler slowly circled the table until she stood behind him. He looked over his shoulder at her and she gestured for him to face forward. A fairly disciplined lot, she noted, and that was good. Without warning, she snatched at his back and held the result up for everyone at the table to see. The look on the surrounding faces spoke volumes to the doubter. With her free hand, she clamped it on to his shoulder and held fast.

"Tell me, child, how do you feel? Speak to me. Now."

He opened his mouth and closed it more than once before choking out, "I'm...cold."

"Cold. Be specific about your thoughts. What are they, what do you wish?"

His eyes darted left and right, looking somewhere between the table and everywhere while his mouth hung open. There was an audible click when his jaw snapped shut and he spoke through clenched teeth. "*I want to make money.*"

"Mmm-hmmm. How much money?"

"More than anyone can imagine."

"I can imagine quite a bit. Tell me how do you feel about doing just that, right now? Be honest."

He looked up and met the eyes of everyone at the table before answering. "Clarity. I feel like...like I can...*focus*. What did you do to me?"

She replaced what had been removed with a slap on his back and left the circle.

"What I did is irrelevant. There's only so long you can go without it, but we need such to divine, to guide your work. Measure yourself, do well, and it goes back the way it came. Do not...Well, know the risks that we may all be profitable.

"All of my sisters are skilled, all of them know what they are doing. When you work with them, you can be assured that what is done will be to the utmost of their ability and benefit you without question. Greed is a beast that must be kept on a short leash and that is your responsibility. There will be quotas, you will be measured and judged against them."

She nodded to the original host and flowed from the room to the waiting elevator without hesitation. She did not look back when she said, "Remember: your success, the profits you earn, are paramount to the success of this company. Your failure is the same, we don't care; Mr. Black here does not lie."

*　　*　　*

What a show this is, eh, boys? Very impressive and something you can be a part of.

Ready to sign? Good, get to it.

Okay, hand 'em in, hand 'em in, there we go.

Oh, what's the matter, pinhead? Still not convinced? Ah, ah! Not a word. Mrs. Kyteler may have suspended the rule for the demonstration, but it remains in effect. You utter one word and you're out of here, the opportunity is off the table.

Let me guess: you *are* convinced, but now you're scared. Well, let me put things in perspective for you because a man of your hesitation might do well or might fail spectacularly by overthinking and making the wrong moves. Here, everyone come here to this side of the room. Everyone except you, Mr. *Carpe Diem*, you stay right there. No, don't sit down.

Okay. See this? All of us over here and you over there? That's going to be *the rest of your life*, boy. Commit to something once and for all, close the fucking deal and reap the rewards.

You want to see the numbers again? They're just an average, remember. Some of you will be above and beyond that, some of you will skew the curve and earn more money than you ever thought possible. More money than can be made at any other firm on this godforsaken planet! That feeling in your chests? It ain't fear, it's potential. Harness it, direct it, be the *best*. You can do that here, at Löckumm & Fixe, this is where it begins and ends.

That's it, boy, that's it, you remember how to use a pen. Just sign your name and you can be *someone*. Be better than everyone before and after you, reach for the goddamned sky and rip it open! Yes! Come on over here, son, join your class, rise together. You give your all to the company and the company gives all back to you. I'm so proud of you, all of you, taking the first step to greatness.

Step right in, step right in, plenty of room. All right. Everyone ready to have their eyes opened? Push that button and head on up, I'll make sure the right people have your signed paperwork. You'll be assigned a witch at reception right off the elevator.

Don't let us down, gentlemen. Remember, Mr. Chairman doesn't like to be disappointed.

The Witch's Apprentice
Morven Westfield

Callie almost succeeded.

She was half out of her body, her astral abdomen tight, her physical head and shoulders flat on the firm, pillow-less mattress. Just as she curled away from the sheet, a shrieking sound interrupted her trance. She jerked back into her body and lay quivering, nauseated by the quick re-entry.

How was she going to make any progress learning astral projection with disruptions like this? Callie was going to be a *real* witch, and do *real* magic, like learning how to travel the astral realms. "I have to learn how to do this, and no stupid car alarm is going to stop me," she muttered.

For the past week, every night before she went to sleep she had practiced. And every night, she was interrupted. The constant disturbance was exasperating. Anticipating the noise, she found it harder to just be able to lie still.

The only thing that kept her from jumping off the bed and casting a nasty spell right then and there was the vivid memory of Crystal, the coven leader, lecturing the coven from an overstuffed chair. "Change should start with the physical, mundane world," Crystal would say, in that saccharin voice of hers. "Don't use magic where physical action will do. Magic won't help get a job if you don't have a resume and fill out an application. Remember: Start with the mundane."

Callie fumed. She thought of making a not-so-neighborly visit to the origin of the sound, but prudently dissuaded herself. The jerk next door could be psychotic. She wasn't going over there and risk getting punched by some nutcase. What if the guy went ballistic on her when she asked him to use the silencer button after 10 PM? Road rage, air rage, why not driveway rage? Wouldn't it make more sense to just do a nice little spell, from the safety of her own apartment? No dangerous confrontation escalating into violence. Just a nice little spell.

She glowered in the direction of the thoughtless car owner. "Why am I spending all this time learning spells if I'm not going to use them?" she said. Why was she spending every new moon, full moon, and every-other-moon-phase in between stuffed in someone's crowded, smelly apartment, choking from incense smoke, learning magic? Didn't Crystal also say that "Learning magic is like learning music; you have to practice, practice, practice?" So, why not start with a tiny spell to quiet your neighbor?

Callie kicked around the floor until finding her slippers. Scuffing them on, she continued her tirade as she tottered down the hall to the kitchen.

What harm would there be? She wasn't going to curse him to his death or make his dick fall off. She was just going to *stop* him. Okay, so she *was* imposing her will on him, and Crystal always said that a witch should never impose her will on another, but wouldn't she be doing that anyway even if she just went there in person and spoke to him? Or called the police? Or, what if she never spoke to him at all and he just kept up with that stupid alarm, day in, and day out? Wasn't he imposing his will on *her*? Either way, someone was imposing his or her will on the other.

"I'm a witch," she said aloud, "and I have powers, and I'm going to use them -- from a safe distance."

*   *   *

On Saturday, almost a week after the full moon, Callie made a dash to the party goods store for a half dozen black candles. Crystal said that black could be used to banish or hex. Callie would try banishing him first, but if that didn't work...

C'mon, lady. Foot tapping, she waited for her turn at the checkout counter. *C'mon! I've had quicker incarnations.*

Everything seemed to be taking too long today. At the coffee shop this morning, the waitress took forever to show up at the take-out counter, almost making Callie late for work, and now this.

She considered walking out without paying, but she could imagine what Crystal would say about that. Witches should always be ethical. What you do comes back to you three times. *Well, fine, let someone come and steal eighteen of my candles, anything. Just hurry the frack up!*

Finally it was her turn. She had the exact change counted out before the numbers appeared on the cash register. Throwing six dollars and sixty-six cents on the counter, she was out the door without waiting for a bag or receipt, and was home in minutes.

Callie flung her coat on the nearest chair, locked the door, and silenced her cell phone. Grabbing a can of diet cola from the refrigerator and her spell books from the bookcase, she plopped down on the retro beanbag chair at the opposite end of her cramped studio apartment. She'd never done a spell for this type of thing before, and she hadn't been studying long enough to know off the top of her head what to do to create one, but she knew she could find *something*. She certainly wasn't going to ask Crystal.

Callie picked up a book that one of her coven-mates had lent her. Greens and blues dominated the color palette of the glossy cover, but the author pictured on the back looked more Goth than Gaia. Callie's interest piqued, she started to read the introduction, but that interest waned quickly when the author recommended performing divination first to find the source of a problem. "Sounds like something Crystal would say. Like I need to do a Tarot reading to find out where the sound is coming from. I don't need a Tarot deck, just ears." She chucked the book irreverently on the floor. "Next!"

Her next choice was a small, hand-produced booklet. The cover sported a crude woodcut reproduction of medieval witches. Warty old hags crouched around a boiling cauldron into which they were tossing all sorts of helpless creatures: toads, snakes, and even a goose. On the simple construction-paper cover, the title *Ancient Wisdom and Master Formulas from the Secret Grimoire of the Ancient and Unknown* was scrawled in hand-drawn script meant to look arcane and mysterious.

This wasn't one of the books on the coven's reading list. Callie had found it on a foray to an occult shop in another city. Crystal hadn't been too impressed when Callie showed her the book, but she was too politically correct to tell Callie *not* to read it. "You have to be careful with spells," was all she had said, and then, "I don't want to censor what my students read, but I wish you would wait until further on in your training before you read that one." Further on in her training. As if that was going to happen. She didn't know why she continued attending coven meetings at all. Recently she'd been missing a few. *Maybe I'm better off on my own. Look at all the books there are.*

Callie thumbed through the pages. The book was redolent of incense and damp. The fragrance evoked a subtle thrill. A vision of a dark cavern overtook her. The sides were lined with tilting bookshelves crammed with ancient tomes and cork-stoppered jars. In the center, a robed figure hunched over a hand-hewn work table. Candlelight glinted off a brass vessel covered in strange symbols.

The hallucination faded and she looked down at the page she had landed on. *To Influence the Mind and Will of Others.* "That sounds good. I could influence him to stop." She scanned the instructions. "Rats! I need a photograph. I don't have a picture of him. Even if I had a digital camera, how would I get the picture? 'Uh, excuse me. Uh, like, could I take your picture? I want to do a spell on you.' Yeah, right. I might as well ask him for a lock of his hair or fingernail parings." Both were listed as preferred ingredients.

She kept looking. Another spell caught her attention, *To Cross Enemies*, but once again, she didn't have the right ingredients. Where would she get dove's blood ink? Yuck! Another one: *To Conquer Those Who Cause You Suffering.* More ingredient problems: War Powder? What the hell was War Powder? Next!

Book after book, it was the same. The spells in the older books required odd ingredients that she didn't recognize, didn't have, and definitely didn't know where to get. The newer books wanted her to do divination and meditation before doing anything else, if anything else. One book didn't even *have* spells. "I can't believe Crystal wants us read this." The author had suggested that, after considerable divination and meditation on the problem, the witch should 'send white light and love' to the presumed offenders.

"Wimps! Next!"

*   *   *

The late autumn afternoon faded to dusk and her diet cola changed to a light beer as Callie continued the research. The evening chill came on fast, and she grabbed a moon-and-stars patterned acrylic throw from the back of the couch for warmth. The book with the rough paper cover was calling to her. She picked it up, and once more the image of a solitary cave overwhelmed her.

As she stared off into the middle distance, she grew drowsy. "Shouldn't have had that beer." Just as she started to drift off to sleep, *beep-beep*, the car alarm woke her.

"Damn you! I've had it," she shrieked in the general direction of her neighbor. She leapt up off the couch, stumbling as her feet caught in the blanket. Angrily she kicked herself free and stood in the center of the room.

She didn't wait to light her candles or cast a magic circle, just started right in, her arms raised and pointed toward the offender outside.

From her feet right up to her arms, she summoned up all the energy she could, breathing deeply and deliberately, focusing all her attention outside, just beyond the wall, to the driveway one house down.

Chants should rhyme; that much, she knew, but her first attempt felt childish:

"Beeper, beeper, go away..."

She tried again. This time she drew on her anger, and not just the anger at hand. From deep inside she dug up old anger against rude and aggressive neighbors and her powerlessness to stop them.

There was the drunk across the hall from her last apartment who used to get so tanked on Saturday nights that he'd vomit in the common stairway and then refuse to clean it up. He'd just laugh at her when she mentioned it. And there was the other guy next door who used to turn his stereo *up* when she'd point out that it was after midnight and *some people* had to work in the morning.

And, come to think of it, it wasn't always just neighbors. She remembered how she almost didn't graduate from high school because that stupid librarian accused her of stealing some book she never even heard of, and wasn't going to clear her for graduation until she paid for it.

Callie was tired of being helpless, tired of being invisible, tired of being just that little girl that no one listened to. She was a witch now, and she didn't have to put up with this crap. Crystal might be afraid of using the Power, but *she* wasn't.

Arms extended, palms pointed in the direction of the noise, eyes wide and burning in anger, she dropped her voice into a low-throated growl:

"By the powers, ancient be,

By the strength of three times three…"

Callie paused for the next flash of inspiration, unsure what to say next. She needed, wanted, more. More energy, more power, more resolve. No longer the spineless, passive sheep, this time she would take control.

Recalling the vision of the cave, she looked deeper at the robed figure. She could feel energy there, a darker energy than she had sensed before. She tried to look into his face, but the hood obscured it. She followed his arms down to his hands where skeletal fingers pulled apart the guts of a dead bird. A black bird. A crow.

His fingers scooped entrails upon the stained work surface with a fierce deliberateness. A low growl of a chant escaped his lips. She couldn't understand the words, didn't recognize the language, but she began to repeat the sounds, even as Crystal's admonitions echoed in her head: *Never chant something you don't understand.* She had to, she was compelled to, and she knew, as she voiced the sounds and mimicked the movements with her own fingers, that *this would be powerful.*

Malfas, zatoz. Ekarri zure indarra. Emaizkidazu botere.

With each repetition, the sorcerer lowered his voice, and pulled more violently on the ragged carcass of the dead corvid.

Malfas, zatoz. Ekarri zure indarra. Emaizkidazu botere.

Callie was almost spitting the words now, listening intently to improve her diction. The sorcerer was speaking faster now, and she followed, making vehement ripping motions with her hand as she watched the ghastly phantom rend the last of the sacrifice's remains, tossing feathers and bones into the air.

The vision disappeared.

Something was wrong. She held her breath as she listened, but all she could hear was the tick-tick-tick of the clock in the kitchen. Nothing else. *Too much* nothing else.

Where were the normal sounds of her city neighborhood? The people yelling across the street to each other? The car horns tooting impatiently? Where were *any* traffic sounds?

Maybe it was just later than she thought. "Damn. I was supposed to go to a coven meeting tonight," she remembered aloud. "Too bad."

She could feel something in the room now, something substantial, something guiding her, pushing her, watching her. She tried to focus her hearing. If there was someone in the room, shouldn't she hear breathing? The apartment felt cold and still, but there was something here, she *knew* it. Something nonphysical. Too late she remembered Crystal's warning about fraternizing with the denizens of the astral realm.

She could feel her earlier anger reflect back on her now, like heat from an old-fashioned fireback, could feel the jittery, metallic tongue of her anger like licking flames. It was strong, stronger, *nine times stronger*, and it filled her with dread, fear, and a hard knot in the pit midway between her ribs and navel. *Something was in the room with her.* She turned to face it.

*   *   *

Crystal glanced at the clock. "It doesn't look like Callie's coming. Has anyone heard from her? No?" Crystal made a mental note to speak to Callie about her attendance - and attitude. She seemed just a little too dismissive at times. "Anyone have any problems with the astral projection exercises?"

River Child nodded, frowning. "Yeah, I have. It went pretty well the first couple of times. I had no problem stilling my mind, or imagining my astral double." She paused.

Crystal smiled and encouraged her with a soft, soothing voice, "Yes, go on."

"Last night, just as I got into it and started the part where you peel away from your physical body, I heard this weird *beep-beep* like a car alarm and it broke my concentration. What *was* that?"

Crystal laughed gently. "Don't you remember our first group attempt at projection? I gave the group a hypnotic suggestion about a beeping noise?"

River Child furrowed her brow, thought for a moment, and then shook her head. "No, I don't remember that."

"When we first covered astral projection, I gave you a lot of detail: how to relax, how to breathe. I talked about wearing comfortable clothing and how to encircle yourself with protective energy. There was a lot to remember. You might have fallen asleep at the point that I spoke the words of the autosuggestion --"

"I'm sorry."

"That's okay. Beginners make mistakes. That's why we work in a group at first, so we can help each other if difficulties arise. I probably should have had you all do a few more group attempts before asking you to try it on your own. The beep-beep was a signal to snap us out of trance whenever there was danger on the astral, like evil entities or something. You heard our astral danger alarm. But at least you're all right. You must have constructed a good circle of protection." She looked around the group as she spoke. "Protection is important, but pay attention to the danger alarm, too."

*　　*　　*

Callie stood before him, eyes wide with fear. She had no magic circle around her, no barrier of salt, no sigils of protection. Though she was clothed, she might have been naked she was so exposed.

"Oh, how sweet," the demon snickered.

"W-what do you want?"

"What do *I* want? What do *you* want? You summoned me." He sidled to his left, cocking his enormous, scaly head as he appraised the hapless apprentice. "Your rage, your anger summoned me. Oh, yes, that and the *Ancient Wisdom and Master Formulas from the Secret Grimoire of the Ancient and Unknown.*" He huffed as he looked at the shaken amateur before him. "He was like you. Inexperienced. Full of anger and bravado. Anytime anyone angered him, he did that spell. Each time I came at his call, and each time he promised me one little favor. That my name would be known forever."

The monstrosity edged toward her. "But each time, I grew more impatient. You know all about impatience, don't you?" He flicked the tender tip of her nose with his claw, drawing a crimson stream. She teared up involuntarily. "Yes, impatient for something more than the regular mumblings of an old man. And then it struck me. He would become the spell; he would live in the pages of that book. And anyone with the same force of anger and impatience as that petty conjurer would awaken him, and together they would invoke me."

He was frightfully close now, the sulfurous stench of his breath sickening her so much that she forgot how afraid she was.

He took her head in his hands. "So, you want the noise to stop? You don't want to hear it ever again?" he cooed. "I can arrange that."

And with one swift snap of her neck, he did.

Going Home
James A. Moore

Several of the locals noticed her as she came into town sporting a modest skirt, leggings and a baggy t-shirt that did not hide her form. They looked and she looked back, smiling pleasantly.

She was pretty and she knew it. That said, she was not in town to meet a man, or anyone else, for romantic reasons. Erika Carmichael had a very different agenda.

The weather was her favorite kind, dry and chilly and with a wind coming in off the ocean that scattered leaves, rustling grass and hair alike. Almost a month until Halloween and already there were decorations everywhere.

Salem, Massachusetts had changed since she'd been there last. There were more traffic lights, more shops, more people and more witches. They were on just about every sign and even on the signs for the city itself. Pointy hats, broomsticks and all. Orange and black was everywhere, even more so than most of the towns she'd been through. Halloween brought out the festive side of people in the town, though that was hardly surprising. Salem was the only town to fully embrace witch hysteria in the United States, even if that was back when the area was a British colony. People had been tortured, hanged, burned, and crushed under stones before it was all said and done. Why not celebrate the festivities with candy and crepe paper?

The little coffee shop where they'd agreed to meet was just around the corner. Not a hundred feet away a statue of Elizabeth Montgomery sitting on a broom and smiling was shining for everyone to see. Erika had practically grown up watching that show. Her mom loved it and played it every day when she was cleaning. That was before the messy divorce, before Erika became a bit of nuisance and was sent off to a private boarding school.

It was one of her old classmates that she was here to see. Amye Hammond had changed her wicked ways and gone full on Wicca, and where better to be if you were a witch than in Salem, Massachusetts?

They'd run across each other on Facebook and after personal messaging for a few weeks had agreed to meet up in Salem. It had been years since Erika had been to the town. So much had changed. So much was still the same. There was an odd sense of déjà vu when she looked around. Behind a scattering of tourist trap museums and just slightly up the hill, she could make out the cemetery where she'd seen several people buried in her younger days. For a moment she considered walking up there to see the headstones and remember the past.

"Erika! My God, you've barely changed!"

She forced a bright smile and looked at Amye. Her friend had put on a little at the hips, almost impossible not to after a few kids she supposed, though she had none of her own.

Well, that wasn't quite true.

Still, Amye looked good. They moved closer and Amye let out a squeal and Erika hugged her affectionately and smelled the same old strawberry shampoo that the other woman had used since high school. Ten years had flown by.

"You look great, Amye. I've missed you."

"Oh, please. There's three of me now. One extra on each hip!" Amye said the words but felt no grief from them, apparently. She was happy to be where she was and happy to have a husband and two beautiful children. At least on the surface. It was what happened beneath the still waters that mattered though, in the end.

"How long have you been married? I can't believe we fell that far out of touch. I should know these things, right?" Erika's smile was warm and genuine.

"It wasn't you, honey, it was me." Amye moved over to a table where she already had an iced coffee waiting. Within seconds the waitress was there and Erika ordered a black tea. When the waitress had left, Amye continued. "I got stupid. I got into too much of the stuff that Lane Hanley was offering and after high school was done I sort of became his little groupie, you know?"

Erika nodded sympathy, but she didn't feel it much. Lane was one of the local boys in Beldam Woods, New York. He was trouble from day one and everyone at the school knew it, but Amye had always liked the bad boys. She felt a compulsive need to fix them, or maybe she just liked to get roughed up. It was hard to say. The Amye in front of her was not the same one she'd known a decade earlier. She was more at peace with herself and seemed stronger, too.

That made Erika happy.

"Anyway, I got away from him when he went from slapping me around to hitting me and kicking me hard enough to break things." Amye looked down and Erika nodded sympathetically. She had that sort of face. Girls wanted to tell her things, to let her be their confidant. Men wanted something different. Well, not all of them, some genuinely wanted to be friends, but they were few and far between.

Erika nodded. She'd stayed in Beldam Woods, though she was seriously considering moving on.

"Lane got himself thrown in a maximum security cell, Erika. He went from fists to guns and tried taking out one of the constables. I know he's appealing, but the sentence was Life Without the Chance of Parole, so there's that at least."

"Well, I wouldn't wish him any harm." Amye said and looked down at her coffee as the waitress brought over Erika's.

"I would. He was a dick then and he's a dick now."

Amye smiled. "You've always been direct, Erika, I admire that."

"It's the only way to be if you want peace in your lifetime. What made you go all witchy on me, Amye?"

"Wiccan." The correction was automatic. "We take that sort of thing pretty seriously here, Erika."

"No offense, I just didn't expect it from you. I mean, your dad's a minister, isn't he?"

"Oh, we had a falling out about it, too. We never did resolve it. He died a couple of years ago in a car wreck." Amye looked over at the statue of Elizabeth Montgomery from *Bewitched*, and then sipped at her iced coffee. Erika sipped at her tea. It was warm and perfect.

"It's not my business, Amye, but you don't seem too upset by that."

"He was never a good man, Erika. You know that. I told you more than I meant to tell anyone. You're the one that got it fixed."

True enough. When Amye had let slide that her father was not always fatherly when it came to their contact, it was Erika who informed the police. She'd taken the liberty of recording the conversation, because Amye would have never said anything in person. At fifteen she was used to being molested. Erika refused to allow that to continue. There had been several fights before Amye decided to forgive her. Having a bit of a history along those lines (nothing as serious, but there were a few boys who tried their luck with getting grabby and suffered the consequences), Erika was willing to lose a friend to save a friend if she had to.

That was, of course, a long time ago.

"I didn't know if you'd made amends with each other."

"We made therapy. That was enough, I guess. But we were never close after that and mom divorced him when it became public."

"When it became public?"

"She knew, Erika. She just never did anything about it."

All around them people went on with their own conversations, oblivious to what was said. That was for the best. Erika hated eavesdroppers.

I like them just fine. They make good fodder.

Erika pushed the thoughts away. Right now was her time. Alvina would wait a while longer.

"How about you? Last time we talked you said you were having problems with, your mom, was it?"

Erika smiled. "More like my grandmother, but we worked it out. She wanted to spend more time with me and I didn't want that at first, but after a while she grew on me. She taught me a bit about witchcraft herself, which was why I was interested when I heard you say you were studying Wicca."

"Oh, I'm not very far along yet. I mean, I attend the celebrations, but I'm not very skilled."

"Maybe you just haven't had the right teacher yet."

"Well, I guess maybe I don't take it seriously enough."

"I didn't want anything to do with it, not at first, but Alvina made me see that I wasn't applying myself." Erika took another sip of her tea and stared into Amye's eyes.

"Alvina?"

"The one I didn't get along with at first." Proper smile as she looked on, her eyes locked in a quiet battle for dominance with Amye. She couldn't come across as aggressive, even when she was holding a battle of wills. "She was patient and taught me a few things, but before then, I swear, it was like being locked in a box and never let out. The thing is, it felt like she was trying to take over my life."

Erika shrugged. The memories were still fresh: The witch taking her body and locking her far down within herself. She was dying by inches every day until Alvina finally let her out to move around again.

"We get along better now than ever. She's more like family to me than my real family is."

"I wish I could say the same about Wendy."

"Wendy?"

A sour expression marred Amye's round face. "She prefers to be called 'Moonlight Greyshadow.' Her real name is Wendy Burton." She shrugged. "Head witch in these parts."

Erika nodded. "Alvina just prefers to be called by her name."

"Kind of an old fashioned name, isn't it?"

"Well, she's kind of an old fashioned witch."

"Wicca." The correction was automatic.

"No. Witch."

"Wicca and witch are the same thing."

"Not always, Amye. Sometimes a witch is something entirely different. Sometimes a witch makes bargains with dark powers and gains personal strength and wisdom from them for a price."

"What, like selling their souls?" Amye laughed. Erika smiled indulgently.

"Come on, Erika. You can't be serious?"

"It all depends on what you want from the world, Amye. I would never sell my soul, but there are ways to get power."

Amye looked at her for a few seconds and then chuckled. It was a laugh, but it was weak and it was nervous. "Come on, be serious Erika."

"I couldn't be more serious, Amye. I'm here because this used to be Alvina's home. A long while back, really. She came from here and went down to Beldam Woods."

"And she's a witch?"

"Of course."

"Remember those old legends about the witch and her three familiars?"

Erika's lips moved. The voice behind them was a little different. "They were her children, not familiars. She gave birth to them in the woods before the locals burned her at the stake."

"I can't believe you remember those old stories so well."

"Not the stories, Amye. The facts behind them. Alvina Bathory was accused of stealing children and eating their bodies and their souls. She was found guilty and she was tied to a tree and burned to death. Her children were burned inside of her house."

Some people wanted willful ignorance. Amye glazed over the use of the name Alvina in two separate parts of the same conversation. The notion that Alvina Bathory might be the same Alvina that Erika spoke of was not entering her head.

"Yeah! That's the story. What were their names? Old Bones, Mister Sticks and Patches?" Amye giggled. "I wonder if every town has legends like those or only the ones here in the northeast."

"Did you know that Beldam Woods is almost a straight line from here? You basically go due west." Erika finished her tea and gestured to the waitress for a refill. The woman smiled and nodded, looking just a little frazzled. Not far away an older man was already yelling at the waitress about wanting his goddamned ice coffee already. He had been seated roughly ten seconds earlier.

"You know, I never thought of that, but I think you're right."

"Of course I am. I just got here, after all."

"Did you take the train or drive?"

"Would you believe me if I told you I took my broomstick?" Erika winked, of course. A little levity.

Behind her, the man who wanted his ice coffee so badly swallowed a fly and started coughing.

"Gawd, Erika. You're impossible." Amye chuckled and took a sip of her drink.

"So how did you manage to get away from the house with two little ones and a hubby?"

"The kids are in day care. Will is at work. He actually commutes by train to Boston every day. It's crazy, but he's making good money, so what can you do?"

"What sort of work?"

A dismissive hand swept the air between them. "He's into corporate taxes or something. He's actually a lawyer, but I could never understand what he does."

"Don't belittle yourself, Amye." Erika smiled, but she meant it. "That kind of attitude only leads to more bastards like your dad and Lane." And there it was, that little flash of guilt. She had married another Lane. This one maybe didn't hit her, but he dominated her world.

Amye sighed. "Will is a much better choice than either of them."

"I believe you. I just don't want you to forget that you are a strong person. I mean, look at what you've already survived. And now you have two beautiful kids." She meant it. They were beautiful in the way that only small children can be. Untainted by life, and not yet ruined by experience. She had seen enough pictures on Facebook to know what they looked like.

"They are cute, aren't they?" She said the words as only a parent can, with a level of pride that was only matched by the quiet awe that something so wondrous could have come from so flawed a background. It was the sort of awe that every parent had to one degree or another, but it was especially potent in someone like Amye who had spent so very long walking a self-destructive path.

"They're as perfect as can be." Erika leaned back in her seat and stared at Amye with a half-smile on her face. "Do they drive you crazy? I don't think I could handle kids. I'm not sure I'd ever want them."

"Oh, they're not so bad." Amye smiled. "I mean, I could use a little sleep now and then."

"How many kids do you and Will want?"

"I'm good with two. Will comes from a big family. He'd be happier with six."

The look of horror on Erika's face was only slightly exaggerated.

"Alvina had three. She said they were more than enough. Of course, hers were all breaches, so that had to be hard."

A small lie. Alvina's children weren't so much breach babies as they were the sort that clawed their way out of her withered body and nearly left her for dead. She'd spent hours trying to recover, holding her own insides where they belonged while she crooned and begged her masters to offer her more time. Three strong servants, boys who would do anything at all for their mother, from caring for her while she recovered to killing anyone foolish enough to come too close.

"I had caesarians." Amye looked down at the table for a moment. "Will wanted to make sure I could keep my narrow hips. He said wide hips lead to a flat butt and thunder thighs."

"Charming."

"Oh, I-he was only kidding." A lie. A blatant lie. Amye couldn't even look at her. She was embarrassed to admit that her husband was a bit of an ass.

"Men seldom understand." Erika shrugged. "I hate to pull that old line out, but men don't understand what being a woman is all about. You have two kids and you're supposed to stay at home and take care of them. You probably have to have dinner waiting for Will when he gets home and that's fine if that's what you want out of the world, but most men don't ask what we want. They just assume that we're okay with whatever they want. I mean, we're in Massachusetts, a state that tends toward the liberal side and you stay at home, raise your children and are expected to make more babies, even if you don't want them. Am I right?"

Amye sighed. "You aren't wrong, exactly."

The old bastard with the iced coffee continued to cough from time to time, his hand going to his throat. He looked around dimly and took another sip of his drink, seeking relief, but it did not come. It wouldn't come, either, until Erika allowed it.

Right then she was too busy focusing on Amye. She had made her point. Now she needed to sell her goods.

Erika nodded and made sure her face stayed properly neutral.

"So, listen. Alvina is thinking about coming up this way for a while. Coming home. She wants to start a coven of her own."

"Oh, I don't think Wendy would like that." Amye's words were serious enough, but there was a slight smile on her round face.

"Well, Alvina doesn't much care what Wendy likes. She's serious about coming up this way and doing real witchcraft, not the simple charms that Wicca sell to the locals but the real stuff. The world has changed. The days when people were hung by the neck, burned at the stake, those are gone. Hell, Amye, most people barely get a slap on the wrist for murder. Imagine how easy it would be to set up a real coven as long as there was a little discretion."

"Okay, but black magic? Really?"

"Please. It's all the same stuff. It's just how it's employed. Have you ever done any actual spells? Have you even tried?"

"Wendy says I'm not ready."

"Wendy just wants to be in control." Erika shrugged. "Will wants to wear the pants at home, Wendy wants to wear them when you're part of her coven."

"Alvina doesn't force you to do anything?"

Alvina's laughter echoed through Erika's head.

"There was a time when she had to work pretty hard to convince me that she was working for our mutual benefit. But you know what? When I had a situation with a teacher of ours, actually with Headmaster Burgess, Alvina took care of it easily enough."

Amye was not surprised to hear about Burgess. The man never actually did anything to most of his female students, but he certainly tried to develop x-ray vision whenever he looked them over. "What did she do?"

"Three words, and he couldn't get hard any more. I mean, did you ever have him try to grind his pants against you? I did. He was always hard. Three words, no more hard on. Not ever again while I was at that school."

Not the whole truth of the situation, actually. The man had been torn apart by her boy, Robert. Then Patrick took his place as the headmaster for the rest of her time in the academy. He hadn't wanted to, but Patrick was her son and he obeyed. The thought brought a smile to Ericka and Alvina both. They sometimes agreed, sometimes disagreed, but were equally happy with how the situation with old man Burgess was handled.

"My point is, it's easy to take control of your own life if you want it badly enough, Amye. No one to call you names, or tell you how it's done." She stared hard at the other woman and made the gambit that would either make or break the conversation. "No one to make you have sex when you don't want to, or to hit you anymore."

The words were spoken without malice or prejudice. There were no accusing tones. It was a sad fact of life that even in a modern era when such things were frowned upon, many men took advantage of their strength and the belief that a man could not rape his wife.

Erika looked away from her high school friend. Amye would look her way soon enough and if she saw her staring back it might be too much. She wanted the other woman thinking, not crying. Not yet.

Soon enough there would be tears.

They were silent for almost five minutes. Long enough for the old bastard to get up from his table and leave, coughing still on the fly that was digging into his throat with unnatural determination. Long enough for Erika's fresh hot tea to show up.

She made sure she stayed aware of where the old man went. She wasn't done with him yet.

"He keeps saying he'll get better."

"He lies, Amye. Men lie. It's what they do. They mean to behave. They mean to do better, but it never really works out, does it? A few months go by and everything is fine and then you make a comment or he decides he wants to fuck and you have a headache and the next thing you know…."

"I fucking hate him." The words were so small.

"Then fix it. Alvina can show you how."

Amye shook her head. "Three times over, right? Whatever you do comes back three times stronger. So if I curse him I suffer three times as much."

"Maybe that's true with Wicca, but not with witches. Believe me, if it was true, I'd be toast by now. Or at the very least frigid, because I've sent several stalkers off with limp dicks who won't ever get hard again."

She knew Amye would not doubt her. The simple fact was that when she was quite young Erika developed more than the other girls and had more guys try to get into her pants than should have ever been possible. Not all of them were stalkers, but there had been enough nonsense going on back then that Amye had commented on it several times.

The good news for Erika was in fact, Alvina, who would tolerate none of that foolishness.

"How do you avoid that curse?" There it was. The darkness Erika knew was there. Amye had never been happy. She just learned to play the part. Amye wanted more than life had ever offered her. Erika understood those feelings very well.

"I'm not sure. I've never been a Wicca. I'm a witch, pure and simple. I don't have to play by the rules that Wicca do. As far as I'm concerned they just took a name with bad connotations and cleaned it up a bit. I couldn't be happier, of course. I mean, without that, maybe there would still be a bias."

Erika sighed and looked around.

"I don't…I'm scared, Erika."

"Of course you are. But I'm here. Alvina's here." She took the other woman's hand and squeezed. "We're trying to make a coven, Amye. You're the first person I thought of, because you're stronger than you think you are. You've just forgotten that."

Amye closed her eyes and nodded her head. Her hand locked onto Erika's painfully.

"I can do it for you. I can take care of Will, but if I do, you get nothing from it. I mean, yes, he's gone, but you'll never know that you can handle yourself."

"I don't know how."

"I do. I'll show you."

Once again Erika looked around. Almost three blocks away now, the old man with the iced coffee coughed once more and fell to his knees in a painful crash. He was out of sight of the café, just as Erika planned. The fly in his throat moved down into his chest and promptly laid a thousand eggs that hatched in a matter of seconds. The maggots that came out of those eggs were hungry, and because Erika wished it, they feasted on the available flesh, ignoring their natural penchant to only eat what was already dead.

He fell to his side and clutched at his chest. A moment later he was face down on the sidewalk. It would be three minutes before anyone noticed. Another ten before the ambulance came around.

That would have to be long enough.

"You can really show me?"

"Five minutes. But nothing gets shown unless you are ready. Not just in your head, but in your heart." Erika stood up. "You have my number. Call me if you decide to, you know, change things up."

Several of the men cast an eye her way. Not all of them, but a few. She ignored their glances. For the moment she had more important things to worry about.

*   *   *

It didn't take long, not really. Amye watched her childhood friend walk away and bit her lip to stop from calling out. Will would have said appearances were important, and so she tried to follow his rules, resenting that he had that much power over her.

Deep in the back of her head she wondered how Erika's hands could feel so dry and cold, the knuckles swollen with age, when they looked so perfect. She pushed the notion away as best she could. Eyes were believed before other senses.

She waited for the sake of appearances and then texted a quick "I'm in."

In response Erika texted the hotel she was staying at and the room number.

Amye waited ten more minutes and then went there.

By the time she arrived, Erika was dressed in running shorts and a top with a sports bra. She was drinking a bottle of water and looking toward the room's window as she let Amye in.

"You're sure?"

There was no preamble. Amye nodded her head.

"So if you look at the notebook over on my nightstand, it's opened to the right page."

Amye walked over and looked, doubtful. She read the words three times before looking up at Erika.

"That's all there is to it?"

"No. Not quite. There is always a cost. Just, in this case the cost is not applied to you."

"So the three-fold curse?" She drew the last word out.

"I still don't know anything about that." Erika looked at her. From only a dozen feet away she seemed different than she had earlier. She seemed stronger. It was the way she carried herself, the look in her eyes. "I told you Alvina is looking for a coven. If I help you with this, you are making a compact with Alvina Bathory. You are agreeing to join her coven. Do you understand that?"

The name Bathory should have meant something—an old story about a countess who bathed in blood? Was that it? Maybe—but she shoved that aside as well.

Amye considered the words. Finally she nodded. "When do I meet Alvina?"

"Close your eyes."

"Pardon?"

"Close your eyes, and I'll let you talk to her."

There it was, that niggling doubt sneaking back in again. Still, she nodded her head and closed her eyes.

A moment later she heard Alvina for the first time. Her voice was strong, old, harsh as a blast of heat from an open oven door. "Do you agree to the terms, girl?" Hands touched her shoulders from behind. They were hands, she knew that, but they felt *wrong*. The fingers were warm and soft, but at the same time almost as if overlaid, Amye felt cold, hard fingers, long, cracked nails and knuckles made heavy with arthritis.

"I do."

"There's always a price to pay, but I can show you how to avoid paying it yourself. There are ways to deal with the devil, child, and I have learned them all in my time."

The lips that spoke brushed along her ear and Amye felt a completely foreign thrill. She had never once in her life been aroused by another woman, but something about that voice, the body she felt press against hers—young and vital and so very alive, but also withered and hard and nearly a husk instead of a body— made her shiver. It was Erika's voice. It was Erika's body. It was someone else entirely, a different creature, barely human, and older than she wanted to ever know.

"Take the paper. Say the words. Think of your Will and no one else. Say them three times."

Barely aware of what she was doing, Amye followed the words. She raised the paper and looked at the simple sentences. "A hundred cuts upon his brow. Tears of blood shed from broken eyes. He has lived long enough now. This is how my William dies." Simple words, but she took in a deep, shuddering breath before she repeated them again. Amye thought of Will. He was handsome. He had moments when he was loving. He could be so very charming when he wanted. She thought of his hand slapping across her face and spoke again. "A hundred cuts upon his brow. Tears of blood shed from broken eyes. He has lived long enough now. This is how my William dies."

The last word choked out of her mouth and she sighed and felt Erika's arms around her neck and shoulders, the press of warm, supple lips against the side of her face. The shadowy feel of cold, leathery flesh. "That's it then. All done."

When she opened her eyes Erika was in front of the window and sipping at her water. Her friend's eyes shone blue in the startling sunset. The angle of the light and the clock on the nightstand both told her that she had been standing there with her eyes closed for at least twenty minutes.

"You should go home, Amye. Your little ones are going to need you soon."

Amye left, a fine, high note whining in her ears all the while. Her skin felt too tight. Her body felt too heavy. There were a dozen physical complaints, though none of them quite made it to actual discomfort. The worst of them was her heart. It felt like it might shatter.

By the time she'd picked up the little ones and reached her house, the police were just pulling up.

Amye felt like a puppet. No, worse, like a ventriloquist dummy. The police spoke and she responded. They asked questions—*Do you have someone you can call to look after your children? Would you like us to drive you to the morgue? Are you all right, ma'am?*—endless questions it seemed, and though all she felt like doing on the inside was screaming and screaming until her voice fractured, she nodded her head and made all the right noises. Was that Erika's doing? Alvina's? Was she doing it herself? She couldn't tell.

For the next few hours nothing at all made sense. Wendy came over to handle the children. Her neighbor, Lisa, came over to drive her to identify the body. Poor Will was dead on arrival at the hospital. He'd forgotten his seatbelt, something Will would never do, and he'd gone through the steering wheel and then the windshield as he tried to avoid a truck that stopped in front of him. Following too closely was the only guess. The coroner had asked her if there were any identifying marks and she'd told him about the strawberry birthmark just under his left nipple. It looked like a boot. That was enough. He would not let her see the body. She was grateful for that. She didn't want to know what was left of Will's face after he

A hundred cuts upon his brow. Tears of blood shed from broken eyes. He has lived long enough now. This is how my William dies.

went through a steering wheel and a windshield.

Lisa, bless her heart, held her while she cried like a baby. Will was dead. Her husband was dead. Her rapist was dead. The man who always knew just the right way to hit so that there were no marks was dead.

She cried tears of sorrow. She cried tears of relief and joy. She cried until she could barely remember how to breathe.

Later that night, when sleep was finally ready to seduce her, the thought came to her mind that with Will's life insurance policies and portfolio she would very likely be a millionaire.

The thought did not bring her comfort.

Sleep remained a distant memory for several days.

*　　*　　*

It was almost a month later when she saw Erika again. She'd spotted her friend at the funeral, but there had been no time to speak. Too many people were around and too many people wanted to comfort her and to be comforted alike. What could she do?

But a month later, life went on as it always did, even after someone died. Breathing became a part of her world. Taking care of her babies without breaking into tears was a possibility.

Almost Halloween and everyone was getting their little ones ready for a night of trick or treating. Little Billy—never Will Junior again, that you very much—was dressed as Captain America. He loved that character and loved the movies. His sister, Lexi, was dressed as a witch. She'd been a clown earlier, because that was what Amye thought she wanted, but as soon as she'd seen herself in the clown outfit the pouting had begun. She would not be satisfied until she was a witch. A small price to pay for a happy Halloween.

The sun was still up. Halloween would fall on Sunday. They did the rounds on Friday afternoon, because Halloween in Salem was rather like Mardi Gras in New Orleans: more for adults than kids. Lisa and Tracy and Sarah and Michelle were all there with their children as well. It was a merry gang of them, moms and their kids. Though he kept his distance, Michelle's husband, Randy, was along as well. He walked behind them by a dozen paces and texted on his phone.

Amye had gotten Will's phone when she cleaned out his car. Turned out the bastard had been having an affair. She couldn't make herself be surprised. She was too numb to be angry or hurt. Deep inside the war continued between happiness that he was gone, guilt that she might have had something to do with it with her little spell, and sorrow that the man she loved—no matter how unworthy he might have been of that affection—was dead.

She hoped Randy wasn't the same way.

The winds were a little hellish coming off the water, and they whipped their way between houses and down streets with a cold roar. The occasional leaf from before had become a blanket of leaves that danced in the breeze, gathering together and making half-seen shapes that hinted at stranger things before they fell apart again.

Amye shivered in her coat, though the children seemed oblivious.

"Can you believe this breeze?" Lisa was forcing a cheerful tone for Amye's sake. She was being amazingly understanding.

Heather shook her head. "It's crazy! Wendy was talking about trying to do something later, you know, around 3 in the morning, but I think it might be too cold for any of that stuff." Heather, who was a mom and also worked as a gym instructor, had the body to get away with getting naked and dancing in the moonlight without worrying about appearances. Amye wasn't quite that confidant.

Besides, she had to stay home. No one to watch the kids.

Besides, if she was going to be a witch, she wasn't sure she could be a Wicca, too.

She thought of asking Erika to watch the kids and had to bite back a bark of laughter.

They reached the end of the block and Sarah looked around, making sure there were no cars around as she took Toby's pudgy little hand in hers. Toby was dressed as a fairy princess for the exact same reason that Lexi was dressed as a witch. Let there be peace on earth, even if Toby's dad, Joe, thought a boy dressing up as Elsa was wrong. Sarah would brook no arguments from Joe. She'd already ranted about that earlier.

Amye envied her that strength.

Will's face bubbled into her mind again, unavoidable, really, as she was still grieving. She pushed thoughts of her dead husband aside and looked at her little ones. They helped at times like this.

Lexi was dancing. Four years old and she danced as wildly as anyone ever had, with complete abandon and no concern about what anyone else wanted.

Billy was looking a few houses down the way, staring hard though his Captain America mask. His eyes were wide and his skin was sweating a bit despite the cold.

Amye looked, too. The house across the way was a landmark, a part of Salem since forever ago, built in Colonial times and likely rebuilt a few times as fires raged and destroyed the port town in the past. It was large and dark and the lights were off. Still, she could see the figure standing there. Small, not much more than five feet at best, with long white hair pulled back in a thick braid and with a face that was as withered and the head of an apple doll.

That figure stood perfectly still, one hand on a long oak staff. The other holding something dark that moved and clawed at the air as if held by its tail. Whatever it was, it struggled feebly in the grasp of that ancient crone's hand.

Crone. It was the best word. The crone smiled at her boy, and Billy looked back and smiled.

"Pretty." That was the word he said right before he collapsed. There was nothing graceful about it. Every muscle in his body seemed to go soft at the same time and he fell straight down in a heap.

Amye looked at him for a few heartbeats, trying to understand. "Billy?" She barely spoke. "Billy?" Better. That sounded like real speech. "Billy?!" She was screaming now, and her son would surely respond. "Billy!!" On her knees next to him, her hands reaching to pull him closer. Lisa, God love her, was already calling 911.

Billy did not move. He was still. His eyes remained as wide as before, but they looked wrong, too dry.

She screamed her son's name a dozen more times but he did not respond. He was dead and she knew it.

Her eyes searched madly for answers, but there were none to be found. The crone was gone. She had vanished. All around her were the faces of women and children that were a part of her world. They looked as helpless as she felt.

*   *   *

Erika was at her house the next day. Amye opened the door and stared blankly for several seconds, her mind not working well enough to allow recognition.

"Amye, I'm so sorry. I wanted to tell you how bad I feel about what happened."

Amye nodded and stepped aside automatically. Erika moved past her, a concerned look on her face.

"It's only temporary, you know that, right?"

"What?" The comment was enough to shock her out of her stupor. "What's temporary?"

"Billy. He'll be with you again soon."

"What do you mean?"

Erika led her to her own living room and urged her to sit and Amye did. Part of her seethed at the idea that Erika could manipulate her that easily. Another part was aghast at her own behavior. Erika had helped her out of a horrible situation, hadn't she?

She couldn't say anymore. The loss of Billy on the heels of William was a shadow over every thought and every action.

"It's Halloween, Amye. That's a special day, you know. The veil between worlds is thinner, fragile, really, and a strong enough woman can change the shape of the world if she wants it badly enough."

"What are you talking about, Erika? Jesus, I just lost my son."

"No. You just finished making your bargain. Every witch in Alvina's coven needs a familiar. Alvina has been working out the details on how to make this work to your advantage. You get Billy back. He becomes your familiar."

"What? Wait, familiars, aren't those supposed to be black cats?"

"No, Amye. Familiars are demons. Minor things, really. They help protect you when you are weak, and they follow your orders. You have to feed them, of course. Milk from your third nipple. They need that to survive and that makes them loyal."

"I don't have a third nipple."

"You will. It'll happen when you give birth to Billy again."

"Birth to...?"

"Billy. Your son. He had to be taken away, but only so you could get him back. Alvina is already hard at work, making sure that no one knows that Billy died. His body is gone from the hospital and the paperwork is all muddled and lost in the system. Parlor tricks, really."

"You took Billy's *body*?" Amye's voice stretched out into a shrill note that bordered on a scream.

Erika nodded and smiled. It was a cold smile, as cold as her friend's eyes. One hand touched Amye's brow. That touch was cold, too. As cold as the emptiness that filled Amye.

"You have your daughter. Don't worry, I'll take care of her while you're busy."

"Busy? Doing what?" The frown felt as numb as the rest of her but that changed when the pain crept into Amye's insides. It started slow and subtle but within a minute the cramps were bad enough to make her wonder if she were bleeding.

Erika helped her lay back on the sofa and moved the pillows around to support her head properly.

"I told you before, you're going to have your Billy back. He's to be your familiar and that means you have to have a connection with him that is as strong as any mother ever had with her child."

"Alvina had three sons. They were hard births. This is going to hurt, Amye, but I believe in you."

The pain was bigger than anything she had ever felt before, and Amye looked at her stomach as it started to grow. Flesh pulled and strained, and Amye rolled back her head and howled.

"Think of how close you'll be, Amye. No son will ever love a mother more."

Erika left the room, heading for the hallway and the bedroom where Lexi was taking her nap.

Amye fell back, already exhausted, and felt something sharp inside of her body pushing at her stomach and her guts and her womb. Whatever it was felt as large as a car. She didn't think she had enough strength left to utter another scream.

She was wrong.

Erika said not a word as she left Amye's house. Some things must be endured alone.

Alvina knew that too well, and as a result, so did Erika.

In time Amye would understand as well. When she had recovered properly they would talk about the next stage of growing a proper coven.

Slow and steady was the way to go.

Alvina spoke to herself as she carried the sleeping girl-child in her arms. "Home," she said. "It has a nice ring to it."

White Witch
Catherine Grant

All babies come into this world the same color—red and squalling for their mother's breast. Annie's newborn was just as ruddy and healthy as any baby I'd delivered as the household midwife; but on first sight I could tell the girl child wasn't Mr. Rutherford's kin. Her skin would soon be the wrong color to inherit Rose Hall.

"Let me see my daughter." said Annie. She gasped in between syllables, trying to catch her breath while she endured the throbbing pain between her legs and the shrinking void in her womb. I cut the cord of life between mother and child and saved it, knowing I'd need the blood inside, especially if the little girl in my arms was to be safe. Jamaica was on the cusp of abolition, but not there yet. That made the child's life *complicated*. Nothing was sacred to me now but Annie and the little one's safety; this precious spark who was my granddaughter in all but blood. Annie was my kin as though she had been born to my barren womb, but to the world I was just her Haitian nanny, a caregiver and a slave. In spirit, I was Annie's mother and father in one, her only family.

"Raeni, please let me see my daughter. I want to hold her." Her eyes pleaded with me, reading my thoughts of preparedness, asking me to wait, to give her time to enjoy the child she'd just carried inside her for nine months.

A spark of anger flared inside me at Annie's selfishness. The baby wouldn't have a difficult life if I acted soon. Strangers would assume she was mine, not Annie's. If Mr. Rutherford would abide it, I could raise the child as my own. Or we could tell him the baby died and I could take her to the servant quarters in secret. I couldn't deny that the thought of having a daughter to raise again gave me a wellspring of joy inside my heart that filled me to the brim. My eyes ran over as I put the newborn, still slick with fluid and spotted with blood, on Annie's chest.

Mother and child stared at one another while Annie cried and cried, be it from joy or from the pain of knowing that she could not keep her daughter like most mothers can. There would be too many questions if the situation was left to chance. Drying her tears with the sleeve of her nightdress, Annie sat up against her pillows, grimacing from the pain, and began to nurse the baby as I cleaned, putting the placenta away for later.

I made Annie drink some water and I applied a poultice to her sore, tender sex to reduce the swelling. She'd done well, my Annie. She was strong like me, stronger than her parents had been. Smart as anyone I knew, too. If she had been born a man with that strength and brains, she could have been a doctor or a lawyer. Maybe even a scientist or a famous scholar. For the months ahead, she would need to be stronger and smarter, still.

"What will you name her?" I asked. I thought the question would distract from the unasked questions hovering in the room like a *duppy*.

She looked up at me and smiled beatifically. Her long, chestnut hair stuck to her forehead with sweat and her eyes were tired, but watching her daughter eat, content and safe, was enough for my darling to look like a queen. She soothed the baby's head, and then kissed her. "Her name is Millicent."

"That's a beautiful name for a beautiful girl." I stroked the baby's forehead, kissed Annie on the cheek, and then finished cleaning before leaving them to spend the last uncomplicated moments they would have together as mother and daughter.

Mr. Rutherford sat on a chair in front of the fireplace, his face red with drink. The room smelled like sweat and whiskey, a sweet, cloying stench that the master carried with him wherever he went. I noticed with a grimace and a hidden scowl that it wasn't yet noon and he was already deep in his cups, a habit that Annie seemed to abide, as long as Mr. Rutherford was more gentle with her than her second husband.

Upon hearing me enter, he stood. His lanky form struggled to keep from stumbling forward and over. "Does the baby live? How is my wife?" He slurred the last syllable and took another gulp of whiskey, almost as though the other end of his word was hiding on the bottom of his tumbler.

I nodded. "Yes. A girl. Miss Annie is fine. She's resting with the child. The baby is a bit weak so they need to sleep as much as possible." I didn't ask if he'd like to meet his daughter, holding my breath to see if he would move toward the room that held his wife and another man's baby.

The Master didn't look either pleased or displeased with the news. He simply nodded, raised a glass to me, and drank deeply. "I suppose I should tend to the cane fields. Tell my wife that I will be gone 'till late. I'm sure you can take care of her better than I can."

He left the room without delay. I wasn't surprised. Despite my cleaning of the birthing room, it still smelled like blood and salt, and Annie was breastfeeding. I watched with contempt as Mr. Rutherford left the house, remembering how my own mother had used her teeth to cut the cords when my sister had given birth to my nieces and nephews. Most white men were squeamish when it came to the act of childbirth, as though they'd like to avoid thinking about how humans came into this earth. I imagined with a laugh asking Mr. Rutherford to bite Millicent's umbilical cord. The man would've fainted dead away.

It is no surprise to me that so many European fables are full of babies emerging, fully grown, from various objects. How did these babies come to be? Not every life is an immaculate conception, no? These men at one point were familiar with the place their babies sprang from in order to make them, yet you'd think the woman's garden was the very origin of evil the way they avoid talking about it or gazing upon it. Perhaps that is why my daughter preferred the company of the bookkeeper Takoo rather than her own husband. Takoo most certainly had no problems gazing upon her form or tasting her fruit.

I went to tend to the baby once Mr. Rutherford was safely away from the house. Takoo was no doubt waiting somewhere in the slave quarters, shut away so he would not be seen agonizing over the state of his child and his beloved.

When I entered her bedroom, Annie beckoned me to come closer and handed me the baby. "Please, Raeni, take her to Takoo. Let him see her tonight, at least. We can figure out what to do in the morning."

"Darling, we need to do something *now*. This cannot wait a day. I told Mr. Rutherford the baby is——.""

Annie wouldn't look at me. She raised a hand for me to halt my plans. Head lowered, hair over her eyes, she said, "I will deal with it when I need to. Please don't press me on this, Raeni."

I did as my daughter asked of me, though every part of my body cried out for me to continue, to move forward with my plan.

Annie had me take the child to Takoo every night for the next three months. Each night I would take the girl child to her real father in his chambers, where he would hold her and sing to her in *patois* and tell her she was going to be the queen of voodoo with a father like him and a grandmother like me in her blood and soul. He was just as careless as Annie, too drunk on love and happiness to care about what would happen when Mr. Rutherford saw that the baby wasn't his, that Annie had deceived him.

I prepared my magic with the placenta that held Annie and Millicent's blood. I brought it to Papa Ghede and asked him to not take my babies too soon. I asked him to give me strength when the time came. Each time I went to Annie to ask that we go to Mr. Rutherford and tell him the child died, she would refuse to listen. She would hold her baby and cry and then send me to Takoo.

"Takoo, you have to listen to me." I pleaded with him one night, clutching Millicent to my chest, away from his outstretched arms. "You and Annie need to start thinking about this baby and what's going to happen when Mr. Rutherford asks to see her. Her skin is already dark."

The candlelight gleamed on Takoo, his fine features creased with worry. Sighing, he sat down, and licked his dry his lips to speak. "How many slaves in Jamaica were born from masters raping our sisters, wives and mothers?"

"Takoo, it doesn't matter——"

"I love her, Mother Raeni."

"Annie or Millicent?"

He looked up at me as though I'd struck him. "Both. Why would you even need to ask that?"

I wanted to take him in my hands and shake him like a coconut tree. He and my daughter were foolish children that had no idea what love was. They were selfish, bathing in their love and ignoring the sharks in the water. I sighed and let him hold his daughter and she laughed and smiled at him, loving him with such depth even as an infant. That was joy, right there in his arms—pure and selfless, without the terrors of the world crowding in on it. My heart cried out in sorrow that Annie and Takoo did not live in a world where they could have that together.

"You both risk too much waiting around and thinking nothing will come for you." I said. "You are like a mouse with his tail on fire, but he thinks it is a cool breeze. You risk your daughter's happiness. That is not love. That is recklessness."

Takoo deflated in front of me. I felt guilty watching it, but the satisfaction at finally getting through after months of pleading was like a breath of life. He nodded. "I'll talk to Annie. Tell her to meet me tomorrow night in the guest room. It has been so long since I've seen her alone."

He looked up at me, and I saw the fight was gone from his eyes. "I just want to be with her and our child in the same room, like normal parents. I don't think we're going to live through this, Mother Raeni. I think the beasts at our doors will devour us. They call us animals and tell us that we're not worth a thing, but who are the ones ready to tear apart a mother and father from their child?"

It was my turn to deflate. I nodded and left him alone with Millicent. I would come back later, gather her up, and take the baby back to her mother's room. Annie and Mr. Rutherford had been sleeping separate since Millicent was feeding around the clock and waking up at all hours of the night.

I had visions in my head of finally getting through to Annie once Takoo had spoken to her, of getting some sense into that foolish head of hers, so full of intelligence, yet void of the common wisdom that would keep her daughter alive. My heart finally relaxed after three months of waiting for the devourer to come and take my world from me. I thanked Papa Ghede for keeping my baby safe.

I breathed relief far too soon.

The next morning, I awoke to screams and the harsh, barking voice of a man. I flew out of bed, covered my nakedness and headed toward the shrill cries of my daughter. When I burst into the room, Mr. Rutherford was holding Millicent, his hands underneath each one of her armpits as she wailed, her chubby arms writhing in discomfort. She wore only a diaper, full and leaking onto the floor, but Mr. Rutherford wasn't paying that any mind. His clothes were ruffled, worn. He looked like he'd slept in them and then stumbled into his wife's bedroom, perhaps looking for her to do her wifely duty now that she was healed. He smelled of rum and whiskey, like a perfume gone to rot. His anger had sobered him and his eyes were a bonfire of anger.

"You lying, cheating *whore*." he said, spit flying from his lips toward his wife. "I am humiliated. I'm sure everyone in Montego Bay knows now that my wife would rather lie with slaves than her own husband."

Annie wailed indistinguishably, her arms outstretched toward her daughter. She dropped to her knees and put her hands together as if in prayer.

"Please give me my daughter." she wailed, holding out her hands. But his grip only seemed to tighten on the infant.

"Mr. Rutherford." I said it with a calm, simple voice.

He turned, startled to realize that I was there. He almost dropped Millicent before catching her indelicately in mid-air. I could see that he was holding her too harshly, his hands just as angry as the rest of his body, making dimples in the baby's soft flesh, pushing against her tiny bones. The infant wailed in pain.

"Please give me the baby, sir." I held out my hands. "You're hurting her and she needs her diaper changed."

His eyes narrowed at me. I could see they were bloodshot as they flicked from one side of the room to the next, never focusing for long on me or his wife who he now knew was with another man, a man he barely recognized as human. Backing away, Mr. Rutherford didn't give me the baby.

"If I throw her down the well," he said, "and tell everyone she died, nobody will question it. Nobody will even ask to see the body."

Annie began to scream.

"Hush, my darling." I said. "Please, you're scaring Millicent." I turned to Mr. Rutherford, my eyes never leaving his face. "Please sir, give me the baby. She never hurt nobody. She didn't have any say in who she was born to. You can give her to me and I'll raise her as my own. I will tell people that she's my daughter, and you can say that your wife's baby died. Sometimes babies die and nobody knows why. I've helped with hundreds of births since I became a midwife and babies die every day. No one will ask any questions." My hands reached out, my heart ready to explode. I inched closer.

Mr. Rutherford turned his eyes away from me, toward the door. He ran out of the room and toward the front parlor. The baby screamed louder as he descended the staircase and struggled for balance. His heavy steps pounded down each wooden stair. Annie stayed behind and screamed for Millicent, her wails echoing off the walls as I chased after Mr. Rutherford, struggling to keep my robe closed against my nakedness.

For a brief moment I thought that Mr. Rutherford would go tumbling down the stairs, feet and head twisting in impossible angles and spilling the baby down with him. My heart almost burst in my chest. He regained his footing and kept running with the baby right out the front door. I chased after him, my old legs feeling slow and feeble underneath me, and I saw him head into the barn.

I entered through the doors of the barn just as he lay the baby on the center of the dusty floor and picked up an axe. Takoo was behind me, gasping for air, wheezing to please not kill his daughter, to show mercy.

"Mr. Rutherford, stop!" My voice boomed in the air. I grasped for my magic, for anything I could do to protect the baby, but voodoo is not a fast weapon. Voodoo requires planning and ritual and is slow to act. I had killed Annie's second husband, a large brute who enjoyed abusing my lovely one, slowly over a period of months. I'd put white oleander in his food. I'd cursed his stomach and his bowels until he shit nothing but water for a month and rotted from the inside out. His death had been just and fitting for someone so cruel.

Mr. Rutherford drank his own poison willingly every day in whiskey and rum. I saw his death as low hanging fruit. It was just a matter of time before his own habits killed him. I bemoaned my lack of wisdom and begged Papa Ghede to forgive my mercy for this man who now threatened to cut up my granddaughter and feed her blood to the thirsty ground.

For now, Mr. Rutherford held his hand. He looked up at both of us and his mouth curled in an ugly sneer. "You did this. You made a fool of me." I couldn't tell if he was speaking to me or Takoo.

Mr. Rutherford raised his axe and I grabbed a knife off the wall and aimed for his guts. The knife sliced clean through, and I pulled it out again with ease. I put it back in him again, and again, the blood flowing down over the front of his pants and staining them the color of wine. He lost his grip on the axe and it fell toward Millicent, missing her by mere inches before Takoo darted forward and scooped her up off the ground, cradling her in his arms and soothing her, brushing gravel and splinters from her soft skin as she wailed.

Mr. Rutherford fought me with his dying strength, putting his hands on my throat and squeezing. Darkness closing in on my vision, I whipped the knife forward and sliced open his gut, the blade sliding through his flesh like over-ripe papaya. A hot pile of entrails and blood gushed onto our feet. He smelled as bad on the inside as he did on the outside, and with a whimper and a choked scream he fell to the ground, clutching at my robe and ripping it off my body as he collapsed.

I stood in the near darkness of the barn, breathing heavy, the blood-soaked knife in my hand. It felt like an anchor, keeping me in one place, my soul threatening to fly from me and stay with Papa Ghede, but I could hear the Lord of Death sing to me that it wasn't my time. I had much work to do.

Already the dry, packed earth in the barn soaked up Mr. Rutherford's blood and his guts, accepting it as an offering. This would be as good a place as any to bury him, away from the prying eyes of the household. I turned to Takoo and he averted his gaze—from my nakedness, or from the gore at my feet, I knew not which.

"Bring the baby back to Annie."

I could tell that Takoo had never seen a dead man before. He was shaken by my composure in the face of his own fear. Takoo was gentle, bookish, two qualities that no doubt drew he and Annie together. He clutched his daughter to him and kissed her forehead, soothing her screams.

I pointed at the door. "Get now, and bring one of the field hands here. I need someone to help me dig and dig fast."

He nodded and fled, glancing back at me as though I were a demon. I suppose that is how I looked, naked and dipped in blood. I pulled my robe off Mr. Rutherford's body and put it back on, feeling the heat and weight of the gore that soaked in. I went to the corner and got a pick axe and started to break up the center of the floor in the barn. By the time the field hand came in, a large fellow named Big John, the center of the dirt floor was broken up and crumbling. Big John glanced at Mr. Rutherford's body, nodded to me, and began to work without question or objection.

I stepped outside into the hot glare of the afternoon sun. The plantation was busy, mulling about as though nothing at all happened, though admittedly Mr. Rutherford had never been that helpful to us. He mostly drank and barked needless orders and annoyed the house servants. My robe was soaked in his blood, stark against the light brown fabric, but the servants gave me only a passing glance, the rumor circulated about Mr. Rutherford's fate. Most slaves do not faint at the sight of blood. We see it daily.

As I approached the porch, I could see Annie sitting on one of the rocking chairs, the baby dressed and in her lap, playing with her own feet and cooing. It was the first time Millicent had been outdoors, out in the open for all to see. She blinked, her small brown eyes observing all she saw as her mother stared out to the horizon, her face expressionless. Annie wore a simple dress of light blue, Takoo's favorite color, and her hair was done up in ringlets.

"What shall I tell them when they come asking after my husband?" she asked, still staring at the horizon.

I paused but did not look toward her. "Tell them I killed him. Just like your last husband, my darling one. Tell them that I am a voodoo witch that will devour all men's hearts and use their blood to fly in the air like a bird. Tell them I am the devil himself, made flesh to steal their souls away to hell. Do what you must, my lovely one. Keep yourself and my granddaughter safe."

I passed by her and went into the house. I went to my room for the appropriate materials: camphor, a dried toadstool top, powdered jellyfish, John the Conqueror root, and went out to the barn and blessed the ground, asked it to seal up Mr. Rutherford's *duppy*, which would no doubt be angry and seek vengeance against me, Takoo, Annie and even Millicent, though the baby was an innocent.

Big John finished digging the grave and we sealed Mr. Rutherford up in the ground. The earth was soft, disturbed. We wet the floor, packed down the grave, then laid out the rest of the earth until it was just a flat, dark patch.

Later that night, I heard Mr. Rutherford's blood cry out. I went in the next morning and prayed over the grave again, asking Papa Ghede to silence that fool in the underworld. Rutherford's blood and bones continued their song every night, despite my prayers, and soon they drew the attention of one of his friends, Mr. Boudreau, who came occasionally to play cards and drink and leer at Annie.

Boudreau came asking after Mr. Rutherford one evening, stinking of rum and swaying in the doorway. Annie turned him away, saying that her husband was sick and in no condition to play cards and drink. Mr. Boudreau returned the next night, and the next. The suspicion, planted deep in his heart, grew like a strangling vine, choking out mercy and compassion and reason.

"I'll be back with the law behind me." The man slurred in Annie's face after she'd turned him away every day for a month. "I know something happened to him. And you have that voodoo *thing* here. She probably killed John Palmer and your second husband, too. Either that, or you are a rather unlucky woman to have husbands that are so ill."

My daughter's face was stone. "My husbands died of sickness, sir. It was unfortunate for me, and I'd ask that you not mock my grief for your own amusement. Raeni has looked after me since I was a child, so please keep your accusations to yourself." Her words were always so precise, like a knife, my brilliant, lovely one.

Boudreau pointed at Annie, his hand getting too close to her. "They died of voodoo from that witch. She should be hanged."

Annie said nothing. She closed the door more, signaling the conversation was over.

Boudreau's hand stopped the door from closing. "I want to see my friend and I want to see him *now*, you simple bitch!"

Takoo heard the shouts, and the cursing, and came from his office and stood behind his beloved in the sliver of doorway. He wasn't much taller than Annie, thin and lanky. But Mr. Boudreau took a step back regardless and his hand dropped back down to his side. Takoo stood here next to Annie, a protective presence, a symbol of unity that didn't need words or violence.

Mr. Boudreau nodded. "I'll see you soon. Both of you. And that witch."

Annie stood in the doorway, shaking. Her face was pale and drawn. When Boudreau mounted his horse and rode off, she collapsed and Takoo helped her to the parlor.

The whole time this stranger stood in the doorway, threatening me and getting dangerously close to my daughter, I heard Mr. Rutherford's blood and bones crying out for vengeance, telling his friend to bring two dozen men with him and to tie a noose around my neck and hang me from the *guango* tree out front of the plantation. I heard him say that Millicent should get thrown down the well, and that Annie should be locked away in a sanitarium, and Takoo should be made a eunuch. We all deserved destruction and misery.

I closed the door, shutting out the vile cries of Mr. Rutherford's *duppy*, and went to the parlor to pour my daughter a strong drink. She was no longer nursing Millicent, so she could have a bit of rum. She drank, staring up at me, her eyes wide.

"What are we going to do, Raeni?"

I shook my head. "I don't know." I'd used up the placenta into as many protection charms as I could around Annie, Takoo and the baby.

That night I performed a ceremony that would give Annie strength, that would protect us all, especially the baby. I knew Papa Ghede had that child in his hand. He hated the death of children and would not take her before her time. The rest of us would need a stronger miracle.

I went into the barn the next morning, and in the center of the floor where we had buried Mr. Rutherford there was a hibiscus bush that had grown overnight. It was possible that Rutherford had a bit of magic in him and his bitter *duppy* was more powerful that I'd thought. The flowers were deep red, the color of blood, with dark black centers. The perfume was heady and thick in the barn so I opened the doors to let in the air.

Takoo came in and stared at the hibiscus bush. "If they come, I'm going to take Annie and Millicent and I'm going to run."

I sighed and my shoulders drooped, weary from pretending to be strong. "They would catch you."

Takoo sighed, silently acknowledging my logic, and then left the barn.

We went about the routine of our day, tending the sugarcane fields, cleaning the house and preparing meals. Around noon, Annie said that we should slaughter the pig Mr. Rutherford was saving for Christmas, that we should roast it tonight out on the lawns and that we should let the entire plantation eat together. The cook, Sarah, saw the roast as a challenge and she created all of her favorite dishes—fried plantain, steamed cabbage, rice and peas, callaloo and yams. We opened the case of rum in the basement that Mr. Rutherford had thought none of us knew was there.

In the fading light of the day I thought for sure would be my last, we feasted, the entire household and every servant on the plantation. I even went to the barn and poured a cask of rum on Mr. Rutherford's grave as an offering, and for once his *duppy* was silent.

We set up a bonfire and danced around it. Takoo and Annie danced together, twirling around and laughing, Millicent between them screaming in delight. We sang songs of love and thanksgiving to God. I prayed as well that Papa Ghede had interceded well for me and that Jehovah would protect us.

In the light of the sunset, just as the velvet blue of the night sky overcame us, we saw men come on horseback from the road. There were three of them, Mr. Boudreau and two young night watchmen, barely men. They all looked rather startled at the sight of fifty slaves and one tiny, beautiful white woman gathered on the lawns in the fragrant night breeze, eating roast pig and dancing around a bonfire with smiles on our faces and joy in our hearts, gifts that slaves had no right to enjoy while they toiled on this earth.

Mr. Boudreau rode forward and pointed at me. "That's her, right there. She's a witch and a murderess. Rutherford never misses an appointment, and he has been sick now for over a month. Just like the other two masters of this plantation."

The watchmen rode forward and dismounted. Annie handed Takoo the baby and stepped out from the shadows of the bonfire, her shawl wrapped tight against her shoulders.

"Mr. Rutherford is sick." she said. "And Mr. Boudreau is an unwanted guest. Please explain to me why you're even entertaining this madness."

The two men disregarded Annie's question. They glanced around at the faces of fifty slaves, half of them young, strong men. One of the watchmen stepped forward and surveyed our banquet. "Looks like you're having quite a party for having a sick husband inside, Miss Rutherford."

"That's Mrs. Palmer. I never changed my name. And I don't

see how what I do with my household is any of your concern. I'm not violating the law by roasting some pig, am I?"

The watchmen glanced at each other. "All of your husbands have been sick? Is that true?"

Annie nodded. "It's not unusual for people to get sick and die."

The watchman smiled and glanced back at Boudreau. They nodded and laughed together as if sharing a joke. "Well then you wouldn't mind if we go inside and talk to Mr. Rutherford, I suppose." He did not wait for permission. The watchmen moved toward the front door.

Their horses turned and I saw all three men brought guns with them, large rifles and clubs for beatings, and a bundle of rope perfect for a noose. I felt my stomach sink, but I was not surprised. In Jamaica, as in many other parts of the world, people like me didn't get a trial. I would never get to tell them how Annie's second husband beat her until she passed out. I would never get to show them Millicent and the bruises on her chest where Mr. Rutherford had squeezed her and broken two of her ribs. People like me are just hung from a tree and left to rot for the crows.

I moved to step forward, to confess my sins, and I felt my daughter's hands steady me. She pressed me back into the crowd, behind Big John, who took me by the arm and led me into the darkness, behind the light of the bonfire that now lit up Annie's short form as she stepped in front of the watchmen to block their path.

"You may not enter." She held up her arms to them, her palms upward as though she were waiting for it to rain. "There is no reason for it. I will tell you that my husband is not in the house. He is dead."

The watchmen stepped back. Mr. Boudreau still sat atop his horse. His mouth hung open and then curled into a sneer.

"All three of my husbands are dead." Annie lifted her chin. "They are dead because I killed them. My nanny is not the Witch of Rose Hall. I am." Her voice cracked and then she steadied it. She took a step toward the men. "I am the witch you're seeking. My first husband did really die of sickness. I truly loved him. My second husband I did not love. He was cruel and brutish. I put poison in his food every single day. I slipped it into his drink. It didn't kill him nearly fast enough for my pleasure."

The watchmen were speechless. They were clearly not trained

to handle such horrors.

Mr. Boudreau dismounted his horse and pointed at Annie . "Arrest her, you fools! She's confessing!"

Annie turned to him. She smiled wolfishly. "Oh, I do confess to killing your friend, Mr. Boudreau. I confess that he was a useless drunk with no love for me. I disemboweled him and buried him in the fields. I took his blood and I bathed in it to keep myself young and beautiful. Then I took our baby and I killed it and ate it for a meal. The flesh of the young has powerful magic that will make me unstoppable."

A house servant, a young girl, stepped forward. "It's true." she said. "She bathes in blood, then flies about in the moonlight like a crow. Miss Raeni taught her everything she knows about voodoo. We are terrified of her."

A man stepped forward and nodded. "She's killed many slaves for her pleasure, sirs. She lies with them and then kills them. I've seen many grown men slain by her magic."

More of the plantation servants nodded and shouted out testimonies, wild tales from old Jamaican myths born of imagination and darkness.

Annie stepped forward and all three men backed away. "I suggest you gentlemen leave here and come back with a dozen men if you wish to take me from my home and away from Rose Hall. Your strength is not enough. The right word from my lips and my slaves will be enchanted. They will step forward at my command and they will tear you limb from limb and bury your bones next to Mr. Rutherford out in the fields."

As if sensing the right moment, every plantation slave moved as one toward the men. The watchmen jumped back as if bitten by a snake. They looked at each other, then to Mr. Boudreau, and got back on their horses. Mr. Boudreau followed suit, his mouth twisted in anger, his eyes focused on Miss Annie. All three rode away back toward the road. When they'd disappeared around the bend, I emerged from behind Big John and went to Annie.

"They'll be back for you." I said.

She nodded. "I know they will. And by that time, you and Millicent and Takoo should be gone." The last word was cracked with sorrow, and Annie fell onto my breast and sobbed. She hugged me with such fierceness that I thought her arms would break. Takoo came forward with the baby and I took them in to our embrace. We all wept bitterly, even little Millicent. It was the last time we would be together as a family.

The rest of the plantation circled around us and prayed for protection, for providence and blessings. We were packed provisions, clothing and whatever money Annie and the rest of the household could scrape together.

I slept in my chamber while Annie and Takoo spent their last night together. In the morning, before dawn, I packed the horses and knocked on Annie's door. Her and Takoo were already awake and dressed. Takoo had Millicent slung to his body, ready for travel.

We stepped out into the morning air, the grass slick with dew, the bonfire burnt out to cinders, a visual reminder of last night's festivities and the threat that could come at any moment and take my Annie away.

Takoo and I were given a letter from Annie with her seal giving us our freedom and ownership of the two mares. It was no guarantee that we would not be taken on the road by bounty hunters looking for runaway slaves or slavers themselves, but with the growing abolitionist sentiment in Jamaica, Takoo and I were hopeful we could make it to a ship, and then to New Orleans. In Louisiana, we would find a community of voodoo practitioners and a place for children like Millicent of mixed blood.

Takoo and Annie embraced, their kiss so desperate that I had to look away to keep myself from weeping. Annie kissed Millicent's forehead, her face haggard from the tears she'd spilled for hours. Then she came to me. I kissed both of her cheeks and wiped away her tears.

"No more sorrow, my darling." I said. "I love you, my daughter. I shall see you again."

She shook her head, then kissed me on the cheeks and we released each other. I blew a kiss to her as I mounted my horse and looked back to make sure Takoo was following. He rode his own horse toward me, his face a stone of misery. I watched and waved to my Annie until we were out of sight and far down the road, past the coconut trees that marked Rose Hall plantation. We took the road toward the safest port.

Halfway there, I broke down and sobbed, a sound of mourning that went deep into the well of my soul. Behind me, I could hear Takoo doing the same.

Takoo and I made it to New Orleans by ship. Annie made sure we had enough money for a private cabin, but after weeks of solitude with a lovesick man and a colicky baby, I longed for land. More than open skies and solid ground, I longed to write to the slaves at Rose Hall and know my Annie's fate. When we docked, I took a step off the ship and smelled the air sweet with Jasmine and I wept. I kissed the ground and thanked God we were safe.

Takoo and I soon found a place among the court of voodoo queen Marie Laveau. Three months after we settled, I received word that Annie was arrested for murder and sent to Bonavista Sanitarium. The plantation slaves spread word of the White Witch all over the island, making Annie Jamaica's most infamous criminal. Rose Hall itself stood abandoned, the locals complaining that it was haunted by *duppys*. Though Annie was very much alive, the slaves said they had killed her out of self-defense and buried her on site at the plantation, but that her *duppy* still lingered, angry with the slaves who had murdered her. No one would buy the property.

My name was lost in the legend that surrounded my daughter. Takoo took my place, his character a voodoo priest whose granddaughter, Millicent, was cursed by the White Witch of Rose Hall. He hated those lies that robbed his beloved of her dignity.

"She saved us, Takoo." I told him one night when we were alone.

Millicent was now old enough to speak, asking about her mother with escalating urgency. "I don't want her to forget our Annie, Raeni. I don't want our story to be replaced with those wretched rumors. I don't want Millicent to think her mother was evil."

I smiled at him. "Write your own story then. Quickly though. Tell the little one now, so she holds that truth in her heart like a jewel."

Takoo nodded. He told Millicent the story I just told you, of a brave woman who, if born a man, could have been a doctor or a lawyer, a scientist or a famous scholar. Instead, she became a witch.

But only for a little while.

 # Baskets
Paul McMahon

A short while after ringing Grandma Shawl's doorbell, Tommy drummed his foot impatiently on the porch. He inhaled slowly and told himself that being made to wait didn't require getting angry. There were worse ways to spend these few moments. The sun dazzled, the birds sang, and the breeze whisked away the worst of the day's heat. He would refuse to leave Grandma Shawl's presence until he got what he was after, and despite expectations, he would keep his cool doing it.

Finally, the lock clicked. Tommy forced a smile and relaxed the muscles in his shoulders. He was still wearing his sunglasses. Too late to return them to the car, he snapped them off and dangled them in the collar of his shirt.

"Grandma Shawl?" he said as the door opened.

Face tightening, her eyes narrowed. "Tantrums."

He clenched his fists at the sound of his childhood nickname, but he forced them open and held his teeth slightly apart to keep from grinding them. Thinking of the picture of Grandpa he wanted, his shoulders relaxed. "I haven't seen you in so long," he said.

"By your own choice."

"Yeah, it was. And I'm... sorry about that."

Distrusting him to the point of hostility, her eyes narrowed even more as she closed the door a little, positioning herself so he couldn't see into her house. He'd known she would treat him this way, and he'd prepared for it, but it would be easier to stay calm if she would stop looking at him like he'd just climbed out of her trash.

"You want something," she said.

Slow inhale, open the mouth slightly, relax the shoulders, admit the truth with a smile. "I do," Tommy said. "But I wanted to see you, as well. I wanted to apologize and see if we can let bygones be bygones."

Grandma Shawl's eyes opened a little. "Bygones," she said. "That's something your Grandpa used to say."

She glared at him a few more seconds. Unclenching his fists again, Tommy swallowed a lump that threatened to grow into a yell.

"You don't want to be friendly," Grandma Shawl said. "Go away. If you want something bad enough to come here, it can't mean anything good for me. Go tell your mother. She can ask me."

"Grandma Shawl, please. I apologize. I shouldn't have said those awful things after Grandpa's funeral."

"You are a hateful brat," she said. "I want nothing to do with you."

He kept his smile, though it felt as if soon he'd have to keep it in place with knives. She started to close the door, and he stopped his foot from kicking it back at her. If he was going to free himself from this bottomless pit of rage, he needed to face her without losing his temper. Just for an hour or so. The crack in the door narrowed some more.

"Do you need help with anything?" he asked.

The door stopped, leaving a gap only wide enough for half of Grandma Shawl's face.

"Help with what?" she asked.

"Anything," Tommy said. "Do you need something moved? Trash gotten rid of?"

"I have someone for that," she said. "Spanish girl. Brought me to the doctor yesterday, then around to do some other... chores."

Tommy opened his mouth to ask something else, but had no idea what. An instant before he shoved himself into her home, Grandma Shawl spoke again.

"Tell me what you want, Tantrums."

"I want to come inside so we can talk."

"I don't want you in my house," she said. "I don't have heaps of money lying around, you know. My money is in the bank, and there's barely enough there to see that I'm buried next to your grandfather."

This time, Tommy left his fists clenched. Accusing him of criminal intent should earn her a punch in the head, damn his constant rage, damn her advanced age, and damn the consequences that would ruin the rest of his life. He wanted to bust in and tear her house apart until he found what he was after.

He forced a smile and tried again. "I'm not here to steal from you," he said. It was as close to an "Aw, shucks," tone as he could manage. Cracking his fists, he forced his palms to press flat against the sides of his legs. "I want to see that picture of Grandpa. The tricky one."

The door opened enough for Grandma Shawl to make direct eye contact. "Tricky one?"

"The one that looks black and white because he's wearing his white suit in the white doorway and there's nothing but shadows behind him. The one where the only color is Grandpa's hand and his... something hat?"

"Panama hat?"

"That's it."

Grandma Shawl looked hard at him for a few moments, as if sizing him up. "Don't know where it is," she said finally. "And if I did know, I'm sure I only have the one, so I'm keeping it."

Tommy raised his hands. "I only want to borrow it for an hour or so."

"Borrow it?"

"There's a photo center down the street. They can copy it for me and I'll bring the original right back to you."

"No. I don't trust you."

Every muscle in his upper body tightened at her refusal. He wanted to throw her to the floor and... no. He would not give in to that urge today. That photo of Grandpa would serve as a reminder of his new choices. Calmer choices. Saddling it with a memory of giving in to his anger would defeat its purpose. Cramming his fists into his pockets, teeth refusing to unclench, Tommy let his smile ease into what he hoped was a pleasant, or at least unthreatening, expression.

"Please," he said. "Please, Grandma Shawl. I need a copy of that picture."

The door opened a little more. "Why that picture?" she asked.

"Serenity," he said.

Grandma Shawl blinked. "Serenity."

"Grandpa was the calmest person I ever knew. That tricky photo captured that about him. His calm... his...."

"Serenity."

"Inner peace."

Grandma Shawl nodded, once. "That's why you want the photo?"

"Yes."

She glanced over her shoulder for a second, then turned back to him. "I don't know where it is," she said.

"It was on the fireplace mantle when I was a kid."

"The fireplace?" Grandma Shawl turned, opening the door even wider. "It's gotten rather cluttered in here over the years."

Tommy leaned in. 'Rather cluttered' didn't begin to cover it. Grandma Shawl's house had always been a little cluttered, but since he'd been here last it had grown downright glutted. Stacks of Grandma Shawl's wicker baskets stretched to the ceiling. Every basket had a lid and nearly every lid held another basket on top of it. The stacks were crammed together, in some places almost as high as the ceiling, making it difficult to see the walls of the room. To her credit, it looked like Grandma Shawl tried to maintain paths through the house, but he had to wonder how she spent her days in this cramped space.

"Will you let me come in and look for it? You don't have to do anything."

"I don't remember if it's on the mantle or not," she said.

Tommy leaned further in and took in a lungful of sweltering, stuffy air. It stuck in his throat like a tangle of brambles. He coughed, put his hand to his mouth, trying to keep his smile.

Grandma Shawl's eyes widened. "Are you all right?" she asked.

Holding up a finger to bide some time, Tommy nodded, still coughing. He grimaced, trying to speak, but could only cough.

"You're not fine by a long shot," Grandma Shawl said. "Come inside. I'll get you some water. Don't touch anything."

Tommy stepped inside, intending to close the door behind him, but Grandma Shawl stepped around and closed it herself. "Follow me," she said.

Tommy glanced toward the end of the room where the

fireplace stood, but the entire thing was hidden behind stacks of baskets. Somewhere over there was one with a green band. His coughing continued as he followed Grandma Shawl.

Entering the kitchen felt like stepping into an open field after being lost in a thick forest. The clutter of baskets didn't stretch into this room, although one lone basket rested on the small table in the corner. Beside it sat plastic shopping bag from the dollar store down the street.

Grandma Shawl took a plastic cup from a cabinet, rinsing it with tap water three times before filling it and handing it to him. Exactly as she had when he was a kid.

Tommy choked out a "Thank you," as he took the cup. He drank slowly, letting the water coat his throat.

"Easy, Tantrums, don't make yourself sick."

He lowered the cup and took a slow breath. Why did old people keep their heat on in the summertime?

He held the cup out to her. "Thank you, Grandma Shawl."

"How old are you?"

"I'm sorry?"

"You can say 'Shirley,' can't you?"

"Of course."

"Then you can say 'Shirl.'"

Tommy smiled. "Of course I can--"

"Then say it. Go on."

"Shirl."

"Very good. That's what you call me. Kids who can't speak correctly call me 'Grandma Shawl'."

"Okay, Grand--"

"No. No 'Grandma' for you, either. You're too old."

"Shirl, then."

"You keep calling me 'Grandma' at your age, you'll kill me before I'm ready."

Tommy forced a smile. "I wouldn't want that."

Grandma Shawl's eyes narrowed. "I'll look around for that picture of Grandpa for you. Maybe when Rosie, my Spanish girl, comes back next week she can help me. When we find it I'll get it to your mother." She took a step toward him, as if to usher him out. Tommy pretended he didn't notice.

"Did you ever learn to make these baskets?"

Grandma Shawl didn't respond for a few seconds. "Make

these?"

"When I was a kid, Grandpa used to encourage you to take a basket weaving class. Did you make all of these?"

Grandma Shawl smiled in spite of herself. She held up her bony white hands, deformed with bulging blue veins and large knuckles. "There's no creativity in these."

"Oh, I bet there is," Tommy said. He stepped up to the small table and picked up the lone basket. "I bet you could've made better baskets than this," he said.

"Put that down."

He went to place the basket on the table, but glanced away and caught the bottom against the edge, tipping it over. The move probably looked more intentional than he wanted, but he managed to make the basket lid slide off. A few marbles rolled out and scattered across the table.

"Catch them," Grandma Shawl barked.

Tommy made a half-hearted reach for them, but they clattered to the floor.

Grandma Shawl tried to elbow him out of the way, but Tommy kept his back to her, keeping her behind him. She tried to reach around and grab the basket, but Tommy pushed it all the way on its side, spilling another marble and a few mini-marshmallows. "What did you put in here?"

"None of your business. Get those!"

"The marbles?"

"Yes, the marbles!"

"All right," he said. Standing the basket on the table, he glanced inside. Two marbles remained, as well as quite a few marshmallows. He reached inside and pulled out a toothbrush. "Are you going on a trip, Grandma Shawl?"

"Don't call me... I told you... put that back... get those marbles..." She snatched at him, finally managing to pinch the toothbrush. He released it but reached into the basket again, this time removing a wallet-sized photograph of a beautiful Hispanic girl with a wide, perfect smile. "This looks like a senior picture, Grandma Shawl. Who is she?"

The old woman looked afraid. "You put that back. That's Rosie, my helper. Now you--"

"Is she single?"

Grandma Shawl swallowed, staring at the photo in his hand.

"Just put that back in the basket, please."

"Maybe you could set me up with her?"

"Please, Tommy. Thomas. Please. Just put it back in the basket."

No 'Tantrums' that time. Finally, he was getting somewhere with her. "I'm sorry," he said. "I didn't mean to upset you." Lowering the photograph into the basket, he executed the movement he'd spent the previous night practicing. Even though the photo was printed on a tougher paper than he'd prepared for, he managed to make a tiny rip in the side quickly enough that Grandma Shawl didn't notice.

"I want you out of my house," she said.

"I'll just get those marbles for you." Tommy crouched next to the table.

"Leave, Tantrums. Just go."

"Wouldn't think of it. You could step on one of these, fall down, and break your hip. Spending time at the hospital at your age, you might catch something fatal and I'd carry the guilt of that for the rest of my life. All because I left these marbles on your floor."

"Thomas, please just go."

Thank God for old, uneven floors. The marbles had rolled into the corner and were easy to scoop up. He paused, listening to Grandma Shawl muttering under her breath. Her cadence was such that if he didn't know better, he'd guess she was praying.

"How many am I looking for?" he asked loudly. When her 'prayer' continued, he yelled his question as if she were hard of hearing. "Grandma Shawl! How many? I found six."

Her voice paused, started, and faltered again. "Damnit," she whispered.

Tommy stood and held his open hand out to her, showing her the marbles. "Is this all of them?" Grandma Shawl glared at him.

"You came here to murder me."

"Six, right? Because I saw two in the basket?"

"Yes, six." She froze. "How did you know?"

His smile came naturally this time, unbidden. "I counted them really fast."

"You bastard," Grandma Shawl said. She paled and seemed to shrink a little. The fire in her eyes dimmed into a look of fear. "Do you know what you've done?"

Tommy shook his head. "No. Tell me what I've done." The plastic shopping bag beside the basket held an open bag of marbles. Tommy quickly dipped his hand in and jammed his marbles among all the others. She'd never find the same six again.

"Don't! What are you--" She caught herself on the edge of the table.

"Are you feeling okay? Should I call a doctor?"

"I feel a lot better than you're going to be feeling in a few minutes, you little shit." She waved a hand at him and looked at the toothbrush she held as if seeing it for the first time. "Get out of my house."

"Okay, Grandma Shawl. I'm leaving."

She nodded. "About damn time."

"Just as soon as I find that picture of Grandpa."

"What? No--"

Tommy walked around her and entered the path through the baskets again. He turned right, heading toward where he knew the fireplace to be, scanning the piles for the green stripe. "It's okay, Grandma Shawl," he called. "I know just where it is." The rage that ruled his entire life seemed further away. He'd torn Roselyn's picture, lost most of the marbles, and stopped Grandma Shawl's incantation. He'd ruined the old woman's chance to transfer her cancer to Rosie, or anyone else. She was stuck with it. Now he could focus on the basket with Grandpa's picture and free himself.

Grandma Shawl called after him, but he ignored her.

He found the green striped basket on the bottom of the furthermost stack in the corner. Carefully, he removed the baskets on top of it, taking them down one at a time and placing them carefully on the floor. Without knowing the spells contained in each, he couldn't afford to klutz up and accidentally open one. No telling what he might unleash.

As he finally lifted the basket with the green stripe, Grandma Shawl spoke from the kitchen doorway.

"You know my Spanish girl, don't you?" she said.

"Roselyn, yeah. We've been dating for six months."

"You're dating that spicaninny?" Grandma Shawl said. "Should've expected as much from you."

The burst of rage kicked up almost too fast for him to tamp down. He kept his grip on the basket and pictured Rosie's smile. "She was the first girl that ever asked me out."

"And this was six months ago?"

"She said I caught her eye because I was living under a curse. You wouldn't know anything about that, would you?"

Grandma Shawl closed her eyes and sighed. "She's been here for two months, digging around behind my back twice a week."

"It took a long time for Rosie to convince me what you are. After the third time I got angry and threw something at her, I began to see she was right. I've been cursed to live my life without peace." Tommy held up the basket with the green stripe. "She asked me if I remembered the first time I got really angry."

Tommy placed his hand on the lid.

"You'll never get it open," Grandma Shawl said.

He slid it off with one finger.

"How did you--?" she asked. Then nodded. "She opened it, didn't she? Chunting bitch already broke the seal."

"You fell asleep in front of the TV yesterday." Inside the basket was a broken glass wrapped in a handkerchief and the tricky picture of Grandpa he'd come for, still in the frame.

"How many has she opened?"

"Couldn't say. Grandpa had a temper, didn't he?" Tommy slid the broken glass aside carefully so he could remove Grandpa's picture. He blew some dust off it and tucked it under his arm. Beneath it, Tommy found a copy of his third-grade photo, striped shirt, cowlick, smattering of freckles. He held it up so she could see it. "This is me."

"That spicaninny knew about the basket I was making for her."

"You used this sh--" he tamped the anger down, "--basket to make Grandpa incapable of losing his temper, didn't you. You transferred his rage to me, cursing me to live with his anger my whole life. You even taunted me about it. You're the one who started calling me 'Tantrums'."

"Did she tell you that disrupting the marble basket would kill me?" she asked. Tommy looked at her as she leaned against the doorjamb, only her face visible over the piles of baskets. She looked old. Weak in a way he'd never been able to imagine. "She sent you to destroy that basket and didn't even tell you the consequences?"

"She didn't have to tell me."

Grandma Shawl gaped at him.

Tommy placed his third grade picture back in the green-striped basket. Due to its age, this one was far easier to tear with one hand. He placed the basket on the floor. "I'll take this along with me," he held up the picture of Grandpa, "but I'll bring it back within the hour." He'd bring her the copy, of course. The original was destined to hang in his kitchen, where he'd see it every day and remember the anger he'd freed himself from. Besides, it really was one of the best shots of Grandpa ever taken.

"How do you not care that your Spanish bitch sent you here to assassinate me? I should think that would make you angry."

Tommy smiled. "Or, if you'd prefer, Grandma Shawl, I can give this photo to Mom and she'll get it back to you."

Grandma Shawl lurched away from the wall. "You're dating a tar-skinned, English-jumbling illegal. You know that, don't you?"

Tommy smiled at her. "Illegal? She was born in Pittsburgh. English is her first language."

"Whatever. You'll never see her again."

He looked at her a long while. "Why do you say that, Grandma Shawl?"

She smiled. "Look around you. Do you know what every one of these baskets holds?"

"Spells. Trickery."

She shook her head. "No trickery. I have lived well for many years because of these baskets."

"You've lived well because you shunted your miseries off onto innocent people."

Grandma Shawl sputtered. Tommy caught the gist of her anger in a few quick syllables. She had justifications and reasons that none of the people she'd inflicted were innocent. At least in her mind.

"I believe you were kicking me out of your house, Grandma Shawl."

"Stop calling me that." She backed away and waved a hand half-heartedly toward the front door. Tommy followed the path to it.

"If there's nothing more I can do for you, Grandma Shawl?"

"Leave!"

Tommy glanced at the photo of Grandpa, then gave the old woman his widest smile. "I'll be seeing you, Grandma Shawl."

"You won't be."

Tommy opened the door and squinted at the sunlight.

Grandma Shawl's house was dim, but the darkness suited her. He couldn't wait to get home and tell Roselyn everything that happened. He'd been more successful than they'd expected. She wouldn't be contracting Grandma Shawl's cancer, and he wouldn't be flying off the handle every few hours.

Tommy unlocked his car and looked back at Grandma Shawl's squat little house. It needed a paint job, moss grew on the shingles, and some of the front hedges towered over the house. He slid behind the wheel of his car and placed the photo of Grandpa on the seat next to him. Slipping the key into the ignition, the sun made him squint, so he lowered the visor and reached beside him to the well where he stored his sunglasses.

It was empty.

He'd failed to take them off when he arrived. He reached up and felt the front of his shirt.

They were gone.

He remembered Grandma Shawl flailing at him for the toothbrush. She must have snatched his glasses away.

"You'll never see her again," she said.

He needed to get them back, now.

He flung the car door open, but before he could stand up the sunlight dimmed as if dusk began to fall. It kept falling. The trees, the house, even the steering wheel dimmed until they disappeared. Tommy heard himself breathing, heard the birds chirping, heard the breeze rustling the leaves. The sun warmed his skin. He ran a hand over his face and felt no glasses, no blindfold, no physical reason that he couldn't see.

The anger he'd known all his life, an anger he deserved to feel right now, didn't come, leaving Tommy to laugh in the dark.

The Saint Of Regret
Nick Manzolillo

I.

The boy, Joseph, claims he saw an old woman wandering the dusty red hills behind the ranch. He says she was a bundle of rags and that her face was as brown as the old savages who built temples all over the country. Ande doesn't doubt that hags wander the desert, hallucinating religious wonders while clutching rosary beads; the only things in the hills and plains around the ranch house are scorpions and cacti. This used to be a place where horses and cattle were bred before it became so hot and barren. There are skeletal remains of thin, starved creek beds scattered throughout the land that were once full of sparkling, mineral rich water.

"No, Tio, no!" The boy, Ande's nephew, kept repeating. Joseph sobbed that the old woman was bleeding from her eyes and spoke "like a crow" with short, whispery chirps. The boy said she kept telling him "when you sleep, when you sleep." At that point, he made the kid's mother, Valeria, take Joseph away. If the old warlord had to hear him whine for one more moment, he'd have strangled the red dust from the boy's neck. When there is a problem, you don't run and cry, trying to find someone who will solve it. Then again, considering the merciless throat slitters that could be coming for Ande, and the fact that Joseph's father was found hanging from a lamppost, headless and castrated, the boy has plenty reason to be afraid.

Ande's paranoia is an old friend that has kept him alive for decades. The boy was surely confused or suffering from heat stroke, but maybe he thought he saw a scary old woman that's really an assassin disguised with a rifle who, even now, is waiting to line up for the perfect shot and send a bullet through the old cartel boss's skull. The wars between cartels take full advantage of shadows and turned backs. Even now a vendetta for something Ande did many years ago could still rear its ugly blood-soaked head.

The rifle in Ande's hands has a custom grip and scope that his lieutenant, Marquez, put together for him as a retirement present. It never leaves his side. Ande knows that carrying the heavy gun up these hills right now might be the excuse his old man's heart needs to explode into a burst of glory no bullet has yet to deliver. But if a killer is lurking, then there must be a confrontation. A man always protects his land.

Marquez and the others are the princes that carry Ande's organization onwards through Mexico and the states, further north, and deeper south. They have left him here like a buried holy relic, at the furthest edge of a lonely town. Ande considers himself to be exotic, one of a kind, because he is free from the game of bloodstained cash and the sharp clatter of gangland gunfire. The law never learned Ande's true name, nor did his enemies. He fully intends to spend the rest of his life withering away in the desert with his indoor swimming pool, collection of finely crafted acoustic guitars, and enough frozen steaks to last until his heart stops—fat, gluttonous, and full of the best deadly sins.

If Ande dies, his story couldn't have a more satisfying ending—though there is much more wine and tequila left for him to drink. Ande's dearly departed brother's wife is still youthful enough to provide him a sweaty orgasm each morning the sun rises and every night the shadows prop the stars into the sky. That is a reason to fight. There is always a reason.

*   *   *

The hills are easy enough to climb; full of natural footholds forged from the floods of a crumbling ice age eons ago. Rattlesnakes could be hiding in the dark fissures cracked across the rocks, which forces Ande to be vigilant during his ascent. When he reaches the flat peaks of the hills, he is met by an intensified gust of heat instead of the soothing breeze he was starting to hope for. The ranch house is a pretty sight, even though the outside paint splotches like rust. Deciding he's wasted enough time, Ande heads back down, but notices something he first mistook for a bundle of rocks.

There is a dead rattler with its tail in its mouth, forming a neat circle. Within the circle is the sun-bleached skull of an infant. Droplets of red that are surely clay, but might just be blood, form a triangle on the crown of the skull. How did the boy find a human bone like that out here? How disturbed must he be to fuck around with it?

Crushing the frail skull with the heel of his boot, Ande lifts the ring of the self-cannibalistic rattler up into the air with his toe. Although he'd thought it dead, the snake twists and hisses mid-air, its tail rattling that haunting melody of danger. The serpent lands on the slope of the hill, quickly slithering out of sight. How did the boy make a live rattler choke itself motionless on its own tail?

Ande takes a long look at the surrounding hills and valleys and then spots something that speeds up his old heart a few beats. There is someone standing in the middle of the plain on the far side of the hill, someone in a torn skirt that's dangling in the wind. He jerks the rifle up and peers down the scope, trying to get some idea of what he's looking at, of who he may have to murder. The thing in the skirt turns out to be a cactus with a towel wrapped around it. While any manmade object is suspicious, Ande recognizes that light blue towel as one of the dozens he keeps by the pool. The boy probably used it and left it on the back porch.

There is no wind today however, so that towel shouldn't be moving. Ande re-focuses through the scope and he realizes he is no better than the boy, it's just the shadows and the distance of the cactus combined with the angle of the sun. It is nothing. He lifts his eye from the edge of the scope and discovers a hunched over, shriveled hag perched beside him.

Ande's not sure what he yells into the bright, blue sky, as he slips back into the dust along the hilltop. The woman isn't much of a threat: red face paint covers her peeling, sun-flayed flesh and scorpions weave in and out of her rat's nest hair. Ande raises his rifle, Bruja be damned. He squeezes the trigger, ready for the rifle crack and gunpowder smell that will precede his bath in the blood of this madwoman.

There is blood, but nothing else. Uselessly pouring out of the rifle barrel is a muddy sputter of red alongside a weak, squealing sound. The hag raises her hand and, filling Ande's nose with rot, falls against him.

"Blessed be," a whispery voice made of sharp, guttural clicks begins to fill his head with contradictions. "The land has reached a verdict." He can't breathe, the hag is weightless, yet she's like a thick blanket wrapped around his throat. "We're not often fed the worthy. Blessed be." The desperate old warlord tries to remember everything his mother ever read him from the bible before she got sick, but he can't. He only remembers the prayers men would stutter as his soldiers turned them into bloody warnings to be left for the opposition.

Ande grabs the hag's hair, and his fingers light with pinpricks of pain that instantly burn and course through his wrist. Persevering through the living needle pricks, he pulls the hag away and gags from the spoiled stench of decaying meat. Scorpions that have fallen from the witch travel up his arms and he shrieks, flinging them away. His stung and poisoned hand becomes useless, but the woman has vanished. The sun grows stronger and the sweat pouring from his body makes him start to believe that this is all just a fever dream. Yes, yes, madness, Ande hoped he'd die before reaching this stage of elderly delirium.

Ande drops the rifle and walks to the edge of the hill. There is no woman. The knuckles along his hand are gone, consumed by the swelling. Below, he can see Valeria through the glass panels above the indoor pool. She's in her white bikini, the one that's a little too small for her. She is something pleasant to march toward. Ande wonders if his brother thought of her just before his throat was mercifully slit and his agony emptied out of him.

He doesn't feel the snake's fangs until the nausea pools in the pit of his stomach at the sight of the reptile twisting and rippling, its mouth tight over his ankle. There was no warning rattle, just a sharp hiss and then, after a long pause, a pain that makes bullets and scorpions alike feel like finger-pricks from a cactus. The new poison spreads, a fresh overdose of fire. There is almost a peaceful moment, as the snake's fangs graze bone. He's barely begun the climb down—hardly taken a single step. What a shame. Ande tilts forwards into the air, over the edge of rock, and plummets.

When it gets bad enough, the hurt turns into a dim buzz, as if Ande's broken body knows he's gotten the message. He's screwed.

Ande's conscious enough to watch as the snake slithers along his chest and gazes into his eyes. He sees her, the old hag, in those black pupils. The snake forms lips and grins. There is a blink of pain, and a woman in rags of dirt is straddling his stomach. She leans forward, scorpions dripping from her hair and clinging to her face. Her toothless mouth opens—an abyss that widens like the snake's detachable jaws.

Valeria is shouting, her face blotting out the sun. "Shoo! Shoo!" A vulture squawks and flies off Ande's chest. With soft hands Valeria begins to gently caress his cheeks as the great black flutters in over his vision. A distant cackling drifts in on a sudden breeze.

II.

The wind is picking up, cruelly blasting the many windows that compose the ranch house. The amount of dust in the air shatters any visibility and it's a wonder they managed to bring the wounded old man inside before the weather turned bloodthirsty. Valeria has no choice but to eventually calm down. Adrenaline is far from infinite. She doesn't love him, Ande is just another man that promised her freedom and then locked all the doors. But she does everything she can to save him. Cruel and as much of a drunk as he may be, Ande's the best thing for her son, for what's left of her family.

The old cartel king's leg seems to be almost three times its normal size, and she fears it will have to be amputated. If he were ten years younger and not as frail and broken as he is now, Valeria and Joseph wouldn't have been able to drag him to the couch in the dim living room. As it is, they nearly break their backs carrying the old man away from the base of the hills. The lighting in the living room is poor because Ande claims this room is for the fireplace to illuminate, which is as silly as it sounds, now that he has to lay in the dark with a fever.

There is anti-venom, of course, filed away in the basement, right beside all the meat in the walk-in freezer. People like Ande dance with death so much they learn to anticipate her moves. Joseph is oddly calm when she sends him to the basement to get antibiotics. All of his crying earlier filled Valeria's chest with the same, lingering panic that's been haunting her since Hector's death.

No, since before Hector's death, when her husband's alcoholism and coke habit had worsened. When he started taking Joseph along with him and his "boys," and wouldn't return until the night had passed and she had wept herself to sleep. When Joseph would wake up screaming even before his father was killed. When her son would scream "I didn't mean to momma, I didn't mean to," she would ask him over and over what he meant but he'd only cry. Valeria can't remember the last time there was no panic.

"Is he going to die?" Joseph asks. Hardly even a teenager, he's a long shot from being a man. Still, he doesn't cry, even as Ande breathes like a croaking frog and that leg continues to swell. Joseph seems to have already gotten all of the tears out of his system.

"I don't know. Maybe." Valeria brushes away specks of dirt from Ande's clammy forehead. There was a gentleness to the old king, despite all the awful things she knows he has done. Maybe his dark side was so savage that his gentle side became extreme too. If you kill enough people, maybe your soft side gets softer. If Valeria had any other option for a different life, one that didn't require her to be on her knees in some brothel, she'd have pursued it, leaving the world of violent men behind. She should be so lucky.

She called Marquez immediately. When misfortune befalls a man like Ande, you want to be clear of it as soon as possible. She has no doubt she would become a suspect in his death if she didn't do everything to keep him alive. You hear about women killing their lovers like this all the time, because in theory, there's a great deal of money in it. If only Hector hadn't painted a target on her and Joseph's backs, they could be living in secluded luxury where foolish old men don't go getting themselves bitten by desert rattlers.

If only Ande's breathing would stop with the raspy, frog-like croaks, then she could carry on with her day and do something, anything with her time instead of sitting around and waiting for Marquez. He's bringing a doctor, he said, but Valeria knows he's probably busy, and the last thing he wants to do is look after a wounded old man. The fact that Marquez will drop what he's doing shows the level of respect that Ande is given for the empire he built. When kings get old they usually get their heads chopped off. That's how it works in Mexico. All of the crooked murderers and young lunatics that have been on Ande's payroll actually allowed him to hang it all up and retire. Valeria still has trouble believing that, but considering the snake bite and his fall, maybe God has a worse punishment in mind.

Joseph stays by her side for a while, but keeps shrinking away from the room until eventually Valeria hears the TV playing in the kitchen. The wind is relenting and the sky outside is growing dark.

Valeria's not sure how long the drums echo outside before she notices. Whether it's the TV or the prospect of the returning, moaning wind or something Joseph has gotten up to, she doesn't realize what's happening until she's in the middle of it. There is a steady, hollow tune like a palm smacking against an empty oil barrel. The pounding of drums seem to come from each corner of the ranch house.

"Mom..." Joseph switches off the TV. With the absence of the TV's chatter, the loneliness and vast emptiness of a hundred miles of desert sets in. The shadows in the living room thicken, as if Ande is stealing the light to heal himself. The drums beat onwards like a primitive heartbeat. "Mom...there are men outside. They look funny..." At the word men, Valeria snaps alert. She sprints upstairs to her and Ande's bedroom and sifts through the several pistols in his nightstand. She takes the smaller one that she's used to practice shooting empty buckets by the dried creek beds. "Mom!" Joseph calls from downstairs and his confusion, fear, and helplessness rips Valeria away from the confidence a loaded gun should bring. She worries about him. She has to protect him.

"Come over here!" Valeria tries to yell but instead squeaks out as she re-enters the living room, crouching. There are too many doors, too many windows. Ande was either overconfident or careless.

"Mom, mom they're wearing animal skins, like coats, with antlers. Are they Indians?"

Boom boom boom. The drums sound like a ticking clock, a countdown to something. Or maybe a dinner bell for death.

"Joseph!" Valeria creeps into the kitchen, trying to hear past the drumbeats but they're deafening, they'll mask anyone trying to get inside. *Oh god the doors...they're all unlocked.* It was a nice day, the pool felt so soothing. Before the wind came, tonight would have been the perfect evening to watch the sun break away into stars.

Joseph is pressed against the kitchen door that leads to the deck, and he's locking it, bless him. Outside there is a hunched figure about twenty feet away, holding something in its hands. The hands are human and maybe the outline of the chin and cheekbones are, but the rest of the figure is clad in light, grey fur and its ears are floppy triangles. Its skull is sloped and dog-like.

"We need to get away from the windows…" Valeria hisses, but Joseph can't look away. There is another figure, just beyond the other, another drummer. *How many of them are there? Are they just trying to be intimidating? They must be…*

The madness of the cartels is legendary. Valeria has heard all of the rumors. Strange rituals involving human sacrifice. Men in masks kidnapping children to dump into sinkholes in the desert. Shrines in the middle of nowhere composed of animal bones and lit by black candles. Violence belies religion and reasoning.

Men filled with bloodlust will eat their enemy's hearts, believing they will gain their enemy's strength. The underbelly of this murdererous environment is the Brujas, and for all Ande's faults, Valeria always respected that he kept his group free from *that* particular madness. Like Robin Hoods, they only ever murdered their enemies and those that interfered in their business, no more, no less. In Mexico, this made them as noble as criminals could get, when compared to their rabid, mouth-foaming competition.

Valeria hauls Joseph back from the window and he trips and falls. "Go away!" Valeria screams to the glass and this time her voice doesn't crack. She keeps the gun by her side, a little surprise for the intruders. The drumming continues, and she wonders if they can even hear her. Adding to the tension, raindrops patter against the roof and the windows. Valeria's vision of the outside becomes water-streaked. She won't be able to see the intruders for much longer, she will only be able to listen with Joseph, and wait.

"Come into the other room." Valeria grabs Joseph by the shoulder. He's crying again. Instead of being ashamed of him, Valeria's thankful he's really not his father's son after all. "If they get in, maybe they'll leave us alone when they see what kind of shape your uncle's in." Valeria's not sure why she lies, but she has to say something and the truth that she will likely be raped before they are both murdered just won't do.

"I want you to hide in the closet, and listen to me, listen to what I say, don't come out, you have to be quiet, and you can't come out, no matter what you hear, you know this, yes?" Joseph knows. Whether he'll actually be able to hide silently is another thing. There could be a chance Joseph survives, if the ranch is not completely ransacked or burned to the ground after the invaders are done with Valeria and what's left of Ande.

There is a steady rumble of thunder that distracts Valeria from the fact that the drums have stopped. Her breath catches as Joseph bangs around in the closet just behind the couch where Ande is laying. Her son pulls the door shut and then there is silence. Headlights flash through the open windows in the kitchen. There are tires on dirt, and then a horn from a pickup truck. Marquez?

"Don't come out until I tell you to. Don't." Valeria hisses, holding the pistol in both hands. Is it worth killing a couple of them? Or should she die a virgin when it comes to murder? Maybe it really is Marquez, but if so, where are the gunshots? Where is the confrontation with those strange men dressed like beasts?

There is a pounding at the front door and the disassociation from reality ends. "Valeria!" Marquez's scream echoes down the hallway as he barges in through the unlocked front door. *Of course, of course! So stupid!* The relief that Marquez is here doesn't wash over her like it should, and Valeria's not sure what's happened to her since Hector was killed. There is a dullness, right beside her panic. There is the expectation that sooner or later, life is going to get so messy that when she finally closes her eyes and her heart beats its last beat, it will be a mercy.

"What, have you been leaving food outside? The coyotes were all over the place!" Marquez, as usual, only knows how to yell. He's a little drunk and he doesn't sound as worried as one would expect him to be. According to Ande, Marquez is his favorite accomplice. "So dark in here." Marquez enters the living room where Valeria stands, still trembling. The stranger that enters behind Marquez makes Valeria's stomach flip-flop. He has feather earrings and wavy tattoo's all over his dirt streaked, unshaven face and he's wearing a short, black and white poncho.

Valeria fills them in immediately, "There were men out there, with drums…did you see them? I think they had something to do with Ande, I don't think it was an accident…" Valeria finds herself sounding calm, and just a little weary. Where is the fight or flight she was feeling moments ago? Marquez carries the shotgun he always has on him, even at funerals, like Hector's. The stranger, who is now looking out the parlor windows, has several knives tucked into a rawhide belt around his waist. Yes, these men will kill whatever threat there is and the circles of violence will keep spinning.

"What's going on here? Ande growing peyote he don't feel like sharing? Coyotes were big, but not men. Have you seen men?" Marquez takes Valeria half seriously. He nods at the gun in her hands and, thinking it might look suspicious, she hands it over to him. He shoves it into his pants and the gun is so small that it might just slide down and end up in his underwear.

"They were men, playing drums."

"No maracas? Was the boy playing his guitar with them?" Marquez scans the kitchen, peering out the windows. He's always been a joker. Valeria is sure of what she saw, right?

"Where is the boy?" Marquez's eyebrows are fat silk worms that salute her. Valeria turns to glare at the stranger, who has crossed his arms and is staring right back at her. The stranger's pupils seem large enough to make his eyes black in the shadows of the living room. The stranger glances down at Ande and rubs a hand through the fever sweat along his cheek.

"This is Lupe, my wonderful friend…he's a doctor, of sorts. If there are men running around in these little hills and caves, he'll also be our vengeful blessing from god, ain't that right?" Lupe smiles at Marquez's praise, saying nothing. The closet door behind the couch creaks open and Joseph tiptoes out, eyeing Lupe before smiling at the sight of Marquez.

"It's true! I saw them! They were dressed like animals and there was a strange woman outside earlier! She made Ande fall!" Joseph glares at Valeria, making her feel all that wretched guilt because she didn't believe him. Now, she believes…there are legends from the Navajo tribe to the north. Legends about shapechangers called *Skinwalkers*, and the flimsy borders between man and beast.

"Okay, okay. I'm going to call up some troops. Get some flashlights going." Marquez pulls out his cell phone, just as Lupe clears his throat.

"Do you dream of the Moon Shack?" Lupe asks Joseph, stepping between Valeria and her son, his eyes pools of silver.

"Who are you?" Joseph asks and begins shivering uncontrollably.

Boom boom boom.

The drums pick up again with that strange, haunting rhythm. Marquez curses, bringing up his shotgun while peering out the kitchen windows.

"Those were just dogs!" Marquez slurs, the alcohol still clouding his blood. He reaches to unlock the kitchen door.

"Brother, don't let her tempt you," Lupe tells Marquez in a flat, emotionless voice. Is he talking about Valeria? What kind of tempting has she done? The stranger in weird clothes places a hand on Joseph's shoulder. The boy's teeth begin to chatter, urine running down his leg and staining the front of his shorts. Primitive, maternal jaggedness grinds and rages within Valeria. Marquez ignores the strange man, and steps into the black night, raising the shotgun like a fool's torch to ward off that cursed, ceaseless noise.

The shotgun roars before Marquez has fully left the house and Valeria jams her hands over her ears. Joseph howls to the ceiling but he doesn't move, as if rooted to the floor by Lupe's hand. "Close the door or I'll be the only one that walks out of here alive. Now!" Lupe hisses worse than any venomous snake. Without thinking Valeria lurches to the door and secures a hand on its frame. Marquez is still out there.

The shadows have been fed by the stars, and Marquez is only illuminated by the orange glow bursting from the mouth of his weapon. Valeria can't make out what he's shooting at, until he starts screaming. The shotgun sheds a flash of light and the coyote gnawing on Marquez's ankle is blown in half. Another is swooping through the darkness, latching onto Marquez's other leg. Valeria can see them now, little blotches on the ground. They're short, no more than foxes. Marquez is fine, if not savagely kicking, stomping and using his gun to bludgeon the mutts. Then a row of teeth slash across Marquez's ribs, and his confidence, his savage glee is gone like an extinguished candle and he crumples to his knees. His face is blotted out by the quick, jabbing beasts that seem to grow fatter and taller and then as big as the ancient bears that once called the desert home. Marquez's screams turn to bleats of frantic agony before ceasing. The drumming continues and via her own will, not Lupe's, Valeria slams the door and twists the deadbolt.

Sweat streams across Joseph's forehead. "You teach men as much as you can but you can never, ever control them," Lupe muses and there's only the faintest tinge of bitterness to his otherwise flat voice. He eases a long, curved, and black knife out of his belt.

"Ande here, for example, is really as old as he looks. He saw the new order coming, and he backed down, like a gentleman."

Lupe waves the knife at Ande's still form, his knuckles growing white over Joseph's shoulder. Valeria's gun is with Marquez, but this isn't a typical country ranch. Every room is designed for trouble. There's a sawed-off shotgun in the kitchen and although Valeria has never used it, she knows it has two shots before needing reloading.

"We have...higher values to worship." Lupe leans down to Joseph's ear. "Like the Moon Shack. Have you stood on its porch in your dreams? Have you knocked?" Lupe grins at Valeria, and then nuzzles Joseph's head like a cat.

"No..." Joseph barely lets out through his clicking teeth.

"It's the only place you, and me, are safe from things like her." Lupe's almost soothing. "You see, we need boys with their father's hearts who know how to make somebody, anybody, bleed. To fight the Brujas of Santa Muerte, the saints of old Mexico that think they own us. Some of them think of themselves as saints, mopping up men like me and silly Marquez. It's already in your blood, whether you've cut your first throat or not. You're as good as guilty in her eyes but if you want to be safe, in the Moon Shack, you've got to be a true killer." Lupe presses the handle of his obsidian blade into Joseph's palm and forces the boy's fingers close around it. "Open your uncle's throat. He won't notice. End his suffering and save your life. The Moon Shack will appear right now, this very night, in all its glowing glory." Lupe pulls away from Joseph with an ominous hiss.

"Baby..." Valeria shakes her head, backing slowly past the kitchen's center aisle. What's the range on the sawed-off? She can't hit Lupe without grazing Joseph, there would be too much of a spread from the sawed-off's blast. Lupe has his hands on his hips. The lights blink as Joseph looks to the "doctor."

"Don't do it..." Valeria doesn't like the glazed look in Joseph's eyes. He knows what Lupe is talking about...this Moon Shack. The cartels have always had their superstitions, their sacrifices to Santa Muerta. Some organizations are run like the militia, the effective ones are run like a religion.

The lights are beginning to dim. Smoke, yes, that has to be smoke rising from the kitchen door, like the door's melting or evaporating. The tan wood is blackening. The shadows are alive beyond the kitchen windows and something is beginning to work its way in.

"We don't have time! It's easy! He's numb. His mind is lost. He won't feel a thing! Do you know what she'll do to you? When she finds her way inside? Those like her always get what they want, they always find their way in. That's why we built the Shack. Do you know what she'll do with your skin? Hurry, she knows she has to hurry." Lupe's voice wavers. He has another knife and this one is in a fancy leather sheath. Valeria wonders how fast he can flick that out.

The very fact that Joseph is standing over Ande with that knife in his hands is too much. Valeria can't find the words, can't form the things she needs to say. There is insanity, there is action and there is very little thought. "Don't listen to him…" She doesn't know how to explain that Joseph is a bright and curious little boy. She doesn't know how to mock Lupe's nonsense and beyond all that she doesn't know a single thing about what's causing the kitchen door to smolder away to the tempo of a primordial rhythm.

The winds rise up and whip at the kitchen windows. With it, comes an ancient voice that is vaguely feminine. The syllables of incomprehensible words are drawn out into prolonged, shrieking nonsense. A series of loose vowels are hurling through the air as the wind whips the chanting between drum blasts and Lupe covers his ears. His eyes are wide and his teeth are grinding. This Moon Shack of his had given him too much confidence and now he's regretting having come here.

Ande begins twitching and Joseph shrieks as his uncle grabs him by the throat. Ande's eyes are white, his pupils rolled up into his skull. The formerly comatose man sits up, lifting Joseph from the floor and what used to be Ande is muttering, repeating the same drawn out vowels as the voice in the wind.

"Stick it in his throat! Stick it in his throat!" Lupe chants, cautiously stepping toward Ande and raising his hands. Valeria has one move to make, so she darts toward the kitchen drawer she's positioned herself behind. The shotgun is heavy. She thought the term "sawed-off" implied less weight, but she has to use both hands to aim it toward Lupe. The resulting blast throws her back across the kitchen's tiles where she cracks her skull against a marble countertop. Her vision flickers as the horrible stench of something burning assaults her nostrils.

Valeria crawls out from behind the center island and it's not the gory mess that used to be Lupe from his nipples up that shocks her into action, but the sight of Joseph's face, going purple in Ande's grip. The dizziness that comes from the jagged gash across the back of her head causes Valeria to stumble as she gets to her feet. She staggers toward Ande, raises her boot and strikes him square in the face with her heel. Joseph drops to the floor as Ande's pupils slide into focus before his eyelids slam shut and he lays back down, a man in the midst of fever dreams once more.

Her skull pounding, Valeria sinks to her knees and cradles Joseph, peering at the red marks across his neck. The lights continue to threaten to go out at any moment and Ande groans within the depths of his fever. The chanting from the wind has ceased, but the maddening drums continue, though seemingly more distant, perhaps receding. The kitchen door creaks open and the lights flicker on and off in epileptic horror. A hunched form appears by the kitchen's center aisle. There is a crackling, popping sound like oil burning in a pan. The hag lurches forward on stiff, creaking joints.

Valeria picks up the knife Joseph had dropped and draws her son against her chest, like a babe. Lupe's nonsense about killers and blood is swirling through her mind, but Joseph is of her more than he is of Hector. Valeria scoots away from Ande, pointing the obsidian blade out before her. The shriveled thing doesn't care, it creeps forward and then the lights go off for good.

The drumbeats cease. Joseph begins to cry as Valeria holds him close. She can't keep back the tears any longer either. Elsewhere in the black, Ande starts moaning, which briefly turns into a wakeful scream before deforming into a gurgle.

"He's *my* son. He's *my* son," Valeria keeps repeating. As a girl, she was never taught her prayers but she learned, from her own poor family, that the world revolves around mothers. From the very earth, the very dirt and forests themselves, it's all about the mother. The wicked old hag limping towards them in the darkness has a vendetta. Maybe she's a mother, too. Maybe the killers of the world have robbed her of something precious.

Joseph seems to grow smaller as Valeria draws him closer. She drops the knife and clasps her arms around him completely. If the hag heralds the coyotes in here, they will have to eat around her to get to Joseph. "I never knocked," Joseph whispers. If anything Lupe said was attractive to him, it was the idea of being safe, of fitting in. The Moon Shack... Valeria can feel the ancient crone hovering behind her back, breathing down her neck. Goose bumps breaking out across her flesh, Valeria holds her breath.

The kitchen door slams and the lights burst on as Joseph's screams mirror Valeria's own, for just a moment, before they realize they are alone. Whatever was left of Ande and Lupe is gone. Only the speckles of blood along the floor and couch remain. Valeria doesn't have the energy to imagine what happened to the remnants of the two men in the dark. She's thankful she had her eyes shut.

In the darkness, a precise circle of desert sand had appeared around Valeria and her son. She squeezes a few of the red grains between her fingers. Marquez's pickup truck is outside. If his body is still out there, she could find his keys. Ande had made them fake U.S. Passports. Maybe that will be enough. Maybe they can just run and run, because their enemies might just have bigger problems then petty boys with guns. Maybe, if they leave right now, they will make it. Maybe, if they step through the front door, they won't be eaten alive.

What could be the beat of drums faintly pounds away in the distance. Perhaps it's only thunder from the storm that has passed, or perhaps it's a storm that is quickly approaching.

To Catsin

Witch
Trisha J. Wooldridge

They called her a witch.

One time,
she nearly wandered into the woods.
The forbidden, dark, bedeviled
woods.

She said
she was following a squirrel.
She liked its little furry face
and the look in its big, shiny eyes,
and the squirrel liked the burnt crusts of bread she'd thrown.
(She was not a very good cook.
Things often burned in her presence.
Or tasted off.)
But the squirrel had appreciated her kindness,
and shouldn't one always do kindness
to all of God's creatures?

They called her a witch.

Never in her presence.
And certainly not in her father's.

He flew to sinful rage
when anyone suggested
his wife's passing in childbirth
was due to anything devilish.
He loved his daughter well,
though she could not cook,
though she did not speak until almost four years of age,
though she often forgot what she was doing,
resulting in burned food
or poorly sewn clothes
or sheep
that got sick
from getting chicken grain
instead of their own feed.
She hadn't meant any harm,
and she cried when two ewes died.
(Too much,
far too many tears,
for a human to shed
over dumb beasts,
if you asked certain people.)

They called her a witch.

Goodman Baker had noticed
the girl
(hardly still a girl.)

She would trade her family's goats' milk
and her father's leatherwork skills
for his baked bread when hers burnt.
(A frequent enough occurrence.)

She trusted Goodman Baker,
as she trusted everyone,
and he taught her that it was important
for good girls never to speak ill of others
and to keep secrets
no matter what.

And if she were not a
good girl,
she would have to be a witch.

And witches belonged to the Devil.

So she kept secret
the things that happened
behind Goodman Baker's house.
When Goodwife Baker was not home.

Even when she stopped her woman's blood.
Even when her clothes grew tight.

Even when she began to hear the others...

They called her a witch.

It was an uncomfortable conversation
for a father to have with a daughter.
Especially so,
when she was trying to be a
good girl
and keep a secret.

She was not a witch.
She did not belong to the Devil.

Even though she still,
sometimes,
followed animals
almost into the dark, forbidden woods.

They all came to her now
after years of burnt bread crusts.
(Why could she never do some things right?)
At least she was never wasteful
and God's creatures did not go hungry during cold winters.

Her father sometimes asked

if she didn't burn the bread
on purpose
to follow animals.

He didn't think to ask
about the bread
she would bring home
from the Baker house.

Goodman Baker
told her she was a
good girl.
To certain others,
he whispered otherwise
after Sunday Services.

He called her a witch.

Her belly grew bigger.
They told her she was unwelcome at Sunday Service
though she quoted
Scripture
better than all but the minister.

Yet,
while she could quote
whatever was asked
to perfection,
she never thought to
use
the sacred words
to prove her innocence.

They called her a witch.

The bigger her belly grew, the more problems she caused.

Now Goodman Baker was burning bread
for no reason,
he would say,

but for what must be a spell or a curse.

An early frost
followed by almost summer heat
and then another scythe-sharp frost
before harvest or the last leaves fell
was unnatural.
An unholy blight.

And rats plagued upon store houses.
(Indeed, some rats were found,
yet to such waning but two or three were a "plague"!)

Had *she* not been seen feeding vermin her enchanted,
bedeviled,
burnt crusts?

They called her a witch.

Her father argued.
Her father defended.
Though he cried,
begged,
at home
to hear the truth.

But she would be a
good girl
and never speak a secret,
never speak ill
of someone else.

They called her a witch.

And then they came
to take her father's property.

To take her to the cells.

Her father fought.

She'd never seen him violent.
Not with angry goats
nor misbehaving mules
nor anything.
He made other men bleed,
but he fell,
trampled,
as they chased her—
Goodman Baker in the lead.

He called her a witch.

"I was a good girl. I was a good girl!"

She ran to the only place
she knew they would not follow.

They called her a witch.

The man in the woods was not much older than she.
But his skin was red,
(like they said devils' skin was,)
so she was afraid.
Yet she was too cold and hungry to do more than tremble.
And accept the food and blanket he gave her.

In time, she came to learn he, too, was chased away by his people.

But he wasn't a good boy.
He was,
sometimes,
but not always.

When he was good,
he taught her about plants,
he held her when she was sick and in pain,
he brought her food and blankets.

When he was not,
he left bruises,

even on her swollen belly.
Even on the small child
that grew from the babe
birthed from the swell of her belly.

They called her a witch.

She didn't return to the village—wouldn't for many years,
but in the few months after she ran,
after they trampled her father
to death
winter came
and even more things began to die.

People grew sick.
Animals grew sick.
Fires would blaze too much or never start.
Crops and stores were lost.
Houses collapsed under frozen water and snow.
The meeting house half-collapsed
during Sunday Service.

She would not set foot in that village
for years,
past when Goodman Baker and Goodwife Baker
were laid to the ground
and their children grew,
married,
saw swollen bellies,
and baked communal bread.

Still...
Those in the village *knew* she certainly must live
in the dark,
forbidden,
bedeviled woods.

Their hardships were not what their God promised;
the Devil must be interfering!

They called her a witch.

She named her daughter Mary.
Mary had a differently-shaped brow and lip.
People in the village would have called her ugly.
But the new mother had once heard someone say
the Devil didn't take ugly children.
It was an odd thing, but she remembered it.
Mary was the name of many important people,
good people, in the Bible.
She would raise a good girl.

And Mary was a good girl.
She learned the lessons her mother taught.
She learned the lessons her father taught—
like what plants would make her sick if she ate them.
What would make her dead.

Mary was a good girl
who didn't like to see things suffer
(like her mother.)
Her mother who threw herself in front of her father's angry,
violent hands
to keep Mary from getting more bruises.
From looking more ugly,
as her father sometimes called her,
when he was being bad.

Mary was a good girl.
She cried when her father didn't wake up one morning,
as a good girl should.
And she promised she would take good care of her mother,
the way her mother took good care of her.

That meant that Mary sometimes had to wander off on her own
to help mother find plants and fruits
that wouldn't kill them.

And sometimes trap the woodland animals,
as her father used to do.

Only he would bring them to their door,
bleed, butcher, and skin them,
while her mother cried.

Mary always did such things away from the house.
(A good girl doesn't make her mother cry.)

But because a good girl doesn't lie,
when her mother asked where she'd gotten a pail of milk,
Mary had to tell her of the place she'd found.

Her mother scolded her—became angry.
Mother was never angry.
Mother told her what happened to her
—save the secret she told no one,
good girl that Mother was.
Mother told Mary
how the village chased her,
how she came to live in the woods
with the outcast red boy
and Mary.

"They would call you a witch."

Mary decided she would not be a good girl
and lied
when she said she would never return to the village again.

They called her a witch.

Her mother.
Who never hurt anyone.
Who cried when animals bled and died.
Who stood in front of punching hands.
A witch.

They called her a witch.

A good girl does not steal,
but if Mary was not going to be a

good girl,
and lie,
she may as well steal too.

Winter came,
as it did every year,
cold and deadly.
The villagers were preparing.
Mother was preparing—worried about food without Father.
Mary was preparing.
She fashioned a hole in the ground and lined it with stones
then dribbled water lightly on the frost-begun days
so it froze faster.
Mary killed animals from other people's barns
as well as those she caught.
And always where Mother wouldn't see.
Neither she nor her mother would die from winter—
nor any of winter's
deadly, natural elements.

Sometimes Mary's father had brought home root vegetables.
He'd said he found them growing wild.
Mary's mother didn't know.
Mary figured her father had stolen them, too.
Mary's mother wouldn't know.
Mary was a good bad girl who didn't want to hurt her mother.

They called her a witch.

Surely a woman wouldn't last so long in the woods.
Surely childbirth, alone, should have killed her.
Animals and food continued to go missing.
People were hearing whispers and movement...
People were seeing shadows and flashes
where there were none.

Except there was Mary.

Who heard every whisper

and saw
every frightened glance.

They called her a witch.

The signs of rot,
the poison plants mixed in with gathered grass,
were not Mary's doing.

But Mary recognized the danger.
These were things her father had taught her,
things that could make people sick
or dead.

She was not so bad a girl that she wished other people harm.
Even if they were cruel.
And apparently foolish
to not realize what was *really* making people and animals sick.

Even her father,
who had made her and her mother bleed and bruise,
who called her ugly,
never let them eat poison or rot.

And Mary was surely not as bad as he.

She saw a child, younger than her—she was hardly a child any
longer—
and tried to catch his attention.
To warn him,
to save him.
To teach him something...

And he was only a child...
Mother always said it was worse
to make children suffer.

But when the boy saw...
Mary,
her face,

her sun-darkened skin,
her wild, uncovered hair,
her animal-skin clothes...
he screamed
and cried
and threw stones
and ran away.

He didn't even call her a witch.

Devil!

Mary knew she should run and hide
but not before
a moment of pride.

"I am no devil! I am a witch!"

Then she ran.
Back to her woods,
back to her dark, bedeviled home—
Leave them to their fate!

She would take what she needed,
as she needed.
But not today.

They called her a witch.

One day,
Mary's mother
saw her tracks in the snow.
Saw where they were leading.
And tried to brush away the frozen tears
as she followed.

A good mother keeps her daughter safe.

She heard the screams.
Anger. Pain.

Mary.

She ran and ran and ran
to the place she'd never wanted to see again.

Outside of the meeting house
a mob
held her daughter.
Barely held her
as they tried to get a rope around her neck.
It wasn't as if the girl hadn't known violence.

The familiar cries pounded in her ears.

Witch! Witch! Witch!

"Mother!"

The mob turned to her.
Mother froze.
Shivering in the snow.
At the end of Hell-Ice stares.
But then a hellfire blazed in her heart
as she saw her daughter
held in hands
that looked familiar
to ones that touched her
long ago
attached to a mouth
that told her to be a
good girl
and then called her
Witch.

A young Baker,
not much older than her daughter.
But the face,
the face almost perfectly the same.
Goodman Baker.

She didn't see the elder Bakers.
The ones she'd known.
She didn't care.
Her daughter was being hurt.
She walked toward the mob.

At her stride,
the fear she felt
fled her,
and preyed upon them.
He told her not to come any closer.
He held a rope around her daughter's neck.
He held her daughter.

She continued forward.

A woman screamed.
Told her to stay away.
Something made her pause
and look.
The woman carried a babe
wrapped in a patterned weave
she'd seen before
on an older, a different, Goodwife Baker's shoulders.

Good wool was always passed to children,
her father once had said,
when he tucked her into bed.
A long, long time ago.

Young Goodman Baker,
who still held neck-roped Mary on that cold, dead-snow day,
shouted to the woman.
Or the babe, perhaps.
He called, *Martha.*
With concern.
The woman-called-witch,
Mother,
found that interesting.

There were many *Marthas* in the Bible intertwined with
Marys.

"What's your child's name?" she asked Young Goodman Baker.

In his moment of confusion
at such a question
from a
witch,
Mary stomped his foot,
snapped her head back against his nose,
and pulled the rope from her neck.
His blood froze crunching crystals
in her uncovered,
witchy-wild,
hair.

She ran to her mother.
So did the mob.

Mary had found freedom.
The mob had found tools.
Weapons.
With which they
thrust,
pounded,
speared,
poked,
and bludgeoned her mother.

Witch! Witch! Witch!

Her mother's blood iced upon the ground.
More fell in its slick,
beneath a town of angry boots.

They called her a witch.

The name took her life.

Mary ran.
Dodging through mad,
blood-blind people
reaching and clawing like storm-grasping branches.
Mary had lived through more than a few storms.

A baby cried.

"He called her Martha."
Mary decided it was the baby's name.

Mary tackled the woman
and took the child
in its blanket.
She didn't know why,
but felt it was *right* thing to do.
Not a choice for a
good girl
or a
bad girl,
but the choice that needed to be made.

And she ran to where the witch-namers would not follow.

The dark, forbidden, bedeviled woods.

Deep, deep, deep away from the people, Mary laid the infant down
in a bed of dried grasses and animal skins,
in a hidden house.

She would protect Martha's life,
with her own,
from all the world that deemed them wicked or ugly or *witches*,
as her mother had done for her.

She kissed Baby Martha's forehead and said,

"They will call you a witch."

Run in the Widow's Hell
K. H. Vaughan

Doughtry parked the old truck outside Bodeen's general store off to the side away from the gas pump and front door. When it was clear no one was around, he hefted a wooden crate of mason jars from under the tarp in the bed and carried it around back to a chicken hutch. Bodeen had left the money in a can just like always, and Doughty added it to the roll in his pocket. The sun was low, and cottonwood fluff drifted lazily in the air, suspended in the hazy gold light. This was his last stop before going back up into the hills. In the hills, it was already dark.

Bodeen's store hadn't changed much in years, and Doughtry didn't expect it to. The old man sat behind the counter reading the newspaper while Wash Bernson held court with Tracie Hitchcock and Honest Bill, eating crackers and sipping on a glass of water. They were nearly as inseparable as the Magi; if you ever saw one, you were likely to see the other two.

"Hidy, Doughtry," Wash said. Doughtry nodded and stepped past the trio to the counter.

"Can I get a coke?" he said.

"Have ye got ten cent?" Bodeen said, looking over the top of his spectacles.

"Yessir."

"Then I guess ye kin. Go on an' pick it out of the case."

"You got peach?"

"I don't know. Ye kin pick it out of the case."

Doughtry let the cool air from the electric case fall over his face for a moment. It was nice. Bodeen wouldn't talk moonshine business with others in earshot, so that was as much of a conversation as they were likely to have.

"That Sutter's old truck I hear you pull up in today?" Wash said. "Fenders on that thing flap like a rusted duck." He probably wanted to know if Bodeen was stocked up with shine, but Doughtry wouldn't put it past Wash to say something to the revenuers for reward money either.

"What you got there, Wash?" Doughtry said. He gestured at the horseshoe on the top of the checker board between the boys. "Didn't think you owned a horse."

"Well, Honest Bill here has got himself a bit of trouble and got to nail this'n here up over his door."

"That right?" Doughtry said.

"I was out sanging," Bill said. He wasn't much for working, but dug ginseng root and did whatever odd jobs were at hand when he needed cash money. "And, I don't know, I must've got turnt around some and I ended up by the Widow's Hell. I didn't mean too, but whenever I figured it out it was too late. Caught a glimpse of her through the woods and I liked to drop dead right then and there. Oh, she got that one milky eye. She's gonna put a spell on me for sure."

"She say anything to you?"

"Did she have to? I know when I done wrong."

Doughtry nodded. Every holler had a Granny Witch, a tough old hill woman who could cure warts and fevers or brew up a charm for love or money. Just a part of life, even though a lot of folks were turning to patent medicines these days. City doctors were hard to come by, and half the time couldn't do a damn thing for you anyway. There was always a Granny near and folks went to them when they needed answers and they wouldn't turn you away if you needed to pay in barter. Doughtry had been treated by more than one over the years.

The Widow was something else entirely. He'd driven through the Pennsylvania Dutch country and talked to locals about the *Hexefoos* painted on barns. Germans, really, not that he held it against them so long as they dealt square. They just weren't in a hurry to change their ways. A lot of folks said the circles were painted just for nice, but some would speak quietly about good luck and warding off evil. That was closer to what the Widow was. She didn't do any midwifery or keep an herb garden. No one went to her except in desperation, and even then not willingly. Most passed her by. She was rarely seen in town, and never in church. Now and again, she might appear at Bodeen's but he preferred to send a boy to deliver her sundries. Doughtry had done this a time or two himself as a child, and always wanted to leave the parcels on her porch and run. Hill people might hang signs and talismans on their doors against her but no one believed that any of it would work if she took a mind to cause you harm. The only sure thing was to let her be.

"You put the sang back?" Doughtry said.

"Hell, I figured it was already too late once I dug it up," Bill said. "I'm gonna have to take what I get for it and give it to her I guess. Maybe if I mail it to her. I got to be careful in the meantime though."

"Well," Doughtry said. "I got to get on."

"You see Sutter, tell him I said 'hidy,'" Wash said.

"You see Bill get turned into a toad or anything, let me know."

*   *   *

Doughtry woke slowly, rolled over in the bed, and smelled bacon frying. By the angle of the sunbeams streaming through the curtains he reckoned it was late, going on ten. Damn, but that store-bought mattress was comfortable. He had slept well, but carried a lingering sense of something forgotten, like the edges of a dream half-remembered. Lights flashing in the dark. Screams. He had gone somewhere he should not. He ran his hand absently along rippled scars on his chest and shoulder until he realized what he was doing and cursed himself silently. No time for that, now. No use. No point. He pulled his trousers on and shrugged his suspenders over his bare shoulders.

Janie was in the kitchen wearing his shirt while she cooked breakfast on the electric range. He came up behind and wrapped his arms around her.

"Hey, Sugar," she said. "You got in so late I reckoned I'd let you sleep a spell. You ain't been out courting some other girl have you?" She leaned back into him, teasing. Sometimes he could hear a trace of her city accent left from when she'd come down from Providence years ago, but her voice was usually smooth as morning mist on the hills. She wasn't wearing aught but that shirt.

"Had to work," he said. "Sutter'd got business needed done."

"As long as you don't go falling in with loose women," she said.

"You're the only loose woman I need," he said, and retreated to the bathroom in the face of her feigned indignation. After breakfast they lay in bed again, tangled in her catalogue sheets. He traced a finger along her shoulder, ran it down along her arm. She pulled it away when he came close to her elbow, the inner aspect blotched and spotted from needles. She'd got shut of it but the tracks remained. Doughtry figured he'd done worse in his life, but it still bothered her. She would let him touch her anywhere but there.

"I'm fixing to go abroad for two-three days," he said.

"Where you going to?" she said.

"I might could guess, but Sutter'll let on when he's ready."

"Don't he trust you, Sugar?"

"Sutter don't trust nobody. Not all the way."

"Well. You ought to get him to pay you more for these runs."

"I'm doing alright."

"It's dangerous."

That was true enough. Doughtry thought about Tater Johnson and Bull McArdle who were machine-gunned by revenue agents driving a load of blockade out of the hills just last month. He hadn't seen it, but knew what a machine gun would do to a man from the Ardennes. That old cod Nathan Dell got himself shot too, threatening government men with a shotgun to get off his land. And Booker Dean crashed his Buick during a chase and got thrown through the windscreen. Lying there in his pine box, it looked like he'd brought a spoon to a knife fight.

"Ain't scared," Doughtry said.

"Ain't never said you were," Janie said.

"Well, maybe you best close your mouth so we don't misunderstand each other."

"Or maybe I'd best open it."

* * *

It was dusty dark when Doughtry kissed Janie to head out.

"They gonna repeal that Volstead Act, you know," she said. "What are you gonna do then?"

"Don't reckon Sutter'll go out of business. Don't matter what the government does. They can put us on a wire and run their telephones and call it 'progress,' but it don't change nothing that matters."

"You think he'll go legitimate?"

Doughtry ran his hand along the stubble on his lantern jaw and thought for a moment. "No," he said. "Not if he can help it."

Starting up the trail in the dying light, he paused and looked back. She stood in the doorway, her form backlit by the electric bulb inside.

"Maybe after I get back we oughta step over a broom and make you an honest woman," he said.

"Oh, Sugar," she said. "That ship sailed a long, *long* time ago."

*   *   *

He had the Ford hidden in an old barn across the unused pasture behind the house. The barn smelled of oil and gasoline, and old dry hay. Smells he loved. He pulled the string for the one bare light bulb he'd run so he could work at night. The Ford was plain and black to look at, like any other on the roads, so long as you didn't look too close. The big flathead V-8 was customized for horsepower and the suspension reinforced to support the cargo. Even with a full load it could outrun any government vehicle he could get in front of. They'd added steel plates in front of the radiator and behind the driver's seat, and a belly plate to protect the undercarriage if he had to run across fields. He stroked the fender and smiled.

Out on the hard road it gave a throaty rumble and he had to go extra light on the gas just to keep it from getting away from him. He drove past small farms and broke-down houses, some empty, all desolate and grey. Places where he'd delivered by the cup or jar as a boy. Past nip joints and pumpkin stands where he'd run barrels. Past a hound dog dead on the pavement, probably having had no idea what a car was or that anything could ever go that fast. All his life he'd been on these roads. You could put down asphalt, but it just meant folks could get the same places faster than before.

Climbing into the hills and onto dirt and gravel roads; the stiff suspension jolted, car straining to go faster. The houses spread out more and more, and lit with coal oil instead of electric light. He turned down a side road so narrow the laurel dragged against the fenders. He stopped to open a gate of corrugated tin and baling wire, and pulled it shut after he drove through. There were many ways to get where he was going and he took care to take different ones.

Up the road was a weather-beaten house slung low and mean. Chickens scratched sleepily in the hardpack and an old-timer sat on his porch in the soft light from the lamp inside.

"Hidy," Doughtry said, getting out of the Ford. "You seen any of them government men?" The old man had a pair of army field glasses and he sat on that porch all day watching, a decrepit smooth-bore musket leaned up against the wall by his side. He'd a done it even if Sutter didn't pay him to, just on general principles.

"Cain't say as I have. Don't reckon ye kin git a dram of the real angel teat for me? This'n here's garbroth."

"Yes, sir. I'll bring you a quart by and by. Get you drunk as a fiddler's bitch."

"I done got this'n from a neighbor; I don't git 'round so much as I used to could. I expect he's mixing carbolic in the mash. That ol' boy'd throw a dead possum in the beer iffin he thought it'd give it a kick."

"Whose is it?"

"I best not name names else he'll up and not sell ary to me anymore, but he makes it in the holler o'er yonder a piece."

"Dixon."

"You done named him," the old man cackled. "I ain't said it myself, now. Nobody can say I did!"

*   *   *

He drove further up into the yellow pine and hit the horn a few times to let Sutter know he was coming. Doughtry started out for him as a boy, carrying jars from house to house through the woods. The blackpot was set up on blocks and the beer was cooking, pure clear shine coming through the condenser coils and spilling into a pail. Sutter waved and a couple of the fellows came over to talk by the campfire set off away from the product.

"Hidy, Doughtry. Hey, Peanut!" Sutter yelled back toward the still. "Do I gotta put a bedpost on yer shirttail? Watch that fire don't git too high!" He shook his head. "That boy ain't got sense enough to poke acorns down a peckerwood hole." For some reason, Sutter's dialect always got stronger when they were getting ready for a big run.

"Well boys, we're fixin' to run to Cincinnati," Sutter said. Doughtry nodded. Cincinnati really meant Newport across the Ohio River, and Newport was easy territory. Outside of a big show by the National Guard in '22, there wasn't any real law enforcement in Newport. Police made perfunctory raids once in a while; never against anyone who was connected or paid up. Hell, the Police Chief was indicted for conspiracy to distribute and the City Commissioner demoted him to foot patrol at least three times. He just ignored it all and kept on not doing his job. The problem wasn't gonna be down there. It was getting out of the hills past the blockade.

"The thing is," Sutter said. "We got to get the load through on account of them prohibition agents got the last one. And they got two of our pots since then too. Goddammit, they even smashed the bottles. Shootin' up the kettle I can understand, but smashin' all the jugs?" He shook his head. "That's just plain mean."

"The buyer barking about it?" Doughtry said.

"He ain't happy about the loss of product," Sutter said.

"That Italian think he's the boss out here, he got another thing coming," Ode Walls said. "Let him send some of them city boys up here to complain and no one will ever see them fellas again."

"Now, Ode, it ain't like that," Sutter said. "This here is a business relationship and we gotta keep the customer happy. The syndicates ain't never gonna try and muscle in out here in the country. Now, we'll send a couple cars to take the law on a chase and ship the whole passel in one car. We'll just pack it to the roof. But we gotta study up the route or they'll do us up like they done Bull and Tater."

They went over where the revenuers had been seen, what roads had the best escape routes, and who was likely to inform on them. Doughtry had to shake his head. Why the government had anything to say about what a man did with his own corn was beyond him. When they got done, Sutter took a sip of the new run from a jar and said "There's one more road we might could use.

Just this one time, and ain't nobody would expect it. Down through the Widow's Hell."

No one spoke. Doughtry could hear the pop and crackle of the fire and the chirring of cicadas. He felt the boys tighten up as soon as Sutter said it. Someone let out a slow whistle in the firelight.

"Now boss, you know she don't hold with no liquor on her land," Ode said.

"I know it."

"How come? She a forty gallon Baptist?" Delmar Roux asked. He was new, up from Greenville. A good old boy, but a city boy.

"She's a damned witch, is what she is," Ode said and made a sign.

"Shut up, you old mountain ape," Sutter said. "She's ain't nothing but a little old biddy."

"Ain't seen *you* run no liquor 'cross her land."

"Y'all don't believe that hoodoo, do you?" Roux said.

No one spoke right away.

"I don't know if she is or if she ain't a witch," Sutter said. "But I always figured it's safest to cover all bets."

"Tell him 'bout that boy-child, Sutter," Ode said.

"This young chap weren't more'n ten year old. This was maybe two-three years gone, now. He done cut 'cross her property delivering a jar and slipped into the crick in the ice and snow and froze to death. He'd been warned to stay off her land but he must've got lost or I don't know what. Hell, he was bluer'n a possum's cod whenever they found him. Everybody said she put a hex on that boy to make it happen. That's the story. Maybe it's true and maybe it ain't, but there's a lot of stories just like that over the years. Making people sick or bringing bad luck. I'll admit it's a chancy thing, but so's trying to bust through a road block. Anyway, who here is willing to drive the load thataway if it looks like it's our best chance? Just this one time."

The men shifted uncomfortably, looking at their shoes.

"Now, fellas, we all done heard them stories all our lives," Sutter said. "But we ain't little boys no more. I ain't much for schoolin', but these are modern times, with all that science and Darwin you hear 'bout on the radio. Doughtry, ye ain't come back from the war all Frenchified have ye?"

He looked up at the trees. Too thick in the deep woods to see the stars overhead. Images of German shells shattering the tall Douglas fir and the feel of sticky clots of sap and blood in his hair rushed in, unbidden and unwanted. Flares and muzzles flashed in the dark. The carpet of pine needles there was much like that at home. Sutter wouldn't let on, but there was a problem with the buyer if he was willing to take a chance like this. Potential trouble with the syndicates, and those fellas were serious as a heart attack, no matter what Ode thought. It was simpler when George Remus was in charge of the whole thing. Everything was orderly and everyone got paid. But then the Feds sent him up for two years and the gangsters moved in. When he got out, it was too dangerous to try and pick up again and he retired. Doughtry spat.

"I reckon I ain't," he said.

*   *   *

As dawn came he drove out by a different route, staying on nothing but dirt roads that wound through the hills and hugged cliffs beneath the trees. Coming down a bend he slowed and eyed the turn-off into the Widow's Hell. He stopped the car at the entrance. Not much of a road, because few people cared to drive through. Twisted old trees arched over the road like a tunnel, and the undergrowth was choked with mountain laurel. The slick of laurel was so thick and deep you'd get lost and never find your way out if you got off the trail. Easier to swim against a riptide than to fight through it. You looked at a map of the mountains and you'd see patches like this, some running for miles and miles, named for people who had got lost in them. The old woman this Hell was named for wasn't lost though. She'd lived in that dark labyrinth for as long as any living soul could remember.

Usually he'd drive a road before a run, just to be sure. But, looking into the shadowed tangles of laurel, his chest grew tight and he pressed the gas pedal and drove past. There'd only ever been one road through there and no forks until it came out the other side. Just have to drive straight on through if it came to it. It'd be alright.

*   *   *

"I'm heading out tomorrow," Doughtry said. He'd slept through the morning and spent the afternoon in the barn working on the Ford. Motor oil worked into the cracks in the skin of his fingers, set in even after washing.

"That right?" Janie said.

"Yeah."

There was nothing but the sounds of eating in the small neat kitchen for a time.

"Well? What're you chewin' on?" she said.

"This fine supper you done cooked us."

"Don't shine me on, Sugar. I know you better'n that. You were calling out in your sleep like you do sometimes and you're all quiet today."

They held eye contact across the table for a while until he looked away and exhaled.

"Alright then," he said. "Sutter wants me to run through the Widow's Hell."

"Oh, baby, you can't do that. That old woman——"

"I don't believe them fairy tales."

"Sugar—"

"That's all there is to it. I'm a grown man, and if I can't do my job, I should've stayed in the army."

"I guess I can't do or say anything to change your mind then, can I?"

"No."

"Well."

They didn't talk much for the rest of the evening, but she held him tight all night and would not let go. The next day she followed him to the barn and wrote on the hood of the Ford in grease pencil.

"What're you doing there?"

"You got to take this charm for protection. That witch'll put a spell on you and I'll never see you again."

He looked and saw that she had written *"Dear Father watch over me that no fiends, no witchcraft and enchantment can harm me. Amen."* And she had drawn three crosses under it.

"Since when you been this much of a Christian?"

"Just 'cause I lie down first and get up second for you don't mean I ain't a Christian," she snapped.

"You know I didn't mean it like that. You just ain't much of a church-going type."

"When it comes to that witch, I surely am. You promise me you'll leave that there."

Doughtry promised and kissed her.

"You ever think about moving?" he said.

"Moving where?"

"I don't know. Maybe to the city. Or maybe back up north."

"Well, hell, Sugar," she said. "I never did come down here by mistake. It was all on purpose."

He nodded. Kissed her again then drove off without looking back toward her or the house. He waited till he had driven out of her sight before pulling off the road to wipe the charm off of the hood.

*   *   *

He took the long way up, driving a good hour before getting to the loading place; enough time for the lookouts to see if he was being followed and warn Sutter. They took the rear and passenger seats out and filled it up as far as they could go, leaving just enough room for Ode to sit on crates next to him. They folded quilts over it all but figured if the law came they'd outrun them. Ode had the Thompson just in case.

"The gov'mint wants it bottled in bond?" Peanut crowed. "This'n here's bottled in the barn!"

"Ye got them tires aired up and the tank gassed?" Sutter said. "Ye ain't gave nothing a lick and promise have ye?"

"It's had the full tune-up," Doughtry said. "You know that."

"I know, I know. I'm just nervous is all. The sheriff is out there with them government men."

"I thought he was all paid up."

"Yeah, but he's got to walk a line with them prohibition agents. He don't cooperate with 'em some they'll fix his wagon. He gets a chance he'll send word what's going on. Somebody out there been flappin' their gums though, 'cause they're looking to get our run."

Come dusk a small boy came running through the trees to tell them where the roadblocks were set up. Sutter scowled and pulled Doughtry aside.

"They got us hemmed in pretty tight here. Ye ain't scared to drive through the Widow's Hell are ye? I wouldn't ask if we didn't need it. I got creditors, and them boys in Cincinnati ain't none too pleased we missed them shipments."

Moe Dalitz and the Cleveland Syndicate had been disagreeing

some with the Lonardo family about who was going to run Cincinnati. Dalitz was in with Lansky out of New York, and Doughtry figured they'd win out in the end. Sutter couldn't afford to cross either one or get caught in the crossfire. Smoke and pine wafted in the air. Doughtry ran his finger along the trench knife he'd got in France. The German boy he'd got it from hadn't wanted to part with it, and it wasn't any kind of fair trade.

"I guess I don't care to," he said. "If it comes to it, we'll make that run. Just this one time, like you said."

*   *   *

"Damn! They's not enough room to cuss a cat without getting hair in your mouth," Ode said once they shut him in. Sutter came round to the driver's side window to see them off.

"That there's a thousand dollar load, boys. Have a good time chasing that red onion down in Newport. Ye get yourselves a ride and tie before ye head back."

"See you boys," Ode yelled out the window as they pulled out. "I'll be howlin' like a curly-tailed wolf!"

Doughtry drove fast over roads curving up and down the hills, through deep trees and brush. Through hollows so deep you'd have to bring the sun in with a pipe, branches whipping at the car in the headlights. Now and again past some cabin, the lamp inside flickering dully, where the occupants might look to see who had come driving so fast out of the dark, or they might not, knowing it wasn't their business.

They made the turn down the ill-used road surrounded by the tangled slick of the Widow's Hell. Doughtry's stomach clenched up as he made it and for a brief moment he wondered if he shouldn't have left Janie's charm be. There in the dark, the road rattled and scraped beneath them and the branches clutched at the fenders. It was weedy and he wouldn't think to call it more than a trail, but the ruts were there even if he couldn't always see them real well.

"Keep an eye out," Doughtry said.

"For the revenuers ye mean," Ode said, nodding, but they both knew he hadn't.

They thundered down the trail in the deep dark, just as fast as the headlights would allow. Doughtry remembered the terror of being shelled or going over the top of the trench line across the wire. Remembered huddling in a bunker with his gas mask on, watching men stumble blindly through yellow-green fog, choking and faltering, that faint smell of bleach and musty hay irritating his nose even through the mask. Hoping the mask would be enough. Now, down in that damp bottom, he felt a different kind of fear. Something older. Darker. The hell was so dark and thick you wouldn't be surprised to meet the Old Gentleman himself. He could be standing next to you in the thick growth and you wouldn't even know it until he took your hand.

It was a surprise when he saw the house, and Doughtry knew it was her the second it flashed into being out of the dark. A dry old form standing on her porch, waiting to see who it was driving down past her house so late in the night, and for a moment it appeared as if her eyes reflected like an owl's. Then they were past and she was gone. The laurel branches whipped the fenders and the trees raced past, but the house and the old woman and the fear raced away in the distance behind them. Doughtry released his breath.

"I don't mind sayin' all that witch talk was getting me a might nervous but I guess we're alright now," Ode said.

"Yeah," Doughtry said. "I wouldn't mind a smoke, if you could light me up one."

"Don't mind if I do," Ode said. "I guess—" he began to say and then the car shuddered as if bumped. Ode cursed, wide-eyed. It seemed as if the dark had begun to close around them, the shine of the headlights smothered, and looking out they apprehended something there. Doughtry had the brief impression of a great slavering maw before the Ford was wrenched from his control and spun out, one of the front wheels flashing briefly in the headlights as it sailed on by. They crashed hard up against an old oak and Ode was thrown against the dash and windscreen.

Doughtry shook his head to clear it, smelled gasoline and shine— an overwhelming vapor that could not quite cover the deep dank smell of the wood around them. Ode moaned.

"You alright?" Doughtry asked, but he could see Ode wasn't. The bones in his forearm were sticking through his shirt sleeve. There was no sound outside of any kind except the ticking of cooling metal.

"Yeah, I'm busted up some, but I—" Ode began to say but then stopped. He stared, face pale in the light reflected off the leaves from the Ford's one good headlight. Doughtry followed his gaze, his mind struggling to put form to what he saw. A tangle of rough ropey vines, tall as a house, was moving slowly toward them. Within, he could see jagged mouths oozing vile ichor and eyes scattered about: mad, bestial eyes placed within the mass with no apparent order but all oriented now on him. Ode began gibbering some sort of prayer and repenting every sin he had ever done and probably a bait of sins he never did, just in case. The thing took a step on a massive cloven hoof.

"You goddamn witch," Doughtry screamed, getting out of the car, blood running down his face. He raised the Thompson and it thundered wildly in the dark, the thing illuminated in the bright staccato bursts. Its thick tendrils lashing the air wildly as it advanced, the bullets chewing at the thick barky stump of its body but doing aught to even offend it, much less slow it down.

Beside him, Ode howled in the car, pure corn liquor running everywhere from broken bottles. Some spark or flame within the wreck caught the alcohol, or perhaps it was just the witch's will that set it alight. The Ford burned with a clear blue flame until the gasoline caught and went up in an orange cloud. The Thomson ran out and Doughtry dropped it, staring at the approaching thing in the glow of the fire, while Ode shrieked in the burning car. The stench of burning flesh and swamp and goat began to make him feel faint and he kneeled down in the road. Beyond the thing he saw the woman, straight and dry like a cornhusk doll, her eyes reflecting the firelight.

"I'm sorry, ma'am," he mumbled. "I'm sorry."

Ode finally stopped screaming.

The thing came on.

Portrait of an Old Woman with Crows
Peter N. Dudar

The crows were never going to stand still, so Marie had to use quick brush strokes to capture their essence and their positions, knowing she'd have to go back and add detail. The crows cawed madly and flapped their wings as they strutted around the old woman's feet. They pecked nervously at each other as they waited for her wrinkled old hand to reach back inside the burlap sack and disperse another spray of corn kernels. The old woman paid no attention to the young lady in the green smock and denim jeans as she dipped her brushes against the blotches of oil paint on her pallet and set upon her canvas. For all Marie knew, the old woman was gazing upon the water in the fountain or at the turning foliage. Deering Park in early October was spectacular to behold, with the fiery red and gold and orange leaves creating an inferno in the heart of the city.

Marie worked with fierce determination. The painting needed to be completed by Monday in order to turn it in for her art class, and Professor Jennings wasn't the kind of teacher who would suffer excuses to allow life to get in the way of art. Beyond the looming deadline for her second big project of the semester, her son Conner needed to be picked up from playschool by noon, which meant she wasn't going to finish the painting anyway. She just needed enough time to capture the old woman's figure and the pattern of the crows around her, and define composition and space. Details could always be filled in later, like after Conner went to bed for the night and before Josh came home from working second shift at the B&M Baked Bean plant. Josh would want a dinner that consisted of anything other than hot dogs and baked beans, and then a few beers and a bit of intimate time before settling down and falling asleep for the night. The old woman on the bench was at least fifty yards away, and after sitting there for hours doing nothing but feeding the crows by her feet, it wasn't like she gave a damn either way. If the old woman got up now and walked away, Marie would still eventually finish her painting and get the grade she needed from Professor Jennings. The assignment had been to capture something nostalgic, and what was more nostalgic in America than an old woman on a park bench feeding the birds?

She dipped her brush against the pallet and swept up a blob of ebony to finish the strokes on her final crow. Marie had not counted how many crows there actually were, but rather embellished both for time's sake and for her own sanity. Those goddamn beasts kept flapping and hopping around and pecking at each other whenever the old crone dropped another spray of corn on the ground. On her canvas, the replication of the old woman was mostly completed; the subject was draped in a long, flowered dress and black shawl and a hat that Marie was pretty sure was called a snood, with a black veil over her eyes and long ebon feathers jutting over the back. In the painting, the woman was holding her hand out and dropping kernels of corn on the ground while the crows gathered at her feet, squabbling and puffing out their tail feathers to show dominance among each other.

The alarm went off on Marie's cell phone. She pulled the device from her pocket, shut off the alarm bell, and started to gather her paints and accoutrements. Conner would be moody if he was the last child to be picked up from Miss Kristina's playschool, and then she'd spend the car ride home listening to the four-year-old pitch a tantrum and wonder why the hell she'd chosen to have Josh's baby in the first place. It hadn't been like Josh put a diamond ring on her finger, or…

The old woman was standing right behind her. It was as if she'd closed the fifty-yard gap between them in the blink of an eye.

"God's eye is on the sparrow," the old woman said, her voice a chorus of bullfrog croaks and formaldehyde. Her bony hand shot out and grabbed Marie's wrist, forcing her to drop her paintbrush in the dying grass below. "But Satan's eye watches from the crows."

Marie stifled the scream from her mouth as she looked through the veil on the old crone's hat (*yes, it's definitely a snood,* she thought for no reason at all, and then the bubble of panic burst inside her and the thought flew away). Behind the mesh fabric was a pair of glazed hazel orbs, laden with cataracts, and she found herself wondering how the old woman could even see. Eyes *that* cloudy had to be blind. Staring into those orbs made her think of wretched, old goats deformed from years of inbreeding.

"You didn't ask my permission before you painted me," the old woman croaked. Her lips formed a distasteful snarl, exposing blackened gums around crooked teeth. She reached her free hand up to the ugly old hat on her head and plucked out a long, black feather. Before Marie could protest, the woman gouged the prickly nub of the quill into the skin of her wrist and carved a long, bloody trail. "You will repay me for taking without asking, young lady."

Marie saw the blood spill down the warm skin of her fingers and onto the ground. Yanking her hand away from the old crone, Marie slapped her paint rag on the wound. The crows over by the bench cawed, screaming bloody murder at the offense, but when Marie turned to face her accuser and protest, the old woman was gone.

*   *   *

"Thank goodness you're here," Miss Kristina said as Marie entered the foyer of the *Amazing Tots* playschool. The unfinished "Portrait of an Old Woman with Crows" was nestled neatly in the trunk of her Honda Accord (although the *real* old woman had never escaped her mind since the assault back in the park. In fact, her heart still racing with fear pounded faster every time she looked at the bloody fabric tied around her wrist) waiting to be completed after her and Conner were home. Miss Kristina looked both frightened and embarrassed as she crossed the romper area to speak with her. The room was quiet -- too quiet -- and Marie noticed the other children sitting around the work table and looking at her son in horror. Their faces were all sealed lips and wide eyes as they gathered away from him at the far side of the table and gawked at Conner. Connor's eyes leaked tears down his ashen face. Marie moved closer and noticed that her son's wrist was wrapped in gauze and a length of eggshell blue bandage. "We were sitting at the table working on tracing the letter Q when Conner took his pencil and started gouging it into his wrist. It was the scariest thing I've ever seen. His eyes rolled back into his head and he just rammed the pencil into his skin...like he was trying to stab a mouse or something. I yanked the pencil out of his hands, but by then he was bleeding all over the table. I got him cleaned up and put the bandage on him," Miss Kristina leaned closer and spoke in a hushed, conspiratorial voice. "As I wrapped the bandage around his arm, he kept whispering, 'This is all mommy's fault.' It's an absolute miracle he didn't puncture any arteries."

Dread filled Marie's belly. She walked past the other children and wrapped her arms around Conner's tiny frame and squeezed him tight. "It's okay, honey. Mommy is here now. Let's get home and we'll figure out some lunch. Maybe we can have a bowl of ice cream for dessert. Would you like that, baby?"

Conner lifted his face to look at his mother.

"You have a booboo just like mine," he said. There was no emotion in his voice; no trace of concern or remorse or fear. He could have been reading lines from a teleprompter or discussing the weather. This was *not* the little boy who threw his arms around his mother and lavished her with kisses every time she picked him up from playschool.

"I'm so sorry this happened," Miss Kristina said from somewhere behind her. "I wish there could have been something I could have done to prevent it. It breaks my heart seeing him acting like this."

Marie slipped her hands under her son's armpits and picked him up. She held Conner close as she moved past the other children and over toward the cubby area to collect his jacket and backpack. Miss Kristina was right on her heals, still talking to her (talking *at* her), but Marie was having trouble focusing on anything other than how her wound and Conner's were in the same exact location. "He's never had behavior issues like this before. This could be leading to something serious. I'm very concerned that he might try something like this again in my classroom. I can't have him hurting himself or hurting the other children. Do you understand what I'm saying?"

"This won't happen again," Marie said over her shoulder. "We'll have him looked at over the weekend." She opened the door as the parade of parents arrived to collect their own children. Her cheeks flushed with embarrassment just thinking about the other children running their mouths off at their dinner tables that evening about what Conner Lynch did to himself at school today, and just what those other parents would speculate about her and Josh and how they were raising their son.

In the back of her mind, she could hear the old woman on the park bench laughing.

*   *   *

It took a hot bubble bath and a bowl of ice cream just to get Conner to return to the happy, vibrant little boy that he usually was. Marie decided to not mention what happened to him (or herself) to Josh, who was still sleeping up in their bedroom when she and Conner got home, and would discuss the whole thing later after their son was asleep and Josh returned from work at midnight. Now that Conner was back to normal, she settled him in the den, in front of the television for the PBS Kids afternoon lineup (in Marie's mind, PBS stood for Public Babysitting Station, with Elmo and Curious George as ersatz conductors on the cartoon railways) and could return to work on her painting.

Or did she really want to?

The thought crossed her mind as she retrieved the painting and her equipment from her Honda. Opening the trunk and reaching in, she noticed that her painting had changed—only a little bit—but enough to make her blood run cold. When she was working in the park, she'd painted the old woman looking out toward the Deering Park fountain, her outstretched hand dropping kernels of corn toward the crows

Satan's eye watches from the crows!

by her feet. Now, the old woman was staring back directly at her. And in her other hand was the feather she'd used to assault her. Seeing it made her wound burn and throb under the new bandage she'd put on after giving Conner his bath.

You didn't ask permission.

"I don't *need* your fucking permission. And I don't have time to start a new painting. I need to get this finished and turned in so I don't fail my course." Marie yanked the painting unceremoniously from the trunk and hauled it up to her studio to work on. If she had to, she would repaint the old woman so that her face looked back out at the water, and she would remove that feather and replace it with a hot dog or a squirt gun or a big yellow rubber dildo if she so chose to. This painting was *hers*, and she would do as she pleased with it. With the portrait in one hand and her easel and box of brushes and oils in the other, she raced up to her studio room above the garage.

*   *   *

Her cell phone rang at 10:17 that evening, long after she'd fed Conner and herself a dinner of fish sticks and broccoli with cheese sauce and tucked her son into bed. Conner had remained happy and animated all evening, as if the whole episode at playschool never even happened. Marie steeled herself to not even bring it up with him, to let himself forget the whole incident, and she found herself shaken when the child in the Mickey Mouse pajamas brought it up anyway.

"I didn't want to hurt myself today," Conner said. His eyebrows furrowed with worry, causing his bright blue eyes to squint. "I tried not to, but she made me."

"Who made you, sweetie?" Marie sat down on the bed next to her son, and stroked her fingers through his shaggy blond hair.

"The old woman. She showed up at school today while we were working on our letters. She told me she could teach me how to fly like the birds." The little boy with blond, curly locks and Mickey Mouse pajamas leaned forward and whispered. "Her eyes were awful. They made me scared so I did what she said."

Panic welled deep inside her. Marie's mind jumped to the nearly completed painting in her studio, where the old woman was once again facing the water. She had to use some heavy oils to correct the old woman's visage (and she added quite a few details as well, like those nasty cataracts that looked more like the eyes of a blind goat than a human's) and improved the composition of the crows around her feet. A few more hours on Saturday and Sunday and the painting would be finished, but where would the old woman be? Could she be watching right now? Did she already know the damage she'd inflicted on her son? There was no doubt that the old woman Conner was referring to was *her...*

You didn't ask permission.

*   *   *

Her cellphone rang.

After Conner fell asleep, Marie decided she did not want to return up to the studio and face the portrait. Doing so would only serve to unhinge her, and that was the last thing she wanted while alone in the house with Conner, waiting for Josh to get home from work, so instead she fixed some sleepy-tea and snuggled up in bed. In the end, sleep won out and she dozed off.

She rolled over and plucked her phone off the bedside table and looked at the number of the incoming call.

It was Josh.

She pressed the on button and offered a sleepy "hello?"

Josh's voice sounded panicked, and she knew something had to be wrong.

"Honey, it's me…Listen, I fell asleep in the locker room during my lunch break and had the most horrible dream. I dreamt you and Conner were here at the bean factory. For some reason, we were all standing up on the roof, just beneath the neon B&M sign. You were holding Conner in your arms, and you had this crazy look in your eyes. When I asked you what you were doing, you told me you were going to teach Conner how to fly. And then…and then you pitched our son off the roof. I watched Conner fall past the windows, flapping his arms like he could fly or something, and then he just splattered all over the parking lot. And you smiled. You smiled the whole time like you were satisfied with yourself. I know it sounds crazy, but I just wanted to hear your voice, and to hear that you are both okay."

"Oh, honey, I'm sorry," Marie answered, secretly thanking the stars above that she hadn't discussed with him what happened in the park earlier or what happened to Conner's wrist at playschool. Josh hadn't even noticed the bandage as he made his routine stumble from the bedroom to the bathroom to do his business, shower, and get dressed for work for the night. Life with her boyfriend meant cleaning up his clothes from the night before (the ones reeking of baked beans and molasses) and getting them into the washing machine before they made the house smell like an Elks Club barbecue. "It was just a dream. We're both fine here. Conner went right to sleep when I put him down."

Josh's voice sounded immediately relieved. "I swear to God, it was so real. Marie, your eyes looked so damned vacant and empty. It was like there was no soul looking through them. It was like looking into a bird's eyes."

That made her shiver.

Satan's eye watches from the crows.

"It was just a bad dream, sweetie. You're probably just overtired. Get home soon and come to bed with me. I miss you."

"Miss you too, hon."

After she hung up the phone she sat up, yawned, and climbed out of bed. She needed to pee, and wanted to stop in Conner's room and give him an extra kiss goodnight. Josh's dream scared her the more she thought about it, particularly after being told she tossed her child to his death off the rooftop of the baked bean canning plant.

When she entered Conner's room, his bed was empty.

*　　*　　*

Marie Lynch tore through the raised ranch on Hawthorne Drive screaming Conner's name as she darted from room to room. The house sat quiet in reply; an icy tomb of quaint New England décor and domestic frailties. The only sound to be heard was her heart pounding in her chest, and the accusatory caw of some lone crow in one of the treetops outside the back window. It called in a shriek that insisted, "You didn't ask permission." She raced up the staircase at the back of the house and burst through the door to her studio, where she found Conner in his Mickey Mouse pajamas, sucking his thumb and staring at the painting.

Tears of relief sliding down her cheeks, she hurried up behind him, throwing her arms around his tiny frame, and then gasped in terror as she gazed upon the "Portrait of an Old Woman with Crows". In the picture, the old woman had vanished completely. Instead was a new figure, dangling from a noose that held taut from a tree limb somewhere outside the picture. The figure was dressed in a green smock and denim jeans, and Marie had no difficulty discerning that this was herself in the portrait, that the old woman had somehow changed things around. Below the cadaverous version of herself was a wooden sign staked into the ground where the crows continued their vigil. The sign was painted in blood-red letters. It read: This Is What We Do To Witches!

"Come on, sweetie, let's go back downstairs," she whispered to Conner. The little boy remained frozen in place, staring at the painting. Marie knelt down beside him and tried to turn him away, but when she did, she noticed that his irises had turned from blue to raven black. Feathers sprouted out of his pajama collar in long, dark plumes that made his neck shine in the overhead light.

Marie screamed in horror.

*　*　*

Her eyes flew open.

The whole thing had been a nightmare. A dream and nothing more. Her family was sleeping safe and sound in their house on Hawthorne Drive. It was nearly six a.m. on Saturday morning according to the digital clock on Josh's side of the bed, and by the smell of the lingering odor of baked beans, Josh had probably fallen asleep with his work clothes still on. This was fine. She could deal with the baked beans scent. She wouldn't even scold him over it.

She picked up her cell phone and examined the call log. The phone showed no record of receiving a call from Josh the evening before, and that was also a good thing. Just chalk it all up to a stressful afternoon, on top of worrying about getting that stupid painting done and turning it in to Professor Jennings on time. Marie realized that she'd been making such a huge deal about obtaining the professor's approval and getting a decent grade that she had put too much stress on herself. Getting the arts degree had been a luxury idea more than it had been about establishing a career. It was getting her out of her house for a few hours every day now that Conner was old enough for playschool. It was a refuge for a stay-at-home mom, who probably should have been working a part time job to help cover the bills so that Josh wasn't always at work. All of this had just been a stress-related dream.

The wound on her wrist prickled in disagreement, and Marie had to stifle the scream to keep from waking her husband up.

The wound on her arm was real.

What happened in the park was real.

Marie sprinted to Conner's room before she could carry the logic any further.

*　*　*

Conner was sound asleep in his bed. The nightlight shined from one of the outlets in the corner, but Marie decided to flip the overhead light on anyway. Her heart racing once again, Marie found herself terrified of what she would see when the room was illuminated.

Her worries were in vain. Connor's eyes were sealed shut with blessed sleep. There were no feathers protruding from his Mickey Mouse pajamas, nor were there any signs that he had gotten up at any point in the middle of the night.

There was also no bandage around his wrist, and no puncture wound where her child had stabbed himself with a pencil back at playschool. There was only warm, pale, unmarked skin. Marie lifted his arm up to examine it close, but when she did, Conner's eyes flew open.

"I'm trying to sleep, Mommy."

"I know, honey. Just close your eyes and go back to bed. I just needed to come in and give you a kiss." Marie leaned down and planted a big, wet smack across her child's forehead. Conner tugged his arm away from her and tried to wipe the wetness of her kiss away.

"What did you do that for? You didn't ask permission."

Marie Lynch stood up and backed herself away from her son in slow, timid steps as his words echoed in her brain.

*   *   *

She staggered down the hall and up the stairs to her studio. Her mind raced in fear and panic as she fought to sort out what was reality and what wasn't. The world was spinning in chaos, and she merely skipped like a stone across its surface. The only thing she *did* understand was that it was time to destroy the painting. It was time to destroy the goddamn thing once and for all, and whatever happened afterward was going to have to be worked out and dealt with. She didn't care if she failed her art class, or if Professor Jennings berated her for wasting her talent. None of it mattered.

Marie threw the door open and flipped on the light switch. The painting sat on the easel at the far end of the room, and even from a distance, she could tell that the painting had changed once again. She sidled up to it slowly, sure that some mystical hex would drag her kicking and screaming onto the canvas, but nothing happened. This time the bench was empty but the crows were still there; only, they had all turned their heads to face her

Satan's eye watches from the crows!

and what she *hadn't* noticed before was now brutally evident. If it had been a connect-the-dots picture, she could have flown right through it without even looking at the numbers to trace the lines correctly. The crows were positioned so that they formed a large pentagram in front of the empty park bench, and just as she noticed it, she felt the ice-cold breath of the old woman on her neck.

Marie turned around and stared into those cataract-laden eyes and whimpered a timid sob.

The old woman cackled in amusement. Her laughter echoed in Marie's ears like the serenade from a murder of crows.

"I'm sorry!" Marie said to the old woman. "I'm sorry I didn't ask your permission. Please forgive me and leave me alone." Tears spilled down her cheeks, and everything went blurry. "I'll destroy the painting if you want me to. Just leave me and my family alone."

The old woman moved toward her, raising her bony old hand out in a beckoning gesture. "It's too late for that, child. You should have minded your own business and left me alone. You took away my anonymity the moment you put your brush to your canvas. Now everyone who sees this portrait of me will know I'm still here...that I never went away."

The old woman reached her other hand into the bosom of her long, black dress and removed a corn-husk doll. The cob fetish had been honed and whittled down to represent a miniaturized version of Marie. The green husks had been folded around it to resemble her artist's smock, and the golden fibers of corn hair had been pulled back into a perfect ponytail. Marie looked at the dreadful figurine and screamed at the top of her lungs.

The witch dropped the doll at Marie's feet and then Marie Lynch, devoted wife and mother, turned into a cascade of corn kernels that spilled all over the studio's floor. Outside the window, a murder of crows cawed and flapped their wings and waited for the old woman to collect their next meal in her little burlap pouch. Their eyes pierced through the window in wicked triumph as the old woman stuffed what remained of Marie Lynch in her little burlap sack.

In the portrait, a young woman with tears flowing from her eyes tried to shoo away the crows around her feet. The beasts fixed their eyes upon her, and Satan watched through them with delight.

Tilberian Holiday
Izzy Lee

Lúcía was unaware of the bustle outside her apartment in the seaside neighborhood of Laugardalur while a happy baby on a catalog of infant products taunted her. She imagined the tiny voice giggling with joy, and a raw wetness seeped into her nightgown; her nipples had expressed milk from a sound that didn't exist. Betrayed by her own body, she choked back a cry. Lúcía rubbed her swollen breasts roughly, trying to make the itch vanish, then shuddered and pulled her bathrobe shut tight. The rest of her body ached badly from labor — all 23 hours of it. But unlike most new mothers, she had nothing but anguish to show for her efforts. The horror of the last few days refused to fade; her delivery room scream still echoed in her memories alongside the doctor's frown. The way he watched her had been unsettling, too calm and clinical in contrast to her raging tide of anguish.

She still felt the slithery, goopy expulsion of amniotic fluid, placenta, and baby Ari escaping her with a slurp-like sound, and it made her want to vomit. Every sense registered in brutal awareness — the immediate tidal wave of wet copper scent, the stabbing brightness of the fluorescent lights... and finally, the tiny body of her child, the color of a deep bruise, with the umbilical cord wrapped twice around his neck.

A rush came up from within the constant gnawing pit of her gut, spewing the morning's tea and toast all over the coffee table and her bathrobe. Lúcía found herself on her knees, the motion of her sudden upheaval having propelled her from the couch in violence. She gripped the slippery edge of the glass table, her skin slipping from fresh bile, and screamed. Tears raged down her cheeks as recently swallowed Xanax dripped from her chin onto her knees. Wailing, she flipped the table with both her feet, sending it flying. It landed upside down, not with a majestic shattering, but with a simple crack as the glass top split into three ragged pieces.

I should join him.

The sharp, crooked glass glinted in the midday light, an open invitation. Lúcía swallowed the rock in her throat. The shining silver and green edges quieted her in a strange way as the buzzing in her head became louder. She wiped away the wet hair pasted to her face, along with the snot from her nose and the last traces of vomit from her mouth, and crawled toward the glass. Only the wooden table frame stood in the way. Gunnar couldn't stand being near her; he'd fled as soon as the stillbirth was announced and had only been home sporadically. He might as well have been dead, too, for all the support he'd given. Sure, he'd been hurting — likely, he was hurting at a nearby pub. *But he should be here. He should be home.*

Lúcía shoved the table frame out of the way.

Gunnar is never coming home. Neither is Ari. You have nothing. You have no one.

Her fingers slipped around one of the shards. She imagined propping up the pointy side and throwing her weight, neck first, upon it. The blood would douse the rug red — very, very red. They'd find her pale and lifeless in a beautiful yet macabre tableau. Gunnar would be free to start a new family somewhere down the line and he would heal. But not Lúcía. Not ever.

She squeezed her eyes shut and tried to imagine a world after death. Breathing deeply, colors and forms began to take shape — a dark place illuminated by fire. More tears slipped down her face as she saw nothing but fire burning in the middle of an empty space. But then the fire grew brighter, and bigger, and fiercer. Within the crackling of the wood and dancing of the flames, Lúcía heard Ari cry out — without having ever heard him cry, she knew it was him, had to be him.

A form materialized in the rioting flames, and a man stepped out. He was tall, naked, and formidable in physique; he could crush her. She felt a flood of confusing emotions, but fear and attraction gripped her fiercely. The man's intense, dark eyes pierced her as he came forward. His skin and his long, dark hair — flowing past his shoulders — were unburned. In fact, he seemed to draw strength from the fire.

Another cry from Ari — this time, a call. It sounded somehow joyful but questioning. Lúcia glanced down and saw her very not-dead child nestled in the crook of the man's arms. He wasn't pale and blue and purple with his eyes and nose sealed shut like he'd been in the delivery room, but glowing and healthy and alive and watching her with big, beautiful blue eyes.

The man stared at her, his jaw set. For a second, she could have sworn he was inside her mind. And then his booming male voice thudded within her chest and mind, all at once, resolved.

Lúcia. Be with me. Join us.

She gasped. Opening her eyes, she saw that she was still crying, back in her miserable apartment, in her miserable life, and screamed.

Maybe this is my karmic payback. Her own mother had died giving birth to her. As a result, Lúcia's father had always been distant. Loving, but always at an arm's length. After the death of Ari — *was he ever really alive?* — the man had given a long, ragged sigh in resignation. Then the old man had squeezed her hand in the hospital room as Lúcia lay in bed. Not a single word had passed from his mouth to her ears, just that one awful, "I've-given-up" sigh.

The heft of the glass was heavier than expected; she pulled harder and it snagged an envelope, one of several pieces of mail that had formerly lain strewn across the table and now littered the floor with other remnants of a broken life.

The crisp white envelope pierced beneath the glass felt like a dare; Lúcia hadn't noticed it before. The letter lay atop the rug, out of place among bills, pleas to switch internet providers and phone companies, and ads for shoes and gardening tools.

Her face pulled into a frown as she released the glass from her grasp. Lúcia fingered the expensive stationary — the return address was from some law office — Magnusson and Associates. There was an odd symbol in the logo… some kind of strange, troll-like face. Sniffling, she wiped an eye with the back of her bathrobe sleeve. *What the hell can this be?*

Lúcia tore open the envelope and took out the letter. The

tasteful muted gold Magnusson and Associates logo shone against the thick, creamy paper. Her finger automatically traced its curved capital 'M' along the top of the document. That weird little face — that same one on the envelope — was larger on the letter. It looked like it had eaten a lemon. Her eyes fell to the type:

Dear Ms. Fjelsted,

> *You are named as the sole beneficiary in the will of Mr. Jón Rögnvaldsson. As such, you are hereby bequeathed with the property of the deceased, located at 3 Víkurtún in the city of Hólmavík on the Strandir Coast of Iceland. You may come to our office at any time between the hours of 8:30 and 17:30 to claim the deed to this property.*

Regards,
Mikkel Magnusson

This has got to be some dumb mistake, she thought. She'd never heard of any Jón Rögnvaldsson; no one in her family had ever had that surname. Nonetheless, Lúcia had never inherited anything in her life. She glanced out the window at the Arctic Sea, rolling the raised logo of the law office beneath her fingers.

*   *   *

Soft leather embraced Lúcia as she sunk into the armchair. A moan escaped her as she rubbed a creaky muscle in her neck. The Magnusson and Associates secretary glanced across the room at her, questioning eyes hovering over her glasses. Even the swinging beads of her eyeglass chain seemed to be shaking each little faceted head "no" at her.

"Something wrong, Ms. Fjelsted?"

Give me a break. Lúcia kneaded the stone knot. "No. Is this going to take much longer? I've been waiting almost an hour."

The secretary shuffled some papers, trying to puff up her importance. "Mr. Magnusson is very busy today. I'm sure — " The heavy mahogany door of the attorney's office opened, and a blonde woman in a green silk dress and black patent high heels shimmied out. A man — presumably Magnusson — stared at her jiggling rear with a fond smile as the woman strode away.

Lúcía grunted, rolling her eyes.

"Mr. Magnusson," the secretary called. The man, dressed in a classic gray flannel suit, turned toward his secretary. "Your next appointment is here." She gestured toward Lúcía. The blond exited the office, and his eyes stayed on the door a moment before he snapped out of his fantasies.

"Oh yes!" He turned toward Lúcía. "Please, come into my office." Lúcía stood and he guided her in with a hand on her shoulder, not noticing that she twitched, jerking from his touch as if her shoulder were a cow tale swatting a fly. He shut the door behind them and they sat.

Was the blonde underneath his desk a few minutes ago? Perhaps bartering special services for attorney fees? Magnusson took no notice of her mood, grinning at her. "What can I do for you, Miss…"

"Lúcía Fjelsted," she mumbled, and fished the letter from her purse. She tossed it on his desk. He opened the letter and skimmed it.

"Ah yes, you're a lucky one," Magnusson said, handing back the letter. "You've inherited some historic property." He went to a row of filing cabinets and Lúcía swiveled in her chair to watch him. The drawers were housed beneath a long row of built-in shelving containing various fancy books with gold and silver lettering on hardcover spines. Many of the books looked old; once-vibrant covers of red, green, and blue were faded around the edges. She wondered if they were there for show, or if he actually consulted and read them.

After a moment of rifling through a drawer, he picked out a file and Lúcía swiveled around again, following him as he slid back into place behind his desk. From within the file, he plucked a weathered manila envelope and withdrew a piece of parchment paper from within it. The ancient paper protested as Magnusson unfolded it. He glanced at it for a second, and then handed it to Lúcía. Satisfied with himself, he spoke as she looked over the document: "With just a few signatures, you're the proud new owner of a home on the Strandir Coast," he smiled, smarmy.

She studied him, and something in the edge of his voice gave her pause. *Was that a hint of knowing?*

However, it was true. Lúcía was indeed named as the sole inheritor of a small property in the West Fjords. "I don't understand," she put the deed down and looked at Magnusson. "I don't know anybody in Hólmavík... Not even anyone in that area." She reached forward and took the battered envelope that contained the deed. It had no return address, but something else was inside the envelope. She tipped it upside down and a big brass skeleton key slipped into her hand. The key's curves and crevices were tinged with green corrosion.

"Who is this from?"

Magnusson leaned forward and glanced at the envelope and then down at the file, which held one more paper. "Oh, this came with the dead — I mean, deed." He handed it over to her. In spidery cursive, it was written:

Dear Mr. Magnusson,

I hereby name the woman Lúcía Fjelsted of Laugardalur, Reykjavik as the sole inheritor of my home at 3 Víkurtún, Hólmavík. Please see that the enclosed deed and key get to her in my stead, for I am not long for this world.

Yours,
Jón Rögnvaldsson

Lúcía looked at the lawyer. He didn't seem like he was trying to scam her; in fact, he had no guile about him whatsoever. An unsettling knot twisted in her gut. "Mr. Magnusson... Who the hell is this Jón Rögnvaldsson?"

She caught the attorney looking at his watch. He shrugged. "It's not really my business. But I'm late for a lunch meeting. I've prepared the papers to sign the property over to you." He rolled a heavy pen to her across the desk, an enameled implement that weighed much more than it appeared. Several spots marked in "Xs" awaited her signature. "Now. If you wouldn't mind..."

* * *

As she gripped an overnight bag, Lúcía looked at the mess she'd left on the living room floor days before. Let Gunnar come home — if he was ever going to — and let him think something awful happened. Let him worry. *Let him suffer like I have.* Lúcía gritted her teeth. The baby catalog, now ripped from her suicidal fit, grinned back at her. Once again, she felt dampness within her shirt.

"Goddamnit!" She slammed the door shut and marched outside to her MINI Cooper. Lúcía threw her bag into the passenger seat, and then the foam donut onto her seat and lowered herself as gingerly as her anger would let her. The traumatic physical effects of the birth left her sore. Behind the wheel, she slammed the door shut and lowered the window to let the cold air in.

Lúcía reached into her bra and used her t-shirt to dry the leaked milk. An old man shuffled by and gaped at her, his eyes and mouth drooping open as he dragged his bones behind him. It was humiliating that her body should be ready to feed an infant that did not exist — and here this senior citizen had a front-row seat to her shame.

She watched as he crept up to the apartment building. He stopped at the door. Then he turned back around, still breathing through his mouth.

"HHHRRNNRNNNNGGGGGGGHHHHHHH!" he yelled, as if he were a human siren and an explosion of crows burst from the nearby trees. She screamed; the odd, shocking drone of sound and crying of birds felt like an assault. He turned back to the apartment building and meandered inside, like nothing had happened.

She pressed her hands to her face to calm the burning heat in her cheeks and rubbed the tears from her eyes. *In… One, two, three, four… Out… One two, three, four…* After several minutes of controlled breathing exercises, she started the car and drove away.

*   *   *

The drive to Hólmavík would have been lonely, if Lúcía had longed for Gunnar's company. Two-and-a-half hours into the three-hour drive through mountains and fields, she regained some of her old self — her anger. Farmlands flew by as she stomped on the gas pedal, pretending it was his face. If Gunnar were to appear in the seat next to her, she didn't know what she'd do. She imagined forcing him out of the car while it was still racing down the road, then revving up the engine and knocking him to the ground and feeling the satisfying crunch of his bones beneath her wheels. Or she could back up for about 10 meters and gun the gas, hitting his body and sending him flying into the fjords off Route 60. Maybe she'd hear the sound of him breaking against the rocks, echoing down until he splashed lifeless into the frigid waters. There was also the possibility of dragging him beneath her wheels all the way to Hólmavík, gifting a red smear to the road; she'd pull into town with nothing but a skeleton tangled up in the undercarriage.

Piercing electronic static burst from the radio, causing her to scream and swerve and slap at the dial. Her heart slammed beneath her ribs as the car danced on the road, wheels skidding as she nearly missed her turn onto Route 61. The ass end of the MINI swung into a cluster of bushes, tearing up vegetation and leaving a haze of dirt in the rear-view mirror.

She thought she saw a figure in the dust cloud.

The Mini's wheels stayed on the ground as she screeched onto the first several meters of Route 61. Her father might have called it a miracle; Lúcia did not believe in such fables. The digital numbers of radio call stations spasmed on the dashboard then disappeared before going blank altogether. She pressed the knob and nothing happened. As she fought to regain her breath, she eased up on the accelerator. Thankfully, there were no cars in sight, either coming toward her, or in the rearview mirror. She swallowed. Maybe she shouldn't have daydreamed about killing Gunnar. Then she remembered his absolute abandonment, and steeled herself, steadying her hands on the steering wheel.

The GPS on the dashboard flickered. Since the electronic voice that provided directions was muted, it couldn't scare her off the road with a violent increase in volume. However, the map fluttered and flailed, switching directions like a broken compass... Except that she was driving in a straight line.

Satellite must be off course. No matter. There was no real way to get lost; it wouldn't be long before the road led straight to her destination.

* * *

A small yellow road sign marked "Hólmavík" pointed right, and so Lúcia turned. The little town rose up as much as it could beneath the huge open sky, and a modern white church loomed over everything on its hill in the distance. *Gotta keep watch on the sheep.*

A combination gas station and convenience store — likely the only kind of each in the tiny town — advertised wine, snacks, and sundries on her right. Its parking lot held only a few cars. The GPS stopped spinning its map, finally loading the correct location.

"Convenient," she muttered. Lúcía passed one bare dirt lot, and then another. The town was really more of a settlement. Pre-fabricated homes dotted the hills overlooking the vast cove, many of which sported red-tiled roofs. Perhaps the color was used to offset the varying gray and blue hues of the clouds, fjords, and cove. The GPS prompted her to turn right, onto a dirt road, and then a second one — Víkurtún. The path rolled forward into a dead end — another bland, gray piece of earth to assault the eyes.

"Let me guess," Lúcía murmured to herself. "The house is going to be gray, too." Only a few houses stood on the road; blue plaques were bolted to the sides of most homes, denoting street numbers. Nine… seven… five… The next building she came to had no number. She stopped in front of it.

Made from large stones, it was clearly older than the other houses, its façade weather-beaten and lighter in color than the other outer walls. The top of the structure was built like a castle, battlements edging the roof. Around the building, the bedraggled grass was the color of hay — if hay could be clinically depressed. A stone staircase led to the front door, a heavy thing made from huge wood planks, held together by brass hardware and adorned with a brass knocker.

She looked to the next house, but there was no "number 1" or any house at all. A crumbling foundation of what had probably been a sister structure was nearly swallowed by ground, begging to be forgotten by history. The road stopped there. She wondered who had lived there, and what caused the home's erasure. Lúcía put the humming MINI into park, turned off the ignition, and stepped out of the vehicle, the ground protesting with a crunch beneath her feet.

She reached into the pocket of her dark olive jacket, which was not quite an army jacket, but a modern blend of fashion and utilitarianism, and pulled out the skeleton key. It felt heavy and rough in her palm, an oversized piece of metal from a long-ago era that dwarfed her car keys. Something was etched in an arc above the key's eyehole. Using her thumbnail, Lúcía began scraping away crumbling bits of sea-green corrosion.

Full Belly!

Between the two words, a deformed, smiling face squinted at her.

"Hello!" someone called, causing her to jump. Lúcia looked in the direction of the voice. A man stood several meters behind her, on the steps of number five. He shut the door behind him and walked down the steps toward her. He looked to be mid-forties, shaven bald with a medium-length, brown beard trimmed to a soft point. "Sorry to disturb you... Are you lost?" He approached, a slight smile on his face. The Scottish accent and slate-blue eyes disarmed her.

"No. I've just come from Reykjavik," Lúcia heard herself answer. *Stupid! Don't tell him anything else!*

"Ah, that's a shite drive. Welcome to Hólmavík, land of oblivion," he grinned, holding an arm out with a flourish to showcase the near-absence of civilization in the cove. He seemed solidly built beneath his thick, navy wool sweater and dark jeans paired with brown boots. "I'm Alastair Hunter."

Lúcia returned a smile despite her mood, and introduced herself. She held up the large key. "I seem to have inherited this... tiny castle," she glanced at the house, suddenly getting the oddest feeling that the structure itself was looking back at her.

"That makes us neighbors, then." He held out a hand. "Pleased to meet ya. You can call me Al, if you like."

They shook. "Likewise, Al. Say... Do you know who the last owner of this place was? A Jón Rögnvaldsson? He left it to me, and I can't understand why. I never knew him."

"Nay, I haven't ever seen anyone live in there." He turned and looked at the building. "Odd little place it is, too," Al considered the structure. "Some folks in this town are mighty superstitious about this lot and building, though," he motioned to the former spot with the ruins and Lúcia's new property. "You know how it is. Small town, small minds," he winked, genuine cheer in the crinkles of his eyes. She couldn't help but smile back. That joke — a seemingly nonchalant gesture from another human being — was the only thing she could recall in recent memory that brought a glimmer of hope. It somehow felt like the first time she'd *ever* smiled.

"Well, I'll leave you to it, then. I'm off to pick up some libations for supper — you're welcome to join if you're around," he began to walk backward in a funny, casual manner.

"That's kind of you. I'll think about it." Al smiled and saluted before turning and walking up the road in the direction of the store. Lúcía chuckled and walked up the old stone steps to her new home.

*   *   *

Lúcía fit the key into the old lock, dislodging some dirt. It took both hands, but she cranked the lock over. The door didn't open on its own. Using her shoulder, she pushed her weight against the wood. It gave way under pressure and swung wide with a loud groan.

Much like the town, the home was empty; no traces of previous inhabitants, knick-knacks, or detritus. Lúcía took a step into the house, testing the strength of the stone floor with the toe of her boot. *What if this is a nightmare and I fell through? Nothing feels real here.*

Dust bunnies rolled across the stones, carried by the breeze. On the far side of the great room past support pillars, a dirty old hearth sat blackened and a baroque gilded mirror hung from chains above the mantle. Lúcía glanced behind her at the street, then stepped all the way into the house. Padding across the floor, she realized that she was almost tiptoeing — the way a child might to avoid detection.

The mirror's glass reflected a maelstrom of cloudy black speckles and mottled blue and bronze hues, not unlike a nebula. She wondered how many decades — or centuries — the mirror had hung in its place. *What have you seen?* Lúcía leaned in and peered into its glass frost; her distorted face was covered in amoeba-like shapes.

The shapes shifted, forming swirls, which began to move. Slowly, they formed furls of smoke and writhed within the glass.

Mouth agape, she rose to wipe a swath of dust from the glass — when a shadow flitted in the corner. She whirled on her heels. Nothing. And it wasn't like there was anywhere anyone or any*thing* could hide, either. *An animal?* She jogged to the window. A narrow wooden cabin stood in the backyard. *Is that an outhouse?* She squinted her eyes and turned.

That's when she noticed the stairs.

She'd been so distracted by the fireplace and mirror that she hadn't seen the stairs at all — but *of course* there was a second story

— no one builds battlements on a one-floor home. *What the hell am I doing here again?* Lúcia sighed. *There's still a chance to leave. Wait — you're acting like a fool.* She charged up the stone stairway. *Stop being afraid. This is yours now.*

*   *   *

At the top of the stairs, a wall lined with a row of empty shelving split the second floor into two rooms. She hesitated before ducking her head into the room on the right. It was empty. Outside the windows lay half the town of Hólmavík, with all its crushing excitement. She turned, just in time to see a snake darting from the hall into the other room.

"Oh my God," she sighed, laughing despite herself. "This is so stupid." Nonetheless, she gave the snake a head start before entering. It disappeared underneath the bed in the second room — *bed?? What is that doing here?* A small bed about the size of a double was pushed against the wall beneath one of the windows overlooking the fjords. Made with a cream-colored pair of pillows and duvet, the bed seemed as though it had been waiting for her. Lúcia took a step toward it. Then another.

She whipped around, expecting to see a charred black shape in the outline of a person, but no one was there. Then she questioned why she would even dream up that specific vision. *What the hell is wrong with me?* She closed her eyes and began the breathing exercise. *In... One, two, three, four... Out... One two, three, four...*

Lúcia opened her eyes, focusing on the bed coverlet hanging above the floor to where the snake had gone. She thought about getting down on the floor and snapping off the covers to scare the creature away, but the rapid beating of her heart and the probability of the snake popping out and biting her in the face nixed that idea.

She turned and walked down the stairs and out of the house instead.

*   *   *

"Hey there!" Al called, walking back up the dirt road. He carried a paper bag. Lúcia, leaning against the MINI while gazing out at the sea, turned and waved. "Still here, are ye?"

"Yeah... I'm not sure for how much longer."

Al's boots crushed the dirt and pebbles beneath him as he

approached. He stopped in front of his own house and raised an eyebrow. "Ghosts so soon?" he joked.

Lúcia laughed. "Maybe!" She sighed. "But seriously," she glanced at the weathered Mini castle. "This place is weird."

"I can't argue with ye there… Dinner?" Al held up the bag and grinned.

"I don't know." Her eyes fell to the overnight bag still in the front seat. "I should get back to the city."

"Aw come on, I caught some fish this morning! And I've got whisky! Keep me company — please?" He grinned, a non-threatening mouth full of white Chiclets. It felt good to smile again. And she hadn't realized that her stomach was rumbling — why the hell not?

*　*　*

"So what's the deal with this town anyway?" Lúcia shoved a forkful of fish into her mouth and hummed as the buttery flakes dissolved onto her tongue. "God, Al, this is great!"

"Aye, agreed," the man smiled. "When it's as boring as it is around here, you learn to cook yourself some nice things — and drink. And read a lot. There isn't much more than that to enjoy here." He swallowed a bite and thought. "I'm sure a lot of people are born here and just never leave." Al paused to pour himself another whisky. "As for me, I got sick of Edinburgh. I needed some place away from people. It gets a bit too quiet sometimes, but mostly, it suits me just fine. I fish and I fix and build things. At night, I cook and I read. And try not to drink too much," he winked.

Lúcia nodded. "I can't say I've ever thought about stepping a foot in a place like this — it's so remote. But I don't miss being around people yet," she smiled. "Maybe you've got the right idea." She plunged her fork into another piece of fish. "I just wish this place … this new house of mine… wasn't so old and creepy."

"Aye. A modern home offers certain comforts. I forgot to mention — I asked the owner of the store up the road what she knows about your place."

Lúcia swallowed another bite of fish. "And what'd she have to say?"

"You're sure you want to know?"

"Are you going to tell me that it's the site of some horrific mass murder or something?"

Al's blue eyes blinked, and his smile faded. "Or something."

Lúcia took a swig of the fancy, peaty liquor Al had poured for her. She sighed. "All right, Alastair Hunter," she rolled her eyes. "What is it?"

Al gave a wry half-smile at the mention of his full name. "The owner freaked out a little when she was ringing up me whisky. She jumped like she was a cat whose tail was stepped on, and the bottle slipped and broke, so I had to get a new one. She asked me if you were a witch." Lúcia nearly choked on her spirits, a cackle escaping from her throat.

"What?!" she laughed. She wiped a dribble of alcohol from her mouth. Al shrugged.

"Some old legend or such nonsense. This Jón Rögnvaldsson who left the estate to you — it's said that he was burned for being a warlock."

Lúcia covered her mouth and let out a full guffaw. "That's utterly ridiculous." She poured a new drink. "When was this supposed to have happened?"

"She also freaked because that was some time in the 1600s, and he couldn't possibly have —" he broke and began to laugh with her, realizing how insane it sounded. "Whatever. Country nuts." He scratched his head. "Cheers," he raised his glass.

"Cheers," she grinned, knocking her glass against his in a celebratory clink before they threw back their drinks.

"Care to spin some records in the other room? I ask because I live in 1975."

"Oh why not? Let's dance to the memory of all the crispy witches and warlocks of Iceland. Surely they miss good music."

*　　*　　*

A fire snapped and popped beneath a midnight sky, and the scent of dead leaves and moist dirt filled her nostrils. A tall silhouette bathed in darkness moved toward Lúcia from within the flames. He held his hand out.

*　　*　　*

This is not my living room. This is not my home!

Lúcia jumped up, throwing off the blanket covering her. She didn't own these book shelves or this art or a record player — *Oh*. She breathed a sigh of relief in remembering where she was. Al's place, next to her own in Hólmavík. She sat up from the sofa and stretched out a very sore neck. Her head wasn't doing so well, either. "Al?" She stood and yawned, walking into the kitchen.

Lúcia helped herself to a glass of water and went in search of the bathroom, where the medicine cabinet was mostly bare. *Figures.* She winced at a pain in her breast, and pulled down her shirt and bra. Her left nipple was red and swollen — and looking closer — bore four tiny scabs evenly spaced around her areola.

JESUS!

She let her bra and shirt snap back into place and scanned the floor for rodents and bugs that could've caused the bite. Shaking her head, Lúcia hurried back to the couch and yanked her boots on, still looking for critters. She grabbed her jacket, then pulled open the front door and stepped out.

Several dozen cats — maybe 100 — lay or stood on the path and on the lawn in front of Al's home. Lúcia stopped breathing as they all turned and looked at her. One large gray cat flattened its ears and hissed. A ginger cat rose from its resting position and fluffed up its fur and tail, growling low guttural warnings. Black, white, gray, tabby, calico, spotted, striped — they began to prowl, a rumble of feline voices growing in decibels. They moved as a pack, narrowing their eyes as if she were prey — until one leaped at her from the path.

Yelping, Lúcia jumped back into the house, slamming the door shut as the cat bounced off door with a vicious scream.

"What the FUCK?!!" Lúcia cried. She ran to the other end of the house, back into the kitchen. A tortoiseshell cat sat in the window on the other side of the screen, flicking its tale, *thwack, thwack, thwack*. Beyond the sentinel cat, more roamed in the backyard behind it; they stopped and swiveled their necks, seeming to notice her presence even though she stood nowhere near the window.

The warning *thwack thwack thwack!* of the cat's tail got louder and more violent. Lúcia stared at the furry appendage beating the windowsill outside the screen like it was chopping wood. She took a step forward. The cat froze and hissed — but the hollow chopping sound continued.

Lúcia took another step and the cat growled. She snatched a saltshaker off the table and hurled it at the screen, repelling the animal. Salt spilled into the sink along with its glass container. The cat ran across the backyard and disappeared into the foliage behind Al, who was splitting firewood with an ax. Myriad symbols — esoteric, swirling, and angular — painted his torso.

She sighed, glad to see a familiar face. Rivulets of sweat cascaded down his heavily tattooed chest, back, and arms as he swung the ax up and let it down, snapping the wood in front of him. It fell away and he replaced it with another log.

"AL!" She called. He paused and looked up, wiping sweat from his upper lip onto his dark brown work pants. Lúcia went to the back door and opened it slowly, waiting for sharp feline eyes to appear in the crack between the door and the wall. When the space was big enough for her to stick her head out, she glanced both ways before stepping outside. The yard was free from cats — or any other aggressors that she could see.

Al split another log but frowned, noticing Lúcia's hesitance. "What's going on?"

She ran to him, still looking for cats — in the bushes, trees, and behind rocks and lumber piles. "The cats," she whispered.

Al put down his ax on the stump and leaned on it, wiping his face again. "Eh? What cats?"

"In the front — tons of cats — hissing and threatening," she took his arm and led him around the side of the house.

The yard and front walk was clear, as was the street.

There weren't even any tufts of fur caught in the grass.

"What..." Lúcia's mouth opened and closed. "There were cats, so many cats!" Tears formed in her eyes and her face heated up. "Where the fuck did they go?!!" Lúcia stared up the desolate dirt road. She began breathing heavier, her voice rising. "What's happening?!"

She felt something falling within her as her limbs began to liquefy.

"Whoa, whoa," Al caught her and pulled her to him, the sweat from his muscles dampening her shirt. "Are you feeling okay?"

Lúcia chuckled and rolled her head back and forth on her shoulder. She laughed again — and again and again. "Let's get you inside," Al said.

*   *   *

"Here now," he soothed, sitting next to her on the couch and handing over a mug, his blue eyes laser-focused on hers. "This'll be sure to settle your nerves, darlin'."

The teacup was warm and comforting in her hands. She sipped, and the liquid rolled across her tongue and down her throat in a medicinal wave. Lúcia couldn't place the taste. "What kind of tea is this?"

Al smiled. "An old family blend of herbs and a bit o' spice, my friend." He reached across and pushed back a stray lock of hair from her face. "My grandmother would make it for us anytime we were upset. Calmed us down straightaway."

Lúcia inhaled a long, deep breath. "Thank you, Alastair," she gazed into the amber tea. "This has been a very strange week."

"No doubt," he smirked, and leaned over to kiss her forehead. When he pulled back, the playfulness was gone. "It will all be over soon. Now drink up."

*   *   *

Lúcia struggled against her captors.

A small army of men dragged her against all her might as she kicked into the ground trying to stave off their progress, but it was for naught. Her heart pounded in her throat and torrents of adrenaline rushed through her veins. A wall of men and women on both sides of her screamed obscenities her way as she fought against the captors. The accents and language were archaic. She didn't understand the words, but she got the meaning; they hated her deeply for something she'd done. Rotten vegetables struck her face and she yelled.

She realized that her voice was that of a man's — the timbre lower, the volume louder and more powerful — and that she was dressed in men's clothing, centuries' old. Long dark hair splayed across her billowing white shirt. She had strong arms and biceps, but those dragging her were overpowering — six of them, altogether. Beyond them, a large mound of wood rose to meet a tall stake. Two more men stood ready with torches.

They were bringing her toward the stake.

She renewed her struggle, but an explosion of hard black pulled the curtains on her sight.

She awoke to the smell of burning hair. Opening her eyes, she saw the group of villagers watching her, yelling. She was tied to the stake and fire was climbing rapidly up her legs. She screamed and writhed and cursed them. She promised them she'd be back to hunt them all. And then she drowned in an ocean of pain.

*   *   *

Lúcía's eyes opened to her own screams. She was damp from perspiration. Fear and drowsiness filled her head and her chest, and then poured down her legs and toes. Gradually she realized she was safe and at Al's. Through the darkness, a faint orange light filtered in from the kitchen. As she stood and stretched, something stabbed her nipple. "OWWW!"

Gasping, she pulled down her shirt — a dark snake-like creature with a woeful human face unclasped its mouth from her breast and looked up at her — blood and milk flowing together from its sharp, circular rows of teeth. "Full belly, Mummy!"

She flashed to the image etched into the skeleton key. It had read:

Full Belly!

Lúcía shrieked, causing the thing to drop and fall to the ground. It gave a scream of its own and slithered away, lightning-quick. The blood was real. The thing had been suckling milk meant for her dead child. It scuttled away through the kitchen and out the back door, which was ajar. An enormous fire blazed in the backyard, reaching into the inky night sky.

A figure near the flames turned and faced Lúcía — Alastair. She stared as the snake creature raced across the grass and circled up his legs, torso, and settled itself on his shoulders, draping around Al's neck like a scarf. The tiny face watched her from its vantage point. "Sorry, Mummy," it squeaked in an odd little voice.

Alastair held a hand out. "Come."

A voice inside her urged her to run — to get into her car and floor it all the way back to Reykjavik.

But yet she went to him, feeling like she was walking through invisible walls of molasses. Why? For an explanation? For a better look at this thing that spoke to her and called her "mummy?" *What am I doing here? This is unreal.* She stopped and stood in front of Al. The creature wagged its tale languidly and smiled at her. *What hell is this?* She stared up at the man before her.

"Am I dead?" she asked.

"No," Al replied. "But you're about to be reborn." He considered her, and pulled up her shirt a little. "He's chosen you. Out of all the women in this country — he called to you. The question is — will you help us?"

"What are you talking about?" Dread churned her insides, and the snake-thing wagged its tail at her. Lúcía stepped back.

Al smiled. "Sorry about the tilberi," he pointed at the creature. "They're a little over-zealous sometimes, these familiars, but they're cool pets that do your bidding. It hadn't been awake long and was really hungry." He petted the thing, and it cooed at him. Al glanced back at her, serious. "There's no need to worry. All that pain can go away now." The fire behind them snapped and a shock of electric blue shot up from the middle of the blaze. Lúcía shrieked as a tall, dark form of a man appeared within the flames. He began to move and to walk.

"Oh my God," she whispered. The scent of dirt and dead leaves wafted up from the ground.

"Just about," Al glanced over at the form and turned back, grinning. "Meet Jón Rögnvaldsson." Al's smile faltered. "He's come back. He *is* real, and he *was* burned at the stake here for being a sorcerer long ago."

Lúcía then understood that in her dream, she'd experienced Rögnvaldsson's demise, and began to weep. At the sound of logs rolling and falling, Al turned.

The dark figure emerged from the bonfire, flames dancing around him. Over two meters tall, Rögnvaldsson wore nothing. Long dark hair fell past his shoulders and the light of the fire bounced off his bare skin — unburned. Lúcía stared. He was the man in the vision — a walking naked sculpture — his presence both attracted and terrified. The tall man looked down at her. She sensed an enormous amount of power emanating from him and knew he could destroy anyone stupid enough to stand in his way.

A river of ice rushed down her spine as she realized that his face was also the face of her delivery room doctor. His somber face had watched her reaction as he held the lifeless Ari in his hands before her.

Lúcía lost her breath as a bolt of white-hot fear struck her. She fell to the ground, but Al pulled her to a standing position and held her up.

"You've met my emissaries," his low voice boomed inside her, vibrating inside her chest, leaving a buzzing in her skin. She shivered. The tilberi gurgled with glee as Rögnvaldsson came closer.

He held a large, strong hand out. "Join us, Lúcia, and you will hurt no more. Your child will be returned to you, and you will walk next to me sowing my vengeance across this land. You'll have any and everything you've ever wanted."

"Why me?" she whispered.

"Your soul cried out the hardest."

The sound of a baby gurgling quickened her pulse. The tilberi on Al's shoulder now had the face of an infant — the face of her own child — that face she'd seen only once before the nurses took him away. Within her, broken tabletop glass and shadows and dust and snakes and teacups and screaming cats melted together and she sobbed. She touched the baby's cheek and it giggled at her in happy chirps.

"Ari," she breathed. It smiled at her.

"Join us," Rögnvaldsson said again. This time, she looked up at him with relief and gratitude.

"Yes," she agreed.

To Dance The Witches Circle Again

Morgan Sylvia

I knew something bad was coming, even before the day I caught Jennet Harlowe spying on me. There'd certainly been no shortage of omens. A few nights prior, the sun had turned blood red at sunset against a dreary, rain-filled sky. Shortly after that, I'd pulled a loaf of bread from the oven, to find it split down the middle. And just the night before, I'd dreamt of walking through muddy water beneath a double moon. These things all warned of ill fortune, and my own scrying only confirmed that the ominous tidings were valid.

But Jennet's appearance was much more ominous . . . and far less cryptic.

I had chanced to look out my cottage window, and seen the pallid, thin face of the cordwainer's wife watching me. I knew it was her: the sallow orange color of her hair would have given her away even if I hadn't seen her face. She stood in a tangle of bracken at the edge of my herb garden, poorly concealed by the branches of my rowan tree, glaring at me with the same vicious look I'd seen at the market that day.

The foolish woman turned and ran as soon as I saw her, branches snapping as she raced back for the village, but the damage was done. As I turned away from the window and looked at the items spread across my wooden table, a cold sense of foreboding cut through me.

Pyewacket twisted in my arms. "Oh, och," I muttered, turning the ferret in my hands. "Ye could've warned me."

I think I knew even then what was coming.

I still clearly remember the day they came for my grandfather. Even now, that bright August afternoon seems like only yesterday. I can almost hear the sound of the scythes sweeping through the barley, the lowing of the oxen, the buzz of birds and tree frogs. The air smelled of rain and earth, a thick, loamy scent that hung over the fields like a blanket. I was cheerful because Granna had promised honey cakes and swan for supper as a special treat, and because I had a new red puppy at home.

The peace was shattered by the thunder of hoofbeats. The minister rode up first, his eyes cold and hard. He brought half a dozen men with him, just to arrest one elderly farmer.

I was very young then, only six or seven. I didn't understand what was happening as the charges were read. I only remember them putting Granda in heavy chains, and shoving him into the back of the cart.

They said he was a conjurer. They said he trafficked in nightmares, and bartered flesh and souls with the lords of hell. They accused him of hexing his neighbor's chickens, and causing four sheep to take ill. After only a few days in prison, he confessed to these things and more. He claimed he'd made a pact with the Devil, and conjured up a storm, and then laid an illness on old Mary Marten. I found out years later that they'd sent for a professional witch pricker to pierce his skin with needles, looking for a spot that would not bleed and was impervious to pain. This would mark the place where the Devil had touched him to seal their pact. A few days later, they'd taken Granna's fine silver, along with our milk cow and several bushels of barley and beer, to pay the witch pricker and executioner, and to account for the expenses of keeping Granda jailed.

The minister insisted the accusations were true. But I recalled only kind eyes and kind words.

Sorcerer, they whispered.

Then they hung him from the tree.

I'd been fool enough to think the hunts were over. Now, as

Jennet rushed back across the moors to the village, I felt a chill settle into my soul.

There was a sudden scratching above me, from the thatched roof, which was followed by the hoot of an owl. The sound startled me and I jumped, jarring Pyewacket. The ferret glared at me. I was tempted to drop him, but I'd learned that lesson already. Once, I'd accidentally let him slip from my arms. As soon as he hit the ground, I felt an unseen hand shoving me, and I, too, took a terrible spill, bruising my hip, twisting an ankle, and spraining an elbow. I'd had to hobble my way into market. Worst of all, I hadn't been able to dance at the Beltane circle. I loved the dances, the freedom of spinning free and wild, the drums and flutes filling the air with song that fueled me like fire.

Pyewacket wriggled in my arms. I put him down gently. Outside, the familiar patter of rainfall filled the air as I brewed a cup of tea and sat down, turning the week's events over in my head.

I'd known even as I refused Jennet Harlowe's request to 'borrow' some corn mash that it was probably foolish to deny her. But she'd proved time and again that such loans would never be repaid, although her husband's shoemaking business was faring well enough. That woman wouldn't have paid her debts if she'd had all the gold in the king's treasury.

So I'd told her I simply hadn't a bit to spare.

She'd peered down her long nose at the baskets of eggs and apples I was selling. "Yer hens are layin' well enough," she said. "None affected by the blight?"

I shook my head. "Nay," I said. "Did ye want eggs?"

She ignored this. She also ignored Jane Henny and Ilspeth Cline, who were waiting to buy eggs. Her daughters, Elizabeth and Margaret, stood silently beside her, glaring at me. They both had the same red hair and pale skin as Jennet, although it suited them far better. They would have been pretty enough, but for the sour looks that never left their faces. Jennet's son, James, peeked out from around her skirt, and smiling shyly, asked for an apple. I knew that to refuse two requests would draw her ire, so I handed him a red fruit. He bit into it greedily as Jennet pummeled me with questions about my goats and chickens.

After Jennet's tenth or eleventh question, I wished her a good day and, looking past her, cheerfully greeted Jane and Ilspeth.

Jennet gave a hiss of disapproval, then turned her back on me and headed off across the muddy market square, her children close behind her. The girls were both carrying several packages. I saw Jennet enter the flesher's shop, and suspected that she'd shortly emerge with a choice cut of meat, mutton or venison, perhaps.

She cast me a withering look as she passed me the next day, but did not stop. I knew full well where the ire had started. I was sorry for the loss of her youngest child—we all were—but the babe had been born with long fingers, a sure sign of a short life, and then the fever had touched him. Our graveyard was filled with those who'd been taken by plague that year, though I dare say I'd kept a good many souls out of it. Jennet had demanded my aid, and then done none of the things that could have helped the bairn: she'd kept her windows locked and her mirrors hanging, and had refused the healing elixirs and potions I'd made for the child. I doubted she'd bathed the babe daily, or given him whiskey or oatmeal and water, as I'd suggested. I did everything I could, but to no avail. She'd even thrown the charm I'd offered back at my feet, saying she'd have no such thing in her home. Never mind that she'd gone to every cunning woman within a day's ride for love charms when she'd first cast her eye on Tim Harlowe.

And now this.

A sharp pain in my ankle brought me out of my reverie. I looked down and saw Pyewacket. He had drawn blood with his bite... and not for the first time.

I put the ferret back into his clay pot. He stared up at me, disapproval clear in his inky black eyes. I got his bowl, filled it with goat milk and bread, then took my bodkin and pricked my finger. Three drops of blood fell into the milk.

The ferret ate quickly and quietly, and then looked up at me, chittering. "Nay," I said. "Best leave that old sow alone for now."

That night I dreamt of black wings and acrid smoke, and when I woke, I smelled ashes and burnt hair, instead of peat smoke. Try as I might, I could not shake the feeling of foreboding.

The next day at church, the Harlowe women glared at me through the entire service, as Minister Stewart warned that the Devil was afoot, and preached about the foolishness of women who had the audacity to assume we could think for ourselves. I couldn't help but notice that, despite Jennet's inability to buy a sack of mash, the three of them all wore brand new kirtles. Elizabeth's was a pretty yellow, Margaret's a sky blue, and Jennet's was a soft green.

And in Jennet's eyes, I saw the same feverish hatred I'd seen in the minister's cold gaze so long ago.

Restless and uneasy, I made charms to protect myself. I wrote a glyph of protection on a bay leaf, and burned it in a candle. I walked all morning in a cold, drizzling rain to find a sprig of white heather for luck. I went all the way around the loch. But it was too late: autumn had already closed in, and the heather was dormant. By the time I got home, darkness had fallen, and it was black as the Earl of Hell's waistcoat.

Not a fortnight later, Gilly came quietly to my cottage. She arrived long after dark, but I didn't ask whether her husband, Thomas, would miss her. I knew she kept a besom, or small straw broom, in her place in bed, which Thomas would think was herself.

"Did ye hear about Isobel Gowdie?" she asked.

I shook my head.

"She confessed voluntarily. There was no arrest, no torture. She went herself to Minister Forbes at Auldearne, and ran her tongue."

I stared at her in disbelief. "You're out of your head," I said. "That can't be true."

"It is. She named her entire coven, and others besides. She admitted to making a poppet to bewitch and kill the Laird's boy, to witching cattle and stealing milk and corn, and to killing three souls with elf arrows. She's wagging her tongue as though *it's* bewitched. I guess the girl's determined to have company on the pyre." She sipped the tea I offered her, closing her eyes. "Pure dead brilliant," she said. "You do make the best tea." A moment later, she slapped her forehead. "Och! I almost forgot what I came to tell ye. The Samhuinn celebration will be at Earlseat Hills," she said. "We'll drink and dance as always. I've a list of things for ye to bring."

My stomach twisted in a knot. My throat was dry. "Isn't it dangerous?" I said.

"Aye," Gilly said. "We could be arrested or killed at any time, any of us. I could take ill tomorrow, or tumble down the stairs and break my neck. But that's all the more reason to dance, innit?"

Leave it to Gilly to look at the bright side of a storm. "I suppose," I said.

"Be happy while ye live," Gilly said, "for ye'll be a long time dead."

We sat for some while, careless of the time, talking. Eventually, as always, we ended up giggling and reminiscing over the fun we'd had through the years. Oh, Gilly and I had sown much mischief together, some gleefully, some coldly. We held a similar view on things: we'd bend over backwards to help those who were good to us, but never hesitated to cast a curse on our enemies, those who'd wronged us three times or more.

At last, she stood to leave. "I must be back," she said. "Thomas will wake soon. Och! I almost forgot. Meet Marie Lamont and Janet Allen and I in the graveyard on the night of the new moon. Ye'll remember what to bring for Samhuinn?"

I nodded. She winked three times, which had been a secret signal of ours since girlhood. She stepped lightly out the door. Then she was gone, speeding through the night to her own home.

Days trickled by, pretending to be normal. Autumn painted the land in red and gold, but it was cold fire: that year was unusually chilly. I kept up about my normal affairs: tending to sick cattle, offering poultices and herbs, midwifing, and selling apples and eggs and cheese and herbs at market. I helped old Dame Crowder clear her lungs of a nasty cough, set the broken leg of Jacob Heady's daughter's kitten, and cured a mean old goat of fever. Each night, I sat close to the fire, wrapped in my thickest blanket, but I just couldn't keep the chill out of my bones. As Samhuinn drew close, I prepared the things Gilly had asked for: I made a bag of spiderwebs, oak galls, toad entrails, some barley, fingernail clippings, a hare's liver, and bits of cloth. I mixed these things together and steeped them in water overnight.

I never made it to the Samhuinn celebration. Nor did Gilly. She was arrested in late October, as Isobel's statements filtered through the courts. Like Isobel, Gilly confessed. She admitted to cursing Elspeth Bitty with sickness after Elspeth had deliberately trampled her seedlings. She also confessed to hexing Adam Taylor's cow, stealing milk and corn from her neighbors with spellcraft, dismembering a man who still hung on the gallows, and healing young Alexander Byrne's crippled leg with a charm. But when I heard that she had admitted to digging up the body of an unbaptized child and casting nightmares on the baker's young daughter, I began to sob and shake uncontrollably, for I knew what those lies meant. They'd only wrest such tales from Gilly if she were in agony. And when I heard that she'd named sweet Old Nan

Hendrick as a witch, I knew for certain she was being tortured.

Twelve more were taken that week.

The hills and lochs rang with the sounding cry of the witch hunts. Word of the craze spread from the Highlands to the shore. At service, Minister Stewart ranted and raved about the Devil. In town, the bells of the kirk rang by themselves one night, and then a hen no one owned was found dead in a pond. I kept to my home, letting my customers come to me. But few people crossed my doorstep in those chilly weeks. Even my most regular customers stayed away, and I knew it wasn't due to the dreary weather.

Isobel and her coven burned together, on one of the only sunny days we had that autumn. Shortly after this, Marie Lamont and Janet Allen brought me word of more arrests, and new instructions from our coven leader.

Then they, too, were arrested.

Marie was accused of sending nightmares to the Laird's wife and sending her pigs to trample her neighbor's garden, and Janet of using her familiar, a red hare, to spoil the milk from a villager's cow. They confessed, in the end, to much more than that. They, too, sang to the witch pricker's needle, saying they'd dined with the Devil and pledged themselves to him, and sent their familiars out to torment people and animals alike, stolen grain and eggs, and made the brewer's ale go bad.

Finally, on the night of the new moon, he came. I heard the flutter of great black wings outside, and opened my door to find him waiting. I dropped immediately into a curtsy, then stood and stepped back so he could enter.

"They're coming for you now," he said. "They've just left the kirk."

I choked back a sob. My knees gave out, and I fell, rather than sank, into the wooden chair. Fear grasped my guts in an icy grip. I was supposed to be stronger than that. But all I could think of was poor Granda.

Seeing him brought me back through the years, to that bright and terrible day. I saw it all again in my mind's eye: Granda hanging in silhouette, a shadow against the sun. His body had turned slowly, moving clockwise with the northern wind. I'd looked up into the sky as the horizon darkened, and seen a rook carrying his soul to the clouds. I ran into the rising storm, looking down the whole time, seeing nothing but the muddy hem of my ragged dress and my bare feet softly crushing the wet grass. I went into the haunted wood near the ruined tower, where I knew no one would follow me.

He was waiting for me there, in the mossy, ancient, forest, wrapped in shadow and sunlight.

He touched my chin with an icy finger, and raised my tearstained face, asking if I should like revenge. I swore my allegiance then and there.

The forest wrapped itself around me, as did the years. When I was of age, he brought me to the coven, and sent Pyewacket to me. I grew from an orphaned child into a bruised and unhappy bride, to a young widow to, finally, a respected cunning woman. I'd controlled my own destiny.

Until now.

Looking back, I saw the threads of time that bound this moment to that. It was all a cycle. I understood that now. Granna's own grandfather had been one of the first to die at North Berwick. In 1589, King James had determined that witchcraft had kept him from bringing his fiancée, Princess Anne of Denmark, to Scotland, by raising storms and sending devils to climb up the keel of her ship. The Devil had told that ill-fated coven that James was their worst enemy, and that terrible things would happen when Anne set foot on Scottish shores. That foreboding had proved true, though in the end, it was their own actions that started the horrors and fueled the king's witch-hunting frenzy. Hundreds had died in that first crazed hunt, thousands since.

And now it was starting again.

I thought of running, but where would I go? Already the leaves had fallen, and the wind was growing cold. I could not afford passage to New Scotland, nor would I survive a winter alone on the moors. Even if I fled to the Highlands, the accusations would only follow me.

He shook his dark head, as though he had read my thoughts. "You canna escape them. You know that."

I looked out the window. Already I could see the dim spark of torches through the trees. They were far off: because of the way the land dipped and rose, it would take them some time yet to reach me.

He held something out. I took it carefully. It was a piece of cloth, upon which certain runes and glyphs had been writ. A thin lock of orange hair lay upon it. A smaller packet lay within it. I did not open it to examine the contents. It had a strange smell, one that was hard to identify, but was not unpleasant.

"Here," he said. "Prick your finger: you'll need to add four drops of blood, one on each corner. Add one of your fingernails and a lock of your hair, braided to the one inside. Tie it with black thread, and then bury it outside, beneath the oak, but not too deep. I'll give you the words to speak when it's done. Hurry."

I cast him a questioning look. But all I saw in his dark eyes was my own reflection.

I did as he said. When it was done, I could see the torches in the valley through my window. They were closer, now.

"Burn the book," he said.

I took the grimoire from its spot under the floorboard. My hands were shaking so badly I could barely hold it, but I cast it into the fire. It had taken me decades to compile the knowledge encased in its hide covers, but the pages—and my life's work—were reduced to ash in mere moments.

When I straightened, he touched my forehead, and breathed a rune into the air. A sense of peace fell over me like a blanket. My nerves calmed. I felt disconnected from my body, as though I were watching these things through a thick glass, rather than experiencing them myself.

I realized suddenly that though I could hear him, I could no longer see him. I reached out, and felt him take hold of my hand. His skin was ice cold, as always: far colder than any human being's should be.

But then, I'd always had my suspicions about that.

"You will dance in the circle again," he said. He kissed me once, and slipped into the night. I heard again the sound of great wings. A moment later, the squeals of startled horses carried across the meadow. He would not have been able to resist frightening them, even knowing that he sealed my fate in doing so.

The hoof beats were approaching.

Pyewacket watched from the shadows. "Aye," I told him. "Best hide, now."

The ferret fled for his earthen container. I carried him outside, and put him in the bracken beyond my herb garden. "Fend fer yerself," I said, scratching his furry forehead one last time. A lump rose in my throat. "'Ware that grey dog. Ye'd make him a good lunch, I think. But I imagine ye'll be sent to another, soon."

I neatened up the cabin, straightening up my herbs. I threw the anise seed, foxglove, plantain, St. John's wort, and ragwort into the fire, along with the things I'd gathered for Samhuinn. I hung my cooking pots neatly from the shelf, and banked the fire, covering the remnants of the book. Though I wasn't hungry, I ate cheese and drank some ale, trying not to dwell on the fact that I might never enjoy a decent meal again.

By the time they rode into the yard, I was ready.

Minister Stewart's voice rang through the night. "Bessie Smith," he said, "You are arrested on suspicion of witchcraft."

Things became a blur at that moment. I only vaguely remember being bound and put into the cart. I was brought to the kirk, and kept in the steeple overnight, while the winds howled around me. In the morning, they made me walk backwards towards the minister, and a long list of accusations were set against me. The Harlowes were there, of course. Jennet insisted I'd sickened James by gifting him a hexed apple. Elizabeth and Margaret claimed that I'd cursed them with sickness as well. Both said they'd had dreams in which I'd danced with the Devil, and called a terrible storm upon the village. Adding to the suspicions were the facts that I had no children, that my animals were healthy, and my clothes were too clean. I had also often been seen talking to my old red dog a few years prior.

Gilly, I found, had also accused me of joining her in hexing the villagers.

I knew what would happen next, but to know something and to experience it are two entirely different things.

I was taken to a dank prison cell to await the Assize, the quarterly courts, where my fate would be decided. They brought me into darkness, into shadows that hung thick with screams and misery.

As they escorted me past the other cells, I noticed a familiar figure in the shadows, hunched and miserable. Gilly's skin was so covered with bruises, cuts, and filth that I could not distinguish wounds from dirt. Her nails were ruined, her face bruised and swollen, her fingertips a pulpy, blackened mess. I saw the witch pricker's handiwork: her body was covered with what seemed thousands of tiny cuts. I broke away from my escorts just long enough to stop and look at her through the bars of her cell. "Gilly?

What have they done to you?"

She looked at me, but her eyes were dead, glazed. "I'm sorry," she said. "I cannae help it. I cannae handle the pain."

I had every reason to hate her for her role in my arrest, but I could not. Looking at her bruised and broken form, I could see nothing of the happy child she had been, back when we'd chased each other across the moors and filled her granna's pewter dish with rainwater for scrying. "It's alright," I told her. Then they shoved me forward, pushing me away from her.

Time stopped. Days, hours, minutes, seconds, and weeks became indistinguishable from one another: there were only cold, dark, moments, filled with fear and pain. The witch pricker's needle pierced a million tiny holes in my resolve, and secrets slipped out through each of them. They ripped the words from my flesh with hot iron and steel, washed them from my hands with boiling oil, shook them from my bones by suspending me on cruel chains.

At first, I told them truths: that we rubbed magical ointments on ourselves, and left our bodies to fly through the night. That we laughed and danced and sang at night, and paid homage to the Devil of our coven, who, we all knew, was really only John Taylor in a mask. I said that we stole wine from the kirk and replaced it with water, and broke into the Laird's house, eating his food and drinking his ale while he and his wife slept sound, due to a potion we'd slipped them.

Then, when they had dug and carved and cut all the truth from me, I offered lies. Mad, delicious lies. I, too, sang to the witch pricker's needle. I told them the most incredible things I could think of, just to make it stop. I told them I flew through the air on velvet wings, sending plagues and nightmares through the land with blown kisses. I told them I raised a demon in the form of a toad, and sent it out every night to wreak havoc on the innocent. I told them that I had supped with the Queen of Fairy herself, and drunk blood from the skulls of the dead under a full moon at the fairy court. I made up a hundred lies, each more fantastic than the next. All of the pleasure and bounty and fortune I had given others was taken from me threefold, a wage paid in pain. Even when I was permitted to rest, the sound of screams echoing through the dark stone passages tormented me.

Eventually, they determined that I had said enough. They left me alone in the dark, and I shed my humanity piece by piece.

At last, it came time for the Assize, the quarterly trial.

It was winter by then, a cold, blustery day. I was brought into the courtroom along with several others from my coven, including Marie, Janet, and poor Gilly, who had to be carried. I kept trying to catch her eye, but she gave no response. The flesh that encased her still breathed and pumped blood, but Gilly was already gone.

The trial did not last long.

They offered Janet a chance to prove her innocence by reciting a prayer, but she fumbled and failed, and sealed her fate. Marie passed that test, but she had a deformed toe and a large brown Devil's mark on her neck, so it made no difference in the end.

Jennet was there, her eyes gleaming as she filled the air with accusations. "She gave my James an apple," she said. "He took ill the very next day with fevers and chills, and still sickens. She hexed my chickens, and cursed my husband's best awl, so that he cannae work." She went on and on, embellishing her original tale, this time adding accusations that I'd had her bairn replaced with a changeling, and that she'd seen me suckling a serpent. I nearly opened my mouth to say I'd only been holding my ferret, but it would have done me no good. If I'd been capable of doing half of what she accused me of, I'd have been sitting on Scotland's throne myself!

After what could have been moments or years, the sheriff depute lifted his thin, bony finger, pointing at me in accusation. I stared at the huge ring that decorated his gnarled skin, wondering where I'd seen it before. Then I remembered. He'd poured our wine at the Beltane celebration, which we'd celebrated with five other covens in the hills above Ocksley Forest.

The voices of the congregation rose in unison. I looked at them as they called for my death. Their eyes were cold, flickering. I shut my eyes and saw them again, dancing with me in the night, witches in the circle at night, churchgoers in the daylight.

The gavel descended with a crack that split my world, my life, into two pieces. I heard them in a daze.

Death sentence.

The next day I woke to a clamor from outside. I could see nothing, since my cell had no window. They brought me again to the torturer's room. I feared another session, but it was only to sign paperwork giving my property to the Laird to pay for my food and upkeep, and the cost of my torture and execution. When they brought me back from the chamber, I saw that Gilly's cell was empty, her blood still on the manacles. But she was gone.

I realized then what all the screaming and cheers had been about.

My heart broke, and the pieces sank to the bottom of my soul. I sat in murky darkness and misery, until, some time later, I felt the tickle of tiny paws on my ankle.

I opened my eyes and looked at my foot, sure that it was another rat. Instead, Pyewacket sat there looking at me, his eyes glittering. There was something in his mouth. I realized, to my surprise, that it was the packet I'd buried beneath the oak on the night of my arrest.

"I've no eggs or meat or milk this time," I said. But I took it, nonetheless. And I heard a voice, clear as a bell, ringing through my thoughts. "Keep it with you," he said. "Be sure you have it when the time comes."

My execution was to take place the next day. As the cock crowed, I swallowed the packet, not sure how else to ensure that it would not be taken from me. Pyewacket watched, and then slipped away into the shadows. Even as the sun rose, they were setting out for firewood, bringing the children forward to watch. I heard the crowd gathering in the market square, calling for my death. I still hear their shouts echoing through my dreams.

Burn her.

Burn the witch.

They pulled me out of the darkness, into the bright white light of day. The sun blinded me: my weakened eyes, which were accustomed by then to shadow and darkness, streamed tears, and I blinked uncontrollably for a few moments. I looked down at my rusted chains, my bloodied hands, my wounded and dirty feet, the stained rags of what had once been a decent dress. One last time, I felt what it was to walk upon the earth. I was thin and weak and in terrible pain, but the cool wind rejuvenated me.

Time did a strange thing, speeding and slowing at once. As they walked me to center of the market square, where the pyre had been laid, my senses sharpened. I took in every detail: the pebbles on the ground, the faces in the mob, the whorls and pocks on the individual pieces of firewood. Crows lit on nearby roofs, watching, waiting for my soul to rise, so they could bring it to him. I saw Jennet Harlowe and her daughters at the front of the throng, dressed in their new kirtles.

He was there, in the shadows, watching silently as they brought me to the pyre and lit it.

He could not save me.

But he made the smoke smell of roses for me.

I looked up at the clouds, trying to read them one last time as smoke filled my lungs and agonizing, searing pain washed over my entire body. My flesh and curses and wishes and dreams rose as one to the sky in billowing smoke. And in the last moments, I felt myself lifted on black wings, and I, too, ascended. I went higher and higher into the sky, until everything below me became tiny and insignificant.

Then, suddenly, I was plummeting down towards the square. I fell back to earth, unexpectedly grounded again, and found myself once more encased in flesh. I did not understand at first. I realized that, somehow, I was standing in the crowd, watching the thin figure of a woman writhing in the flames.

I looked at my hand, and found it once more sound and whole, encased in pale, healthy skin. They were not my hands, at least, not the ones I was used to. They were much smaller and the nails were rounder. The skin was soft and smooth, not calloused and worn down by gardening and work. I looked down, and saw that I was wearing a yellow kirtle. My long thin feet were encased in soft new shoes. I wiggled my toes, and realized they were tiny.

The screams coming from the inferno changed in pitch, suddenly becoming more insistent. I squinted and looked back at the figure writhing in the flames.

Someone beside me spoke. I found Jennet Harlowe facing me with a creased brow and a worried look, her face inches from mine. "Elizabeth? Is something wrong? Ye're pale."

Not trusting my voice, I only nodded. A murder of crows took to wing, cawing all at once. I watched them go, hoping that they would carry Elizabeth somewhere fair.

"Ye'd best not be bothered by a witch burning." Jennet's eyes glittered. "Breathe deep, girls: that's the stench of evil being cleansed. This round of hunts will catch the lot of the ungodly. And they will burn. All of them will burn, this time. I know it. We'll pray to that, tonight. The minister's coming for dinner, so pay attention, in case he asks questions."

The screams stopped. The figure on the pyre went still.

Beside me, Margaret reached for my hand. I looked at her, puzzled. She winked three times. I let a smile spread across Elizabeth's—my—face, and then I winked back.

Margaret leaned over to speak to Elizabeth, but it was Gilly who whispered into my ear. Gilly, as she had been at twelve, bubbling with glee and laughter. "We've some mischief to make tonight," she said. "We're too young for the Sabbat, but we can amuse ourselves well enough. I think we should hex the dyer's pots, so he can only make black clothes. Wait 'til ye' see the girls' room. It's lovely! We even have our own ponies and proper riding kits! And our familiars: mine is a kitten now. Och, and we should heal little James: he's a good boy, despite *her.*" Her voice dropped, and I saw a mischievous gleam in her eye. "I think our mother's a *witch!*"

The crowd was beginning to disperse. As the fire died and Jennet led us away, I looked back one last time.

He was standing quietly beside Minister Stewart, watching us go, his priest's collar shining bright white against the pale blue sky.

Another Plane
Patrick Lacey

Crowley the parrot said, "Welcome home."

Matt said, "Fuck off."

Walking through the front door and slamming it behind him, he called Kelly's name. Once with no answer, then again with more silence. It had been three days. Not her longest departure, but it was enough to make him anxious after the fight.

He thought that maybe she was in the backyard, sitting on the porch and drinking lemonade, having forgotten all about the other night. For a long time he looked through cupboards and tidied up, hoping that if he entertained the idea for long enough it would come true.

He checked the back porch. There was a squirrel biting its way into an acorn and pile of bird shirt on the stairs. No Kelly.

Matt poured himself a glass of whiskey, skipped the ice.

The parrot stared, a gift from Esmeralda, and no, he still didn't believe that was her real name. But he *did* believe she had something to do with this, believed it enough to want to go down to the shop right now and confront her.

The note was still on the fridge, scribbled in letters that didn't quite match his wife's script, but resembled it enough.

The whiskey burned his empty stomach as he read.

I stopped looking, Matt. I stopped like you told me to. But it turns out they found me first.

The signature seemed the most familiar, bubbly letters and a few X's and O's tossed in for good measure.

He grabbed his keys. Yes, he'd go to the shop and inquire, alright. He'd lock the doors behind him too.

Crowley squawked from inside his cage. "Welcome home."

Matt gave him the finger and stepped outside.

*   *   *

Three nights ago, while Kelly was in the shower, Matt found the dead thing in a box beneath their bed, rotting and reeking. He reached a hand under, looking for a work shirt that had gone missing, when he felt the wooden edge. There were etchings on the outside, circles and stars and little eyeballs. A fly flew out when he opened the lid. It was a jewelry box, but there were no rings inside, only a dead pigeon, its head bent at a crooked angle. There was a red slash down its neck, a vertical slice that traveled the distance of its belly and abdomen.

Its soulless, orange eyes were open.

He dropped the box and cursed. Son of a bitch.

They'd talked about this and not just once. First it had been candles, then incense. And then came herbs and the spell books. It was a phase, he'd told her.

The dead pigeon stared up at him accusingly.

Some phase.

He waited for her to finish up in the shower, listened while she brushed her teeth and blow-dried her hair. Dressed in a robe, she stepped into the bedroom and her eyes opened wide.

He held the box up. "How many times? How many times do we need to have this conversation?"

She tossed towels into the hamper and sat down at her vanity. "As many times as you'd like. We can have it once a week, twice a week. We can have it every day if that's what you really want."

"I thought we were done with this."

"*You* thought we were done with this. I never said a damn thing. You know it's important to me."

"Kelly, there's a dead bird in this box. A dead fucking bird. And the cut seems a little too precise to be a cat scratch. I thought your little spells and your rituals were bad enough, but this—this is on a different plane."

She didn't turn around. She stared into the mirror and applied eye shadow. "Funny you should say that. If you'd listen to a word anyone else said besides yourself, you might learn a thing or two. That's what all this is about, being on another plane."

"Why was there a dead bird under our bed? Answer me that."

"It's a sacrifice."

"A sacrifice? For what?"

"Forget it. You wouldn't believe me anyway."

He saw her reflection and though it was hard to put into words, he thought a piece of him might have died in that moment. From the outside she was still the woman he adored, the woman he'd met at the dentist's office ten years ago, so nervous about his root canal he could have pissed his pants in the waiting room. But she'd put down her magazine and asked if she knew him from somewhere. Later, lying in bed after they'd made love, she told him she could tell he was on the edge of cracking up, that she'd just wanted to take his mind off of it.

To this day he couldn't remember an ounce of pain from that root canal.

But in the here and now, sitting on the bed and watching that same woman be taken over by something so silly, that was pain. Real pain.

He shut the box. "When will you stop chasing things that aren't there? What is it you're looking for?"

"I told you, you wouldn't understand."

"She's dead, Kelly. You know it, I know it, so just give it a rest."

There was just one moment of quiet, when every noise on earth seemed to halt, and then she was up and smashing things, throwing jars of lotion and hairbrushes. She toppled her vanity over, the mirror shattering. He wondered if that was bad luck.

She held a trembling finger toward him. "Now you listen. Just shut your mouth for one goddamn second and listen. I know what happened to my sister because I was there. I saw her go through the window. I saw her hit the ground. I saw her bleed to death in front of me. I know she's dead. But no matter how far gone things are there's always a way to get in touch. Nothing's ever *really* gone."

That night he slept on the couch, asking himself over and over why he'd gone and brought up her sister, her sister that had been thrown through a windshield while they'd been driving home from a concert. A drunk driver had managed to pull onto the wrong side of the highway, through a turnaround the state police used, and hit them dead on. Kelly's head had puffed up to resemble a bruised squash.

Her sister's head had left its body.

He felt sick to his stomach when he finally fell asleep.

Matt woke once during the night with icy cold sweat clinging to his clothes. Though it was dark in the living room, he was sure that someone stood at the foot of the couch, watching, observing, so he dove for the light.

There was no one there, save for Crowley, eyeing him like he was keeping a secret.

*   *   *

Esmerelda's Olde Magic Shoppe stood downtown among other tourist traps. The sign, rickety and peeling, had probably cost a thousand dollars to have some graphic designers make it look that way.

Matt watched from outside, saw the girl at the counter, pitch black hair, pitch black lipstick, pitch black nails, flip through a magazine and stare at the clock. Ten minutes to five. They would be closing soon.

A woman walked by and went into the shop, bells jingling overhead as she opened the door. The girl at the counter pointed toward the back, where Esmeralda came out of one of two curtained rooms, and led the woman out back to have her fortune told.

Matt waited.

Five minutes later the girl at the counter stepped outside to have a cigarette. He moved quickly, coming from the side and going in through the door before it shut, making sure he wasn't spotted before he looked around.

There were ingredients on the sidewall, basil, oak, holly, blood root, snake skin.

There were candles and incense, and above the counter hung a poster of something called the pentagram of elements.

In the back corner of the shop there were mugs and t-shirts, a few gag gifts. He wondered where those fit in.

He could hear Esmeralda through the curtains, telling the woman happy days were coming her way.

Outside the girl was finishing up her cigarette. Matt went into the other curtained room and knelt down. It smelled of old incense, the scent not quite settled, like dust in an abandoned house. There was a split second where he wondered if he was really alone in this dark room, as if he could turn around and find something hovering above him with eyes that bored through the blackness. He pushed the thought aside, told himself not to be so stupid, not to entertain anything but rational thought about all of this.

A few minutes passed. Esmeralda finished up with the woman, charged her fifty dollars, and saw her out. She told the girl she could take off early. The bells above the door jingled behind her. Matt heard the front door lock and the sound of the open sign being switched to closed.

He risked a glance into the shop, but couldn't see Esmeralda, couldn't see her brightly colored robe or dangling gypsy jewelry.

The curtain pulled aside and he almost fell back on his ass.

Esmeralda smiled. "I can tell the future, Matt. Did you really think I couldn't hear someone breathing up a storm in my own shop?"

Matt smiled back. "Nice to see you too, Esmeralda."

"I've got to close things up. Might as well come out and give me a hand. Here." She handed him a box of fliers and told him to put it in the storage room. "What brings you to the shop? Did you want your palm read?"

"That will be the day." He threw the box out back. "Kelly's run off again."

"What a surprise."

"What was that?"

"I said 'I'm so sorry to hear that.'"

"I wanted to know if you've seen her at all. She's been gone three days now. I'm starting to worry."

"She always comes back, Matt. Though I don't quite understand it, she always comes back." She took money from the register, beginning to count bills and coins.

"You're sure you haven't seen her at all. It seems like she would have paid you a visit before she left."

"Why's that?" she asked, not looking up as she leafed through the money.

"Because she sliced up a pigeon and fit it nicely into a box underneath our bed. She said it was a sacrifice. Sounds like something you'd put in her head."

Esmeralda looked at him as if she'd just received bad news from a doctor. She walked toward him, away from the counter. "Matt, there's something you don't understand about your wife, something you probably ought to get through your thick dome of a skull. She's very…receptive."

"Receptive to what?"

Esmeralda held her hands out. "You see all this? This is the light side of what we do. Come on in and let me read your palms. Buy some ingredients for a love spell on your way out. This is the safe stuff. But Kelly, she is beyond all of this. You probably think I'm the one who turned her on to magic, but it's the other way around.

"We were in high school when we first started to dabble. We'd go for long walks through the woods after school, sometimes even sneaking out after bedtime. One night we built a fire and added some ingredients, not sure exactly what we were doing but eager just the same. We waited. Kelly tried calling out, asked if we had made contact with something. Nothing answered. Not at first. But your wife is persistent. We sat there for three hours and just as I was about to tell her my ass was halfway frozen off, we heard something, some leaves rustling.

"And the fire turned black, Matt. To this day I don't want to believe it, but the fire turned black, and the smoke was even darker and it started to form something, a face. We couldn't understand what it was saying, but we pinched each other and it sure as hell wasn't a dream."

"What are you saying?"

"I'm saying that Kelly has a gift. She can communicate with other planes."

A chime rang out in his head. "Funny. She used that same phrase the night I found the dead bird. Any idea why she'd want to go and do something like that?"

"A sacrifice. She's trying to open a doorway."

"A doorway to what?"

Esmeralda shook her head and walked back to the register. "Hell if I know, and I'd like to keep it that way." She went back to counting money. Matt wanted to tell her that he didn't believe in her bullshit, despite the sweat on his lower back that felt like a cold hand.

*　　*　　*

Crowley welcomed Matt home and he ignored him. All these years he'd had to put up with that damn parrot and the thing could say a handful of phrases at most.

He went into the den and called work, told them he'd be taking a few days off. He was middle management and he could work from home if need be. Half the time he sat at his cubicle and stared at the computer screen, answering emails and making calls when he needed to, but mostly he just stared off into the distance.

He went downstairs into the basement. There was a workbench down there and it would be good to get his mind off things. His road bike, needing oiling, was propped upside down. Matt spun the rear wheel and winced at the high-pitch protest it gave.

Then he almost bit his tongue at the noise upstairs. A voice, familiar. It was hard to make out, but there was no denying it.

Kelly was upstairs and she was talking away. He walked to the foot of the stairs, holding his breath and feeling faint. He listened.

"Here is what you desire. I am your servant. Allow me to cross over." Kelly kept repeating these same three phrases, chant-like.

He ran upstairs, calling her name, ready to apologize and scared as hell.

But there was no one upstairs, just empty rooms and a parrot that eyed him too much like a human, a human that knew a little too much for his own good.

When he slowed his heartbeat down he turned to go back downstairs.

Another voice spoke out, this one much deeper. "Join us."

Matt spun around and saw that Crowley was speaking. "Join us. Join us. Join us." He sounded less like a parrot and more like something Matt didn't want to imagine. He grabbed a coat from the rack and threw it over the cage. The bird stopped speaking.

Matt's throat was like a dry sponge. He needed a drink.

When he stepped outside into the evening, he tried to tell himself he was only going crazy.

Because it was better than the alternative.

*　　*　　*

"Where the hell you been, Boss?" Matt set his beer down on

the table and pulled a chair out. Greg Fournier was his next door neighbor, had moved in a few years before he and Kelly, and on most nights he couldn't stand the sight of the man. But tonight was different.

"Been busy at the office." Matt sat down, looked around the bar. Every time he saw a woman turned away from him, he swore it was Kelly.

"How's the house coming along?" Greg sipped at something that smelled like sour apples, managed to spill some onto his beard. "Any new projects?"

Matt drank his beer. The glass was ice cold and seemed to cool his entire body down. He wished he'd brought a coat, but he left it at home, resting on Crowley's cage.

Join us.

"Nothing right now. Kelly wants an addition on the living room. Sounds pricey but her uncle's a contractor, said he would give us a good deal." It felt harder to breathe when he said her name aloud.

"How is Kelly anyway? I swear that woman never stops moving. Every time I look out my window she's either planting something in the garden or jogging up and down the street. Hell, just yesterday, I must have seen her circle the block five or six times."

Matt's beer threatened to come back up as his hands shook underneath the table. "What was that?"

"Oh, I was just saying that yesterday your wife was jogging up a storm. Seems like a real health nut." A drop fell from his beard, unnoticed.

"Yesterday, you said?"

"That's right. Had some vacation time. Decided to take the day off and sit on my ass all the day. Every time I looked outside, there was Kelly pumping her legs."

He stopped listening then. The entire bar receded into the background and it was only him at that table.

Before he realized what was happening, he was outside in the night, walking as fast as he could, toward home.

His tab was still open but he'd stop by tomorrow.

Right now, he wanted to go home and find that everything was normal again, that he'd just flipped his rocker and Kelly was there in the kitchen, cutting up something for supper. He'd check the fridge door and there would be no note and underneath their bed, there would be only boxes of old, neglected things.

But no dead things.

*   *   *

There was another box waiting for him on the front step, not a jewelry box with etchings but a dusty cardboard package. He picked it up and wondered if anything lay inside with its eyes open. He lifted the tabs. There were small Ziplocs filled with powder and tiny jars with leaves and roots. A piece of paper rested underneath it all.

This is a protection spell, Matt. Use it. If Kelly opened up a doorway, you'll need it.

It was signed from Esmeralda and as he looked up he could see a car pulling away from the curb and driving off. He threw the box into the yard as hard as he could. A few of the jars clinked inside and shattered. "I don't believe in your magic bullshit! I just want my fucking wife back and I don't want you filling her head with anymore tricks!" He knew she couldn't hear him this far away, but it felt good to say the words anyway.

Matt went inside and slammed the door shut for the second time that day. It felt final. "Kelly?" His voice sounded weak, scared, but he told himself otherwise. She was here somewhere, hiding in one of these rooms, because she couldn't be gone. Kelly, who did the bills, who remembered when his blood pressure medication was running low, who calmed him down when he was ready to strangle his boss.

"Kelly?" He sounded desperate now, searching through every room, under every piece of furniture, until he tripped over the rug in the living room. A corner of it had come loose. He lost his balance and fell against Crowley's cage. The coat fell and he saw the bird's eyes, actually looked into them for the first time in a long time.

They were not birds' eyes. He was not sure what that meant, but they were not birds' eyes.

He turned away, wiping cold sweat from his face, and noticed something on the floor, something peeking from beneath the rug. He kneeled down. At first it looked like someone had just spilled ketchup, but he knew better. Matt's pulse raced. He lifted the coffee table, moved the couch and lazy boy. Then he rolled the rug up and tossed it aside.

There were symbols written on the living room floor, symbols that matched those on the box with the dead bird inside it. These were much bigger, some of them looking a lot like pentagrams and not innocent like the one hanging in Esmeralda's shop.

They were not written in ketchup.

"Join us."

Matt almost fell again when he heard Crowley, his voice deeper than the grave this time.

The house shook and his first thought was an earthquake, but when the symbols on the floor started to glow, he pushed that thought aside. They lit up in neon shades of red and green and under normal circumstances it would have reminded him of Christmas.

But under *these* circumstances, the shades made his bowels run cold and a few drops of piss squeezed out onto his legs.

The shaking stopped and the entire surface of the floor in front of him rippled, like waves at the beach. It was calm somehow, and he could've watched for a very long time if the hand didn't reach up. It was smooth and pale and he recognized the shape.

"Join us," Crowley said from behind in a crocodile's voice. "Join us. Join us. Join us."

Kelly reached her hand out, then her elbow and shoulder, until she was out of the floor, somehow floating on top of the rippling floorboards. She was naked and he thought that she'd never looked more beautiful.

"Kelly," he managed in a whisper.

"I heard you calling me." Her voice was too calm.

He nodded. "I missed you."

"I missed you too." Her skin seemed too dry, not an ounce of wetness dripping down her body. "They found me, Matt. I called out to them, just like you called out to me, and they let me in. This is the doorway, the doorway to another plane."

"Your sister?"

Kelly nodded. For the first time, he noticed her eyes were black. "She's here too, but she's only the beginning. There's so much to see down here, Matt." She held her hand out to him. "Join us."

He brought his hand forward, trembling. In his mind somewhere he pictured the ingredients that lay on the front lawn, the protection spell.

Kelly smiled. "Everything you could ever dream of is down here. It's been right beneath our feet this whole time. They welcome anyone into their kingdom. You need only to call out to them, to say their name, to build a doorway, and to knock. I knocked, Matt. I knocked for a long time and they finally let me in."

"Who are they?" Matt's hand touched Kelly's.

Her fingernails slid off her fingers. He pulled away and in the process the flesh from her right hand pulled off, stuck to his skin. He wiggled it off and saw that her hand was a maze of grey scales.

Kelly's smile grew impossibly wide. "Now you're beginning to see." She ripped the rest of her flesh off, a decoy skin that hid the truth.

And the truth was ugly.

When she was done, Kelly no longer resembled his wife. Her nose that she'd thought too big, the nose he'd adored, was now a vacant hole. He thought there were things climbing around inside. Her teeth were chipped and rotten, and he could have sworn there were hundreds of them. Her breasts were not there anymore. In their place was grey slithering flesh.

Matt pinched himself, as his wife and Esmeralda had done in the woods that night.

He turned to leave, except he didn't move at all. His feet were submerged in the puddle where the thing stood. It grabbed his arms and pulled him close. "You called us. You knocked and we answered." It was no longer Kelly's voice, but the voice that matched Crowley's, that deep groan.

Matt struggled.

"Nothing's ever really gone," the thing said. "Just on another plane."

It dragged him forward and then down, into the puddle that should have been hardwood floor. He fought with every muscle in his body and the thing laughed.

His head went under for a moment and he saw things, hundreds of squirming things with grey and scaly flesh. Some had loose pale skin hanging from their limbs.

He struggled back up and saw one last glimpse of the living room and Crowley in his cage. Then he was submerged, on another plane, and the things were closing in on him.

"Welcome home," Crowley said.

Access Violation
Jeremy Flagg

"We're starving, you bitch."

"We at Ration Distributions are dedicated to providing rations to the residents of Boston."

"You--"

"Sorry, please hold."

Click.

Emile slumped down in her chair. If she leaned too far to the right, the missing wheel would send her to the floor. It was funny to think about until the image of the rats scurrying along the carpet sobered her. The monstrous rodents seemed to fit in with the peeling paint, dirty gray carpet, and struggling ventilation system. Food distribution, the most important business on the planet, and her bosses couldn't even spring for a tacky motivational poster. She imagined this is what the public relations office would look like for Satan's asshole.

She kept herself sane by practicing her craft in the privacy of her cubicle. Her pointer finger spun around in a circle. The complimentary pen given to her by her douche boss started to spin around on the table on its own—homework given to her by the coven, utilizing her ability to see beyond the physical. It wasn't a complex equation, but she figured she might as well get in the practice while on the company dollar. She got a smug sense of satisfaction as small parts of the world bent to her will.

Emile stopped spinning the pen and took a deep breath. The

light continued blinking. There were hundreds of calls waiting for her to make excuses and explain why there was no food. Customers wanted answers, and she perpetuated the ruse that help was coming. The other dozen customer service reps on her floor repeated the well-rehearsed lines, trying to maintain an upbeat attitude. With each call she tried to talk as if she was smiling, but it was nearly impossible, people were dying because her company couldn't produce enough food. She debated on marching down the aisle, past the dozens of cubicles, into the elevator, and saying good riddance.

Ignoring her current call, she began another.

"Hello, you've reached Ration Distributions, my name is Emile, what can I do you for?"

"Hey, I work for the distribution center in the Chicago Loop. We were supposed to open our doors an hour ago and there still isn't a shipment from you guys."

"Okay sir," she attempted to sound positive. "I am going to put you on hold while I locate the delivery truck."

"Please hurry, the people are starting to get rowdy."

"I'll alert the authorities, sir. Please hold."

Nails clacked against the touch-screen on her desk. With a few clicks she saw the route of the distribution truck. It had another four hours before it reached the center. She pushed aside the application and opened a new window. Pressing a button, she alerted authorities that a distribution center was about to be torn apart by locals. The screen flashed as a receptionist in the Chicago police department acknowledged receipt.

"Sir, the food truck is several hours away. The authorities are on their way. They are sending in a response team to neutralize your threat. Do not open your doors. Enact your riot protocols. They will be with you shortly."

"But, they're starving. They are going to kill me."

"Please hold, sir."

Emile punched the hold button and tore off the headset, crushing one of the finely sculpted spikes of hair on her head. Swearing under her breath, she threw the headset onto the desk. Today, she celebrated her six-month anniversary at Ration Distributions. The paycheck didn't cover the headache of this job. At first, she couldn't argue with the money and an additional food ration per week. Now, each day seemed longer, the hours dragging by. It reached the point where she stared at the clock on the wall counting seconds. She counted each second, each moment of life stolen from her, moving her closer to death.

Emile tapped her finger on her phone's blinking wait button, debating how long she would force the guy on hold to listen to their static filled, turn of the century, pop hits. Emile's chipped nail polish mesmerized her as she tapped the hold button again and again. Returning to reality, she moved her finger over and clicked the "disconnect" button.

"I hate my life."

The light on her phone blinked. The contraption looked as if her company stole it from the 80's. The bulky phone lacked modern necessities like artificial intelligence or even solitaire. The small red circle incited a rage deep in the pit of her stomach. She'd get a moment of peace before it'd blink again. It was obvious why her occupation prompted a freakishly high suicide rate. No, if she was going out, she'd go postal and take the whole office with her.

Three dings sounded in her ear. One for family. Two for everybody else. Three for the coven. She pressed the sub-dermal node just to the right of her eye. She blinked and as she raised her eyelids, an image of her email inbox showed in the right eye. The sensation was dizzying as her inner ear adapted to seeing a computer screen in one eye and the office in the other. The optical illusion allowed her to click on the inbox with her pointer finger. Thumbing through the thousands of saved emails, she reached the most recent one.

!Urgent: Grove. Now.

"Shit." It was rare the coven members reached out to each other before the full moon. It was extremely rare to receive a summons from anybody other than the High Priestess. Reaching under the seat of her chair, she pulled the lever, dropping it several inches so she could access the computer mounted under her station.

"Mother fucking Christ," Emile cursed as she tried to locate the internet connection. It was bad enough they didn't have neural gel connectors, but the lack of wireless simply pissed her off. "Goddamn, cheap ass suits."

She fished behind the archaic box and grabbed the blue cord, following to where it fed into the back of the computer. Snapping it out of the port, she turned over her wrist. Hidden within the lifelike tattoo of bionic bones, wires, and metal muscles, she felt for the opening. A wired connection might be her last resort, but she always came prepared. Emile shoved the wire into her arm. The click in her inner ear confirmed the handshake between her bioware and the network. The second click confirmed that her bioware overcame the company's firewall and she accessed the internet.

Pressing the bump beneath her skin to the side of her left eye, she blinked, opening her eyes to a white empty room. In the infinite white, Emile stood naked. Hundreds of tattoos cataloged her life story. Each significant moment, detailed in a cacophony of black ink, from the logo of the first band she saw in concert to the three times she had fallen in love, each memory etched just beneath the surface of her skin. Several of the alien-esque tattoos on her right shoulder moved as if the ink were alive and angry. The dragon wrapped around her left leg moved, the gears composing its heads turning, releasing wisps of smoke. The empty white space flickered, her brain giving her a sign it loaded her local construct.

A cough from the next cubicle in her office reminded Emile that Janice refused to take a fucking sick day like a considerate coworker. She ignored the sounds coming from the office, the yammering on outdated telephones and the chipper lies the reps spouted. Her body might be trapped in the office of the damned, but thanks to technology and a bit of witchcraft, her mind didn't have the same limitations.

Standing exposed in her computer program, Emile's hand slid across her bare flesh. Fingertips touched a techno-organic skull inked just beneath her collarbone. The software accessed her hardware, submerging her in the program. The eyes of the skull flickered red as Janice's coughing fit ended and the sensation of being naked rippled across the skin of her physical body. The hair on her arms stood on end as a simulated breeze caressed her. A small gasp escaped her lips. The restraints of the physical and depressing world she lived in fell away. The perfect silence was a welcomed change as the office became a distant memory. Her physical self became her avatar, a digital representation of herself in the virtual world.

Pixel by pixel, a neon blue circle slightly wider than her wingspan materialized on the floor. Symbols surrounded the circle, burned into the ground. Each of the runes resembled a letter, part of a long forgotten alphabet. The angular 'R' ignited as dark blue robes faded into sight, suspended in the middle of the circle as if by magic. Her hand touched the clothes, her fingers dancing through the rabbit fur lining along the edge of the hood. The robes disintegrated, pixels breaking down into tiny blocks, moving along her arm and along her back. .04 seconds later, her body was clothed in the heavy fabric. She couldn't hide the slight grin. She continued to be impressed with her coding skills and the elegant transitions of her scripts.

"Grove," she stated.

A seam flared to life in the empty vast white, burning along until a rectangular portal hung in the air. The door opened but she didn't need to move further. The seam denoted a secure connection, a visual cue, connecting to the Grove's server and her construct. An empty field of grass filled in beneath her feet. The crickets chirping and the scent of fresh dew on blades of grass invaded her senses. Amidst all this beauty, she found it difficult to recall that her body remained in an office with Janice, the wheezing hell-beast.

In the center of the field, a grand oak tree stretched into the sky. Emile walked closer. A woman wearing near identical robes faded into the Grove. They continued the walk, more avatars appearing until eleven brothers and sisters in robes strode side by side. The bottom of Emile's robe turned a darker blue as it dragged along the damp grass. As she continued toward the tree, the smell changed subtly, more like earth soaked after a rain shower. Emile longed for the chance to experience these sensations in the real world. Between the lack of green land and the threat of acid rain, she was certain she'd only be able to enjoy these simulated experiences nowhere but here.

They approached the tree where a woman and man waited. The man had robes similar to theirs, the woman, however, wore powder blue robes. The light blue cloth denoted her rank above the other coven members. Her avatar showed her age, the lines carved deeply around her mouth giving away her love of laughter. On the side of each eye, crow's feet sprouted, adding to the air of wisdom about her.

"Welcome brothers and sisters," the Priestess greeted them with a slight nod of her head.

"As we welcome you," they returned in unison.

"The time for formalities has passed, my sacred children. Caleb is in grave danger." The elderly woman eyed the initiate standing next to her. She held out her hand, waiting for Caleb to return the sentiment. The members moved into a circle, their hands emerging from the depths of their robes. Emile took her place, locking her left hand with Gabriel and her right with Monique. The warmth of their hands gave her a sense of peace. These twelve, over the course of the last three months, formed the core of her family. With each encounter, they reminded her that she belonged to something bigger.

"Simul nos unum sumus." Together we are one.

As their leader spoke, light materialized about her palms. The light from the Priestess coursed through each of their hands, connecting them as one. Emile tightened her grip as the light sprung to life in both of her hands. Every member of the coven reacted in a similar fashion, and then their eyes flashed white.

The processor attached at the base of Emile's skull, a small box no bigger than her thumbnail, computed the information being passed between them. Like her, everybody in this coven had the gift of witchcraft. It wasn't like in the books, not nature loving, herb growing, broom riding hags. Each of them held the ability to see through the veil of reality, the source code, and with enough effort, they could alter the code. The virtual meeting place had been an amalgamation each of them coded, written from the ground up. In the real world they went by the name witch, here, in the bowels of the once revolutionary internet, they were known by another name: hackers.

Data streams opened.

In their shared vision, they saw Caleb cowering in the corner of a small room. The man's legs were drawn against his chest as he held his mouth closed, suppressing an impending scream. The image of the thirty-year-old male was live, happening somewhere in the world that very moment.

The small room where Caleb sat frozen flashed blue. Emile's processor sifted through the information dump. The packet contained all the sensory input Caleb experienced in the last two minutes. The memory inside the file contained all the data his conscious and subconscious recorded in the time span. She moved the file backward looking for clues.

The scene moved backward in time, a blurry flash of motion

stopping once Caleb stood in a long room with windows along each side. It took Emile a moment to process the scene. The seats in rows, the overhanging storage racks, and the patrons sitting quietly gave her contextual cues. The humming vibration underneath her feet revealed the final hint. He was on the bullet train.

She stood in the middle of rapid transport from Chicago to Boston. The passenger train, with runes etched into every bit of glass, had been deemed the only safe travel through the badlands to and from the cities of men. Somewhere on the train, in a cabin near the technical operator, a mage meditated, expending his energies, keeping the evils outside at bay.

The mystical energy flowing through the train was palpable. Thin blue lines, no bigger than a spider's web flowed around the outside of the train. If she examined them long enough, she'd see through the magic and be able to identify the source code, the raw essence that made magic work. Each mage had his own visualization preferences. This mage treated the strands of energy as a cocoon engulfing the train. The sigils carved into the windows glowed, pulsing with light as if they breathed energy.

"So beautiful," Emile whispered as she waded through Caleb's memory.

Whether Caleb saw them or not, the badlands earned its name. Swarming with vile creatures from lower levels of existence, travel through them required magic to keep the demons at bay. Between the cities of men, the bullet relied on magic to prevent the fiends from breaking into the train and devouring the passengers' flesh. It didn't matter if the demons could be seen or not, little explosions against the blue strands were proof something was attempting to push its way inside. The only things keeping the demons at bay were a mage, and his stubbornness.

Caleb stood in the center aisle of the passenger car, nearly two minutes prior to the huddled mess in the sleeper cabin. The train shook. Caleb staggered, grasping the storage compartments for support. Another rocking motion wracked the train. The people in their suits, sporting expensive Rolexes, reading the news on their electronic devices, nestled in plush chairs, didn't flinch at the shaking. Their faces didn't react to the disturbance in the slightest.

The thin blue lines sputtered, the continuity vanishing for half a second. The strands broke and fluttered away from the speeding train. With each shudder and tiny explosion, the elements protecting the exterior weakened. None of these passengers had the gift. For them, the sigils appeared to be nothing more than decoration. Even with the knowledge that a mage protected the train during transportation, they couldn't sense the man faltering at his job.

The blue vanished. The sigils died. The magic ceased. The terror erupted from Caleb's mouth as he screamed. They ignored him. He pointed. They continued. He took steps forward, not sure how to proceed. A man watching a news segment about the promotion of a technomancer in the army barely glanced in the witch's direction.

The passengers turned their heads at the distant sound of tearing metal. It originated somewhere in the cars behind them. The rumble made the train jerk, sending everybody bouncing in their seats. Caleb fell to the floor. It was coming for them. It was going to kill them.

Demons.

"Our wards are holding. We are approaching Boston. Estimated time of arrival is seventeen minutes."

There were no wards left. The announcer had lied. The conductor hoped they could make it to the city before the demons broke through. He tried to keep the passengers calm. He failed. They were going to die before they reached the station.

Sparks flew in the back of the train car as the demons moved forward. Dents spiked downward in the ceiling as they attempted to punch their way through the metal exterior; and the passengers screamed. They dropped their books and cell phones, brought back to reality as the back end of the car tore open. The roof was peeled back; the stench of sulfur filled the air.

The panicking started.

A man sitting near the window ripped at his seatbelt, scrambling to climb over the girl seated next to the aisle. The young lady struggled to get out, but the man shoved her backward as he fell into the space between seats. A woman near the back clawed at the seat, trying free her leg from a duffle bag sitting at her feet. Another man grabbed her by the arm and dragged her into the aisle, trying to rescue the woman from the inevitable.

They were mundane, to them an invisible force was intruding, threatening to eradicate them. They didn't have the optics or the abilities to detect the demons. They couldn't see the grotesque human-like figures pouring through the cracks, couldn't see the distorted faces and melted body parts that oozed as the beasts pulled themselves into the train. Mundanes couldn't see the extended jaws clamping down on a man's head.

Caleb could see.

He pushed backward, trying to move toward the front of the train away from the carnage. Caleb pulled himself past a man trying to remove his seatbelt. He only turned back when he reached the door to the sleeper compartments. The sickly red figures clawed at the stragglers in the car. The blood was real even if the passengers couldn't find the cause. Gashes opened on torsos, and limbs tore from their sockets by invisible attackers. The smell of frenzied panic filled the cabin, a mix of sweat and piss and shit. Struggling to open the heavy door between the cars, passengers lent their strength. Several ran through. Caleb tried to save who he could.

He stepped into the next train car and closed the door, drawing down the lever that locked it. On the other side of the glass, a massacre was taking place. Bodies smashed against the sides of the car. Entrails painted the walls. Those who could still draw air, screamed. They were lost. He rested his hand on the door, touching a sigil in the glass. As he mumbled, green lines surged through the symbol, branching outward like vines. Caleb's abilities as a witch were minimal, but he had some ability in the physical world.

A demon hurled itself against the door, the impact startling him. Its head resembled a ravenous dog with part of its head rotted away. It beat its head against the door, saliva coating the glass. It clawed at the door, the protective green energies knocking its talons away.

Caleb's ankle gave out as he turned to run. Toppling to the floor, he grasped at air to pull himself away from the door. He pulled at the wall, dragging his body along until reaching the first cabin. Grabbing onto the doorframe, he hefted himself through. Slamming the door shut, he locked it. The sound of glass shattering erupted through the cabin. He traced sigils in the air, leaving a trailing light as he drew. Gasping for air, Caleb murmured a phrase, power surging into his air writing.

The door cracked under the weight of the frenzied demon; the glyph was failing. The infection wanted in. He backed away, drawing up his legs until he was a tiny ball against the wall. Seconds separated the blood hungry demon from burning through the energy of the sigil. It was going to tear into him and, if he was lucky, kill him quickly.

*   *   *

"We gather to protect our own," said the Priestess. The coven returned to the present.

The Grove. Thirteen members. Each opened their eyes as their cerebral processors disconnected them from the live stream of their brother. Caleb's avatar held itself together, his hands still firmly in place with the others. He reached out to the coven. Together, in this virtual sacred space, their energies converged and through the bond they shared, through witchcraft, they offered themselves to their brother in need.

"From the many, we bestow upon one," they started. Several members broke off, resorting to native languages. The High Priestess had always encouraged them to bring their true selves into the circle. Emile recited the line several times and stopped. She imagined Caleb, curled into a ball, cowering in the sleeper cabin. Standing next to the frightened man, energy flowed into her terrified brother, bathing him in a brilliant radiance.

Broken down into ones and zeroes, they poured their magic into their brother. Emile's innate abilities were reduced to code and pushed through fiber optic wires until it reached Caleb. With the joint energies of the coven, Emile hoped Caleb could defend himself until the train made it safely to the city.

Caleb's avatar's hands slipped from his neighbors. The man staggered, crumbling to the ground. His avatar resembled his physical self, trying to shrink into obscurity. He opened his mouth to scream but no sound emerged. With a final reach toward the coven, the fingers on his hand stretching as far as they could. The man blinked in and out, his avatar flickering as the program terminated his connection.

He was infected.

In a bullet train speeding toward Boston, the demon had reached its target. Its claws penetrated Caleb's physical skull, infecting his body, leaving nothing more than a husk of a human. The hellhound didn't kill him but spread its toxins through the witch's veins. He became one of them, a replica of his creator, a blood-thirsty denizen craving destruction and fear. His avatar's veins pushed to the surface, and what should have been deep blue burned a saturated crimson. The demons weren't smart enough to access the computer from a terminal, but they had evolved and learned new ways to procreate.

The avatar's flesh turned red as it convulsed on the grass, hands pounding the ground. Skin boiled and melted away, pouring to the sides, leaving his stomach exposed and gaping. Caleb twitched and stopped moving.

All but the Priestess froze. Her hands moved furiously, mumbling an incantation. Roots moved up from the ground, binding Caleb's corpse. Caleb had become infected, the demon using his body as a portal into the virtual world. Seeing the man die in front of them was one of only a dozen terrifying things about this session. The potential for the demon to access the Grove made them uneasy as they waited for a command from their matriarch.

A hand reached up from the dead man's torso, emerging from his guts. A second hand shot upward, latching onto the ground, struggling to break free of Caleb's entrails. The High Priestess held out a closed fist and flung open her fingers. Flames rolled off her hand until she held a ball of fire. She hurled it at the beast, striking it in the head, causing a spray of fire to rain onto the once immaculate grass. It snarled a blood-curdling growl, bringing the coven back into the moment. Others in the coven cried out, throwing up magical shields to ward off the invasion.

"Children," she cried, "daemons."

Demons were not witches. They had no abilities for complex coding. Their digital replica had no minds, but only one purpose: multiply. Demons reached into the code, using daemons to do their bidding. Daemons, the virtual computer code embodiment of hell.

Emile was pissed. The infection already tainted the Grove. Where its hands touched the grass, rot set in. From the rot, two more of the beasts pulled themselves to the surface, determined to spread more of their vile infection. The High Priestess stepped back, wanting to make sure the creatures didn't touch her avatar. A sister panicked, grabbing her forearm, and with a guilty look, disconnected from the grove. Fear rippled through the remaining members of the coven.

"Familiar," Emile remembered. Reaching into the folds of her robe, digging deep into the right pocket, she pulled out a small rock carving of a black bear. She thrust it into the ground. The processor pulled from an internal library and executed the script. A life-sized bear blinked into existence, half of the totem resembled a lifelike bear, metal joints and gears filled in the rest. Her hand rested on its head, fingertips clutching its fur. The black animal roared, the sound bellowing from the pit of its stomach filling the air. "Kill the fuckers," she hissed. Each of the remaining coven followed suit; a horse, wolf, falcon, elephant. Much like daemons, familiars served one purpose: to protect their creators.

As the animals charged in, the High Priestess pointed at Caleb's corpse. "Emile, patch the breach."

Their firewall separating the Grove from the physical world lay in ruins, decimated from the demon's brute force attack. Emile frantically cycled through a library of programs. Her collection of security software was formidable. She watched as the High Priestess dodged a daemon before a beam of pure white light from her hand pulverized the corpse. The virus had been scrubbed, but the doorway between the Grove and Caleb's attackers remained. Emile reached into a pocket on her robe and threw two acorns at where the corpse had been. Both programs initiated themselves as they landed in the grass. The acorns sunk into the ground, and two small trees broke the surface, their roots consuming the spot where the rot originated.

"Our firewalls are active," Emile yelled to the Priestess.

Emile turned her attention to the daemon absorbing a familiar. The creature vomited a red syrupy liquid, leaving pools of it on the ground. With each ragged step of the beasts, the ground turned a dark brown, the saturation of color diminishing until their wake appeared black and white. More daemons pulled themselves out of the pools of putrid liquid.

A scream erupted from Gabriel. Emile turned, and one of the less human daemons shoved its fingers into the man's chest. It pulled back and continued walking toward its next victim. The witch fell to the ground, his body convulsing as the infection spread. Emile didn't have time to access her emotions, she could only react to the chaos swallowing her safest of safe spaces.

"Momentum impede," Emile shouted the words of protection. The program executed, throwing up a containment field around several of the daemons, locking them inside. The bubble shimmered with each strike, preventing the creatures from getting any closer to the survivors. She sifted through software for a program to scrub the daemons from the Grove. Her palms grew sweaty as she realized nothing would stop them short of a clean wipe of the Grove.

The shield tinted red.

She grit her teeth and growled at the relentlessness of the daemons corrupting the code. First, one hand, then a second, reached through growing holes in the bubble. Another sister screamed as a daemon clutched at her ankle, tearing at her foot with its claw. What started as a single intrusion had grown to a dozen, each of the daemons seeking out more living victims.

Emile jumped backward as a bony hand reached out. Stored in her library; weapons, software, swords, programs she 'liberated' not available to the general public. Panic prevented her from being of any real use. Flesh seemed to be flayed from the bones of the daemon reaching toward her face. A scream stuck in her throat. She knew she should run and not let it make contact, but she couldn't move. The muscles in her legs twitched, her flight response reduced to slight spasms. She wondered what it would feel like to have her processor corrupted as it eradicated any sense of self. She wondered if it would hurt.

The daemon crumpled to the ground as the bear latched onto its outstretched arm. Emile's familiar clawed away at the infection, it's metallic paw crushing the daemon's head as it tried to tear the arm from the body with its mouth. The moment it bit into the arm, she knew her familiar was lost. It was only software, but it had been one of her first programs. Black fur started to fall off its body, and its metal parts rusted as the virus consumed it.

"Disconnect," screamed the High Priestess.

The woman in blue threw her arms out wide. Mirror images of the elder woman appeared, folding out like paper dolls. Stealing the idea from the daemons, the woman's replicas charged in, hurling themselves at the beasts. The witch yelled again for the others to disconnect from the Grove. One by one the remaining members vanished. Emile and the High Priestess were the last of the coven connected to the Grove. More than half of their coven lie in bloody piles on the ground.

The Grove was lost. The files containing their sacred space riddled with corrupted data, the code itself damaged forever. The daemons would remain until there was nothing left. The fallen witches would wake, demented versions of their original selves. None of them could stop the virus. There was nothing they could do but sever their connection. The High Priestess reached to her forearm and motioned for Emile to do the same.

"May the mother take perch upon your shoulder," said the elder woman as she pulled her cord.

"Blessed be." Emile reached for the wire feeding into her arm. With a yank, she disconnected.

<c:/grove.exe -terminate>

T.S. Eliot Burns In Hell
GD Dearborn

1.

How often does a man get to meet the goddess that he had worshipped as a young man? Once in a lifetime? *If* he's lucky! What would happen if a man were to bring a dead goddess back to life? He'd become a demigod! Christian knew the score. America loves to see its gods fall, but it loves bringing them back even more. Robert Downey Jr. at the turn of the century? A B-list crack-head who'd already blown one comeback. Now? The idol of millions, sex symbol superstar, a prince of Hollywood, and one helluva nice guy. Little kids had his posters on their bedroom walls. The corn king dies, the corn king is reborn: it's magic!

So if that happened for a superannuated brat-packer, how much more would happen for the great Sara Hazel if she released a new single nearly twenty years after she went missing? What would happen for the man who convinced her to do it? Christian Leonard knew the answers. Soon everyone else would too, as soon as he got off this dirt road and spoke with her.

Sara Hazel had been the queen of the music world back in the day. She'd come out of nowhere and had risen to the top of the charts less than a month after the release of her first single, "Invisible Color." Talent incarnate, she'd written her own songs, had played guitar like Hendrix, and had even painted the cover art for all her five albums. Her vocal style was all her own, but her blues numbers were often compared to Janis's, and her folk rock ballads to Sandy Denny's. No one rocked harder than she.

Sara could have been a fashion model with her long legs, perfect features, and peaches and cream complexion. Her most striking feature, though, was her emerald green eyes. Christian had spent hours staring at them on the covers of her albums and pinup posters.

Christian counted himself lucky that he had been in the audience of her last performance; he could bear witness that she'd never sung better. He'd spent his last dime for front row seats and was rewarded for it when, for just an instant, their eyes had locked. Sara had stared directly into his soul at the moment she sang the high note of his favorite song, "Shadows All Around." It gave him shivers just thinking about it.

Her sudden and unexpected—some said precipitous—exit from stardom shocked the music world. The rumor mill went into overdrive when she walked off the stage mid-song at her last performance. The rest of her tour was postponed, then cancelled. The consensus was that she had burned too brightly and was on hiatus. The quiet aftershock to her fans came years later with the realization that she wasn't coming back. No press releases came from her management after the first week and none of her celebrity friends knew where she was. Her organization declared chapter 11. She was just *gone*, disappeared, whereabouts unknown. Had she gone into hiding? Or was foul play involved? It *wasn't* a hiatus; it was a mystery.

Christian would be the one to crack the mystery, and he'd be the one to bring her back to stardom. The music industry would sing his praises and he'd write the exclusive for *Spin* or *Rolling Stone*. After that, a multi-book deal with a New York publisher. Then, Hollywood. He'd be able to sell his own screenplays, direct his own movies. If that hack Crowe could do it, why not him?

He'd chased his quarry through the years of earning his journalism degree at "Podunk U," his state college alma mater that opened no doors but still dunned him for alumni donations.

Through the years of writing for two-bit mom-and-pop newspapers, glorified weekly shoppers, the walking-dead news outlets of the internet age. Through the years of boring, soul crushing assignments: countless police blotters, school board meetings, and ribbon cuttings. Through the years of self-publishing his poorly selling music zine, and then his poorly viewed music blog. He had planned to take both to the next level and go pro, but neither one earned much money, and thus they perished.

Through it all, nothing he did mattered to him as much as solving the mystery of Sara Hazel's disappearance. On his Obsession Top 40, it was always number one with a bullet. He followed every lead, cataloged every internet rumor, pieced everything together on his bedroom wall with pins and yarn, like a deranged conspiracy theorist trying to link 9/11 to the Campfire Girls. After twenty years of investigation, what did it all mean? Nothing.

He had all but given up. Then yesterday the tip came, out of the blue, that unlocked the mystery. An anonymous note—written in a spidery hand, on pale purple stationary that smelled of violets—revealed all. She was hiding in plain sight, living in a farmhouse in the Vermont Green Mountains region, not far from Brattleboro. The house had passed down for many generations of her birth family, the...?

He drew a blank. Why couldn't he ever remember the family name? Whitely? Wheatley? He'd have to check his notes for the article. Sara had renounced her family and changed her name before she became famous. It had taken him months of research to find it. She refused to talk about her family to the only interviewer that had asked, but she'd implied that they weren't nice people and that they kept to themselves.

An announcement from the GPS broke his reverie. "You have arrived." Christian hoped that the GPS was speaking as an oracle, metaphorically. But its message was also welcome literally; he was thrilled to be off the unpaved, unmarked road, a glorified wagon trail cut out of the dark woods. *Out of the woods.* He hoped that was a metaphor as well, for his expected change of fortune. As he exited the Subaru to meet his destiny, Christian prayed that Sara would be as beautiful as he remembered.

2.

The ancient farmhouse looked like its best days were a century gone. It aspired to ramshackle-ness. He rapped on the screen door. "Hello! Sara Hazel? I'm a journalist and I'd like to talk to you. Is anyone home? HELL-O!" His shouts went unanswered. The door was ajar, the handle missing, and he'd come too far to stop now. Rusty hinges creaked as he pulled the door open and crossed the threshold unbidden.

An overpowering stench staggered him. The house was overrun with cats. The beasts were everywhere; some lolled about, some chased invisible mice, or their own tails, or each other. A dirty, white, Persian kitten rubbed up against his leg and mewled but was driven away by a large Calico. Christian had always thought of cats as being clean animals, but he never would again. Everywhere were piles of cat feces: fresh ones, desiccated old ones, and some in transition. The pheromones of a hundred cats, living and recently dead, mixed together, trying to tell a hundred insane stories that only cats could interpret. The combined odor was nearly, but not quite, masked by the strong, ammonia reek of urine.

It was all he could do to stop his gorge from rising. He remembered a trick a homicide detective had told him over beers, back when he was still trying to break into writing the crime beat. He took two of his cigarettes from their pack and tore off the menthol filters, then stuffed one up each nostril. It felt strange, and didn't do half enough to quell the stench, but at least he could breathe without fighting the urge to vomit.

The few beams of sunlight that forced their way through the layers of grime covering the windows offered the only light. Each ancient pane of glass was thicker at the bottom than at the top. The glass bent the light so that shadows of the cats were cast into caricatures as the felines leapt or sauntered past the windows.

Entranced by the shadow play the cats staged on the far wall, Christian momentarily forgot to watch his step. Something underfoot crunched, crackling as it broke. Startled, he backed away and stared at what he had stepped on. It was a kitten's leg, with a few scraps of fur still, but most of the meat chewed away. It occurred to him that he had not heard a bird within miles of the place, nor seen any small woodland creatures. He looked about the room and saw in the corner a midden of bones, with feline, rodent, and bird skulls represented in abundance. A pitiful screech yanked his attention back towards the door. The Calico had caught the Persian and casually snapped its neck. With horror, Christian realized that the fattest cats in the room preyed on the thinner and weaker ones. They, in turn, feasted on kittens and on the scraps left behind after the fat cats had their fill.

A husky voice startled him from his gruesome epiphany. "Marley? Is that you?" An old woman sat in a rocking chair in the corner, wrapped in shadows, grinning at him. She was far too decrepit to be Sara Hazel. Perhaps it was her grandmother?

Then he saw her eyes. Those impossibly beautiful green eyes, unmistakably Sara's.

He'd imagined thousands of scenarios about how he would finally meet his idol, but he'd never foreseen this. His composure blown, he forgot what he had planned to say. He was reduced to stammering, like an improv player suffering a panic attack on stage, dying in the spotlights.

"Sara… Ms. Hazel? I'm a freelance journalist, I'm Christian… uhh, I mean my name is Christian… I'm a huge fan! I was hoping you'd be willing to give me an interview? Your fans want to know what happened. Uhh.. I mean they want to know what you have been doing with yourself since you retired from the music business."

The woman laughed raucously, clapping in glee. "Of course, of course! Please, sit down. Rest a spell. You must be starving, dearie. What can I offer you? Yes… I will make you a sandwich and tea. BLT? Everyone likes those." Christian heard her bones creak and her joints grind as she got up out of her chair.

Christian's heart sank. Was this crone *really* her? How could it be? He hadn't expected her to look like the fresh-faced girl on his bedroom posters, but he'd assumed that her looks would be better preserved than this.

"Not aged well" would be the most polite euphemism for the ravages the years had wrought on this woman's face and body. Every hair she had left on her head was dirty white. Her nails and eyes were yellowed, as were her remaining teeth. Her crepe-paper skin sagged off her bones, and even her wrinkles had wrinkles.

And yet her eyes, those hypnotically alluring green eyes!

He slumped onto the chair. "I'm fine, thanks. Don't go to any trouble."

"Oh, no trouble at all. Shall I go make it now?"

The thought of eating in this breeding ground for germs brought a fresh taste of vomit to the back of his mouth. "Thanks, really. But, no, I had a big breakfast," he quipped. It came out more sarcastically than wanted.

Her face fell. She sank back down in the Boston Rocker and hung her head, avoiding his gaze. She muttered something that he could not make out. He was sure that his churlishness had offended her, and his mind struggled to find the *bon mot* to fix it.

A large brown and grey tabby jumped on his lap, startling him. "Jesus!" he shrieked.

At this she looked up and stared into his eyes, cackling. "Oh, dearie! Not Jesus! Hee hee! That is Marleybones! He likes you!"

The cat must have rolled in something foul. Even over the background stench, his nose wrinkled from the fresh assault. Christian normally could keep his aversion to germs in check, but suddenly becoming forced furniture for a feline pushed his comfort boundaries to the limit. But to placate his hostess, he forced himself to stroke the cat's matted, smelly fur. He yearned to douse his hands with the small bottle of Purell that he always kept in his pocket and fought the urge to hurl the beast to the floor.

"Marleybones... what an *enchanting* name," he said, with his best manufactured smile. The cat rewarded his stroking with a low purr that hid the threat of a growl, should Christian cease to please.

She nodded her head amicably, his *faux pas* apparently forgiven. "Yes, yes. Marleybones is Number Two. Not the big kahuna, but he keeps the others in line." She flicked her hand in a gesture aimed at a coterie of smaller cats that had gathered in the hallway. "Get'em Marley! How rude! Can you imagine? Staring at our guest! Make them mind their manners!"

Marleybones leapt off Christian's lap and dove into the cluster, scattering them. She cackled and clapped her hands in glee as Marleybones chased after a cat, then quickly changed direction and nipped another. With yowls and screeches, the mob dispersed.

"Don't you pay them any mind Mr. Leonard. They were just curious about you. They meant no disrespect. We don't get many visitors anymore. Now what did you want to ask me?"

Christian smiled awkwardly, relieved that he would get his interview after all. He pulled a micro cassette recorder from his jacket. "Do you mind if I tape this?" Without waiting for a reply he asked "You shocked your fans back in '89 in Boston when you stopped singing in the middle of your number one hit, "The Silver Key," and left the stage without a word. The rest of your tour was cancelled without explanation. Your management refused all requests for interviews, and announced that all tickets would be honored for rescheduled performances which never happened. None of your celebrity friends had the faintest idea where you had gone. You vanished, as if you had dropped off the face of the earth. I simply want to ask you, why? What happened? How could you walk away from your life so quickly and completely?"

"Well, Chris, thank you for asking. But you have to understand something about show business. You have to understand about this business we call *show*. They show you the money, but then they show you the business. And it's really none of their business, no sir. But the money…it's not really about the money, is it dearie? It's about the love. The love of the fans. The fans that I love. The fans who loved me. The fans who wanted *too much* from me. They wanted to take, and take, and take. I took more from them, at first. Yes, all the cheering and the applause, I took it from them. It was a rush! It made me high!

"But then it started, Chris, it started to go south. It was the merch, I know that now: the jewelry, the tee shirts, my designer label clothing line, but most of all, the posters. The damn posters! The kids would gaze at me. I could see them do it. I saw you too, Chris, hee hee! Right through the posters I could see you all! And you wanted *me* so much. It drained me. The cheering at the live shows was great, a charge. But I needed more than that. I needed my get my 'mojo' back.

"My mojo, that's what the black man gave me all right. Not for free! He demanded far too much in return. My soul! But how can you sing if you've got no soul? So what was I to do? What? What else *could* I have done? I signed my name in the book. I made a contract! What would *you* have done? You don't know… No one *knows*…" She rocked faster and faster, keeping tempo with the words that maniacally spilled from her mouth.

"He showed me his book. I read all the words. I learned every line by heart. Because I am a fucking professional, aren't I, dear? A pro knows her lines! I drew the lines. Not in chalk, with my own blood. And I said the words: I said them to the East, I said them to the North, I said them to the West, I said them to the South, the beautiful South! I got the power! But it was no use, it didn't last. My fans...they nearly took it all!

"In my dreams I see him. He's waiting for the day of glory! Not one of them are dead. Not one! Not dead, just asleep... He'll lead them all in. I will make my comeback! He promised me so. I will sing again, for my fans. My fans! But not as the star attraction. No! I am just the opening act..."

As she ranted on, ever faster, Christian shrank into his chair. How could his teenage idol have become this mad, sad hag? She had been larger than life back then, celestial. It wasn't supposed to have gone this way. This wasn't what he wanted!

"But what was I thinking? How rude! Tea! I must make you some tea!" she shrieked.

What should he do? Call social services? No, he couldn't. It would take too long; what if they wanted him to stick around and answer questions, sign papers? The urge to escape was overpowering. The hissing and shrieking of dozens of cats, the nauseating smell...he had to get away from here, right now. "No, really! I don't want any tea!" he shouted. And then softer, "I am— I'm sorry."

He shut off his tape recorder and stood. "This has been...terrific. Thank you so much. I am sure your fans will be thrilled by the news. I've taken too much of your time already. I really must be going. It's been an honor, truly. Thank you. Thanks."

His words fell on deaf ears. The mania of a moment ago had boiled away. The woman in the rocking chair was like a rag doll that had lost its stuffing. Her head sagged down on her chest, oblivious to his presence. She rocked back and forth rapidly, arms across her chest, as if she was trying to hug herself. She had returned to muttering and mumbling under her breath. Christian struggled to make out her words, but it was just blather and nonsense. *Finn gluey muggle-one-naff hulahoo Riley wagon-naggle fit agon.* Meaningless babble.

What a pity! he thought. *An interview with a lost legend would have been my ticket to the major league.* Rolling Stone *would have gobbled it up. But who'd print this mess,* The Weekly World News? *They went out of business years ago. Too bad, she could have shared the front page with Bat Boy! But then again....* He took his camera out from the other pocket of his jacket.

"Mind if I take some pictures? For the fans?"

She didn't seem to hear him, or if she did, she didn't think it worth it to stop her insane muttering. He moved away from his chair to make the best use of the dirty sunlight. The camera automatically filled in with the flash. It tried to dispel the viscid shadows, but could only do so much. Good! It made her look eerie. Not that she needed much help in that department. Her pupils had rolled straight up so her eyes were nothing but bloodshot whites. *I just need to change the spin! "Lost Superstar Now Crazy Cat Lady."*

He paused a moment and considered this. Nice way to pay this woman back for all the good music she once had made, for being the object of his adolescent fantasies. *She ran away from the scene, I should respect that. I should try to get her some help.*

Then he looked at her again; a thin line of drool ran down her chin. Disgusting! He squeezed his eyes shut, trying to banish her from his sight. A sudden flash of anger boiled in his thoughts. *No! The bitch! She did this to herself. She gave up! Maybe she ate too many magic mushrooms, snorted too many lines, or just drank too hard, but she could have gotten help. Time in a celebrity substance abuse resort is a rite of passage in her business. That business we call* show! *She owed her fans more than this...betrayal! This will be my big break after all. She wants to hide, but I'll show her to the world!* His anger ran hot, his face flushing. He wiped his brow on his sleeve, opened his eyes, and noticed that all of the cats in the room had stopped whatever they had been doing and were staring at him. They were still and waiting for...something. They studied him with feline curiosity.

"Dearie? Are you alright? You don't look so well. Maybe you should sit."

He sat. The woman in the chair was perfectly calm now. She smiled at him with her pearly teeth, nearly perfect. A concerned look marked her face, which was mostly smooth, with just crow's feet and laugh lines to gently texture it. No wrinkles. Her hair was almost the way he remembered it in his favorite poster of her— long, red, and luscious—though now streaked with a hint of grey. *Why did I think she was so old? A trick of the light?*

"Now how about that tea?" Dumbly, he nodded his affirmation.

"That's a yes? Cat got your tongue?" She smiled evilly at her own joke. She got up from her chair and patted him gently on the arm. "There there, sweetie. You'll be right as rain again soon. You must have had a terribly long drive. Were the roads bad? I don't drive so much lately." She walked away.

Christian smelled propane and heard the pop of the stove lighting. Sara hummed a tune: bars of her greatest hit, "Dreaming In My House," wafted in from the kitchen. Her song was mellifluous, just as it should be. The words played in his head... *I've waited so long... Under strange stars... But soon they'll be right again... Until then I'm dreaming... Dreaming of you...*

Marleybones and ten of the larger cats crept back into the room while she was singing. Each claimed its favorite place on the floor, forming a circle around Christian. They purred as they watched him. It made Christian recall *The Tailor of Gloucester*, his third grade play at school. He had played a mouse.

She returned, still humming the melody, carrying a tea tray. She set in on a table and poured him a cup. "Lemon? Sorry, no cream... I buy it by the gallon, but it doesn't last long in this house."

"Thank you. That would be fine," he croaked.

She put the teapot down and got a broom, sweeping the floor furiously. Cats scampered away from her as she approached them, then reclaimed their spots in her wake. "I am so very sorry about the mess. You caught me just before spring cleaning. I just can't keep up with all the cats. Most of them are strays. I should get rid of some of them, but my heart couldn't bear it. I just can't say no to a stray. I become attached to them too easily. They are my children."

He nodded again and sipped his tea. He was more of a coffee drinker and could only guess at what he was drinking. It was bitter on the first taste; Earl Grey? *Who was Earl Grey anyways? Tarzan? No, Tarzan was...* Before he could recall, he drained his cup. "Could I have more, please?"

She seemed delighted. "Of course, my love! You must have been parched. Would you like an animal cracker?"

"Yes please." He gratefully accepted his refill, this time with a cookie. He liked cookies. He stared at it. It was a goat. *A black goat?* He munched it greedily. She sat down in her chair and started to rock.

"I do hope you've gotten enough on your tape recorder for your interview. You should come back again soon, I could give you the dirt on everyone. Jagger, Bowie, Jimmy Page, Debbie, Cobain, Alice Cooper, the Ramones... I have enough stories for you to write a book. For ten books! I know that you will be a great writer. You could write for the *New York Times*. Or *Esquire*, or *Rolling Stone*. Or screenplays! That's you, the next Cameron Crowe!" As she spoke she continued to rock rhythmically, back and forth, back and forth.

As he listened, a tear rolled down Christian's cheek. He sprang from his chair, dropping the cup and the saucer. They smashed on the floor. "Yes. Thank you! You understand. Finally, someone gets me. I'd be *honored* to work with you. It's a dream come true."

"Wonderful! I am so happy!" She laughed. She stood up, took a step, and embraced him. He wrapped his own arms around her, returning her embrace. Her chest felt cold, but that made him want to hug her all the more. He gazed into her emerald eyes. Without thinking, he bent his head and kissed her.

She took a step back and took both of his hands in hers. She was beautiful. She looked just as she did on the cover of *Cammie & Cassie*, his favorite album, her first. Skin like fresh cream, long scarlet tresses, big green eyes. She was even wearing the same gauze dress. He knew then that he truly loved her, that he'd always loved her and always would. They were soul mates.

"I know what we must do. Let's start right away. Right now!" She walked over to an oaken chest next to the wall and shooed away a cat that was sitting on its lid.

"Yes. That's terrific. Where do we start?"

"With a blessing! A good luck ritual. And we should sign papers, make our arrangement legal. And then, dearie, you must have me."

Have *her? Oh!*

He paused and tried to think. How could he have been so wrong about her, the goddess of his late teens? This was moving so fast; every one of his dreams, all coming true at once. He thought he should do something, but he couldn't think what.

She stooped to open up the chest and rummaged through it. She pulled out items and set the ones she didn't need on the floor beside the chest. A portable reel-to-reel tape recorder; a long knife; small glass tubes with various dried plants held in a wooden box; an antique cut glass bottle with a rubber bulb spritzer; a black Led Zeppelin concert tee; a violet box of stationary; a hookah... "Ah.

Just where I left them." She scooped up five black tallow candles and a piece of chalk. "Marleybones!" The large tabby re-appeared and once again started chasing the other cats. In short order, the room was cleared of them. She started humming again—a song he did not know this time—and drew a large circle on the floor. Christian watched her, fascinated, rooted to the spot. She drew a star in the circle, and then adorned it with shapes and symbols that he did not know, but feared anyway, like baby chicks fear the shadow of the hawk.

Her artwork finished, she casually slipped out of her dress. He did not resist as she removed his jacket, unbuttoned his shirt, unbuckled his belt. He felt her gaze on his body and then heard her soft sigh. "Well dear, you're no Robert Johnson, but you will do."

She went back to the oaken chest and removed a book, bound in leather, handmade, with another symbol he did not recognize engraved on its front. With it she brought a raven's feather with a sharpened nib and a silver censer filled with aromatic herbs and resins. With one spoken word, smoke emitted from the censer and the candles lit.

Carefully she stepped into the circle, opened the book, and chanted strange words; words he could not understand, words that filled him with dread. *Agak gnarly ho tep. Perfidia Satanicus...* She placed the book, the feather and the censer precisely, and carefully stepped out of the circle again. Sara led him by the hand to the center of the circle, admonishing him to not step on the lines she drew for the sake of his mother's back. He followed her like a child being led by his nanny into a stranger's house, fearful, but eager to please. She bade him to kneel before her.

"For my love, wouldst thou sign this book of thine own free will and agree to its covenants, now and for eternity?"

"I will," slipped from his lips.

"In exchange for thine heart's desire, can thou forevermore pledge thyself to the Black Man, to do his will forevermore?"

"I can."

"To glorify the Old Ones, do thou renounce all claims to your astral essence and give it gladly to Those Who Wait on the Threshold, to do with as they please?"

"I do."

"Then mote it be. Sign the book." She jabbed him on the chest with the quill, but it was so sharp he hardly felt it. She held the book open before him; he saw a list of names, some of them familiar to him. He signed his name below theirs.

She searched for a page and started chanting the words on it, then sang them. The tune sounded familiar, but the words were strange. The melody was the same as the B-side of her 1987 hit single, "Black Cherry Wine." What was the name of that song? It didn't make it to *SeaStarHead*, the '87 album that featured BCW. She bade him with a nod to sing with her. He read the words in the book and followed along. *Sanctus Satanas, infernalis. Niger caprarum in silvis. Mille paries filios. Tres portas amentibus. Delirium Macedo, Callium Hibernia, Digitus Aurum...* In a sudden flash of insight he grasped the significance of the woodcut illustration on the page and stopped singing with a gasp. The things in the picture would haunt his dreams nightly for the next seven years.

Christian's head swam, his senses reeling. The thick incense seeped into his brain. She guided him into a sitting position on the floor and then sat on his lap. Her long copper locks nearly swept the floor. She was a vision, as lovely as the most beautiful virgin that ever captured a unicorn. Her voice was transcendent as a Siren's, and as perilous. She sucked the last droplet from the quill, tasting his blood. She kissed him hard, sharing the blood with him. Sara wrapped her legs around his back and they joined.

The cats returned, all of them, and lined up behind Marleybones. He led the parade around the room until it encircled the lovers. The cats slowly walked widdershins around the circle, tails held high.

A strange music filled the room, but he saw no speakers. Electronica? No, more like violins, or pipes. The cats sung a dirge to accompany it. Their caterwauling was discordant, yet kept with the music. The cacophony would soon drive him mad, he knew. His lover's hips bucked and ground to the rhythmless dirge. Her fingernails raked his back, drawing blood, but he didn't care. A bolus of energy, like an electric charge, was building at the base of his spine. His every nerve sang in resonance to its frequency. "This is nice, isn't it Chris? So much nicer than just by blood!"

The pitch and the tempo of the music built higher and higher. As it did, the feline horde chased around the circle keeping time, racing ever faster, until their chase became a dance. Cats split into pairs, dancing tarantellas that orbited the large circle. They became a blur of black, orange, grey, and brown.

The black candles cast their shadow on the wall. He gazed on them, mesmerized. Christian felt as if invisible entities also watched. It was a pornographic shadow play, meant not for his amusement but for some darker audience.

With fresh horror, a new player entered the stage. Christian saw the shadow of a huge cat, not one of the dancers, but what could only be their chieftain. The shade of the beast moved ever closer to the frenzied shadow lovers. *It walked on two legs.* Christian closed his eyes, dreading to witness the moment when its shadow merged with theirs.

He could hear her chanting again as they writhed and twisted. Her voice, once a beautiful soprano, lowered in pitch until it was octaves lower than a baritone, a throaty growl that would put any Death Metal vocalist to shame. He dared to open his eyes, glancing at the censer behind her left shoulder. It now emitted a dark acrid smoke—the color of a liver ripped from a festering corpse—that would not disperse into the open air. It gathered in a cloud above the censer, becoming denser, until it thickened into a tangible shape. As it coalesced, it formed appendages, a bulbous head, and then, at last, crude facial features: humanoid, but not human.

This final horror was too much to acquiesce. This was all wrong—horrible. What had he done? What else was written in the book and what had he helped escape from it? His mind renounced this wretched phantasmagoria. Repulsion set his will free, and he felt himself again. For the second time today, he knew that his only salvation would be to escape this house at once and flee from his dark goddess and her nubilous master.

They were locked together, like a dog and a bitch in heat. He felt sick. Christian tried to push her off, but he could not budge her. Her claws burnt him now as they dug deep into his sides. "No!" he screamed. "Stop! Let go!"

She started laughing. "Soon, soon! Almost there, dearie." Her laughter devolved into hideous cackling. "All... Most... There... Give me a kiss, lover, and then give it up!" She bent backwards a bit so she could kiss him, and he clearly saw her face. She was a hag after all, decrepit and all-but-toothless. "Pucker up for mama!" She leaned in and moved her hands to his shoulders. He thrust his hands under hers and grabbed her around the throat. His fingers laced around her thin neck, and his thumbs pressed hard upon her larynx. He squeezed as hard as he possibly could. If he could not choke her out, he would snap her neck. The electric charge that gathered at his spine surged into his groin. He never felt so alive, so potent! He knew he was about to get off and the realization filled him with dread.

"No! No! No!" He released the grasp on her throat and shoved her away hard, and thrusted his legs like pistons against the floor, ripping his way out of her. She gasped and fell back on the bare wooden floor. He scooted away from her, as fast as he could. Sara wailed. "No! It's mine! Give me what's mine!"

Christian scurried across the old pine floor, smudging chalk marks and knocking over a candle. The cats shrieked in unison and ran about in all directions, toppling the other candles and upending the censer in their panic. Hot coals spilled across the floor, setting it aflame. Christian found his feet and looked wildly around the room for the exit. He saw the humanoid shape of fog and shadow give him a final look—it almost seemed wistful— and then dissipate into formlessness, mingling with woodsmoke.

Grabbing his pants and jacket, Christian ran out the door. He stumbled over a dozen cats with the same idea. Others caught fire, or choked to death on the smoke and the fumes. Soon the house was ablaze. Christian fished his keys from his jacket pocket. He threw his clothes onto the seat next to his, not taking time to dress until he was safely miles away.

He caught a flash of movement in his rearview mirror as he sped away from the burning house. He tried to tell himself it was a dressmaker's dummy blown clear from a window when the propane tanks exploded. But in his dreams, it was always a black panther smashing through the window with a bundle tucked under its human arm.

3.

The years that followed his escape were good for Christian. He didn't think often about the source of his change in fortune and even less on the events of that day. He had vague feelings that he'd been rewarded for some deed virtuous, heroic even, but his mind wouldn't let him specify what. It was easier to fabricate the notion that his new, rapid success was his rightful due for long years in the trenches of journalism. The recompense that followed was overdue acknowledgement of his vast talents, as a writer and visionary.

He called a cleaning company the minute he'd gotten back to his apartment. He then went to the doctor to get a large splinter removed from his butt cheek, his genitals checked, and the scratches on his back disinfected. He told lies about his injuries. To his ears they sounded weak, but the lies seemed to satisfy the doctor. He spent the night in a hotel. When he returned the next day, his teenage obsession with the pop star was gone, a puff of smoke, along with the mementos on his wall.

Sitting in a booth at a bar six months later, he couldn't remember his forsaken's name. That was the night he'd signed the contract his agent handed him. As they say, hilarity—along with wealth, celebrity friends, and fandom —ensued.

Words came easily. He instinctively knew the right thing to say and writer's block was nonexistent. He made hundreds of new friends and enjoyed a universal reputation for his wit. He collaborated with pop stars and film producers; wrote authorized tell-all biographies that topped the NYT Bestseller list; found success with novels of his own; bought a loyal Rottweiler and lived with it and a series of beautiful young women: on Martha's Vineyard in the summer, in the East Village in the fall and spring, and Laurel Canyon in the winter. His vitality and power, in and out of bed, exceeded even his peak at nineteen. Even the grey at his temples disappeared and his hair grew in thicker. For seven years, his life was a dream. It was worth the nightmares.

4.

Christian was tired from the awards banquet, but it was a good tired. Instead of picking up a young wannabee, he opted for a good night's sleep. As he swiped the keycard through the slot in the door of his hotel room, a thought unbidden echoed in his mind. *You have arrived.*

The last thing he heard was Sara Hazel's cackle as he was torn apart and devoured by sixty-six scorched cats.

Black Forest, Black Heart

Joshua Goudreau

The spring of 1168 was a relatively dry one in the high Rhineland, and that was just as well for Brother Augustus de Parma. Since his exodus began, he had traveled many a spring trail ankle deep in mud making the firm ground a welcome change. He wore his Benedictine robes with the hood up to protect his albino skin from the sun and ward him against the brisk air. Snow still clung to the ground in the deep glens and a frost was common in the mornings but overall, the traveling was comfortable.

He stretched his long legs and moved along at a brisk, comfortable pace. Aside him, the cat trotted silently. The animal had slunk away into the trees when he first broke camp but soon returned to the monk's side. The lanky, black feline was an odd companion, having come to him one day uninvited and simply never departed. The beast had its own agenda, sometimes disappearing for days, but it always returned to accompany Augustus on his journey once more.

The forest was strangely still this morning. He was accustomed to the quiet tranquility of alpine mornings but this one tugged at his subconscious in odd ways. The cat seemed on edge also, occasionally darting forward or scampering into the bushes only to return after a moment as if nothing had occurred.

Augustus paused to take a haul from his water skin and sit on a rock in the sun for a time. The sun had fully risen above the mountains and warmed him. In the valley below, the pitched roofs of a small hamlet puffed smoke into the still morning air. He decided to make his way there but had no suspicion of the horrible, black presence that hung like a shadow over the sleepy, little village.

*　　*　　*

The trail down the hillside was steep but manageable and before long, he passed the waterwheel of a small granary and entered the town. It was a curious and lonely sort of place. The buildings were of typical stone and mud construction with peaked roofs of thatch but the lichen covered stones gave the impression that the homes were hundreds of years old, perhaps even dating to the time of the Romans, though none of it bore the skilled mark of Roman construction or planning.

The folk of the place were few indeed. They stared at him, their dirty faces, each shying away from the albino monk. Astride the town green, a longhouse had its wide doors open to the spring air. The building was a stone and timber affair and was the only building in town without a thatch roof. Smoke rose through holes in the ceiling from a low fire on the hearth and the single room inside was dominated by a sturdy timber table.

To one side a barrel-chested man of middle years swept the soiled hay from the night before. He stopped when Augustus entered and simply stared for a moment. The monk waited for his eyes to adjust and for the man to become accustomed to his peculiar appearance. His pale skin, white hair, pink eyes, and prominent scar on his cheek caused disease in some, though Augustus never took offense.

After his eyes fully adjusted to the dim interior of the longhouse, Augustus turned to the man, smiled, and started toward him. "Guten morgen, friend."

"Hallo," the man said.

"My name is Augustus de Parma of the Order of St. Benedict. It's a pleasure to meet you."

"You Roman?"

"Venetian. And you are?"

"German."

"I meant your name, friend."

"Ah, Heidenricht."

"Well met. And what is this quaint village I find myself in?"

"This hamlet's Schwarzherz. I'm alderman if you have business. You just passing through?"

Augustus felt an unease about the man. He could not exactly say why, but things were not right here.

"I may stay the night."

"You can sleep in the longhouse if you like. We got no supplies fer you though. You'll have to go to Nürtingen for that."

"Aside from use of your well, I am not in need of provisions."

The man simply nodded.

"Might you have a meal for a hungry traveler?"

"Ja, I can get you some bread and mead if you like. We don't have many travelers but prices are cheap."

"That sounds wonderful, thank you."

The man moved toward one end of the longhouse and Augustus settled onto one of the benches alongside of the table. He placed his traveling bag beside him and rested his banded oak walking stick beside him, well within reach. The stout stick was as tall as he was and banded with iron. It served double duty as a quarterstaff and Augustus had made use of it as a weapon on several occasions.

The cat made himself comfortable in Augustus' lap as Heidenricht returned with a plate of bread and a wooden tankard of warm mead. He thanked the alderman, who returned to sweeping the soiled hay and replacing it with fresh straw. As the monk warmed himself with the fire and mead, he closed his eyes and let the pulse of the town speak to him.

A strange presence tugged at his subconscious. Something was rotten in Schwarzherz.

*　　*　　*

Augustus spent most of his day exploring the tiny hamlet and the fields to the east, avoiding the forest that crept to the west edge of town. The townsfolk shunned conversation with him, with the exception of one humble farmer named Bors, who wished to receive the sacrament. Augustus tried to explain to the man that while we was, indeed a man of God, he was not a priest and so did not, by common rule provide such services. When the man failed to understand, Augustus gladly provided him with the comfort of a simple blessing.

As the day slid into evening, Augustus returned to the common longhouse in hopes of mingling with the populace. He had seen nothing outside the ordinary but the general sense of unease persisted. The monk's intangible sense of the presence of evil had never failed him and had in recent months, grown stronger. The cat had left his side, presumably in search of a meal. With the sun sinking low the longhouse filled with many weary peasants, tired after a long day plowing and sowing the fields. Augustus sought out Heidenricht and found the man passing mead, bread, and stew to the gathered folk.

"Ah, monk," he said, "I see you're still about. Have a seat if you'd like a meal."

"Thank you, friend. Your hospitality is welcome."

Augustus sat next to a woman who shied back from him. Across the room, he caught sight of the lanky black cat dart into the room and under the table. Scraps were a favorite of his.

Somewhere in the hills, there came a baying as of wolves. It sent a chill through Augustus as it sounded like no wolf he had ever heard. The entire room went silent, tense, terrified. Near the door, Heidenricht stood watching the darkness of the green. He placed a hand on the wide door and behind it a stout timber leaned against the wall, ready to bar the entrance if necessary.

Augustus tensed. There was trouble about.

Across the green, a light emerged. It was Bors, holding a lantern aloft and running for the longhouse. Only a moment after he broke cover, a great, black form was upon him. Augustus leapt to his feet, his staff in hand, and ran into the darkness.

The lantern fell to the ground. Of the attacker, Augustus could only discern shaggy fur, gnashing teeth, and glowing yellow eyes. It was over so quickly there was nothing Augustus could do. The beast lifted Bors and fled the scene. Lost to the darkness beyond the green.

Nearby a low bass rumble brought Augustus to a stop. On either side of him, he spied two more of the big wolves, growling malicious intent upon him. Behind him, the alderman released a terrified gasp, standing beside the door to the longhouse was still open. The beasts each took a step closer, closing in on the monk.

Deciding to seek safety rather than clash with the terrifying beasts, Augustus broke into a sudden run toward the light. As soon as he passed the threshold, Heidenricht and another man swung the door shut and dropped the bar with practiced precision. A moment later, the door shook as a massive form slammed into the outside threatening to break into the building. The door held.

Augustus stood cautiously listening. The cat was at his side. Its ears and head twitching and twisting about, watching and listening for enemies he knew were nearby. Augustus could feel the wolves circle the building twice before moving away, back into the forest.

With the immediate threat retreated, Augustus turned and surveyed the folk before him. The town boasted maybe three dozen people total, most were present. They were terrified. The state of the town became clear, though he found it curious none of them mentioned wolf attacks when he was about earlier.

He turned to Heidenricht. "Alderman, if I may?"

The man nodded and they moved to the rear of the hall where a small fire warmed a pot of mead. He poured two mugs and handed one to Augustus.

"How long has this been going on?"

"The wolves started just before the thaw. They've taken six folk so far."

"Why has there been no gathering to hunt them?"

Heidenricht shuffled on his feet and looked to the floor.

"There's a darkness that hangs over Schwarzherz."

"That much is clear."

"Them wolves first took gentle Osana, the daughter of Castellan Gerhard. Poor child. The Castellan was here last time Bishop Sigmund came 'round, but ain't been back since."

Augustus looked around the hall. The only sound was the crackling of the hearth fire. Most of the folk had their heads down as if their stew were their only solace. Near the far end of the hall, a group of women clustered and spoke among themselves

"Assemble the town quarter at dawn and we will hunt these beasts."

The alderman shuffled again.

"What is it?"

"They won't enter the forest. That wood is cursed."

Augustus sighed. "Fine. Assemble the quarter for defense and

I'll go after the wolves myself."

"There's only death in that wood."

Of that much, Augustus was well aware.

*   *   *

Augustus took his morning prayers alone as the rest of the townsfolk began to stir from slumber around the hall. By the time he finished, Heidenricht had assembled the quarter and they opened the door. The air was chill and a mist hung close to the ground. The men of the quarter left and returned promptly with spears in hand.

Augustus called the alderman over. He pressed into his hands his traveling bag, tied tightly closed. "Keep this safe, friend. It is of the utmost importance that no one aside from yourself even approach it, and do not open it. It is dangerous to do so."

Heidenricht nodded, a palpable sense of terror about him. The cat looked back and forth between the two men. Augustus gave a slow nod to the animal. It did not seem pacified.

Augustus surveyed the hall once more. The folk were all looking to him. "Stay in the hall. Leave only if necessary. These beasts will die."

One of the women spoke from the back of the hall. "Your god can't protect you out there."

Augustus nodded. "These are not the first beasts I have hunted."

*   *   *

Among the trees, the cat was a mere shadow in the low-clinging mist. Alert, Augustus scanned his surroundings. The tracks of the great beasts were easy to follow despite the morning frost. They had moved briskly and there was no sign of a body dragging through the blanket of crimson leaves.

The beasts were powerful to carry a man so far, and large based on the length of their stride, though not quite as large as they had seemed while cloaked in the shadows of night. Still, the animals were larger than the wolves of this land were commonly known to grow.

As they passed through a stand of evergreens the cat stopped, its tail straight and head forward. Its ears pivoted, scanning the trees about them. Augustus stopped.

Something was upon them.

Augustus took a cautious step forward, hoping to determine the threat's location. The cat broke its pose and darted forward. It was airborne before Augustus even saw the great, black wolf, emerge from the trees. The cat landed squarely on the thing's face. Its rear claws tore long furrows across its eye and snout.

From his peripheral, Augustus saw movement and spun, his staff swinging in a deadly arc. It met the snout of one of the lunging beasts, staggering it sideways. Behind him the third wolf struck, knocking him to the ground.

He rolled onto his back as the beast lunged, its massive jaw snapping for his face. He brought his hands up in time to clutch the things nose and prevent it from sinking those foul teeth into him. He did not see the cat until the wolf reared back, the cat attached to its flank, tearing madly, rending great furrows in its flesh. The monk slammed his fist into the wolf's exposed throat. When it reared back, he saw a wicked scar across the beast's chest.

Augustus did not have time to press his attack. The wolf he had struck with his staff sank its powerful jaw into his shoulder and dragged him away from the other beast. It snapped its head to the side, tearing the monk's shoulder, slamming him back to the forest floor. Blood poured freely from his shoulder and soaked his black robes. The beast with the cat on its flank spun and snapped at the air, unable to catch the vicious feline. The first wolf charged, its left eye reduced to a ragged wound. Through a haze of pain, Augustus saw the beast did not bleed. It lunged toward the cat but the small animal was faster, leaping away as the two wolves collided in a tangle.

In a blink, the wolf with the missing eye was back on its feet, lunged for Augustus, and sunk teeth into his thigh. The two attached wolves pulled away from one another and Augustus screamed at the overwhelming pain.

His vision blurred and grew dark at the edges. Somewhere in the forest came that terrifying baying. The wolves dropped him and became a still as statues. As consciousness faded, Augustus saw the great beasts lope away, disappearing among the trees.

*   *   *

When Augustus' eyes fluttered open, he was face to face with the cat, its nose mere inches from his own. The animal sniffed him and when he stirred, hopped off his chest.

The ravaged monk rolled over, pain coursing through him. Blood soaked his shoulder and leg and he could move neither, though both wounds seemed to have stopped bleeding. Without a close examination, he could not be sure of the extent of his injuries but he was well aware he had hovered very close to death and would be recovering for some time. He dragged himself to a tree and used it to prop himself up and looked about.

A few yards away, the cat was sitting, watching him. Despite the pain, he smiled. The animal had again saved his life. The shadows had grown long and the fog around them had risen, obscuring the more distant trees.

He retrieved his staff from nearby and used it as a support to stand. His right leg was a mass of ragged flesh that could not move nor support his weight. With the use of the staff however, he was able to move away from the tree.

When he seemed able to leave the scene, the cat trotted away and looked back to him. Trusting the animal's judgment, he hobbled after it.

The cat led him deeper into the forest for a time before stopping before a clearing. Augustus spied a dilapidated cottage. Its gabled roof sagged and most of the stonework was covered in thick lichen. The timber door was partially green from moss but seemed stout regardless. The dwelling could not have been less than two hundred years old. There were no lights inside but the ground outside was disturbed, indicating the place was inhabited but currently empty.

Aside him, the cat looked between he and the cabin. Augustus hobbled forward and tried the door to find it unlatched. He limped inside and allowed his eyes to adjust to the gloom. The scene inside however, was not one he expected.

The one room abode sported a dirt floor and rough furniture. In the middle of the room was a great, iron cauldron suspended above a bed of glowing coals. From the roof hung bunches of dried herbs giving the room an unsettling smell.

The cat prowled about the room, sniffing and looking in and under things. Augustus gravitated toward what appeared to be an altar. It was dusty with herbs and speckled with dried wax. In the center of the altar sat a tattered collection of rough paper bound with leather cord, surrounded by various implements of witchery: a silver dagger, balls made of sticks, pen and ink, candles, a brass bowl, and a clay jar bearing an odd symbol perched on a shelf above.

He gingerly inspected the pulpy book. Within were strange symbols and text in a scrawling hand. Much of the book was ancient but some of the writing was much more recent. Augustus could not easily read much of it as it was written in the local dialect of German. The symbols seemed to swim and contort in a maddening dance making Augustus dizzy. He recognized some of them however and could read enough of the writing to see the dreaded name of Shub-Niggurath, the Magna Mater, the Black Goat of the Woods with a Thousand Young.

He shivered.

The monk closed the book and tucked it in a sack found nearby. With his injuries, the sack would make carrying it back to town much easier and the tome was in need of study. He removed the clay jar from the shelf and opened it. He recoiled from the stench that erupted from within and saw three small hearts, worm riddled and decaying in a morass of herbs. Clearly not human, he suspected they were the hearts of wolves.

In the hills, he heard that mad baying again. Not of wolf and not of man. It was the call of something different, a sound that ought not exist on this Earth.

Augustus was in no condition for combat and knew he needed to return to town where he could properly tend to his wounds. More time among these trees would certainly be the death of him. As quickly as they could manage, the monk and the cat left the cottage behind.

*   *   *

Due in large part to his injured state, Augustus did not return to town until after dark, finding a nervous populace. The spearmen arrayed around the longhouse in rigid vigil, but the day seemed to have been uneventful. Heidenricht met him at the door and assisted him to a bedroll near the hearth. Upon lying down, Augustus promptly lost consciousness.

He awoke to the sound of dripping water. A young woman was crouched over him, cleansing the wound on his leg. His shoulder was wrapped in soft cloth. A pungent odor of herbs hung about him.

The woman reached her hand forward and placed it gently on his chest. "Rest now, my friend. You will feel better in the morning."

He placed his head back and was soothed to sleep by the soft purr of the cat.

*   *   *

The next day Augustus awoke about mid-morning. He was stiff and sore but felt surprisingly well. His leg and shoulder ached and were wrapped in moist cloth, but he appeared to have no limitations of movement. The cat still lay next to him.

Near the door, Heidenricht stood speaking to a group of women. The young nurse was among them. These women had been about, near to the administration of town since his arrival. There was something suspect about them. He started toward the group but stopped abruptly when he saw men in heavy armor standing just outside, swords on their hips and halberds in their grasp. The soldiers seemed to be guarding the longhouse but he could not say who they were nor why they were here.

The alderman and the women ceased their conversation when Augustus approached. On the green, he saw three fine coaches. The horses tethered nearby were nosing at the ground though there were no grass shoots to graze upon. A handful of other soldiers milled about the wagons. A green and yellow pennant hung limply from the wagons but Augustus could not see the coat of arms upon it.

Heidenricht was the first to speak. "The Castellan arrived early this morning. He must have ridden through the night."

One of the women, a comely peasant of middle years and auburn hair who seemed to be their leader, spoke up. "He hasn't stepped foot in Schwarzherz since the wolves took his daughter. If you must look at me so, I am Bertrâdis."

"Augustus de Parma, 'tis a pleasure."

The group watched the coaches for a time but there was no movement from within.

"Please fetch my bag, my friend," Augustus said. "I have some reading to do."

Augustus made his way to a bench and sat. Bertrâdis brought

him the old book collected from the cottage even before the alderman returned with the bag.

"You tangle with dark things, monk."

"Of that I am well aware."

Augustus thanked Heidenricht for keeping his bag safe. Heidenricht nervously left before more could be asked of him. The monk watched him, studied the cluster of women at the door, and finally turned his attention to the woman across the table. The cat hopped onto the table and sat nearby. Augustus steepled his fingers in front of him and leaned on his hands.

The curious situation in Schwarzherz was more than wolves and even more than a witch lurking among the deep glades.

"You seem very knowledgeable, my friend."

Bertrâdis leaned forward and locked her eyes on him. "As do you, monk. Let us drop pretences. Why does a Benedictine wander and carry the *Al Azif* with him?"

"You have gone through my possessions."

"I can feel its vile presence."

"This tome has killed greater men than I. It is my burden to bear. How does a peasant woman know of the *Necronomicon?*"

"I am of old blood from these hills."

Augustus nodded. "Tell me about the witch in the forest."

Bertrâdis took a deep breath. "There has long been a shadow over Schwarzherz. She had a name in ancient Gaulish but it has been lost to time. The Romans called her Nigrum Melificus de Silva, the Black Witch of the Wood. It is said she follows the will of things older and darker than man, things with names I will not utter here."

Augustus took a moment to absorb it all. An ancient cult of one. The generations old shadow hanging over the hamlet perfectly explained the palpable fear about the townsfolk. This peasant woman across from him and the others of her group who seemed to have the ear of the alderman and the respect of the townsfolk, were not so easily explained.

"What of the nursemaid?"

"Heske. She is also of old blood."

"As are the rest of your circle, I assume."

Bertrâdis nodded. "You seem strangely calm for a Christian. It is 'suffer not the witch to live' is it not? Or to quote the *Al Azif*, 'happy is the town at night whose witches are all ashes.'"

Augustus took a moment to form his answer. "There are more things in Heaven and Earth than any man may know. Not all are the enemy."

She put a hand on his when he reached for his bag. "I have no desire to be in the presence of that cursed tome if it is opened."

She stood, stroked the cat, and departed. Augustus then carefully removed and unwrapped the beautifully illuminated copy of the cursed tome *Al Azif*, known in Latin as the dread *Necronomicon*. This tome had indeed killed men and terrorized friends. The monk had not yet studied it fully but planned on doing so eventually. He dared only tackle small pieces of the tome at a time as the words and revelations hidden within were dangerous.

He set about correlating the witch's grimoire with the knowledge within his. There was indeed dark knowledge about the thing the witch worshipped. Shub-Niggurath, the Black Goat of the Wood was an ancient entity said to pour through her dark young into the world of men, making way for her eventual return.

The witch learned and recorded many dark rituals in her book. Augustus would not study the runes and formulae too closely as it tugged at his sanity just to skim the contents. One spell caught his attention however, it was a dark rite to gain control of a being by the ritual murder and removal of the heart. A cursed black crystal was then inserted into the creature, warping it and putting it under the witch's control.

The rest of the book was too blasphemous to study in detail. There were black rites of corruption, vile resurrection, and sacrifice. Augustus tossed the ragged tome into the hearth and watched it burn.

After collecting his things and securing his own blasphemous tome back in its wrappings and inside his bag, there was a clamor at the door. Jostling his way inside was a tall and robust man of regal bearing. From his shoulders hung a fine fur cloak and atop his head was a fur trimmed cloth cap, blending almost seamlessly into his bushy, grey beard.

Augustus approached the Castellan. "Hallo m'lord."

The man looked Augustus up and down. "You seem quite well for a man half dead only a few hours ago."

"The tender ministrations of Heske here were quite recuperative."

The man sneered and looked sideways at Heske who simply

shied behind Bertrâdis.

"Hm. Regardless, Schwarzherz is in no need of monks. Report to Bishop Sigmund in Nürtingen for duties."

"I plan to see this business with the wolves resolved before I depart."

"There is no need to concern yourself. My huntsmen and I will slay the beasts on the morrow."

"If it's all the same, I will be staying."

The Castellan scowled. "Have it your way."

With that he turned and staked away. Bertrâdis stepped up beside Augustus, the cat draped in her arms. "Pay him no mind, the man is a pompous blowhard."

"I have learned as much."

*   *   *

The remainder of the day saw the Castellan remain within one of his wagons. His soldiers and green clad huntsmen lingered but made no attempts to interact with the townsfolk. As night closed in the peasants gathered in the longhouse as they had the night before. The soldiers commandeered some of Heidenricht's spiced mead but otherwise left the folk in the longhouse unmolested. Augustus joined them for dinner and led them in prayer. The folk had quickly grown warm to him, glad to have not only a man of God among them, but also a fearless defender looking over them.

The danger that came upon them however, came without warning, no unearthly baying in the hills, no growls in the night, only the terrified screams of the soldiers and the horrible tearing of flesh. Augustus grabbed his staff and bounded for the door. Behind him, the men of the quarter clutched their spears and moved to protect the entrance.

On the green, the Castellan's men had placed a number of standing torches to push back the darkness. In the sputtering light, the great wolves tore through the rank of soldiers. The trained men slashed and stabbed with their halberds but did little except slow the beasts. Only one of the wolves succumbed to the assault and collapsed in a bloodless heap.

Augustus felt a surge of terror and spied a great form moving in the darkness only a moment before it emerged and smashed a mighty fist into the side of one of the wagons, splintering wood and tearing away the wall. The thing stood more than nine feet high when fully erect and while bestial, had the distinct features of a person. She was almost beautiful in her horrific visage. Her legs twisted back like those of an animal and her arms were elongated and ended in wicked clawed fists. Her skin was alabaster and long clumps of ragged fur hung from her hide.

Two of the huntsmen emerged, shooting arrows into the witch's back. She paid them no mind, pulling the struggling form of Castellan Gerhard from the wagon. Augustus could not help but notice unmistakable familial resemblance in her cherubic face and the great, ritual scar across her chest.

The Castellan struggled in her grasp but her fist was tight around his neck and his feet well off the ground. "You are nothing without me."

Her voice was both light and childlike and also deep and feral. She was neither beast nor man but some kind of twisted corruption between the two. "Your control over me ends now."

Before Augustus could move to intervene, her clawed fingers ripped the man's intestines from his ample belly. From his right Augustus saw one of the wolves break through the soldiers and charge him. It was the beast with no eye. He spun his staff and met the wolf head on.

The witch tossed aside the Castellan's dead body, slamming it into a coach with a wet thump. She strode forward but stopped as Bertrâdis, Heske, and the other women of the circle stepped together onto the green, their arms lifted above them. "Ia! Ia! Shub-Niggurauth! Cast away your darkness! Ia!"

In the door, the cat stood poised, its tail whipping angrily behind it. Augustus delivered a powerful blow to the injured wolf and heard the witch scream in an ancient tongue he did not recognize. The circle strode forward continuing their chant of banishment. A nimbus of shadow rose up around the witch as she continued her own chant. Her face curled in a vile and victorious sneer as one of the circle dropped, blood pouring from the woman's nose and ears.

Augustus leapt and brought the staff down on the wolf, satisfied when its skull cracked and the beast collapsed. He scanned the scene, looking for an object he hoped was present. The witch took another step forward and another of the circle dropped. The duel would claim more lives if he didn't act soon.

Among the debris from the demolished wagon he spied a clay pot with a strangely familiar rune carved upon it. A pot just like the one he had inspected within the witch's hut. He ran forward, momentarily brushing the witch's nimbus. He staggered, his head throbbing, but he pushed on as his vision blurred. With a leap, he crushed the jar under his boot and the rotting heart within it.

Behind him, the witch screamed a bellow that was eerily similar to the braying heard among the hills. Sinking to her knees, her skin cracked and split spilling a vile smelling, black ooze from her wounds. With a final, human and child-like whimper, she collapsed into a lifeless heap.

All was quiet as the body of the witch, the last in her line it seemed, sizzled and popped, dissolving into a mound of brackish sludge that then slowly, evaporated into a black smoke which drifted off into the night.

*　　*　　*

Brother Augustus de Parma remained with the folk of Schwarzherz for a fortnight. The shadow over the little hamlet had lifted. He led daily prayers and gave blessings to the people. As a show of respect, the women of the circle even attended his services though they took no blessings. He eventually bid a fond farewell to the simple folk and left the little hamlet behind him.

The Jatinga Effect
Doug Rinaldi

Swirling shapes in her refrigerator's reflective shine grabbed her attention as she walked by; the woman knew something was wrong. An immediate feeling of loss, a parental phantom limb sensation, made her go limp. She swayed, grabbing the countertop for balance and staring into the remnants of the tiny water splashes in the sink. In those minuscule drops she found more trepidation. Though vague in details, maternal instinct rarely lied.

With focus renewed, she plugged the drain and turned the faucet on full blast. Something horrible happened and she needed to know what—immediately. She stared into the maelstrom where the flowing water met the rising pool and muttered in her native tongue.

Less skilled at scrying than her other *daayani* abilities, her power of retrocognition was limited by her devotion to other spells and incantations. Gazing into the running water, images moved fast and clear, creating a more cohesive vision. Performing this advanced witchcraft drained her of considerable energy, yet, she knew—not knew, *felt*—that the direness of this situation would require all of her strength and concentration if it was to work.

* * *

As usual, Edson sleepwalked through his day, start to finish. If it wasn't for the trash compactor inside his skull squeezing his bloodshot baby-blues through his sockets, he would've thought he was in a perpetual dream-state. The fringe of his vision blurred as he gazed at his computer monitor wondering if he *really* needed to finish this report today.

His thoughts drifted to his new habit of sleep driving. It happened again today, becoming all too frequent for his liking. Then he recalled his doctor's visit for his sleep study results. A quality of life disrupting sleep disorder is what she had called it. He called it just another reason to eat a bullet. *Another heaping portion of shitty life, please. And an extra order of I'll just go fuck myself then, too.*

His phone rang, drilling into his skull. Cursing, he scanned the phone's LCD screen but didn't see any numbers, no extension listed. And all the lines appeared to be ringing at once, the red lights flashing like the warning of a runaway train hurtling toward an intersection.

"Hello?" Nothing but a weird digital silence answered back. "Hello? May I help you?" A shrill spike of noise pierced his brain through the ear piece. He yanked the handset away, cringing and confused. *What the fuck!*

"Hello," a faint voice on the other end replied.

Edson put the phone back to his ear and listened for a second before speaking. "Hello? Can I help you?"

"It's all *your* fault." A female with a thick Indian accent spoke. "You *will* pay for what happened to my Anusha." Edson had trouble following, but her intonation was fluent enough to make her point. "She was my morning star and *you* snuffed her out."

"I'm sorry ma'am…." Edson scrambled for his words. "You must be mistaken or have the wrong number. I don't understand what you're talking a—"

The voice cut him off. "You ran her down and left her to die. Prepare yourself, Edson Doherty."

"Excuse me? How do y--?"

Click.

Edson stared at the phone for a few seconds, cockeyed and more confused. "I need a nap," he said, dropping the handset back in the cradle.

His cell phone buzzed, rattling against his keyboard. He snatched it up and flicked open the text app.

ba arlte l! d'dio yhe tho onwd tiviar o'yu t'ra fer?

Edson shook his head, trying to set the sluggish marbles in his skull back into place.

hey dildo! you down for trivia later at the bar?

"That makes much more sense." He grumbled into his hands, rubbing the fuzz from his eyes. "I *really* need a nap."

As if hearing Edson mutter was an invitation to converse, Bogdan poked his head over the shared divider between cubical spaces. In his thick Russian accent he asked, "You observed Celebrity Dance-Off on the television last night, yes?"

He looked up into the fifty-something's brown eyes. "No, Bogdan. I didn't *observed* Celebrity Dance-Off last night." Edson's eyes pleaded for the man to leave him alone.

"That is too bad. It was hash-tag amazing-spheres."

"I think you mean *amaze-balls?*" Edson replied.

Then Edson heard Tim plodding down the carpeted aisle like an elephant. He grumbled again. *Please... keep walking.* Life was unfair.

"Hey fellas!" Tim, over-caffeinated and preferring to go by 'T-Bone', asked enthusiastically, "you catch last night's—*don't say it!*—Celebrity Dance-Off?"

Fuuuuuckkk...

Bogdan's eyes sparkled at his comrade in commercial bullshit. "Yes! It was awesome cream."

Edson sighed. "It's sauce, Bogdan. Awesome *sauce.*" He glowered at Tim. "If you're gonna teach him these obnoxious catch phrases, Tim, can you make sure you teach him right?"

Tim scowled. "Remember, it's T-Bone there, buddy." He tossed Edson a wink and a shot from his finger gun.

"You're literally a special brand of stupid, aren't you, *T-Bone?*"

Tim's face dropped.

"I mean like special order, third-party, mongrel brand stupid you can only find at the Dollar Store."

Insulted, Tim scrunched his forehead. "Well... Your mother!" With that, he stomped away and Edson smiled, throwing his arms over his head in victory.

Yet, he was still beyond exhaustion, feeling it in every fiber, from the tippy-top of his head to the nappy straggles of hair on his big toe knuckles.

Bogdan's square head lingered above the partition. His eyes unblinking, they hovered somewhere between confusion and anger. "Why do you holler at your boy?"

Edson tried blinking the annoying Russian out of his field of vision. "That's... that's not even—*why even bother*—what that... means." Bogdan made a hideous face, contorting his lips into some frightening debutante-duck hybrid before slowly dropping behind the divider as if his noggin was on an invisible elevator.

I'm surrounded by dolts.

He returned to his monitor and grimaced at the spreadsheet screaming at him with all its arbitrary colors and numbers, begging him to finish the calculations. He ran his fingertips over the keyboard and then banged ALT-TAB with burning hate. His FriendFace page filled the monitor screen. "Politics. Politics. Racist. Asshole. Racist asshole. Somebody's cat walked across their keyboard." He went down his news feed, sneering as he read the myriad of pointless comments. "So stupid... blockity, blocky, block-blocked."

As he was about to remove the latest digital "friend" from his account, the image of his boss' face, a pale red brick of a head topped with ginger sprigs of hair, popped up in the bottom corner of his screen. *What now...?*

Nothing but scrambled gibberish filled the instant message window. Edson's eyes burned and the pressure behind his sockets swelled. He squeezed them shut and rocked his head around and then opened them once more.

Come to my office... when you get a chance.

"That's just great on two different levels." Because he knew his exhaustion was possibly making him crazy and a 'when you get a chance' from his boss meant, without a doubt, right this damn second. He stood up and stretched. The fatigue dizzies continued to make his head pound and eyes fill with dancing glitter. When it wore off he marched towards his fate, wondering what he'd done this time.

"Hold down the fort," he said as he passed Bogdan's desk. "I got called to the principal's office." Out of the corner of his eye, he spotted Bogdan thrusting his fist up in the air in a circular motion. "Thanks, Arsenio." Edson wondered what decade Bogdan lived in inside his bulbous head.

On his travels to the wonder-filled office-wing of middle management, Edson passed Veronica's office. The door was open but it was dim inside save for the natural light of the outside world filtering in through the windows. Veronica stood facing the glass, staring out over the parking area. Edson lingered in the doorway for a second and noticed that his coworker was shivering. He peeked his head in—*not cold or anything...maybe there's a draft.*

"Hey, Ronni," he said expecting a response, a vacant head nod in the least. "You cold or something?" Nothing. "Should probably get away from the window then, late spring and all."

She shivered, facing the window and ignoring him.

"Good talk." Edson huffed and continued on his way to the boss' office—but not before noticing a distant fog rolling in over the tree-lined horizon.

Edson arrived right outside the office of douche-master extraordinaire, boss-man Aaron Hill, and paused. He dreaded any interaction with this bane of his working class existence, but he sensed an abnormal amount of horror with this summons—no sense in making it any worse. He stood at the semi-closed office door, frowning as he rapped his knuckles on the window.

"You wanted to see me, boss?"

"Ah, yeah. Eddie." Pecking away at his keyboard, Aaron barely looked up at him. "C'mon in and have a seat." He finally hit the ENTER key and perked up, leaning into his high-back, leather executive chair. "Come, come. Sit."

"If this is about my email to Ops about having a working coffeemaker in the break area," Edson began as he sat in the chair, still feeling uneasy. "I apologize. You don't pay me enough to afford Café Beanery every day. I just *really* need my caffeine." He let loose a tiny chuckle, hoping some levity would break the ice. Then he spotted the large Café Beanery cup on Aaron's desk....

Aaron politely half-smiled, his way of saying 'shut it down'. "Actually... I asked you in here today because..."

Edson's jaw dropped, his eyes widening. On the opposite side of the building now, the fog he saw earlier from Veronica's window was creeping towards the office complex from this direction as well. It left him awestruck and he had no idea why—it just felt...off. Ominous.

Seeing Edson's face, Aaron followed his gaze out the window behind him to the low hanging clouds filling up the landscape. "It's just a fog bank, Eddie. You know, the collection of water droplets suspended in the atmosphere near the earth's surface?"

But Edson wasn't listening. His eyes were locked onto the incoming mist which darkened by the second. He realized he was gripping the armrests too tightly when he swore he felt the building vibrate and the windows shimmy.

"Eddie…." Aaron didn't seem to notice and grew annoyed. "Back to business. We have important stuff to talk—"

"Boss. Look." Edson raised a pointing finger to the window. Aaron just glared. "Jesus! Would you just fucking look?"

As Aaron turned around, Edson climbed from the chair and backed up to the doorway, half in the office and half in the hallway. "Why are you being so diffic…?" Aaron's words dropped off as he saw the darkening fog thicken. Within the gray haze, organic things moved making the mist look alive. "What the… hell…?"

They weren't the only ones in the office witnessing the event. Everyone was up and looking outside, but what really bothered Edson, what made his blood freeze in his veins, was the that all his female coworkers appeared dazed or entranced, shivering—or *are they vibrating?*—just like Veronica was when he walked by her office.

"Boss," Edson called. "I think you need to come out here."

Aaron stood, placing his hands on the glass, mesmerized by what he was witnessing. "Do you *see* this? What on earth…?"

"Aaron!"

"What?"

"Something's wrong!"

Aaron tore away from the window and walked towards Edson. "No shit. Ya think?"

The floor resonated and for a moment everything seemed to pulsate. Edson's ears popped and his vision blurred in unison with the shallow vibrations passing through his feet and up into his core. Aaron braced himself against his chair as a wave of nausea rolled his stomach. A quick glance into the main office alerted Edson to the same phenomenon affecting all the males. Yet, the women remained in their awkward trance-like state, rippling like rung bells.

"They look like they're phase shifting. Or changing frequencies or some shit," Aaron said, sticking his head through the doorway. "Just like on *Star Trek*!" Bogdan came around the corner, his eyes glued to the window at the end of the hall.

"Bogdan! What's going on out there?" asked Edson. "What's wrong with them?"

"I don't know, but—how do you say—fans are about to spray out the shit."

Even before Bogdan had nodded to the window for them to

look, Edson already knew many shits were about to spray. The sky blackened, casting erratic shadows inside the office and dimming everything despite the overhead fluorescents.

"What *is* that noise?" Aaron had to raise his voice over the incessant droning emanating from the fog bank.

The murkiness in the whole office deepened. Something pelted the windows and building, pinging off it in patternless intervals. The sound echoed on all sides, some sounding stronger than the others, little tectonic percussions rattling the structure.

Edson peered out the window in Aaron's office. "Are you fucking *kidding* me?"

Out of the fog, swarms of bugs—mere specks at first—rocketed toward the windows. Splat after splat, bugs of all shapes and sizes flew into the glass like insectoid Kamikaze pilots. Edson almost laughed aloud. *What's the last thing that goes through a bug's mind when it hits a windshield?* "Its asshole," mumbled Edson, his mind floundering.

Within the span of minutes, their suicidal onslaught against the office building smeared the windows in grotesque shades of greens and yellows and purples. Aaron gawked as well, shaking his head and shrugging his shoulders with a complete inability to respond to the situation. Behind the furious swarms an even darker collection of swirling blackness barreled out of the mist still crawling toward the complex.

From across the office, Bogdan shouted, "Birds!"

Aaron moved closer to the window because he didn't believe his ears *or* his eyes. The birds flew so fast that he couldn't identify them. In an endless frenzy of feathers, they crashed head first into the building on all sides, shaking the inner walls. Beaks smashed into windows, causing the glass to spider-web near the point of shattering. In some spots, their beaks broke through, but the birds were oddly silent until they plummeted to the ground.

"Christ, Aaron! Get away from the window!" Edson shouted.

"Holy shit," Idiot Aaron blurted, his face pressed against the window, straining to see the ground. "C'mere, you gotta see this. If they're not breakin' their necks the first try, they friggin' get up and try again!"

The more birds and bugs that flew out of the fog and into the building, the colder Edson's blood grew. The silent bombardment of the birds was what terrified him the most. Not a squeak or a squawk—just the thuds and the crackling sound of the windows giving way. And the finality of thousands of tiny snapping necks.

Another beak penetrated the window, almost stabbing Aaron in the eye as he gaped at the chaotic world outside. "Whoa, shit!" He jumped back a foot and turned to Edson who stared at him with disbelief and disgust. "That was clo—"

The window shattered. A shockwave of transparent daggers shot inward, ripping into the side of Aaron's face before he could cover up. As he squealed in pain, birds flooded in—black and brown streaks of avian death-wish—crashing headfirst into the walls, the furniture…and Aaron. He dropped to his knees in futile defense as the birds continuously struck him, gouging and stabbing with their beaks.

Edson stood frozen, his blood finally going full glacial. Before he could snap out of it, a strong arm shoved him from the threshold and slammed Aaron's door shut before any more birds could escape into the office proper. "The birds are very angry today," said Edson's Russian savior.

Angry, possessed, or what have you, it didn't matter; neither could divert their eyes as Mother Nature ran amuck on their boss. Yet, as far as Edson could tell, Aaron wasn't the target of their fury. Even though the birds' pummeled him, shredding his flesh during his vain efforts to wave them off, their trajectory seemed aimed at Edson. Thud after thud, hitting the wall and door at maximum velocity, the birds exploded upon impact, filling up the office with an eruption of feathers like some hellish pillow fight gone wrong.

With the bird tornado situation igniting his nerves near the point of spontaneous combustion, it dawned on Edson that he hadn't heard a peep from his female coworkers. In fact, he didn't hear or see *any* of his colleagues. All that registered was the sickening cacophony of bug and bird versus brick.

"We must hide." Bogdan's abrasive voice bore into Edson's head.

"Hide?" Edson blurted. "Where? Where exactly would you like to go?" Edson didn't mean to take his frustration and fear out on Bogdan. After all, the man did just save him from becoming an avian pincushion. "I'm sorry, man. Between this bullshit and my eyes just wanting to close, I've just about had it."

The building was totally engulfed in the thick fog. "I understand, but this is very bad news, my friend." Bogdan paused and listened. "The birds are no more hitting the building."

"That's good news, though. Right?" Edson looked around. "Where the hell is everybody?" He was about to call out when Bogdan slapped a meaty hand over his mouth and swiftly pushed him into an alcove between offices. The Russian gave him the international hand signal for "shut the fuck up" which only confused and angered Edson more. He peeled Bogdan's hand away. "What the hell, dude? Even if I swung that way—"

"Please, shut up."

Edson zipped it; the intent in Bogdan's eyes drove the point home. Something moved down the hall in the center office space. Bogdan peeked around the corner after letting go of Edson's shirt. "No more angry birds," Bogdan whispered. "Angry womans."

Edson recalled the disturbing vibrating thing all the office girls were doing during the bird-storm. "Are they… you know. Still all?" asked Edson, mimicking their jerky movements.

Bogdan snuck another look and bounced right back into the alcove, smushing Edson into the door handle. "Yes. And walking like they have the poop in their pants."

Edson sucked in from the pain of the handle jabbing his side. "We need to get out of here." He jiggled the supply closet's handle. "Shit! Locked!" The noise echoed through the office, but a weird humming sound filled the void, getting louder—or closer—every second.

"Oh no!" Bogdan grabbed Edson's arm and dragged him out of the alcove and into the corridor. "We need to go now."

All the noise Edson had made caused the women to organize and zero in on their target. Edson had no choice but to follow Bogdan, who was dragging him down the hall and away from the twitchy women. Retreating, he managed to glance back at them. Each one was indistinguishable from the next except for the piercing glow of silver eyes that fixated on Edson, despite their undulating bodies. As the two turned a corner, trying their damnedest not to step on any of the bird carcasses littering the floor, Edson swore he heard them utter his name.

The boom of the door smashing open mattered little to Bogdan as he pulled Edson into the stairwell. Edson peered over the railing to the lower floors. A strange grayness swirled below them accompanied by some otherworldly magnetic resonance.

Bogdan took a peek as well. "Going down is not option. We

must go up."

"But what if we get trapped up there?"

"Good point," Bogdan said as he eyed the upper floors. "But nothing good will be down there to greet us I am certain."

"Point. Counterpoint."

The Russian yanked on Edson's arm again. "We must go up and hide. Find a place to collect thoughts and make strategy."

They bolted up the flights of stairs trying every door on every landing until one opened. Once through, Bogdan grabbed a nearby folding chair and braced it against the door handle for whatever security it could offer. Even through the steel door they could hear the whirring sound funneling up the stairwell.

As they gathered their bearings, they realized they were on the unfinished floor of the office building. An outside company had leased the floor but ran out of funds and now the whole space stood in unfinished disarray. Through the hanging plastic sheets they found the one finished room complete with a door that locked. The only problem was that it was a tight fit full of building supplies, let alone that it was the most obvious place to hide amidst the chaos. Regardless, they barricaded themselves in before slumping to the floor, exhausted and terrified.

"What the hell is going on?" said Edson, catching his breath. "I mean, I can't be going any more insane than I already am because you're seeing this shit, too." He felt like crying he was so tired, but being on the verge of hyperventilating kept the tear valves shut. Instead, he balled up his fists and pressed them into his clenched eyelids. "What in the holy fuck?"

"Jatinga," muttered Bogdan.

"G'bless you?"

Bogdan rolled his eyes. "No sneeze. Jatinga."

"Thanks. Cleared that right up."

"In 1971, my Uncle Arcadi was in Soviet Army during India-Pakistan War. His troop was stationed in Indian state of Assam near small village called Jatinga."

"That's great, but this is *the* worst time for war stories, dude."

"I have point to make if you would keep your mouth silent," Bogdan snapped. Edson huffed, but zipped his lips. "He told me of a strange, um…" He struggled for the word. "In Russian we say 'yavleniye', like something odd you can't explain, like UFO or Bermuda Triangle."

"A phenomenon?"

Bogdan's eyes lit up. "Da! Exactly." As he shifted closer to Edson, the Russian looked like a crazed man telling a campfire tale in the weak light from the overhead construction lamp. "One night, he was at his camp inside his tent. It was monsoon season and the troop was frightened of being swept away by floods. When weather cleared, he heard odd sound coming from village. He called it "a magnetic vibration." All of a sudden hundreds of birds started flying straight into the ground and into all the homes and buildings in the village, knocking out lights and hitting people—killing some."

"Sounds familiar," Edson said.

"Uncle Arcadi said scientists blamed it on atmospheric conditions and heavy fog confusing birds, but he said villagers knew better. Evil spirits in sky controlling the birds to do their bidding... an endless battle of witches—*daayans* they call them— and their covens that'd been raging for years and years for control of the villagers' souls. White magic versus black."

Edson rubbed his temples. *Yeah, okay. Witchcraft. Why not?* "Jesus...."

"Exactly. Jatinga."

Bogdan returned to his history lesson, but Edson no longer listened, the words fading to a dull mumbling in his ears. All he could think about was that phone call.

It's all your fault. You ran her down and left her to die. Prepare yourself, Edson Doherty.

He buried his face in his palms.

You snuffed her out

"No!"

You will pay

"I didn't do anything wrong!"

Prepare yourself

Edson smacked his head desperately trying to rid his mind of the voice.

You ran her down... left her to die

His eyes popped open, but not from the pressure on his temples. From recollection.

You ran her down

Ran her down

He shook his head. "No... can't be..." Mental images of his

car hitting a bump, the icy sweat from snapping awake while driving, his hands gripping the steering wheel assaulted his mind's eye.

Prepare yourself

Edson Doherty

The image of rain making it hard to see; the blood and chunks of hair and scalp washed away by that rain. No evidence, no crime. Snuffed out. Just like that....

Edson... Doherty...

He was shaking. A deep voice shouted in the distance.

Edson

The shaking wouldn't stop.

"Edson!" Bogdan gripped his shoulders and shook him. "Snap out of it.

Glossy eyed, Edson looked up at him. "It's my fault."

Bogdan glanced over his shoulder at the barricaded door. "I believe they found us."

"All my fault."

Again, Bogdan yanked on Edson's arm to get him moving, but Edson wouldn't budge. "Nonsense, my friend. But we must now go."

"I thought it was just the curb or a pothole." Edson's eyes welled up. "I was so tired. Only closed them for a second. One second!"

Bogdan finally got Edson to his feet and pulled him towards the exit. "You can tell me all about it later, but for now we must go!"

Edson jerked his arm back. "You don't get it, you big retard. The phone call, the birds. She said *I* killed Anusha." He began to shake, tears streaming down his cheeks. "I fell asleep driving and ran over her daughter!"

"Oh." Bogdan's face went slack. "Well, you made real bad fuck up then." The Russian's face turned cold and he scowled. "You have a curse on you! And you have taken me downtown with you."

"I know. I'm sorry. It was just an accident."

Bogdan huffed. "Sorry...? *Pizda ti jopoglazaya!*"

* * *

The woman walked through the fog; it seem to part for her as she neared the offices. Higher in the sky, well above the building, the sunlight struggled to pierce the dense clouds hanging over the area. The grayness swirled with each step as she traversed the field of dead birds, crunching the shells of dead bugs under her feet.

She rolled three smooth, tumbled stones between the fingers of her left hand while clasping onto the ornate amulet around her neck with the other. Her lips moved, working the chant she barely knew and had hoped she'd never have to speak. Though her words were inaudible, the magnetic resonance fluctuated with her intended inflection.

Layers of leaves, feathers, and fallen insects flittered away on a ghostly breeze. She looked up, mesmerized by the sound waves that only she could see swirling around the building. The magnitude of the spell she had cast to exact her vengeance on her daughter's killer left her not only stunned, but more importantly despotic.

"Edson Doherty!" she finally shouted, her voice ricocheting off the fog until joining with the funnel of magnetic interference. "I know you're still in there… alive. Have you made your peace?"

Enthralled by the terrifying power she never thought possible to harness, but now felt coursing through her, she twirled the smooth stones in her hand until they rose from her palm. All around her, the fog joined the churning magic and grief emanating from the center of her soul. She quivered, her whole body blinking in and out of focus.

And then the three smooth stones shot from her palm into the building.

* * *

"You hear that?"

The Russian nodded. "Of course I heard that."

Edson paced. "She knows I'm still in here. She knows who I am and what I did." Fear and guilt painted his face, his cheeks burning with shame. "I'm dead… and she's gonna kill me."

Edson's voice echoed onto itself in the closed quarters of the unfinished room. His words melded into each other forming nothing more than incoherent gibbering. The fullness of the sounds pushed on their ears as if they were rising to the surface from a great depth.

As the structures around them vibrated to the point of

blurriness, Bogdan grabbed Edson. "We must escape," he mouthed. "Now!"

Edson allowed himself to be pulled and guided, letting Bogdan act as momma bear protecting her young. Through fading mental faculties and crippling exhaustion, his adrenaline dump cramped his brain. All around, exposed metal studs rang like tuning forks, shaking dust throughout the abandoned work zone.

Edson Doherty

The syrupy tone of the voice rumbled as the words crawled closer. Around one corner was possible escape. Around the other—perpetual madness and unknown doom. Surely, for them both now. Edson felt terrible for unintentionally involving Bogdan, let alone the uncounted number of employees who most likely fell prey to some form of the witch's vengeance. Beleaguered, he succumbed to his pitiful uselessness, content with solely relying on Bogdan's strength and will.

Edson... Doherty...

The voice got closer.

Killed my Morningstar...

They were right around the corner... coming for them.

Vengeance is mine...

A hand breached the turn, gripping it until the whole wall trembled along with it. From the shadowed corridor a pulsing group of shapes appeared. Barely recognizable as the women from his office, he swallowed hard when he realized the lead writhing mass was most likely Veronica.

"Ronni?" he said. "Please, no. What's happening?" The shambling figures lurched forward, each individually weaving in and out of the one closest until almost forming one congealed voltaic mess.

"Stop! You don't have to do this," Edson begged as Bogdan ran to check around the far corner for safety or escape. For all his insight and perceived strength and bravery, Edson knew Bogdan was just as terrified. The formless thing continued forward, shifting in spectrums like television interference. "*Please...* I'm a good person. Tell her I'm *sorry.*"

Bogdan's scream split the air loud enough to cut through the electric din of the witch's messengers. The scream faded fast, ending with a cracking thud. When he allow himself to tear his eyes away from what was in front of him, tore down the hall, almost meeting the same doom as Bogdan who had fallen through the floor and into the office below.

Edson grabbed an exposed beam just in time. While the height was not that great, Bogdan's size and weight contributed to the force of the impact, splitting his skull open and twisting his neck so that his dead eyes stared at the backs of his legs. Edson's body shook from fear and nausea.

As much effort that it took for him to look away from the nebulous mass of static, the effort it took to return his gaze was overwhelming. "I'm begging you," he said between snorts of wet snot. "I'm sorry! Tell her!"

"Tell me yourself...."

Three stones rocketed out of the center of the spectral flux, sending the bodies rippling in fluid diverging circles. In succession, they slammed into Edson's shoulders and abdomen, propelling his body backwards and pinning him to the wall. Struggling did little as he watched a form step out from the chaos. The mass of bodies violently flickered before separating and each falling lifeless to the floor, around the witch.

As she stepped out of the ring of bodies, she looked just as mortified as Edson assumed he must. Yet, he detected a spark in her eyes—not only one of genuine surprise at what just happened but a glimpse of madness he knew meant nothing good. Her eyes became an afterthought as the dull drill bit sensation of the three stones pushing into his flesh set his nerves on fire.

"Tell me *how* sorry you are!" Her voice boomed.

Edson grimaced through the hot pain crushing his body and his vision sparkled, the salty taste of tears in his mouth. He knew he was speaking, mumbling more useless apologizes to the woman stalking closer to him, but he heard nothing, just felt his jaw moving soundlessly.

The woman released the amulet and the stones released their pressure, rushing back to her palm but sending Edson slumping to the floor. She smiled, pleased with herself in ways she never imagined. Why had she never pursued this path of her gift? Why had she always stuck to the *white ways* of her family's coven despite their meager place amongst families darker and more powerful? Now with the thrilling ache of untapped potential and authority, she would exact vengeance and walk towards legend amidst the great mystics of her culture.

Once to his knees Edson fought for focus. Even with all her flickering pawns now motionless behind her the magnetic whirling didn't dissipate, as if she was the source of it all. He watched the three stones spin in her hand as she gripped her amulet again and grinned. That maniacal expression made him feel weak and pathetic.

"I said tell me!"

Edson jerked. "Yesyesyes! I'm so-so… sorry. You have no idea." If he could've pushed himself inside the wall behind him just to get farther away he would have. "I swear, if I could swi—"

"Don't you *dare* say you'd switch places with her." One of the stones shot from her hand into his stomach, knocking him back down and windless.

Through his violent coughing fit, Edson heard her mocking him, ranting about the beautiful life he had taken from this world. Edson noticed a small hunk of two-by-four behind his feet, and reached for it. He was careful not to alert Anusha's mother, fumbling, refusing to take his eyes off her while he formulated his feeble plan.

The woman chanted louder now, the harsh tongue of her native dialect accentuating the key phrasings. As the stones swirled in her hand and a gray mist wafted behind her, she clenched the talisman. Her cadence and volume increased, rising over the static din. Edson finally had a sure grip on the hunk of wood and waited for the perfect time to strike.

Her sneer faltered mid-chant and for a fleeting moment Edson spotted panic and uncertainty in her face. The words—or her memory—failed her and the smooth stones slowed their rotation, wobbling and clanking together. Edson, not squandering the moment, launched the block, side-arming it with all his might.

Lost in her confusion as she struggled with the phrases, the witch couldn't avoid getting clobbered. The chunk struck the hand clutching the talisman, gouging her skin and cracking the charm in half. She roared as the pieces fell and broke into even smaller shards of crystal.

Edson dared not move. He stared, waiting for her reaction and wondered if he just made things worse. The whirring sound and foggy mist intertwined, thumping and contorting the air into a living thing, hemorrhaging from every fracture in the building. The air turned thick and Edson felt as if he was stuck in quicksand.

The building shook, rattling worse than it ever had. A staticky boom filled Edson's ears, covering the whole Earth with its deafening howl for all he knew. His skin tingled and all his body hair stood at attention; more waves of nausea seized his innards. He covered his ears, hoping his drums wouldn't pop, as he balanced against the wall.

Frantic, the woman dropped to her knees, ranting through her tears as she tried to scoop up what remained of her talisman. In her rancor she seemed oblivious to or unfazed by the surrounding calamity—including her wounded hand—and failed to notice how her blood sizzled and seeped into the dirty, uncarpeted floor.

Edson swiveled as he searched for an escape route. To his left was the deathtrap that took Bogdan and to his right was a pile of construction material concealing a fire door.

"Shit! Shit! Shit!" he shouted, barely noticing the background noise diminishing, becoming more of an intermittent zapping or revving sound. He turned back to the witch and her current state of confused despair. She was mumbling, declaring that she spoke the spell correctly as she played with the puzzle pieces that were her amulet.

The only way out is through her….

Edson skidded to a stop.

Despite the uncertainty he saw in the witch's face, she still held a rage in the glowing embers of her eyes. Edson knew nothing about witches or spellcraft. Hell! He was dumbfounded such insanity actually existed. But he felt certain something was amiss— he knew the look, no matter how brief, of terrified bewilderment well enough to tell she had fucked something up.

Enraged, she stood before him screaming her infernal words. In each hand were the two biggest halves of the bloodied talisman, and as she pushed them together against their magnetic resistance light erupted from the space in between.

He saw movement behind her through a curtain of sparks. His coworkers' bodies (or what had become of them) were gone. No corporeal traces remained. Some clothing, some hair and stains—as if they had dissolved into the floor becoming one with the structure.

Their surroundings took on that disorienting in-between television stations sensation again. As everything pulsated, the two halves of the witch's amulet sucked together and disappeared into an orb of blackness, dark unlike anything either had ever witnessed before. It hovered between them emitting a hot wind before imploding in on itself into exquisite brightness. Then a horrible rumble like that of a detonation tore open the floor beneath them, giving way to a jagged hole through the center of the building.

The woman plummeted into the breach but snagged her shirt on a sharp beam, managing to grab hold before falling deeper. Edson dropped to his stomach as the building around him swayed and shimmered. Perhaps out of guilt—or instinct—he reached down into the pit to help her.

"Grab my hand!" He shouted over the noise, anchoring his foot against some fallen beams. "Please! I'll help you!"

The orb-light intensified. Murmurs whispered from nowhere and everywhere at once, indecipherable to his ears, bouncing off the trembling walls.

"C'mon! Stretch!"

She strained to hoist herself up higher, her lips quivering and eyes full of fear.

"You can make it!"

The light brightened.

The voices coalesced, mimicking the light's growing potency.

Their hands finally touched, fingers interlacing at their tips. "I got you." The building rattled almost breaking his weak grasp on her. He was having trouble seeing her now as his eyes would no longer adjust to the increasing brightness. "Hang on!"

In an instant, the blinding whiteness shifted in color, turning red then blue then back again. Oscillating. Strobing. A stiffness overtook his body and his hand seized, releasing his tenuous grip on her fingers. Yet, he didn't hear her fall or scream... just a distant wailing. As the light pulsated—red blue red blue—he felt nothing but pain in every part of his body, tasted blood trickling down his throat. He tried to cry out but nothing happened; he felt asphyxiated.

Hang on buddy... We'll get you out of there...

He heard the other voices more clearly now, panicked with a sense of urgency. And the wailing grew louder. A woman crying, shrieking in a foreign language he didn't understand. As the white light faded, pain sharpened his vision and the scene came into view almost triggering an anxiety attack. And with his difficulty breathing, he was on the verge of going into shock.

He was in his car. The front of it had hugged a tree; steam hissed and smoke wafted from the engine block. Blood—his blood—smeared all over the steering column and dashboard. The radio was spitting out nothing but weird static and fuzzy squawks and buzzes. Surrounding him were multiple emergency vehicles all with their lights blazing—red blue red blue. A paramedic was standing by as the firemen pried open the door.

"Hang on. You're gonna be okay."

He was fighting for words, something to say—to ask—about what had happened, but the howls of sadness gave him pause. In the dangling rearview mirror he saw a woman kneeling over a white sheet steeped in red. She held a bloodied hand in hers as she screamed the dead one's name.

The firemen had to tear the door off its hinges before the medic could wrap a collar around Edson's neck. Then they gingerly pulled him out of his driver's seat. Though he was able to stand on wobbly legs, his knees buckled and he vomited all over the orange spine board waiting for him on the sidewalk. The rescue workers did their best to calm him down, assuring him it was okay as they called for the other paramedic to bring the gurney.

Edson looked back to the crying woman. The swirling lights danced off something crystalline hanging around her neck. Everything slowed to a crawl. She looked up from her dead daughter's body to Edson with laser focused anger and contempt assaulting him like a physical blow.

"No, no, n—no. This can't be happening!"

"Calm down, sir," said the paramedic holding him up. "We need to get you to the hospital."

"It's… It's her…" Edson shook his head and started shivering. "No!" he repeated, getting louder each time until he was yanking himself out of the medic's grip. "It was a fucking accident!"

You bitch!

Edson shoved the medic sending him tripping over the stretcher. Despite injuries, he snatched the fireman's Halligan bar leaning against his car before anyone could react. Gripped tight with the axe blade on the business end of the tool shimmering in the police lights, Edson snarled and took off running towards the woman and her talisman…determined to get to her first this time.

The Place of Bones
Barry Lee Dejasu

When the conversations began to die around the campfire, I suggested that we tell ghost stories.

"*And*," said Kenta, a history sophomore, "I think *you* should tell the first one, Margaret."

There were a couple of throaty approvals from around the fire; I'd expected nothing less.

Several days ago, Kenta had come to the school library and told me that he and some friends were gathering for a woodland party. He was quick to emphasize that no alcohol would be present and that I was welcome to join them. I suspected he wanted me along because of my penchant for local folklore, but it had been quite some time since I'd had a chance to socialize with anyone; so I told him that I would be honored to be his party's token hippie lady.

We'd met at dusk at the base of a long trail that led from the dorms, then walked around the base of the nearest mountain, until we were nearly a mile into perfect isolation. I must've seemed like a complete kook when I met Kenta's friends, including a girl he'd met in town who'd introduced herself as Sharon; I stammered a lot, and had to excuse myself as they started the fire, claiming to feel a little dizzy. I'd retreated along the path and stared into the woods for a few minutes, fighting back tears as memories came to me, memories that I'd not thought about in almost thirty years, as overgrown and shadowed as the forest around me.

Those dark and painful memories had haunted me all evening.

"Well," I said, standing and grabbing a log from the pile to shove into the fire. "I *do* have a story that I could tell, but I'm not sure everyone would appreciate it."

"Well, *I* have a good one," Sharon said.

I turned as flames leapt out to taste their fodder, and saw her round, pale face beaming in their orange glow.

Earlier, Sharon had said she was a dropout; she'd claimed that her love of the land had been more than enough of a reason to stay, even when her education had come to a grinding halt for reasons that she hadn't divulged. I'd kept an eye on her, wondering at times how she felt being among students who were doing what she was not; although she'd laughed at the occasional joke or tale of misadventure, she'd mainly kept to herself all evening—until now.

Sharon turned, the corners of her mouth twitching upward in a controlled grin. "Any of you ever hear of the Bone Witch?"

Jake and his girlfriend Sophia snickered at the name.

Kenta asked if Sharon was referring to a video game character, but she shrugged. "I wouldn't know," she said.

Then she glanced at me, and I shook my head. I was actually *very* familiar with this story and curious to hear her take on it.

She grinned, throwing her long, blonde hair back over her shoulder, and I caught a glimpse of glistening metal—a pretty, gold necklace, half-hidden by the top of her shirt, which I stared at as she began.

"This is a ghost story from a long time ago," she started. "There's supposed to be a strange figure that haunts the woods throughout this area, from Stamford on up through Manchester, and even some places out by Hoosick. People have claimed to see a woman in the woods, watching them from between trees and in caves.

"There's been different versions of her over the years. Nobody really knows when or how it all started, but since the late 1600s, every thirty years or so, people go missing. Sometimes individuals, sometimes groups."

"The Vermont Triangle," I muttered.

Sharon turned to me, looking a little annoyed at the interruption. "Yeah."

"The what?" Kenta asked.

"Back in the mid-'40s," I said, blinking hard at a sting in my eyes, "at least six people disappeared in this area. It's how the Vermont State Police got started."

"That's right," Sharon said.

"Oh shit..." Jake's eyes widened as he whispered, "Weren't there two hikers who vanished over in Bennington recently?"

Sharon grinned at this. "Told you it was a ghost story."

Everyone fell silent, and she continued.

"Every once in a while, hunters and hikers sometimes find little *objects* in the woods...like this." She removed what looked like a pale, uneven star from her jacket pocket. She offered it to me, and I took it, frowning—then almost dropped it when I realized what it was.

Bones. Several small bones, perfectly clean and smooth, their middles bound together with some kind of dark string. I gingerly handed it back to Sharon, but she nodded past me, so I turned and passed it to Jake. Frowning, he offered it to Sophia, who shook her head in refusal. Curiosity piqued, Kenta stood up and reached around the fire to have his turn.

"Are these...*human?*" Kenta muttered, staring at the bone fetish in his hand.

"For the sake of the story, let's say *yes*," Sharon said. "I wound up with it just a couple of years ago, from a girl named Becky who was driving up from Massachusetts. We don't talk anymore, but knowing what happened to her, I've never wanted to get rid of it." She took the bone-star back from Kenta and stuck it in her pocket.

"It would've been a three hour drive for her, but it took her almost five in the end, and not just because she ran into a ton of construction work. Not long after she crossed the border, Becky had to pee really bad.

"So she's driving along, hopping around in her seat. It's early evening, and it's late September, so it's getting darker earlier in the day. She's praying that she can find a rest stop somewhere, but there's just more and more highway, and she doesn't want to pull over and risk squatting in a shrub of poison oak. So she keeps going until she can't hold it any longer, and pulls into a ditch and gets out of her car.

"Becky *really* doesn't want to do this, but it's gotten pretty dark by now, and she figures that she can just go out of sight from the highway and do her thing. She locks her car and goes behind some bushes, turns around and looks. She sees a car go by, and she can see the driver, clear as day. So, she thinks, in turn, anyone could see *her*. So she goes deeper into the woods, and she finds a little bundle of bones, like this one.

"It's *weird*, she thinks; maybe it was from road kill somehow, but no matter. She can't worry about that right now. She's got to *pee!*

"So she walks deeper, and then she trips on something and falls, and almost pees herself. She stands up, expecting it to be a root or a stick or something, but lo and behold, it's a *bone*, about as big as my arm here. *Now* she's getting a little weirded out.

"Becky decides to get it over with, and steps behind a bush. As she's going, though, she sees a big, white rock nearby. It's hard to see in the light, because it's almost nighttime now. She finishes up and moves a little closer to the rock. It's about as big as— Like that tree stump there. Then when she gets close enough she sees it's *more bones*. I'm talking dozens of them, a whole *pile* of them. And there's no skulls or anything, either. Becky can't tell if— Well, she *hopes*, that they're not human. They're all perfectly clean, no gristle or gore on them."

Sharon paused for a moment. In that split second, a pin could be heard dropping.

But before she could continue, someone said: "Could...?"

All heads turned.

Sophia, her dark eyes wide, asked in a low voice, "...Could it have been hunters? Like, after they skinned them or... Something?"

Sharon inclined her head, frowning. "That *would* make sense, I guess, but these were so carefully put together, not just randomly thrown on top of each other. It was done with such deliberate design that it looked like a *cairn*. You know those piles of rocks you sometimes find in the woods? So imagine a cairn...of *bones*.

"And as scared as she is, Becky can't stop looking at it. And then she sees there's *another* one nearby. And *another*. There's a whole bunch of them, at least half a dozen. She's in a whole *field* of these bone-cairns."

"And then she hears something, and turns. Behind a couple of trees, she thinks she sees something white. It's really tall and really high, *way* bigger than the bone-cairns. But before Becky can get a good look, she hears something again. She turns...*and—*"

"Shit!" Kenta bolted to his feet, startling everyone. He was looking past me, down into the woods.

I twisted back for a peek, but saw only the orange-grey of the surrounding trees and the shadows between them.

"¡*Mierda!*" Sophia snapped, then sighed heavily. "Don't *do* that!"

Sharon giggled. "Good one," she and Jake muttered at the same time, and they shared a laugh.

Kenta raised a hand, frowning, still staring into the woods.

I mirrored the look on his face. "What are you...?"

"*Shhh*," Kenta hissed. "I'm serious guys!"

I stood and turned to looked down the path, but it was a jagged tunnel of nearly perfect darkness.

A branch snapped, and then a stranger sound: a quick series of dry clicks, coming unmistakably from the path.

"You heard that," Kenta breathed, to no one in particular.

I nodded, swallowing hard.

Everyone rose to their feet.

"What is it?" Sophia asked, her voice barely a whisper.

Another series of clicks came—from somewhere *behind* us.

Everyone spun around, crowding each other beside the fire.

"Fuck this!" Jake hissed, and pandemonium broke out.

Sharon panicked. "Let's get out of here!"

Scrambling to pull out a flashlight, I blurted, "Just stay close to the fire!"

"Oh my God, oh my *God...*" Sophia recited continuously.

Trying to raise his voice over all others, Kenta said, "Hold on! Maybe it's—"

Something crashed loudly in the undergrowth behind us, and everyone screamed. Chaos erupted: Feet shuffled, heads twisted in every direction. There were curses and gasps, pointing fingers and harshly-whispered questions. The woods remained silent, an amused audience to our panic.

Tearing the fabric of my jacket pocket, I tugged the flashlight out, clicking it on and pointing it unsteadily. In its pale glow I saw a blur of trees—and caught a glimpse of something white that shrank back between their trunks. I fixed the beam on the spot again, eyes widening, but it was gone.

Another horrible peal of clicks came from somewhere *above*, like the forest was laughing at us.

Kenta grabbed my arm and I jumped. His mouth was working

quickly, pronouncing indistinguishable nonsense.

Then that dry tittering came from beside me, and I yelped and spun around.

My beam caught something on the ground, a clump of pale roots beneath a nearby shrub. It twitched—and then the knot lifted from the ground and began to spread, blooming like a giant white flower—or a terrifyingly wide *hand.*

Kenta pulled on my arm. I staggered back, the flashlight beam fixed on the giant bone-hand as it snatched at the space I'd just vacated, far too many digits clutching at the empty air.

Another clicking laugh from behind us, and we quickly huddled together.

And then came a piercing cry, and something rammed against my side, knocking the wind out of me. I staggered back, hearing a thump and more screaming, and turned to see Sophia had fallen, her red jacket puffing out with the impact. At first, I thought she was kicking one of her legs back, but then I saw something wrapped around her ankle, something big and lumpy and pale that began to *drag* her toward its owner's hiding place in the forest.

Shouting, Jake grabbed at Sophia's hands. I looked around for something, *anything*, and saw Kenta diving for the woodpile.

Sophia screamed again, her face a grimace of terror and tears. Reaching past Jake, I grabbed her forearms and *pulled.*

Kenta stumbled back, swinging a log like a baseball bat. He roared, the log connecting with the bony arm with a satisfying *crack*, and then, swinging again and again, each impact made a resounding snap. There was a blur of white as the hand released Sophia's leg, and she seemed to fly forward, and she, Jake, and I crashed into each other, falling into a heap on the ground.

Shouting and cursing, we scrambled to our feet and regrouped. Sophia was hysterical, and Jake, hugging her fiercely, cursed incessantly. Kenta's gaze was hopping from one spot in the woods to another, and Sharon—

I cursed and spun in a full circle, but I already knew what I'd find—or rather, what I wouldn't.

Sharon was gone.

*　　*　　*

"No!" I ran to the tree line, looking around, but couldn't see a sign of her.

Kenta glared back at me. "*What?*"

"She's gone!" I stamped my foot on the ground. "*Sharon.* She's gone. *Dammit!*"

"Someone mind telling me what the actual *fuck* is going on?" Jake said.

Sophia: "It's the Bone Witch!"

Jake: "No, *no!* That—"

Kenta: "You *saw* that thing— Those things."

Me: "Guys—"

Jake: "Those had to—"

Sophia: "*La mierda fantasma me agarro! Me tenía de los—*"

Jake: "Shut up!"

Kenta: "*It's fucking real, okay?*"

Everyone fell silent at this.

"The Bone Witch is *real,*" Kenta continued, "and it *took* Sharon, and—"

"We need to go find her," I interrupted, only to hear Kenta finish, "—the *fuck* out of here."

Jake and Sophia took turns looking from me to Kenta and back.

"No, no, and *no,*" Kenta spat. "No fuckin' way am I playing rescue ops after—whatever the hell those things were."

"Sharon!" Sophia shouted, and I echoed her. We called out repeatedly, and a moment later, Jake joined in.

"This is ridiculous," Kenta muttered.

Sophia spun on him. "*What if she's hurt?*" she snapped. "*Or—*"

"The fuck…" Jake muttered.

"We don't know that," I said, and shouted for Sharon once again, straining my lungs.

Jake: "Fuck!"

Sophia: "We can't just let her get—"

Kenta: "Look Margaret, I'm sorry, but we—"

Jake: "*Holy shit, help!*"

Everyone turned in time to see a terrified Jake pitching forward, his arms swinging up into the air, hands trying to grab anything they could as he hit the ground. He was quickly lifted by two sets of those horrible bone hands, and shrieked until his voice cracked. We all lunged for him, but he was already out of reach: we watched with dumb, horrified wonder as he was lifted up, up, *up* into the trees, until his feet disappeared between the branches.

Sophia and Kenta found their voices, shouting and screaming after him. I shone my flashlight beam up in time to see Jake being tugged backward through the thick branches and clumps of dark brown leaves, toward something enormous and pale and far, *far* too high up to sanely comprehend.

And then Kenta howled, and I saw another massive bone-claw smash out through the forest and grab his upper body, yanking him backward. I charged after him, Sophia wailing beside me, and then something grasped me around my midsection and *squeezed*.

There was vertigo and a blur of branches and leaves around me, smacking my face and tearing at my hair. I shouted, kicking wildly as I was lifted higher and higher, the night sky rushing toward me, I thought I saw the heavily-distorted face of the moon up there, big and jagged and white and *so* terribly close—and then my head collided with a heavy branch, and everything went dark.

*   *   *

A blink of light and sound.

A glowing blur, something pressed against my cheek.

Screams in the darkness.

Movement as I'm lifted upright, and something hard ramming into my back.

Someone—I think it's Kenta—screeches like a wounded cat, louder and louder.

I murmur something, but I can hardly hear myself.

I can see little points of light all around me, and something big and white floating behind it all.

Then my head dips forward, and all is dark again.

*   *   *

I was half-aware of the singing for some time before I became fully conscious. It was dissonant, warbling, foreign-sounding.

I felt dull pain in my neck as I moved my head to the side— then groaned as it burst into brilliant fire, waking me fully up. I opened my eyes and realized that I was sitting upright, my head resting on my chest. From the hard, painfully lumpy surface pressed against my back, I gathered I must've been left lying against a big rock. I slowly lifted my head up and back, gritting my teeth as

I did.

Then I realized that it wasn't *singing* I was hearing—it was a series of sobs and ululating whimpers, the voice very familiar. As I listened, the whimpers stopped.

Blinking in the darkness, I could only tell that it was night, but there were blurs of softer shadows around me. I realized that they were points of light, and squinted at the nearest one, trying to concentrate on it until my vision returned.

The light swam in and out of focus, growing wider and narrower, seeming to shift and twist. I recognized it as a flame—a candle, set on the ground by my left foot. I stared at it until my vision cleared...and saw that it rested upon a small, star-shaped bundle of twigs.

No. *Bones.*

Jerking my leg away from the candle, I tried to sit up, but something hard pressed against my sore chest. I looked down, and gasped.

I was tied down to the rock not with rope, but with several layers of bones—thick ones, thin ones, curved and straight, all bound together with some kind of black thread. They held well, too; despite all my struggles, I was kept firmly in place against the rock.

There were many more of those wicked candles placed on the ground around me, I now saw. There were several big, pale shapes nearby, nearly as tall as people, and I remembered Sharon's story from earlier: *a whole* field *of bone-cairns*. I didn't have to look to know what I had been bound to—or what was holding me. I could feel, could *hear* the shift and scrape of so many bones piled upon each other, pressing into my back and making my skin crawl.

Adrenaline surged, panicking me. It took everything I had to push that down and try to calmly examine my surroundings.

It was a clearing, the encompassing trees forming a jagged circle beneath the night sky, from which the stars distantly regarded this horrifying place of bones.

The whimpering voice came again. I turned and looked for its source—and my eyes bulged.

Several yards away from me was a low, dome-shaped hut or hovel, the crooked black opening in its side facing me like a gaping, hungry mouth. I immediately recognized the lumpy, mottled surface that made up its wall, riddled with holes: skulls. Human skulls. Hundreds upon hundreds of skulls, neatly stacked upon one another, some with jaws, some without, and more than a few of them far too small to have come from adults.

When the voice spoke again, I tore my gaze away from the hovel. Although my eyes had adjusted to the candlelit darkness, I could only make out a big, pale shape, with something low and dark resting against it. I squinted at it until I recognized the red jacket.

"Sophia!" I cried, but my voice came out in a harsh, dry croak. As I cleared my throat, she yelled something back to me. "Are you alright?" I asked.

"I—I think my leg is broken!" she whimpered.

"Hold still!" I instantly realized what a silly suggestion that was. "Where's Jake? Kenta?"

"I don't know, *I don't know, I—*" Sophia lowered her head, sobbing again.

I tried to stretch my arms as wide and as strong as they could go, but it was useless. I looked around, setting my jaw as I tried to find something, *anything,* to change our situation—and then I heard a low, guttural moan from nearby.

From the hovel.

I couldn't recognize the voice, but it was definitely male, and from the sounds of it, he was in death's embrace.

I turned to Sophia, saw she was also looking at the hovel. I shook my head, hoping she could see me—but then she started shouting.

"Jake! Jacob!"

I tried to hush her, tried to calm her, but she was too far away and too scared.

And then I heard the laughter from the hovel, and the blood froze in my veins.

It wasn't quite the high, nasal cackling that I somehow expected. No, it was a deep, lyrical laugh that trailed off with an unmistakable tone of mockery.

Through the door of the hovel, I saw quick movement, just the barest change of shade in the blackness, then it was gone—

Something was hurled out at me. I yelped and tried to duck, but the bones held me in place, and I could only cringingly turn my head as something struck my shoulder and fell to the ground. I didn't dare look at it; instead, I stared at the doorway as its thrower emerged, laughing. Sophia's hysterical shouts died out as the Bone Witch stepped into view, a pale, grinning specter.

It was the girl who'd called herself Sharon.

* * *

She was naked but for her gold necklace; somehow, I was expecting her to be wearing jewelry made of bones. In fact, I was more surprised by this than I was to see *her* casually striding out of the hovel toward me, slowly shaking her head.

"Let them go," I said.

"What, these?" she asked, raising her hand. She was holding something red and glistening, and it had smeared blood on her arms and body. I swallowed my nausea and forced my gaze to meet hers. Her smile broadened. "Too late."

"*They're* kids!" I shouted. "*They're just damn kids, and they didn't deserve this!*"

"They're young and strong," she said.

"*Jake?*" Sophia said in a tiny voice. "*Jake...oh my God...*"

"No!" I shouted.

The Bone Witch's smile widened; despite her young and pretty features, I could see something far older and incredibly ugly behind that horrible grin as she turned and slowly stepped toward Sophia. She dropped the red object, which landed on the ground with a revoltingly wet *splat*.

She started speaking as she got closer to Sophia, but I could only make out the words, "*...you, child...*"

Sophia began to loose a drawn-out, warbling cry.

"Please!" I cried. "*Please*...you don't want to do this!"

"Oh? *Don't* I?" she called over her shoulder. "Haven't you heard the legends?"

My thoughts racing, I hollered, "Wait, my story!"

The Bone Witch stopped and turned to face me, her eyes skull-like pools of shadow as she frowned.

"I never got to tell *my* story!"

She stared at me for a long moment, then turned back, the grin returning to her face as she approached me. "How right you are," she said, crossing her long legs and lowering herself to the ground before me. "Please, tell it to me *now*." She spread her bloody arms, grinning. "I have all night."

I wasn't sure if I was ready for this; but then, it was all I could do.

"It's a sad story," I started, looking down at the ground. "I don't remember all of it, other than what I've heard and pieced together over the years. I was only five years old at the time." I looked up at the Bone Witch, and saw the perplexed look on her face.

"There was a girl who went to college right near here," I said. "Her name was Patty. She was eighteen."

"No," the Bone Witch said, and I looked up to see a new look crossing her features—exactly the look I expected. I continued.

"One day, Patty went for a walk, and she never came back."

"*No.*" She raised a hand to her forehead, and damn if it wasn't *trembling.*

"She never came back. Her family got so worried."

"*Stop it!*"

"Her Ma, her Pa, and her sister went through the rest of their lives wondering what happened to her."

The Bone Witch jumped to her feet with a snarl.

"Ma died in 1961," I continued. "Heart attack. Pa was taken only a few years later from a stroke. And her sister—"

My tongue went still in my mouth as I heard a familiar series of dry clicks and rattles from nearby.

One of the vacant bone-cairns appeared to be crumbling open, as if something was bursting out from inside it. Then I realized it was *shifting.*

Before my eyes, bones dropped, tumbled and crawled noisily over one another, slowly forming a hodgepodge shape. For a brief moment, it looked like a person bent forward on hands and knees; but then the head—such as it was—began to take shape, and it was like nothing I'd ever seen.

Sophia began to shriek, and the Bone Witch turned to her, grinning.

The bones had formed something between a bull and a bear, and it slowly turned around, horrifyingly silent but for ripples of clicks, taps, and clatters.

I turned back to the Bone Witch and snarled, "*Leave her alone!*"

"*Enough, you!*" she snarled, and something shifted against my side. I heard a few bony clicks, and then a point of tremendous pressure formed against the left side of my abdomen, then exploded into pain. I started screaming. One of the bones had twisted and rammed into my side like an improvised dagger.

I desperately squirmed against my terrible restraints, the pain worsening, screaming louder, wet warmth seeping into my shirt and pants as I bled. I couldn't fathom what was happening to me, how much blood I was losing; but then I heard a high, keening sound, and realized that I wasn't the only one screaming.

Sophia was.

"*No!*" I managed. Sophia's shrieks got louder and louder, until I was sure they'd spare the Bone Witch and her horrible creature the trouble of tearing her throat apart.

Trapped in a world of pain and horror, I screamed the only thing I could think of, the only thing I had left.

And then there was sudden, horrible silence.

I squeezed my eyes shut, knowing what was surely happening. I listened for the wet rips and gurgles of slaughter…

…But there was only more silence.

I heard the soft crunch of bare feet padding on dead grass and leaves, and opened my eyes in time to see the Bone Witch looming over me. "*What?*" she asked in a low voice.

I coughed, and damn, if I couldn't taste the life bleeding out of me.

"Her sister. *Your* sister. It's me, Patty."

*   *   *

We stared into each other's eyes for a long, silent moment.

"Midge?" she breathed.

Then the silence broke with a loud crash, and I saw the bone-creature collapsing. It didn't return to its previous cairn structure, however; all its pieces simply crumbled apart like a kid's popsicle stick model, landing in a haphazard mess all over the ground.

When I turned back, she knelt before me, eyes wide and frantic. There was a cacophony of clicks and what felt like the rush of air around me, and suddenly, the bones that held me fell apart, littering my legs and my hands and the ground beneath—and then I cried aloud as the one piercing my side twisted, then went still, firmly wedged inside me.

"Midge, oh no, *Midge!*" she said, dropping to her knees and bending forward. I turned away—somewhere, I'd heard an injury is easier to handle if you don't look at it—but when she tore the bone out of my side, spheres of blackness swam into my vision that were so dense, I was sure that this was it.

"It's…" I shook my head, but everything seemed so *slow*, so laborious, and more of those black spheres were crowding in around me now.

"*Shhh, shhh*," she whispered, and her voice began to form low, strange words.

"*Just…*" I managed, but it sounded like two long, drawn-out syllables.

She continued to speak, and I sank into the dark, hearing a voice echoing, calling out one final plea:

"*Just…let…her…go…*"

*　　*　　*

I don't know when I came around. I wasn't sure if I was still alive.

Hell, for all I knew, this was some kind of purgatory, a purgatory in which my long-lost sister was sitting naked with me in a field of candles and bones. And a fire—I saw a fire had been built nearby; it took me a moment to realize that I could feel its gentle heat seeping into my cold limbs.

She was speaking again, but all I could hear was a low, droning sound, punctuated with the occasional syllable or pause.

I blinked, and there was a little more light now. I spent a long time with my head turned to the side, staring at the horizon, and could see the veil of stars beginning to lift at its edges. I could feel the familiar texture of earth against my back, and realized that I was lying down now, no longer resting against that damned bone-cairn. I tried to sit up, but pain exploded in my left side, sending fireworks through my senses.

"Midge, don't move," she said, a slight echoing lisp to her words.

"What the hell…happened?" I asked, meaning something far bigger than the moments—or hours—that had just passed. I took a heavy breath, then winced and let loose a grunt as deep pain lanced through me again.

A hand pressed to my shoulder. "Don't move. You're bleeding bad. I was able to make it stop now, but you've…"

I nodded sadly. I understood.

Then an image flashed through my mind: a terrified girl's face. "Sophia!" I groaned.

"She's gone," she said, and from the sour tone in her voice, I felt ready to eat my pain if it meant I could throttle her, but then she added, "I…I let her go. She had a bad limp, but she'll be fine."

I let out a heavy breath, then nodded weakly.

"Midge," she said, "I didn't recognize you."

"I got old." I snickered, intending to add, *and you didn't*, but pain shot up into my abdomen, and the rest of my breath escaped in a soft wheeze.

"Why did you come back?"

"You and those other people vanished back in the late '40s. The next group disappeared in the '70s." I shrugged weakly. "When those two hikers disappeared last month, I did the math. What…what the hell happened to you, Patty?"

I had spent most of my life asking this question, to Ma and Pa, to the authorities, to God, to anybody who would or could give me any semblance of an answer. Even the concept of death had been easier to grasp than the possibilities raised by this question. Asking it now, however, seemed so minuscule, so fickle, so *normal*, that I might as well have been asking about a disastrous choice of a boyfriend.

She sat back, looked to the distance. "You wouldn't understand."

"Try me," I said.

She looked away for a long moment, then took a shaky breath and said, "I don't know where to start."

"For one thing," I said, "can you put on some damn clothes?"

*　　*　　*

She re-emerged from the hovel moments later, her feet bare and her jacket discarded, but thankfully not the naked, bloodied horror she had been earlier. She sat down beside me and regarded the fire for a long time, her necklace glimmering in its flickering light. She'd been wearing that necklace in an old photo that my parents had kept hidden from me until I was almost as old as her.

"So?" I asked.

She regarded the fire for a long time, then spoke.

She'd told me how she'd followed the Long Trail into these parts, where she'd found a wide, deep pit dug into the ground; but as she spoke, I started to have trouble making sense out of what she was telling me. It may have been my lost blood, or maybe she was just speaking in circles; but I didn't stop her. I kept listening; I had a feeling that this was a story she'd never told anyone, and would probably never tell again.

She told me about a strange voice that seemed to call her toward that pit, how she'd stared down into it so long that she'd lost track of time, and how quickly the night had fallen. She told me how she'd not been scared, only *curious*, the whole time. She told me about the figure that had appeared in the darkened woods, a bald, naked, grinning man with flashing orange eyes and something like a giant black spider growing out of the middle of his chest. She said something about being "augmented by the black," and something about the power of *structure*, of the power that lurked in everything and how you only needed to pick something apart to tap into it.

I had to hush her when she began to grow excited with the specifics. She remained silent after that.

The sky was still dark, but there was just the faintest difference in shade in the distance.

"I can't do anything in the daytime," she said. "And...Midge, I'm so sorry, but..."

"But what?" I looked up at her.

She was crying, I now saw, but no tears touched her cheeks or even her eyes. She shook her head and sniffed. "When the sun rises, I'm powerless, and you..."

I closed my eyes, took a heavy breath, and nodded.

"I'm sorry," she repeated, pressing her hand on mine. I took it and squeezed.

I looked up, and could see the stars had begun their slow retreat behind the first hint of blue in the sky.

Then I snickered weakly.

"What?" she asked.

I twisted my mouth into a sour grin. "My story. I never finished it." I coughed harshly and turned to her. "You'll like it. It's a ghost story."

Patty's trembling lips twisted into a smile that I had only ever seen in old photographs, and I felt her hand squeeze mine harder.

I coughed again. "This is a ghost story from a long time ago…"

Creaking Through Salem
Ogmios

Creaking, creaking there in the shed.
Footsteps creak there in my head.
The lantern shows but no one knows,
I see no creaking where it glows.
Did I see a hobgoblin thing,
His minions creak, creaking?
On the roof and in the air,
Biting, stinging, without a care!
That WITCH there, she commits Sin!
SHE let the creaking D'evil in!
My friends here, they saw it too.
How could all three have visions untrue?
Bound and chained the witch did go.
But the creaking still persisted so.
WITCH! WITCH! How each did fight!
Creak, Creaking keeps me up all night.
Bound, drowned, tortured and pressed,
The witches died all failing their test.
Horrors and creaks did still abound,
Whilst most… heard not a sound.

The hunt was on and pyres set.
Those which witches will all burn yet!
Stinging, creaking, how could this be?
I think they think the witch is ME.
I went with that woman into the wood.
Her stories and wisdom sounded good.
Creaking I hear since that night.
CURSED as a witch, perhaps they are right!
I eat my last, not eating for days.
The pyres are set in the sun's final rays.
My head creak creaking, the creaking does grow,
As all of we witches are tied in a row.
The flame licks my toes, I can see with the light.
Who's that in front, she does not look right.
Her pyre's creaking while ours are just bright.
I dare not believe this wicked sight!
All we witches, we burn I will tell,
But flames delight those spawning from hell.
The earth-born demon smiles through the blaze,
As villagers panic to avoid its gaze.
Clenching for air as my body dies,
I see the creaking through squinted eyes.
The stinging creak, creaking rose to a din.
Who let that ancient D'evil in?
Too late to see, it spawned from within;
And that time, I fear, D'evil did win.

Blessed Be & Kick Ass
Jan Kozlowski

Kass Wewal glanced out the window as the Cessna Mustang descended over the lush, green landscape of central Connecticut. She took a deep breath and tried to find her calm, peaceful center, but her higher senses had already switched on in anticipation of this latest predation case.

There was a slight bump as the landing gear grabbed the earth. She fidgeted as the plane rolled to a stop in front of a battered green Quonset hut she assumed served as the tiny airport's terminal. Kass unbelted and stretched her long legs.

"Flawless flight as usual, Char," Kass called as she moved forward towards the door. "I'll shoot you a message when I'm ready to head back."

Charmaine poked her head out of the cockpit. "Broomstick One and I will be ready and waiting, Kass," she said with a grin.

"You know I hate it when you call it that," Kass volleyed back, enjoying their long running routine.

"Yep, I do. Blessed be and kick ass."

*　　*　　*

Descending the stairs to the cracked asphalt tarmac, Kass's grey eyes swept her surroundings, her senses taking in everything. She felt rather than saw her contact moving toward her from behind the building's tinted glass doors. A blur of bright color and even brighter energy barreled out into the sun.

"Kass Wewal?"

Kass had a moment to nod before being enveloped in a massive hug that almost overloaded Kass's white light circuits.

"I'm Pauline Markham, I'm the one that contacted you," the kaleidoscope said upon releasing her. A tweedling sound erupted from somewhere within the generous folds of fabric. Pauline dug out her cell and motioned for Kass to follow her as she began walking toward the parking lot.

"Yes, dear. No, dear. I'll be there, don't worry. I'm just picking up a friend first. I wouldn't miss seeing you get your poetry award. Okay. Love you, too."

Pauline made the phone disappear again just as they reached a large, grey sedan that reminded Kass more of a cruise ship than an automobile.

"Sorry about that. My granddaughter Tory. She's very excited."

"You contacted me about your granddaughter's friend, right?" Kass asked as they settled in and weighed anchor.

"At first it was just Gina, Tory's friend and her older sister Abby, but since I contacted you...I...I did some snooping through Tory's social media accounts and found some conversations where they were talking about "things" that had happened during sleepovers at the girls' house."

"What kind of things?"

"From what I read, Tory saw Gina and Abby's father grab their breasts as they walked by him in the hallway and every time any of the girls went to the bathroom, he managed to walk in on them, always by accident HE said. He blamed it on the girls not locking the door properly."

"Has he harmed your granddaughter in any way?"

Pauline's eyes sparked, her face darkening. "He creeped her out and she's scared for her friends, but I don't believe he actually did anything to Tory. And believe me he will never get the chance. As soon as I found out I surrounded that girl with every protection spell I could summon. I know I never was blessed with your special talents or power, but I can still throw some mean mumbo-jumbo when necessary. No one fucks with my family."

Kass sat quietly, listening to Pauline and watching her aura corroborate every word, like a multi-colored lie detector. There was no deception or hidden agendas here, just a grandmother who loved and feared for the safety of her granddaughter and her young friends. Pauline was also being very modest about her powers…from the strong red and black pulses that arched and crackled every time she mentioned the predator, Kass knew this particular asshole's days of hurting little girls would soon be over. Even if Kass somehow failed her mission, Pauline would find a way to end him herself.

*   *   *

The parking lot was full by the time they got to the school. It had been a long time since Kass had been near a public educational institution and she was surprised by sleek, ultra-modern look. To her it looked more like a city office building than a neighborhood school and that wasn't a compliment. They finally found a spot in a back corner and she had to hurry to keep up with Pauline as she race-walked for the side door.

"My daughter-in-law is supposed to be saving us seats and since she's friends with Abby and Gina's parents, Brian and Debbie Nyland, both families will probably be sitting near each other."

Kass followed Pauline into the large multi-purpose room that she heard referred to as the Caf-a-gym-atorium. Kass smiled to herself, it sounded like one of her old Latin alchemy spells-Caput Mortuum, Caf-a-gym-atorium.

"There they are, over there," Pauline said, waving like a mad woman and rushing forward. Kass made her way along more slowly, sliding through the crowd of milling parents and siblings, trying to keep her sensitivities in sleep mode and her cloaking shield in place. In groups, it was particularly easy to be overwhelmed by auras and emotions being thrown off by all those around her. The cloaking shield, while not quite an invisibility device, did mute her physical features, making her difficult to remember or identify even seconds after meeting her.

Kass caught up with Pauline standing among a knot of people spread out over two rows. The girl who must be Tory was hanging onto to her grandmother like a monkey on a banana tree. Pauline kissed the top of her head and brushed the curls out of her eyes as the girl looked up at her adoringly. Standing directly behind the two was a younger woman who had to be Rachel, Tory's mother. Kass didn't need any special powers to see the jealousy on Rachel's face as she watched Pauline and her daughter.

On the other side of Tory and Pauline stood two young girls, one Tory's age and one slightly older. The younger one, Gina, was thin and frail with a haunted look that Kass was unfortunately way too familiar with. The older girl, Abby was overweight and collapsed in on herself, her limp hair hanging down in front of her face, her eyes locked on to the floor in front of her, except for the seconds they'd flicker away to search for the location of her father's sneakers.

The parents, Brian and Debbie, stood on the other side of Abby, talking and laughing with another couple in the next row. Brian kept his eyes on his daughters though, and they wilted a little more every minute he stared.

"Kass, there you are!" Pauline called. "I want you to meet my granddaughter Tory and her mother Rachel. Rachel, Tory this is an old friend of mine, Kass."

"Pleased to meet you, Kass," Tory said, offering a polite handshake.

"Thank you, Tory. I'm very glad to meet you too, your grandmother talks about you all the time." The girl beamed.

"Kind of weird that Pauline dragged you along to an 8th grade awards ceremony," Rachel spat out. "You must be really hard up for company, but then again, if you're hanging out with Pauline…"

"Actually, Pauline and I are going out to lunch after the ceremony and I loved the idea of finally getting to meet the little girl who means the world to my dear friend."

"Yeah, right…whatever." Rachel pulled out her phone and began texting someone. Out of the corner of her eye Kass watched Debbie jump a little as her phone must have vibrated. She fished it out and after squinting at the screen, looked over at Pauline and Kass, smirked and began to text something back. Thankfully the lights flashed and everyone busied themselves getting the kids onstage and family members in their seats.

It turned out that Rachel had forgotten to save a spot for Pauline, but luckily, the nice couple who had taken seats directly behind the Nylands, suddenly decided they'd rather sit somewhere else and were happy to let the women take their chairs.

The lights went down and the principal strode out to center stage to polite applause. Kass arranged her body comfortably, softened her gaze and through half-lidded eyes, focused on the backs of the girls' heads. She lifted her right hand and with her index finger made a subtle circling gesture. The sound in the auditorium receded to a dull hum in Kass's ears as a bubble only she could perceive formed around her and the two girls. It was now safe for her to make the connection. Kass tuned in and watched as the colors of grief and pain, anger and fear exploded out of Abby and Gina like volcanic eruptions.

Kass couldn't exactly read minds, but she could touch and interpret the energy generated by strong thoughts, experiences and emotions. Over the years she'd gotten very skilled at her readings, to the point of being able to go beyond auras, deep into her subject's emotional center to what some called the soul.

She sank deeper into meditation and reached out with her vibrational field until she could visualize the girls' hearts. The shimmering, opalescent vapor that normally resided deep in a human body's chest cavity had been reduced to dull-colored shreds. The disintegrating wisps reminded Kass of a delicate lace handkerchief used for target practice. Abby's and Gina's souls had been all but obliterated.

Kass slumped back in the hard plastic chair and let the bubble evaporate. She had witnessed enough to confirm Pauline's fears and then some.

* * *

By the time the awards ceremony ended Kass had decided on a plan of action. She had learned from simple eavesdropping that both girls would be going back to their classrooms. Debbie would be heading back to work and Brian had a date with a squat rack at the local gym, though he'd be certain to be home before his girls.

As Pauline collected a final hug from Tory, Kass caught her friend's eye. Pauline gave her a questioning look over the girl's head and Kass nodded sadly. Pauline smothered the girl in kisses and hugged her until she squirmed to be let go.

"What do you need me to do?" Pauline asked, walking with Kass back to the car.

"Just drop me off near the Nyland house. I'll take it from there."

"I'd like to help."

Kass turned, putting her hands on the older woman's

shoulders, and looked her in the eyes. "Pauline, you've done more than anyone else would or could. I won't disrespect you by putting an amnesia spell on you, but please, just go home and forget about everything today but your granddaughter and her poetry award. You have my word everything will work out the way it's supposed to."

Both women were silent as Pauline navigated the labyrinth of suburban streets. "There it is, the white ranch with the black shutters at the end of the cul-de-sac," Pauline said.

"Where do the woods behind their house come out?"

"Ironically, they back on a small cemetery we call the Burying Ground. The entrance is one street over on Nettle Spring. It's not active anymore. I think the historical marker says the last internments were Civil War casualties."

"Perfect. Let me off at the top of Nettle-whatever."

Pauline pulled the car over as instructed and Kass got out and walked around to the driver's window.

"Thank you, Pauline and blessed be."

"Won't you need...?" but Kass was already striding away.

*　　*　　*

After traveling and being stuck in one form of a chair or another all day, Kass enjoyed the feeling of being on her feet, moving through the fresh air with all of her senses snapping and crackling as she extended them in all directions. They told her the area was safe with very few people around, which made slipping into the Burying Ground a simple matter that didn't even require a body shift. She hurried through the woods as quietly as possible, slowing down only when she spotted the rear of the white house through the trees.

She found a large maple set back from the edge of the yard and lifted herself into its lower branches. She sat quietly, watching the house, listening, smelling, and tasting all the information that was coming to her. Outwardly, there was nothing special to be seen. The house and yard were unornamented and slightly neglected, the grass and weeds long and the ground dry. It was a place where people existed, not a home where lives grew and thrived.

Kass knew time was getting short and now that she had made sure there were no surprises like visiting relatives, large dogs or motion detectors to interfere; she prepared herself to do the things she needed to do before the family returned home. From her perch, Kass had spotted an air vent leading into the home's attic that would suit her purposes. She breathed deeply, whispered a few words, swept her arms wide and pushed off the branch into the late spring breeze.

If anyone had been watching the Nyland's backyard at that moment, they would have seen a beautiful, iridescent green Luna moth glide gracefully from the woods, leisurely circle the property and then land on the moss-encrusted aluminum siding just under the attic louvers. She stayed there for several minutes, the small eyes on her wings helping her evaluate her surroundings. Finally satisfied that she was safe and undetected, she entered the building.

The attic was dry, dusty, and large enough for her human self to stand up in. Kass shifted quickly and immediately began to repeat the words and sounds for the Search and Seizure spell. Any pieces of evidence related to Brian Nyland's nasty predilection would now throw off a neon glow like an 'Open' sign at a 24 hour highway choke and puke.

Kass scanned the storage space and when nothing lit up she headed down to the main floor. The kitchen, bathroom, and shared living spaces were all clear, as were the two open bedrooms. The third room off the hallway though had a closed door with a heavy duty deadbolt on it. She tried the knob but it was locked. She smiled. *Got ya, you asshole*, she thought as she flicked her finger over the keyhole and heard the snick of the bolt snapping back. Opening the door, she almost had to take a step back from the red, pulsing glows that seemed to come from all corners of the room.

Kass gathered up all of the electronic devices, flash drives, DVD's, cameras and boxes of photos that had pinged and piled them on the desk. She rifled through them all, growing angrier and more nauseated with each passing second. These were all images of Abby and Gina, from infancy through what could have been this morning, doing…or being forced to do…things that would make a Hell's Kitchen hooker vomit.

There were thousands of pictures, all total, but a niggling feeling in the back of her mind told Kass that this wasn't all. He had another stash somewhere in the house. She checked the time and decided to do a quick recon down to the basement, the only area she hadn't searched yet.

Sure enough, even before she reached the bottom stair step, the muted red beacon coming from the farthest left corner drew her attention like a lighthouse in a hurricane. This time it was an old military style footlocker, hidden behind a false panel in the wall. Kass dug it out and moved it to an open spot on the floor. A fast pass with her hand threw the padlock against the wall and popped the lid. More pictures, older, the edges of some curled and faded, others spotted with fluids she didn't want to think about. None were of Abby or Gina, but there were dozens of other little girls with the same terror-stricken eyes staring out at her. These were his earlier victims, the ones he had to hunt and trap, before he decided it was easier to just breed his own.

Kass returned to the office, adding the footlocker to the collection. She made a few adjustments to the circle she had drawn in the center of the room, moved a few objects to handier locations and then, as a car turned into the driveway, she sealed the room with an Impenetrable spell. A quick click of her tongue and she was airborne again, her long wings lifting her up to the top of the kitchen curtains.

She watched as Brian let himself into the house and hurried down the hallway. She expected him to head for his office, but he breezed by it and hooked a right, straight into his daughters' bedroom. Kass swept out of the kitchen and followed him, landing on the top shelf of the girl's bookcase. Any fear she had that Brian had noticed a five inch long green moth flying around his home evaporated when she realized what he was focused on. He had already stripped his shirt off and his pants quickly followed. There was no underwear. He looked over at the dresser on the other side of the room and that's when Kass noticed the small video camera and its red blinking light. He considered the angles and carefully lowered himself down among the stuffed animals, pulling them in close, his erection bouncing up and down between them in anticipation.

Both Kass and Brian heard the sound of the front door opening and closing at the same time. Brian smiled, his cock jumping again. Kass launched herself off the bookcase, threw a Locked In spell at the bastard and sealed the door behind her. The girls were in the kitchen, their heads up like wild animals, listening and looking, trying to gauge where the threat would come at them from today. Their body language said there was no IF for them, just where and when.

Kass scrambled for a new strategy. Debbie wouldn't be home for an hour or two. The girls couldn't go into their bedroom and they'd be spooked if they thought their father had just disappeared. They were almost at their bedroom door when they heard what Kass hoped was a reasonable facsimile of their father's voice being thrown from behind his closed office door.

"Abby, Gina-your bedroom's off limits today. Make yourselves a snack and go watch television until your mother gets home. I've got work to do."

The girls were confused, but they were well trained. "Yes, Daddy," they said in unison and did as they were told.

*   *   *

Debbie pulled into the driveway two hours later. Kass waited until she got inside before she put the girls into a deep, peaceful sleep and then materialized directly in front of the Mother of the Year.

Kass had often heard the phrase "scared the piss out someone" but this was the first time she'd seen it in real life and she'd be liar if she didn't admit she enjoyed the hell out of making this woman suffer that little extra bit of humiliation.

"Who…what…what are you doing in my house? Where's my husband? Brian? BRIAN?"

Kass made a swiping motion with her index and middle fingers and Debbie's lips slammed shut as if she had slapped a strip of duct tape across them.

"Has no one ever told you that you learn more by listening than by talking?" Kass asked, pushing her face within an inch of Debbie's.

Debbie's eyes widened and she made small choking sounds in the back of her throat.

"For example, just now, do you want to know what I heard? I heard you ask about your husband. I heard you call for your husband. I did NOT however hear you ask or call out for your girls. For most mothers, that would be their first instinct, but that's not how you're wired, is it?"

Debbie moaned and tried to sink to the floor.

"No Debbie, stand up. We're going to take a little walk and

you are finally going to listen… and see… and truly, deeply understand, what's going on here in your happy little suburban paradise."

Kass hauled Debbie up by her shoulders and propelled her down the hall to her daughters' bedroom. She unsealed the door and pushed Debbie through, walking her right up to the bed where her husband lay, and forcing her to look. Debbie turned her head away, and even through her closed mouth, Kass could hear the word No, repeated over and over again.

"LOOK at him. THIS is what your daughters have been coming home to EVERY. SINGLE. DAY. This is what he does to them EVERY. SINGLE. DAY. Do you understand?"

Kass flicked her fingers and Debbie's voice burst out, still chanting No, No, No.

"Do you UNDERSTAND?"

Debbie dropped to her knees beside the bed, her head shaking from side to side, tears raining down her face. Brian was quiet now, frozen in mid-wiggle among the stuffed animals, his erection still at full mast. His eyes though were wild. He was completely aware in there, but unable to move anything but his ocular muscles.

"One more time Debbie, do you understand what Brian has been doing to Abby and Gina?"

Debbie turned her head and looked up at Kass, her eyes flashing hatred, her hands curling into claws. "What did you DO to him, you bitch?" she screamed, "What did you DO to my poor husband?" Debbie tried to stumble to her feet, but Kass pushed her back down, hard. It felt good to use physical force, and it took every ounce of self-control she possessed to refrain from beating this woman until there was nothing left but a meaty pulp. Instead, she satisfied herself by making sure Debbie shared the Locked In experience with her beloved.

This was not going the way Kass had hoped. There was no way she could trust the girls with this pedo-diva. Even if she permanently removed Brian from the situation, Debbie would find another male, and there was every possibly he could be even more of a nightmare than this asshole. These girls would never feel safe or protected or truly loved as long as this pair were part of their lives.

Kass stared down at these two poor excuses for humans, disgust and rage urging her to use one of the ancient incantations to flush them both out into the universe like the pieces of shit that they were. But there were the girls to consider, and they deserved so much better. They deserved a chance at a good life with decent people who would keep them safe and do everything in their power to help them heal. Kass took a deep breath and reached for her cell phone.

Pauline flew through the door a few minutes later. She rushed to the sleeping girls and knelt between them, tears streaming down her face. "I'm so sorry. I should have known. I should have protected you. I should have known. I should have known."

Kass let her grieve for the girls, knowing that there was nothing she could say that would make Pauline feel better. She would always blame herself--good people always did. When Pauline quieted, Kass walked over and put her hand on the older woman's shoulder.

"Would you like to help me make this situation right?"

Pauline looked up at her, eyes blazing. "Fuck, yeah."

Kass gave Pauline a quick tour of the bedroom and office, explaining her plan. Pauline made a couple of suggestions, they settled on a meeting time and place and each went off to complete their tasks.

*   *   *

At midnight, a solemn procession of thirteen dark clad figures emerged from the woods and made their way into the Burying Ground. A large circle had already been laid out along the edges of this hallowed place, shielding the entire space from all those not involved in the ritual.

The thirteen joined Kass and the Nylands at the base of large Civil War memorial obelisk and gathered around the pyre she had erected there. When everyone was in place, Kass took the hands of the two girls and led them forward. Their minds were technically still in a twilight sleep, but they were able to move and obey simple commands.

"Blessed be!" she intoned.

"Blessed be," the group responded.

"We have gathered here among this community's bravest ancestors to ask their help in the protection of two of their own. Abby and Gina, known now as Nyland; granddaughters of the Barretts and Everlys; great-granddaughters of the Calhouns, Longs and Mannerlings; and great-great-granddaughters of the Nelsons, Fortniers, Paines and Holcombs."

As Kass listed the names, the ground around them vibrated, like a large machine had been turned on. Kass felt the voltage surging up through her body, and looking around she could see the others were experiencing it too. She stretched her arms out and slowly brought them back together in front of her body, feeling the energy gathering and coalescing between her hands into an orb of cobalt-blue cold fire.

Chanting the ancient words, Kass brought the blazing sphere to the pyre stacked high with the physical and digital evidence of Brian's perversions. She carefully placed it in the center of the pile and stepped back as the flames devoured the photographs first and then moved on to the electronic and storage devices. The thirteen chanted louder and the shuddering from below grew stronger as the inferno roared upward into the night sky, consuming everything, cleansing everything.

Kass reached out and took the girls' hands again and walked with them to the edge of the crucible. She reached into the flames and scooped out a handful of blue fire, holding it out first to Abby, who eagerly took it from her and then to Gina who accepted it more tentatively.

As soon as the girls touched embers, the cold fire roiled over their bodies, enveloping them for an instant and then winking out as if it never existed. The girls' eyes widened and they turned and stared at each other as if waking up from a shared nightmare. They held each other's gaze for a minute, communicating wordlessly, the way only siblings can and then both broke into the goofiest grins Kass had ever seen. For the first time, they looked like young girls instead of broken, dead-eyed dolls. Kass knew that even magic as powerful as this wouldn't be able to wipe the memories of their abuse from their minds completely, but it would help. Hopefully, one day, it would all be little more than a passing cloud scuttling across their mental skies.

"Abby, Gina, I'd like you to go with Tory's grandmother Pauline now. She's going to take you back to her house for a sleepover, if that's okay."

Pauline stepped forward and the girls smiled shyly at her. As Kass watched them walk through the cemetery gate, a very clear visualization rose in her mind. The shreds of their souls lengthening and growing, beginning to knit themselves back together and with every step they took, another new stitch was cast.

Once the girls were safely away, Kass turned her attention to the parents. Their immobile bodies had been covered and placed behind the obelisk, out of sight of their daughters. Kass now motioned for them to be carried forward and laid out on the ground in front of the pyre.

The coven, with Kass taking Pauline's place as the thirteenth, formed a circle around the two and recited an incantation that stretched back to the very origins of humanity. Their voices rose and the earth beneath them began to boil. Streamers of golden light rose from individual plots scattered around the cemetery and rushed toward the prone forms of Debbie and Brian.

Ribbons of energy poured down over the two, writhing around them, touching, tasting and probing their every fold and orifice. Although neither could move or speak, Kass could see their eyes as they rolled wildly, their pupils huge with terror, primitive, guttural sounds muted behind closed lips. More luminescent strands appeared, intertwining with the first wave, forming thicker bands of light that wrapped themselves around the pair's bodies, encasing them like fossilized insects trapped in amber.

Kass and the others watched, transfixed, as images began to appear within the light. Horribly deformed human faces, hideous monsters, snapshots of war and death, torture and abuse flooded past. Kass wrenched her gaze away, as did the others, one by one. Brian and Debbie were not in a position to do the same. All they could do was lie there, eyes open and acutely conscious but physically helpless, completely at the mercy of others who were more powerful than themselves.

The light swirled and pulsed around them wildly for a few moments and then the ancestors decided it was time to take their errant kin home. A fissure opened under their bodies and the light sucked them down into the moist earth below. Seconds later, everything was as it had been before. The lights were gone, the pyre was gone, and the Nylands were gone. The thirteen ended their ritual, broke the circle and went their separate ways.

*   *   *

A week later, Kass finished up her final report closing out the

Nyland case. The girls were thriving under Pauline's care and due to the combined efforts of the coven --whose members included a lawyer, a judge and a real estate broker, as well as several successful business folks-- all the legal and financial details of the children's care had been quickly settled.

For the few that had asked, the story was that Brian had finally gotten that big, important job out west that he had been angling for. Unfortunately, he had had to leave immediately and Debbie, being the loyal wife she was, decided to go with him so they could get the family settled before uprooting the kids.

Temporary guardianship papers had been signed, the house had been put up for sale and a trust fund established for the kids' expenses until such time as they were reunited with their parents...or came of legal age.

Kass sat back in her seat and allowed herself a smile.

The intercom clicked on and Charmaine's voice filled the cabin. "Broomstick One on final approach. Buckle up Kass, touch down in two minutes."

Moving House
Rob Smales

The sun shone warmly, the day filled with the buzzing roar of a two-stroke engine and the clean scent of fresh-cut grass. Tommy leaned against the rounded edge of the huge birdbath, folded his arms, and watched Anthony work. Shouting would be useless, Tommy knew, both because of Anthony's ear protectors and the machine he strode behind: a Cub Cadet 33-inch, rear wheel drive, self-propelled mower with a 420cc overhead valve engine, four speeds forward, one back, eight-inch castor-style front wheels for easy maneuverability, a mulching blade, and a two-gallon gas tank for hours of grass-cutting fun.

Tommy chuckled. All he knew about his own battered Toro was that it took gas in one hole, oil in another, and cut grass with the whirlygig underneath—but most people in the neighborhood could recite the Cub Cadet's stats. Some folks told you about their kids: Anthony told people about his *stuff*.

Anthony reached the end of his swath, turned the big yellow machine, and tossed off a jaunty wave as he caught sight of Tommy. He mowed his way back to the middle of the lawn, a bespectacled man preceded by a prodigious gut—Anthony referred to himself as *post athletic*—shirtsleeves neatly turned halfway up his forearms and long khaki pants, despite the summer heat.

"Hey there, neighbor." Anthony dropped his ear protectors

around his neck as the engine sputtered off. "What can I do for you? That old Toro finally kick the buc—"

"Hi, Anthony," Tommy said, heading off any criticism of his own mower. "I saw you out here and thought I'd ask if you needed any help with this." He thumped the cement beneath his hip, but the water didn't even ripple; between the five-foot bowl and the three-foot pedestal, the birdbath had to weigh five or six hundred pounds. "What are you going to do with it, anyway?"

Anthony squinted. "What are you talking about?"

"The birdbath. Where are you going to put it?"

"What? It's perfect right here!" Anthony rubbed the birdbath rim affectionately. "*Beautiful Communities* even said so. Their review said this little baby made Crystal Street 'undefeatable,' remember?"

"Yes," said Tommy. "But what are you going to do, give it to the new . . ."

Anthony's face went stiff. "New . . .?"

"The new owner," Tommy said. "Catherine sold . . . Anthony, Catherine finally sold the lot. I thought—"

He spun toward his own house, bordering the lot on one side. One of the kitchen curtains twitched, guiltily: Jenny, watching him talk to Anthony. Jenny, who'd told him of Catherine's sale and suggested he go offer to help with the birdbath. "How did Anthony take it?" he'd asked. "How do you think?" she'd said—which he now realized wasn't actually an answer to his question. *I've been set up to be the bearer of bad news*, he thought, glaring at the twitchy curtain. *Dammit.*

"I thought you knew," he said to the reddening Anthony. "Catherine sold it, and it was some kind of hurry-up deal: the new owner's taking possession by the end of the week."

"But—"

"You'll have to do something with your birdbath."

"But—"

"I *told* you not to put this thing on land that wasn't your own. Will you be calling in professionals?" he asked, in the somewhat desperate hope that it would sound like a good idea: Tommy didn't relish throwing his back out helping a man who probably wouldn't even think to say *thank you.*

Anthony sputtered. "I—you—it—we'll just see about this!" He stormed off toward his own house, bordering the lot across from Tommy's own. "I'm calling an emergency neighborhood meeting!"

Halfway across the lawn he spun and marched back, punched the electric starter on the Cub Cadet, revved up the throttle and threw it into fourth gear. "One hour!" he shouted over his shoulder, trotting for home behind the speeding mower. Tommy turned toward home with a sigh.

In the kitchen window, the curtain twitched again.

*　　*　　*

"How did I not know about this?"

The eighteen people gathered in Anthony's living room—all the residents of the neighborhood he'd been able to get hold of on short notice—just stared. "I mean, here I am, *president* of the Crystal Street Neighborhood Group, and I find out by *accident!*" He waved a hand at Tommy, who shot Jenny a withering look. Jenny, to her credit, withered a bit. Anthony didn't notice; he was leaning down to place his hands to either side of the cell phone resting on the coffee table, the screen's green speaker icon indicating that a call was live and the speakerphone engaged.

"I thought, Catherine," Anthony enunciated, "that all potential additions to the neighborhood were to be vetted by me?"

"And I've explained to you," came the voice of Catherine Wright, the realtor who'd handled all the properties in the neighborhood since before Tommy and Jenny moved in a decade earlier. "On numerous occasions. My office is under no obligation to run anything by you whatsoever. That I have done so in the past was merely a courtesy on my part. This client paid to expedite the process, and there just wasn't time." Though her tone had been clipped and professional thus far, Tommy detected a bit of smile creeping in. "I'm sorry if this is discomfiting to you, Anthony."

Though Anthony's head was down, the flesh along his ruler-straight part went pink. "This is because of the birdbath, isn't it?"

"Ah, yes," said Catherine, the smile in her voice now wide and toothy—she lived over in Pinehurst, one of Crystal Street's major contenders in *Beautiful Communities* every year. "The 'undefeatable' birdbath. I *told* you to get that out of there—you really should have asked first, rather than just apologizing after the fact."

"I—"

"I'm sorry, Anthony, I have another call. I'll have to let you go."

"Wait!" Anthony shouted. "When does construction start?"

"No construction. She's moving her house in there on a flatbed—should be there by the end of the week."

"A prefab?" Anthony was horrified.

"No, no, she's *moving her whole house*, Anthony. Apparently been in the family for generations. Look, I really have to go. Good luck with your birdbath. And good luck with Barbara Yeager. You're in for a treat."

She cut the connection and for a moment they all stood around watching Anthony breathe, which seemed to be giving him some difficulty. Jenny made what Tommy recognized as *significant eye contact*, and subtly jutted her chin at Anthony. Tommy gave a somewhat helpless shrug. The eye contact grew more significant while the chin grew less subtle.

Tommy sighed. "So," he said, his enthusiasm sounding almost as false as it felt, "you need a hand moving that—"

Though he remained bowed over the coffee table, Anthony's hand shot into the air, reminding Tommy of a televangelist about to tap the viewing audience for cash. "No. Not right now. I have until the end of the week. I'll think of something."

"Okay," said Tommy. "If that's what you—"

"This isn't over." Anthony's head came up, eyes slitted, mouth curved into a smile Tommy found somewhat unsettling. "I have until the end of the week to find this . . . what was her name? Yeager? Barbara Yeager? I have a week to find her and work my magic." He rubbed his fleshy palms together in a wholly unappealing way, and some of the people, reading the way the meeting was going, were already filing out the door.

"Wait," Tommy began, concern creeping in around his relief at not having to help move that birdbath. "I don't think there's anything you—"

"A week," Anthony said, voice smooth once more, but palms still massaging each other unsettlingly. "I can do a lot in a week. Mrs. Yeager might decide she likes the birdbath. Who knows? She may decide she doesn't want to live on Crystal Street after all. It's happened before, right?"

Tommy was about to ask *what* had happened before, but Anthony struck first.

"Listen, Tommy, thanks for the offer, really, but I have some calls to make. Would you excuse me?" He waved a hand at the door. Jenny stood waiting for Tommy, the last to leave.

Well," he said, "if that's what you want—"

"It is. It is what I want. Please." Tommy followed Jenny out the door, but before he was gone those palms were back to rubbing each other in small, almost excited circles. "Oh, she won't know what hit her," Anthony said as Tommy closed the door behind them.

*   *   *

Tires screeched; both Tommy's feet left the ground for an instant and—if he was ever completely honest about it, which he *never* would be—a tiny spurt of urine shot into the front of his jockeys. He'd pulled the Honda into the driveway after work, glanced toward the recently sold lot to see if Anthony had done anything about that birdbath yet—and froze right there, stunned. He'd wandered to the sidewalk in front of the old lot like some sort of zombie and just . . . stared. He'd still been there, staring, when that car in the street behind him had—

"What the *hell* is *that?*"

Anthony's scream was, if anything, even louder than his tires had been, but Tommy had a firm grip on his bladder by then. He assumed the question was rhetorical, so he merely stood silently as Anthony's car door opened and closed with extreme vigor. There was scrabbling, the skid of shoe leather on cement, and Anthony stood beside him, gut jouncing like a nervous man's Adam's apple with every barely controlled breath.

"*What* is that? What *is* that? *What* is *that?*"

A hand smacked Tommy's shoulder, and he realized the questions *weren't* rhetorical. He tore his eyes from the scene and looked at Anthony. The somewhat smarmy, self-confident look from the night before was gone: behind his slightly crooked glasses, the president of the Crystal Street Neighborhood Group's eyes were wild as he stood in a slight crouch, hands spread as if looking for someone to wrestle. His normally perfect hair had a cowlick from the speed at which he'd exited his Mercedes, and Tommy restrained a strange urge to reach out and smooth it down. Instead he offered the only answer that came to mind.

"Uh . . . it's a house, Anthony."

It *was* a house, but it wasn't like any house Tommy had ever seen—*especially* on Crystal Street. It was a cottage. No, a hut. No, that wasn't it either. *A hovel?* Tommy thought, but then Anthony's shocked whisper gave him the word his mind was looking for.

"It's a fucking *dump!*"

Yes, that's it! Tommy thought, feeling an almost stoned sort of happiness to have that little dilemma solved. His own breathing was odd, he realized, and the skin on his face felt asleep. *Shock?* he wondered. *Was the sight of this dump enough to put me into shock?*

The peaked roof was uneven—and not due to any architectural daring. The right side sagged like the back of a broken-down mule, but it took a moment to realize it because of the windows. They were also uneven, but in the other direction; the window to the right of the porch was noticeably higher than the one on the left. The aforementioned porch—if you ignored the zig-zag stairs—was as perfect and square as if it had been plumbed and leveled by God himself, which only exacerbated the roof and windows, giving the right side of the structure a strange, squinty look, like it was in the throes of some kind of housy stroke.

The dump—that word was coming in *so* handy—didn't appear to have ever been painted beyond its original color, which was dirt. They had done the trim in mud, then gone for broke when they painted the porch, and chosen muddy dirt. The color scheme made details difficult to make out in the dim light under the two—no four, with those two in the back—spreading oak trees that must have also come in on the truck with the house.

And there had been trucks, no doubt about that! Muddy tire marks—some better than a yard wide—showed where something related to WWII tanks had driven about, backing in and pulling out. Smaller ruts showed where heavy equipment had gone to drop the trees—and the full-grown bushes Tommy now saw all around the base of the house as his eyes adjusted to the riot of non-color. The lawn, once so meticulously groomed—Anthony had gone so far as to crawl about trimming the border with hand shears—now looked like a teething puppy's favorite chew toy after a hard day's use.

Perusing the destruction, Tommy followed one set of smaller tracks—*probably a Bobcat*, he thought—to a sight that snapped him out of his semi-daze.

"Oh, Anthony," he said, mouth in motion before he'd thought it through. "Man, I'm sorry."

"This is bullshit," Anthony muttered, still hunching as if

prepared to take on all comers. "That bitch said I had 'til the end of the week. I had a week!"

"No," Tommy heard his mouth say, still running merrily ahead of his brain, "that's not what she said. She said Mrs. Yeager would move her house in *by* the end of the week. That meant any time from then *until* the end of the week."

Anthony wheeled on him.

"But that wasn't what I was talking about," Tommy blurted, thrusting a finger toward those Bobcat tracks. "Look!"

Anthony spun, following the line of the finger—and his gasp was almost a scream in reverse. He straightened, hands drooping to his sides, then one lifted, groping the air before him as a small, helpless sound filtered up from his chest.

"Eeeah?"

Though they didn't cross over onto Anthony's property, the small earthmover tracks led right up to the line and then away, making an arrow in the earth pointing out something *just* to the other side of the line.

"My . . . my birdbath," whispered Anthony.

Tommy couldn't see if it had been chipped or cracked, but the individual parts were separate, the pedestal lying on its side, the bowl leaning, upside down, upon it. The bowl was intact, but even from this distance Tommy could see the churned-up earth around the heap: the birdbath segments had been simply dropped—and Tommy figured Anthony'd be hard-pressed to remove it without some kind of heavy equipment tearing up his own lawn.

"That's my birdbath . . ." he said again. "That's . . . that *bitch*!"

Tommy, staring at how deep the pieces had sunk into the ground and a little lost in wondering just how to get out of his offer to help move the damn thing, was surprised when Anthony launched into motion. Head lowered, shoulders rolling, arms swinging wildly, Anthony chugged across Mrs. Yeager's devastated lawn like the Little Engine that Could climbing that hill—if the little engine had filled the air with enough curses to make it shimmer.

"Anthony," Tommy called, tottering belatedly after him. "I don't think you should do that right now. Let's give it a little time and approach this thing with cool heads."

When Anthony shouted back what he could *do* with his cool head—an anatomical impossibility—Tommy brushed the suggestion aside and followed anyway. He'd need to know what had happened for Jenny. Because she would ask.

Anthony's forward momentum was disrupted when a loose board on the stairs sent him reeling left, then another nearly pitched him into the bushes to his right, but he made it to the porch—still strangely level and solid, Tommy noted. He balled a fist, skipped right past knocking, and *pounded* on the door.

"Mrs. Yeager! I want to talk to you! Come out here so we can talk . . . please?"

That last was said in kind of a whimper as he tucked his pounding fist under one armpit, with a muttered "Son of a bitch." He'd really thrown his shoulder into it, and from where he stood at the foot of the stairs, Tommy didn't think that door had sounded at all ramshackle: it had sounded like Anthony was pounding on a bank vault. The door remained closed.

"I, uh, I don't think she's in there, buddy," Tommy said. "She probably won't move *into* the house until tomorrow or the day after, you know? C'mon, let's go home."

Anthony glared at the door a moment longer, then pivoted on one heel and stomped down the stairs—where he promptly stumbled sideways and right off into the bushes. He struggled out of the shrubbery, informing the whole neighborhood at the top of his lungs that yes, there were indeed fucking *thorns* in there, *huge* fucking *thorns*. He flailed back into the open, plucked away a couple of twigs still clinging to his torso via unintentional piercings, and stomped wordlessly toward home, right hand still tucked under his arm.

"So, about that birdbath, buddy," Tommy called after him. "Maybe we should get the name of the company *she* used to get it out of there? You know—just something to keep in mind."

Tommy had just reached his own front yard when the ratchet and squeak of an ancient door opening carried to him through the evening air. He whirled, and though one of the looming oaks partially obscured the front door to the new house, the stooped figure of an old woman stepped down onto the crooked stairs. She wore black or brown, and was hard to make out with the distance and the shadows cast by house and tree, but the figure quickly swept the steps, then scuttled for the door.

She doesn't have any trouble with the stairs, he thought, as Anthony hove into view. Wounds forgotten, the president of the Crystal

Street Neighborhood Group sprinted across the tattered lawn, broken-field running around and over the worst of the destruction in a manner that gave credence to his *post-athletic* claim. The *cha-thunk* of a heavy door closing came just as he leaped at the foot of the stairs, flying over treacherous treads to disappear onto the shadowy porch.

Tommy heard shouting, then thin pounding, then more shouting. Silence loomed—and suddenly the evening was filled with the most terrible screams; awful shrieks, the only words that made any sense being a repetitious *fuck-fuck-fuck!* The screams died, and Anthony limped into view, now clutching his *left* hand under one arm. He paused halfway across that destroyed front yard, twisted about with a groan, and ripped free a thorny creeper that had been stuck in his back. He flung it toward the little house with a weak "And *stay* in there!" before turning and limping—with both legs, it appeared—toward the safety of his own home.

With the show over, Tommy entered his own house to find Jenny carrying groceries in from the garage. She gave him a quick peck, but it was with eyebrows raised.

"What was that commotion? It sounded like someone kicking a bag of cats that had been taught the F-word."

"Well . . . have you been home yet today?"

"No," she said. "I stopped at the store after work, and"—she hefted the bags in her arms—"just got in. What's up?"

He sighed. "Well, to begin with, we have a new neighbor."

*　　*　　*

Urgent! read the flyer. *Imperative! Your presence is required!* And there wasn't just one hastily printed flyer in there: there were *five.* Tommy looked up and down the street: bundles of paper stuck out of most of the mailboxes, the red *Urgent!* at the top fluttering in the breeze. The garage door suddenly ground upward, and Jenny pulled the Toyota into the driveway, lowering her window when she saw Tommy on the front porch.

"You okay?" she shouted.

He waved the flyer. "Anthony's called an emergency meeting."

"Are you serious?"

He nodded. "Get this: our presence is 'required'."

Her eyes rolled. "Oh, Christ. When?"

"We have"—he consulted the flyer—"an hour." He looked up but the Toyota was already moving, his disgusted wife muttering behind the rising window.

*　　*　　*

It was standing room only in Anthony's living room, thirty-seven people having responded to the flyer—the entire Neighborhood Group, minus a single absentee.

"Where's Mary?" Anthony asked Joe Burgess after a quick head count.

"The hospital," said Joe. "With her cancer."

"But this is an emergency," said Anthony. "Couldn't she—"

"No," Joe said, eyes flat.

Anthony turned to the rest of them. "Well, as you know, this *is* an emergency."

"Is it *really?*" said Joe. "It's just a new neighbor. It happens all over the country every damn day. You're blowing this way out of proportion."

Anthony wheeled toward him as best he was able, casting a hand down his own body with flourish. "Does *this* look blown out of proportion?"

Anthony was, to put it mildly, a mess. A heavy-duty strap-on brace supported one knee, and a splint wrapped one wrist. His upper lip was split, and his eyes looked like he'd never been taught to keep his hands up in a fight. What skin they could see was covered with small Band-Aids and what looked to be splots from a styptic pencil, and that cowlick from the night before still stood at attention.

"I saw you run over there last night," said Carol Standish, who lived across the street from Anthony. "I thought an old woman lived there. She did all that to you?"

"Yes! Well . . . no. I . . ." He looked at Tommy, who stared back blandly. "I never actually met the woman."

The room erupted into murmurs of disbelief.

"But all this happened just trying to knock on her door," Anthony shouted, pointing at himself. "The place is unsafe! It's a mess! It's . . . it's a *shithole!* I—"

There was a heavy knock at the front door. Anthony's head whipped around, though the move made him wince. He looked at Joe. "You don't suppose Mary . . .?"

"No."

"Well, whoever it is, I'm busy," Anthony said, hobbling to the door as the knock came again, loud and evenly spaced. Anthony grabbed the knob and flung the door wide, already in mid-dismissal.

"I'm sorry, but we're all *terribly* busy right—gaaaah!"

He staggered back, nearly falling due to the knee brace. Framed in the doorway was a nose.

The nose was large. The nose was long. The nose had warts, which, in turn, had warts of their own, though some of the smaller, younger warts had decided to break with tradition and grow thick, wiry hairs instead. These hairs were black, unlike the iron-gray bristles fluttering in the cavernous nostrils, caught in the current of some very audible breathing.

"There is meeting?" said the nose—and Tommy became aware of the woman behind the prodigious proboscis. Though a voluminous brown robe concealed her body, the hand and arm protruding from her sleeve to clutch her walking stick were nearly skeletal, and even bent beneath the obvious hump on her back she still matched Anthony in height; if she'd stood straight, she may have had to duck through the door. Her hair was the same gray as the follicle florets dangling from her nose, and beneath it were a pair of sickly yellow eyes, the left riding significantly higher than the right.

The eyes made the connection for Tommy, having noticed a similar trait in the windows of the new house next door. He stepped up behind the open-mouthed Anthony. "Mrs. Yeager?"

"There is meeting?" the woman repeated. "Yes?"

Her words were easily understood, but her accent was thick and strangely familiar. "Yes," Tommy said.

"Emergency meeting?"

The word *emergency* made it click for Tommy, with its rolling R and clipped vowels: she sounded just like Mr. Chekov from the bridge of the starship *Enterprise*. Before Tommy could respond again, Anthony lurched to life like one of those animatronics at Disney, when somebody gooses the juice.

"I'll say it's an emergency! It's a *travesty*! Your house is—"

"My house is emergency?" She hadn't raised her voice, but her question cut Anthony off as effectively as a shout, her strange, mismatched eyes still staring toward Tommy. "What about inspection? Wright woman said inspection once house has settled. How can there be emergency before inspection?"

"Have you *seen* your so-called house?" Anthony shouted. "Your *lawn*? We're the Crystal Street Neighborhood Group—*I'm* the president—and we're meeting to determine what you should do about it!"

It was odd, Tommy thought, to watch her offset eyes, designed to be permanently out of focus, finally lock onto Anthony with a precision and intensity that rocked him back a step. Even with the warped gaze and hump on her back, she reminded Tommy of a snake looming over a battered, limping mouse.

"*You* will determine what I will do. About *my* house?"

"But it's an eyeso—" Anthony began.

"Is *my* house, yes?"

"Well, ye—"

"Is my *land*, yes? I pay for, is *mine*, yes?"

"But it's not safe," Anthony tried. "I fell on your stairs. Twice. I could sue!"

"Not inspected. But I use stairs, not fall down. Perhaps you're just clumsy?"

"Why didn't you answer your door last night? I knocked, and—"

"Is law I must answer door? Is law I must open to stranger shouting the fuck on my porch?"

"No," said Tommy, trying to calm things down before they got out of hand. "Of course not. We—"

But she took a step toward Anthony, her long and lumpy nose stopping mere inches from his. "Pounding on my door. Shouting the fuck. Tromping through my bushes with more the fuck. 'Fuck-fuck-fuck!'" she roared, in a shockingly good impression of Anthony in the thorns. "And now, deciding what I will do with *my* land. *My* house."

She reached out a twisted twig finger to poke Anthony's chest, one stiff tap emphasizing each word. "You. Are. *Rude*."

She spun to the crowd packed into the living room, and if her voice had been forceful before, now it practically overflowed with authority. "Emergency is over. Meeting is over. Go back to your homes. *Now*."

She blocked their path through the front, but the back way was free, and people began filing out through the kitchen as fast as they could, some trying to maintain a sort of dignity, others simply fleeing.

"But—" Anthony began, his emergency meeting disintegrating before his eyes. Mrs. Yeager looked his way, head cocked like some hideous RCA dog. Anthony stopped, swallowed, then found courage enough to speak.

"But you broke my birdbath . . ."

He trailed off as she broke into a grin as iron gray as her hair— a strangely predatory expression Tommy stepped back from, even though it wasn't aimed his way. She took a slow step toward Anthony, who tried to take a compensatory step away but found himself hemmed in by the stairs up to the bedrooms.

"*Your* birdbath. On *my* land. *Rude.*" Her voice turned sly. "Also, I think, illegal? Perhaps *I* should sue *you.*" She snapped dry stick fingers with a disgusted sound as she turned away. "Pah! Was not broken. Was returned to you. We are done."

She moved to the front door—which still yawned open to the night—the robe-thing she wore hiding her lower limbs, making her seem almost to float across the threshold. As she passed out of his home, Anthony came to himself once more, hobbling to the doorway and thrusting a finger toward her retreating back.

"This isn't over!"

"No," came her answer. "But it *will* be."

Silence fell.

"Well, at least it was a *short* meeting," Tommy said. Anthony merely stared blankly into the night, muttering.

"How did she even know? I didn't drop off a . . . and how did she know it was my . . . and it *is* unsafe, it has to—the inspection!"

Tommy was almost through the door when a hand clutched his forearm with fevered strength, and Anthony stared at him from a foot away, one eye squinting slightly in unconscious imitation of their new neighbor. "The *inspection,*" he said. "That's it! She'll *never* pass! I'll talk to the guy, make *sure* . . ." he turned, hobbling deeper into the house, already lost in his scheme.

"I'll, uh, I'll just let myself out then, okay?" Tommy called after him. "I'll just . . ." he shook his head, and closed the door as he left.

* * *

"I'm telling you, she *did* something to it!"

Tommy stood in Anthony's garage examining the blackened remains of a Cub Cadet 33-inch, rear wheel drive, self-propelled mower with a 420cc overhead valve engine, with four speeds forward, one back, eight-inch castor-style front wheels, and a mulching blade. The two-gallon gas tank was noticeably absent— well, not so much *absent* as melted down the side of the scorched machine. The yellow paint had either burned or peeled away from the heated metal as the lawnmower had fried.

"I just don't see *how*," Tommy said. "Tell me again. Slower."

"I went out this morning," Anthony began.

"You didn't go to work?"

"Do I look fit for working? Anyway, I gassed up the Cub, and—"

"You can't go to work, but you're okay for that?"

"Look," Anthony shouted, "do you want to hear the story or don't you? So I broke out the Cub. Even with all the ruts and tire marks, you could see I'd left the job only half done. It made it look even *worse*! Unkempt. So I fired up the Cub and headed over there."

"Oh, for Christ's sake! She made it very clear that is *her* property—what made you think she'd be okay with you messing with her yard?"

"I've been taking care of that lot for—"

"But it was never *yours*!"

"I have to keep marking my territory, don't I?"

Tommy was incredulous. "What are we, *dogs* now? But whatever—you stupidly went over there with your big, expensive lawn mower. Then what happened?"

"Well, the next thing I know, she's shouting from those goddamn death-trap steps of hers."

"You *heard* her?" Tommy said, recalling the loud motor and oversized ear protection.

Anthony made a face. "Well, no, not *heard* really . . . I guess I was just suddenly *aware* of her, you know what I mean?"

Recalling the woman's massive presence at the meeting the night before, Tommy nodded.

"So she's standing there, waving her arms, and I can see she's shouting. I ignored her and kept on mowing . . . and I guess I *might* have given her the finger. A little. You know, kind of as one does in these situations."

"When you're illegally cutting someone's lawn."

"*Then* I *did* hear her, shouting a bunch of Russian nonsense at me. Except for . . ."

Tommy raised an eyebrow.

"Rude, all right? She called me rude. I looked at her then—I mean, that's rude right there, name-calling—and she was waving her broom at me, you know, shaking it like a threat. The next thing I knew, *whoosh*, the Cub was on fire—and I don't mean there was a little flame that grew, I mean just . . . *whoosh*. The whole thing was ablaze."

There was a thoughtful pause.

"Well, you *do* have a bad hand. Maybe you spilled some gas—"

Anthony's gaze was cold. "I have *never* spilled gasoline on the Cub. *Or* oil."

"Sorry! But it might explain how—"

"*She* did it!"

"How?"

"I don't know *how*, but she *did*."

"Uh-huh," said Tommy. "Good luck explaining *that* one to your insurance adjuster."

"There's more!" said Anthony, eyes manic. "I was worried that it might blow up or something, so I left it there to burn itself out. I came home to put some ointment on my hands—I *did* try to save it, you know—and I'd been here about an hour when I smelled smoke. For a minute I was afraid the house was on fire, but I followed the smell, and found it sitting right here."

Tommy was baffled, but still trying to be the voice of reason. "So she pulled—"

"It weighs over three-hundred pounds and it's frozen in gear."

"She got someone to help?"

"It was still smoking and too hot to touch when I found it here. With the garage door closed."

"So . . . she . . ." Tommy began, but wasn't sure where to go from there.

"How did she get a three-hundred pound smoldering wreck all the way over here and into my garage *without me hearing the garage door going up and down?*"

"She's a resourceful old woman?"

"No." Anthony stared off at nothing. "She's more than that. She's . . . *different*."

Tommy didn't like the way he spat that last word: *different.* He tried to get Anthony engaged in something constructive. "So, you want some help moving this thing?"

"My birdbath. My Cub. My marriage. The *Beautiful Communities* award. She even undermined my position with the Neighborhood Group." He turned toward Tommy, eyes afire. "*She's ruining my life!* But I'll get her. Her home inspection is tomorrow. We'll see who has the last laugh! We'll just see! Ha! Ha-ha!"

Tommy left Anthony standing over the ruined corpse of his Cub Cadet, and though the man laughed maniacally, unchecked tears rolled down his face.

* * *

"She *passed!*"

Tommy yanked the phone from his head with a wince, then spoke into the mouthpiece with the speaker still a good six inches from his ear. "Anthony? Is that you?"

"She *passed!*"

"Are you talking about the inspection?"

"Yes! I talked to the guy. I pointed out the stairs, the roof, made sure to point out that she has no electrical service. Did you notice that? No wires at all? No gas line, either."

"I had not," said Tommy, but now that Anthony mentioned it, it *was* strange. "So how did she pass?"

"*She has a dispensation!*"

"A what?"

"A *dispensation!* She has special permission from *somebody* or other to not have gas or electrical service! She—get this—uses lamps and a wood-burning stove! So I said 'Isn't that unsafe?' and he told me that was her insurance company's headache."

"Huh. But the roof? The stairs?"

"That idiot said everything was structurally sound. He must have been paid. I can't believe she thinks she can just flout the rules like this!"

Tommy was tempted to tell Anthony that *his* flouting the rules was what had gotten him into this mess in the first place, but he worried the man's head might actually go nuclear, leaving the entire neighborhood nothing more than a radioactive crater. He clamped his teeth tightly shut.

"But that boob gave me an idea—*the* idea! I know just what to do now, and tonight we'll see! We'll see who has the last laugh! We'll all see!"

"Anthony," Tommy started, "don't do anyth—" But the connection went dead. Tommy stared at the phone.

"What was *that* about?" said Jenny.

"I think Anthony's lost his mind."

Jenny smirked. "No great loss there."

"I'm serious. I think this is going to go very wrong."

*   *   *

Though Anthony had dressed like a television burglar—black shoes, pants, turtleneck, and (despite the summer heat) watch cap, the chalky white Styptic patches on his face shone like tiny searchlights under the streetlight as he skulked toward casa Yeager.

Oh, and the yellow plastic five-gallon gas can stood out like a sore thumb.

Tommy jogged straight in from the street, across the devastated front yard, and easily caught up with the lurching figure. With the brace on one leg and hands bandaged from trying to put out the flaming Cub, Anthony was focused on carrying the obviously heavy can over the rough terrain, and never even heard Tommy's approach until:

"What the hell are you doing?" Tommy stage-whispered.

"Gaah!" Anthony shouted, dropping the can, which thunked solidly to the ground.

Yup, it's full, thought Tommy as Anthony whipped about with a finger across his lips, hissing "*Shhhhh!*" as if *he* hadn't been the one doing the shouting.

"What the hell are you doing?" Tommy repeated.

"I'm taking my life back." Anthony hoisted the can again. Big and yellow, *Cub Cadet* scrolled across the side, the can had come with the expensive machine that sat, scorched and stinking, in Anthony's garage.

"What are you going to do, burn the house down?"

"Yep." Anthony limped into motion.

"You can't *do* that!" Tommy said, tagging along.

"Why not?"

"Because, well, you just *can't.*"

"Watch me. That inspector said her lamps and wood stove

were a fire hazard. I'm just speeding up the process."

"But they'll be able to tell it was gas! Lamps don't run on gasoline."

They were skirting the thorny bushes at the side of the house, and Anthony paused just at the corner to the front. "I know." He shook the sloshing can. "That's why I bought kerosene. I get some of this in one of her windows, and it'll look like she had a little 'accident'."

"I can't let you do that." Tommy gripped Anthony's arm. "Come on, we'll—"

Anthony's palm met Tommy's chest and *shoved*. Tommy stumbled, fell on his backside, and looked up at Anthony in stunned silence.

"This is my *life* we're talking about, here!" Anthony's whisper was almost a shout. "It's my *life*, and I'm taking it *back*!" He limped around to the front of the house—and stopped dead. "What the *hell*?"

Tommy scrambled to his feet and over to Anthony's side—where he, too, stood dumbstruck.

"Where are the stairs?"

The stairs, the same ones that had thrown Anthony into the thorns and been pronounced rock-solid by the house inspector, were gone. The front of the porch was smooth and unbroken, and the porch itself higher than Tommy remembered; there had been three steps leading up—Anthony had taken them all in a single leap—but now the platform was shoulder height, which was—

"Impossible," Anthony whispered.

Tommy had seen the house from the front when he'd crossed the yard. Hadn't there been stairs? He couldn't be positive. The shadows cast by the great trees were deep and dark, sure, but wouldn't he have noticed something like this?

Anthony hoisted the heavy can to the porch. "Give me ten fingers."

"What?" said Tommy, startled.

"Give me ten fingers. Boost me up there."

"No, man." Tommy raised his hands. "No way."

"Pussy." Anthony placed his bandaged palms to the porch and, amid pained grunts, began slowly levering his gut up and over the edge. He was about halfway up when he suddenly fell back to land flat on the lawn, the air whooshing out of him. A moment later the yellow gas can hit the ground next to him, kerosene fumes filling the air as the cap popped loose, the contents glug-glugging out to darken the soil. Anthony struggled over and righted the can, wheezing like an asthmatic.

"What . . . the hell . . . happened?"

"Loose board?"

"I . . . was thrown."

"Very loose board?"

"Why . . . didn't . . . the can . . . fall when I did?"

"Look, man, I don't know!" said Tommy. "I don't even know where the stairs went. Can we just go?"

"Side window." Anthony lurched away, can in hand. Sighing, Tommy followed back the way they had come until Anthony stopped, pointing to a pane of glass nearly obscured by the tall bushes. "That one."

"You can't get at it." Tommy said. "Thorns, remember?"

"Oh." Anthony drew his brush machete from its black sheath, invisible in the night. "I remember." He went to work hacking the dense thorny growth, sweat running from beneath his watch cap, flailing viciously until—with a startling crunch—one bush fell away, then another, and he suddenly had a clear path through to— nothing.

The house wasn't there.

"What the . . ."

Tommy followed Anthony through the new gap and found the house—the *front* of the house, not the side—a good ten feet back from the bushes. They stood in a new rectangular front yard, completely boxed in by the tall thorns.

"The house moved!" Tommy wasn't even trying to whisper any more, feeling that warm squirt in the front of his jockeys again. "It was right on the other side of the bushes—Anthony, *the house moved!* Let's get the hell out of here!"

"Impossible," Anthony said. "That's *impossible!*" He lurched through the gap in the bushes and Tommy followed, relieved Anthony was coming to his senses—and nearly ran into the Crystal Street Group president as he returned, full steam, bearing the half-empty gas can.

"*Fuck* getting it in the window," he shouted, unscrewing the fill cap. "I don't *care!* All I know is this fucker's gonna *burn!*" He swung the can, flinging a great arc of kerosene toward the house . . . which moved.

With an alacrity unusual for a house, the peaked, boxy structure lifted up on two thin legs, and—with a cracking of bushes— scuttled back another ten feet and stood bobbing slightly like a wary boxer unwilling to stand still.

The yellow can fell to the ground, though Anthony stood with arms outstretched, frozen in the act of splashing.

"*Enough!*"

The door burst open and Barbara Yeager strode onto the porch. Unfazed by the swaying house, she planted her feet wide, back straight and almost inhumanly tall, stabbing a long finger at the frozen Anthony.

"Long, long time I live alone. No neighbors. Nothing. So bring house to this country, try to retire, try to live by your rules, but you don't leave me alone. All I want is nice neighborhood to live out my days, but always men like you, you don't leave me alone."

She stomped a foot.

"Of course house ugly. House *starving*. House on *diet* so we fit in. But you, you will not stop. You want house handsome? You want house *healthy*? Fine. We do it your way. House must *feed*."

She shouted harsh syllables Tommy couldn't understand, and though he desperately wanted to run, he couldn't even avert his gaze as the house leapt forward, frighteningly quick. The front of the porch opened, and stairs came out, but twisted and bent into great wooden teeth. The mouth—for that's what it was, Tommy had no doubt—opened as the house pounced on the paralyzed Anthony like a cat with a mouse.

Anthony's top half disappeared into the great wooden gullet, two-by-four teeth punching into him—*through* him—front and back, like wooden chisels, and amid the horrible crack of breaking ribs and Anthony's muffled shrieks, Tommy heard the patter of falling blood slapping pooled kerosene. The great jaw ground twice, with a snapping of bone that had the wet heat in Tommy's pants spreading. The house gave a quick jerk, flipping what was left of Anthony up and in, again reminiscent of a cat with a mouse, and the crunching of bones went on and on as Tommy stood and wept, unable to move, unable to flee.

When it was over the house settled to the ground. The teeth became stairs, though Tommy couldn't help but see the bits of . . . *stuff* . . . smeared across the risers. Mrs. Yeager shuffled down the steps, hunched and leaning on her stick once more. She moved right up to Tommy, trembling where he stood and unable to stop. "So . . ." he said, voice high and tremulous, "we, ah, we good here? Please?"

She fixed him with the full force of her mismatched gaze; behind her the windows shifted slightly as the house did the same.

"Almost good," she said. "You will do something for me. Yes?"

"Yes," said Tommy, nodding like his life depended on it . . . which he was pretty sure it did. "Yes. I will."

* * *

"Let the meeting come to order," said Tommy. Jenny stared at him with red-rimmed eyes.

"Where's Anthony?" said Joe Burgess. "He'd never let a meeting go on without him. What's going on?"

"Well . . ." Tommy took a breath. "You may have noticed him acting funny lately? Apparently his mom is sick, and he had to go take care of her. So he's not going to be around for a while." He swallowed. "Maybe *quite* a while."

There was murmuring, and Tommy noticed quite a few smiles around the room. He raised his voice and grabbed their attention again. "Now, though, we need to elect an interim president for the Crystal Street Neighborhood Group, and to that end let me nominate our newest member, Barbara Yeager!"

The front door opened, and the crone flowed in as the murmurs died.

"*Spasibo,*" she said in her rough voice. "I am new neighbor, but I have much experience. I have plan—starting with fixing of my house." Her eyes found Jenny, weeping quietly, unnoticed by the rest.

"Seconded," Jenny whispered.

"Excellent," said Mrs. Yeager, and then power filled her voice. "*All in favor?*"

Faces blank, everyone in the room raised their hands, making the decision unanimous. The new president of the Crystal Street Neighborhood Group looked at Tommy, who felt terribly ill. "Now," she said, "we are good." She faced a room full of people lowering their hands, confusion on every face. "I must correct,"

she said. "My name is not 'Barbara.' Is Baba. Baba Yaga."
And the old witch smiled.

About the Cover Artist

Mikio Murakami is a Japanese-Canadian graphic designer. He specializes in cover art, T-shirts, logos and drinking bad coffee. His design company, SILENT Q DESIGN was founded in Montreal in 2006. Melding together the use of both realistic templates and surreal imagery, SILENT Q DESIGN's artistry proves, at first glance, that a passion for art still is alive, and that no musician, magazine, or venue should suffer from the same bland designs that have been re-hashed over and over. The evolution of artwork ranges both locally and internationally. SILENT Q DESIGN has commissioned work for Montreal and surrounding area bands such as SYNASTRY, EPOCHOLYPSE and REDEMPTION. Likewise, SILENT Q DESIGN also boasts work for musician international musician BOB KATSIONIS (TOSHIBA-EMI / LION MUSIC / CENTURY MEDIA) as well as Montreal Radio station 90.3 FM's SOUNDS OF STEEL music program. Their works go beyond fantasy landscapes and surreal imagery, offering their customers personalised service. SILENT Q DESIGN prides itself on being a multi-faceted entity that can serve even the contemporary business world.

About the Contributors

Scott T. Goudsward: By day Scott is a slave to the cubicle world, by night a slave to the voices in his head. He writes primarily horror but has been known to branch out with Sci-Fi and Fantasy. Scott is one of the coordinators of the New England Horror Writers and an active member of two local writers' groups. His short fiction has most recently appeared in *Anthology: Year 3* and *Atomic Age Cthulhu*. His latest novel ***Fountain of the Dead*** came out in January 2016 from Post Mortem Press and a new non-fiction book ***Horror Guide to Florida***, also from Post Mortem is out. Upcoming releases from Dark regions press are ***Return of the Old Ones*** and ***Horror Guide to Northern New***

England. Find Scott on Facebook and Twitter @scottgoudsward
www.goudsward.com/scott

David Price lives in Biddeford, Maine and has worked as a
hardwood floor contractor for more than twenty-five years. He is a
member of the Horror Writers Association, the Science Fiction &
Fantasy Writers of America, and the New England Horror Writers.
David is author of the paranormal suspense novella, *Dead in the
USA*, and has been published in several anthologies. He can be
found on Twitter as @_David_Price_ and at davidpriceauthor.com

Daniel G. Keohane is the Bram Stoker Award-nominated author
of *Plague of Darkness*, *Margaret's Ark* and *Solomon's Grave*,
as well as the **G. Daniel Gunn** horror novel *Destroyer of Worlds*
and novella *Nightmare in Greasepaint* (with L.L. Soares). His
short fiction has been published in a variety of professional
magazines and anthologies over the years, including *Borderlands 6*,
Cemetery Dance, *Shroud Magazine*, *Apex Digest*, *Madhouse*, *Coach's
Midnight Diner* and more. You can visit Dan and keep up-to-date
with prior and future work at www.dankeohane.com

Penny Dreadful is the eerie witch horror hostess of *Penny
Dreadful's Shilling Shockers*, a cult TV show which features
classic horror, sci-fi, and fantasy films. Penny Dreadful won the
Rondo Hatton Classic Horror Award for Favorite Horror Host in
2007 and again in 2010. She was inducted into the Horror Host
Hall of Fame in 2014. *Shilling Shockers* airs in over 200 cities and
towns throughout New England and in various other locations
throughout the country.

Suzanne Reynolds-Alpert writes speculative fiction in between
driving her kids around and meeting the incessant demands of her
feline overlords. She's a published author and professional editor
who loves to write and read creative and unusual stories with
unforgettable characters—usually while drinking coffee. Visit her
online at http://suzannereynoldsalpert.com.

John M. McIlveen is the author of the paranormal suspense
novel, *Hannahwhere* (Winner of the 2015 Drunken Druid Award

(Ireland) for high literary merit and Nominee for the 2015 Bram Stoker Award (HWA) in the First Novel category. He has also the author of two story collections, *Inflictions* and *Jerks and Other Tales From a Perfect Man*, and the well-received novelette *Got Your Back*. A father of five daughters, he works at MIT's Lincoln Laboratory and lives in Haverhill, MA with his wife, Roberta Colasanti.

Born and raised in Boston, Massachusetts, **Errick A. Nunnally** served one tour in the Marine Corps before deciding art school would be a safer—and more natural—pursuit. He remains distracted by art, comics, and genre novels. A designer by day, he earned a black belt in Krav Maga and Muay Thai kickboxing by night. His work has appeared in several anthologies *Doorways to Extra Time, Wicked Seasons, Inner Demons Out, A Dark World of Spirits and The Fey, After the Fall,* and *In Vein*. Errick's novel, *Blood For The Sun* is available wherever fine books are sold.

Morven Westfield first became fascinated by the unseen in her childhood, delighting in superstitions and ghost stories. Her interests are reflected in her writing. She penned two novels, *Darksome Thirst* and *The Old Power Returns*, (Harvest Shadows Publications) in which vampires battle modern witches and she regularly contributes articles on folklore and the supernatural to *The Witches Almanac*. Her supernatural-themed short stories have appeared in *Northern Haunts* (Shroud Publishing) and *Snowbound with Zombies* (Post Mortem Press). Morven lives in Central Massachusetts with her husband. Like many writers, she keeps a messy office and drinks way too much coffee. www.morvenwestfield.com

James A. Moore is the award-winning, bestselling, author of over forty novels, thrillers, dark fantasy and horror alike, including the critically acclaimed *Fireworks, Under The Overtree, Blood Red,* the *Serenity Falls* trilogy (featuring his recurring anti-hero, Jonathan Crowley) and his most recent novels, *City of Wonders* and *The Silent Army*, both part of the *Seven Forges* series. In addition to writing multiple short stories, he has also edited, with Christopher Golden and Tim Lebbon, *The British*

Invasion anthology for Cemetery Dance Publications. Moore's first short story collection, **Slices**, sold out before ever seeing print. He is currently at work on several additional projects, including the forthcoming **The Last Sacrifice**, book one in the **Tides of War**, series. Along with Jonathan Maberry and Christopher Golden, he hosts the Three Guys With Beards podcast and currently he lives in Massachusetts.

Catherine Grant is a speculative fiction writer who lives in Providence, Rhode Island with her husband and two cats named after Game of Thrones characters. She writes in bed before the day job and probably drinks too much coffee.

Paul McMahon has been writing since his Junior year in high school, when he won an argument with his English teacher by writing his first short story in second-person narrative. He is a member of the New England Horror Writers, and has appeared in all three previous NEHW anthologies, *Epitaphs*, *Wicked Seasons*, and *Wicked Tales*. His work has also been published in the anthologies *Flesh Like Smoke* and *Caped*. He writes two monthly columns for CinemaKnifeFight.com, where he's known as The Distracted Critic. Currently, he is hard at work on numerous stories and a novel that's giving him fits, but will not beat him... as long as that basket on his desk stays covered.

Nick Manzolillo hails from Scituate, Rhode Island. His writing has appeared in *Nebula Rift* and *Thuglit*. He's currently working on an MFA in Creative and Professional Writing from Western Connecticut State University. If he's not reading and writing in his spare time then he's probably busy refueling with chicken wings and craft beer.

Trisha J. Wooldridge is the former president of Broad Universe and a freelance editor, writer, and journalist. She also writes grown-up stories and poems, including EPIC award-winning *Bad-Ass Faieries* contributions. As child-friendly **T.J. Wooldridge**, she's authored 3 novels, **The Kelpie**, **Silent Starsong**, and **The Earl's Childe**. Find out more about all aspects of her writing and editing at www.anovelfriend.com.

K. H. Vaughan writes dark fiction and has been published in a growing number of anthologies. Appalachia looms large in his heritage, even if he was born on the Left Coast and raised in the heart of Yankeedom. He lives and teaches in New England with his wife and three children. Information on convention appearances and new releases can be found on Facebook or at www.khvaughan.com

Peter N. Dudar is the author of the Bram Stoker Award nominated book *A Requiem For Dead Flies* and the Solstice Award-winning novella *Where Spiders Fear To Spin*. A graduate of the University at Albany, Dudar now resides in Lisbon Falls, Maine, and is a founding member of the writers group The Tuesday Mayhem Society. His story in this anthology marks his third inclusion in the Journals of the New England Horror Writers. He is a fan of all things Halloween.

Izzy Lee is a freelance film festival programmer and writer for *Rue Morgue*, *ScreenAnarchy*, and *Fangoria*. When she's not writing, she's making scary little films, often from an outsider perspective. Her films are frightening, strange tales that often have a socio-political bent that have screened with Baskin, Antibirth, Tales of Halloween, They Look Like People, The Love Witch, The Lords of Salem, and The Sacrament. "Tilberian Holiday" is her first published short story. Visit Nihilnoctem.com for more madness.

Morgan Sylvia is a writer, a metalhead, a coffee addict, an Aquarius, and a work in progress. A former obituarist, she is now working as a full-time freelance writer. Her work has appeared in *Axes of Evil 1 and 2*, *Eternal Haunted Summer*, *Forgotten Places*, and *Tales From The Moonlit Path*. In 2014, she released her first book, *Whispers From The Apocalypse*, an apocalyptic horror poetry collection. Her debut horror novel, *Abode*, will be released in 2017.

Patrick Lacey was born and raised in a haunted house, and just so happens to be the author of *A Debt to be Paid*, *Sleep Paralysis*, and *Dream Woods*. He lives in Massachusetts with his Pomeranian and his muse, who is likely trying to kill him. Follow him on Twitter (@patlacey) or find (stalk) him on Facebook.

Jeremy Flagg is the author of the dystopian superhero science fiction series, *Children of Nostradamus* and the zombie satire series, *Suburban Zombie High*. He spends his free time immersed in geek culture and watching b-rate horror movies.

GD Dearborn loves cats and donated the fee for his story to Alley Cat Allies, http://www.alleycat.org. Please spay and neuter your pets! This is his first fiction sale.

Joshua Goudreau is a life-long writer, adventurer, and gentleman nerd about town. He was born and raised in Maine and resides there still, banging on keyboards, exploring mountains, and showering affection upon his furry feline lifemates. Check him out on Twitter @JoshIsAwesome42 and Facebook.com/JGWriting where he shares news, waxes philosophical, gets nerdy, and shares a bit too many cat pictures.

Born and raised in Connecticut, **Doug Rinaldi** received his art degree in Computer Animation and Special Effects for stage and screen. However, writing dark fiction was always his passion. At the turn of the millennium, he bid Connecticut a final farewell and relocated to Boston, Massachusetts where he's been honing his writing and artistic skills ever since.

Barry Lee Dejasu has previously had stories published in *Shock Totem* magazine and *Anthology, Year Three: Distant Dying Ember* (2014, Four Horsemen LLC). A native of Providence, Rhode Island, he attended college in Shirley Jackson's hometown of Bennington, Vermont, where a number of inspirations for "The Place of Bones" occurred. He currently lives in Providence with his wife and cats.

Ogmios is a story-teller, artist and the publisher for OTB Comics. His comic Splicers ran weekly in *The Sun Chronicle* for three years. He's had a number of poems/short stories published in anthologies and is a regular writer for OTB Comics. Art by Ogmios can be seen on many book covers and interior illustrations including New England Horror Writers' 2015 release, *Wicked Tales*. Currently, the main thrust of his creativity is to develop OTB Comics producing *Summerlands*, an anthology comic for mature readers. Ogmios is focused on horror, mythology, sci-fi, and fantasy. See more from Ogmios and OTB Comics at www.OTBcomics.com.

Jan Kozlowski is a freelance writer, editor and researcher who lives in CT with her husband, five cats & neurotic German shepherd. She is the author of ***Die, You Bastard! Die!***, edited by the legendary John Skipp and published by Deadite Press. Her short stories appear in *Hungry For Your Love: An Anthology of Zombie Romance* and *Fangbangers: An Erotic Anthology of Fangs, Claws, Sex and Love*, both edited by Lori Perkins; *NECON EBooks Flash Fiction Anthology Best of 2011* edited by Matt Bechtel & Bob Booth; *Weird Noir* and *Noir Carnival* edited by Kate Laity. For more information, check her website, jankozlowski.com.

Rob Smales is the author of ***Dead of Winter***, which won the Superior Achievement in Dark Fiction Award from Firbolg Publishing's Gothic Library in 2014. His short stories have been published in two dozen anthologies and magazines. His story "Photo Finish" was nominated for a Pushcart Prize and won the Preditors & Editors' Readers' Choice Award for Best Horror Short Story of 2012. His story "A Night at the Show" received an honorable mention on Ellen Datlow's list of the *Best Horror of 2014*, and was also nominated as best short story by the eFestival of Words. His latest work is a collection of short stories entitled ***Echoes of Darkness***, published by Books & Boos Press (2016). More about his work can be found at www.RobSmales.com, or you can look him up on Facebook at www.facebook.com/Robert.T.Smales.

The New England Horror Writers (NEHW) provides peer support and networking for authors of horror and dark fantasy in the New England Area. NEHW is primarily a writer's organization, focusing on authors of horror and dark fiction in all mediums (novels, short stories, screenplays, poetry, etc) in the New England area. We are also open to professional editors, artists & illustrators, agents and publishers of horror and dark fiction. NEHW activities include book signings, readings, panel discussions at conventions, and social gatherings. With members ranging from Maine to Connecticut, NEHW events take place in varying locations in an effort to provide support for our members throughout New England. Find us on facebook or at www.newenglandhorror.org.

35700664R00196

Made in the USA
Middletown, DE
12 October 2016